# London
# E1

*To George B., who brought me down from the wall when I was up it: and to Tess, who wanted to be first; to Reg, and to those of my family and friends who still live near the brewery. My thanks and gratitude also to Russell Braddon and George Greenfield, without whose help and encouragement I would never have started.*

# London E1

*Robert Poole*

*Introduction by
Rachel Lichtenstein*

**New London Editions**

**London E1** was published
by New London Editions in 2012.

New London Editions is an imprint of
Five Leaves Publications,
PO Box 8786, Nottingham NG1 9AW
www.fiveleaves.co.uk

*London E1* was first published in 1961
by Martin Secker & Warburg
and is reprinted by permission
of The Random House Group Limited

Cover image: John Chillingworth
Picture Post collection/Getty Images

ISBN: 978 1907869624

Five Leaves acknowledges financial support
from Arts Council England

Typeset and designed by
Four Sheets Design and Print

Printed by Imprint Digital in Exeter

# Introduction
## Rachel Lichtenstein

On the back cover of the first edition of Robert Poole's long-forgotten first, and only, published novel, *London E1* (Secker & Warburg, 1961) is a black and white head and shoulders shot of a slim white man, with a high forehead, a slightly receding hairline, a long square jaw and prominent ears, who looks remarkably like the English comic actor Stan Laurel. He is looking directly into the camera and appears to be suppressing a smile. Underneath the photograph are instructions for the reader to look inside the book jacket for some details of Robert Poole's 'highly unusual career.'

Here we learn the author was born in Stepney in 1923, 'about fifty yards from Brick Lane.' After leaving school without any qualifications, he worked as an office boy, a telegram boy and then in a war factory making gun brushes, before volunteering for the Navy where he became a wireless operator on anti-U boat detection and was later involved in the Pyu landings in Burma. After being demobbed he spent some time as a garage store assistant and an estate agent. At some point he fractured his spine in a car crash and, whilst recovering in hospital, he began writing short stories. Then he joined the Merchant Navy as a steward, jumped ship in New Zealand, changed his name 'to dodge police' and became a successful broadcaster and scriptwriter for N.Z. radio, as well as a radio actor, whilst also working as an import agent and a sub-editor on a daily paper. The police finally caught up with him in New Zealand and after spending four weeks in the 'clink' he was deported back to London.

He sold clothes in Oxford Street for a while. In 1958, at the age of 35, he moved to Margate and ran the bingo stall in Dreamland, which he described as being 'fabulous!' Eventually he showed his short stories to his friend, the bestselling Australian author Russell Braddon, who 'liked them.' Encouraged, Poole developed these stories into *London E1*.

A search for further information on Robert Poole drew a blank. He seemed to have vanished without trace after publication. However, after trawling through various genealogical websites, I found some brief entries on his family history. A relative of Poole's had traced the family tree back to the 1830s, discovering generation after generation living in Whitechapel, Stepney or Bethnal Green. His parents, Elizabeth Peddler (a domestic servant) and George Poole (a barrow boy and peddler) had eleven children in total. Robert was the ninth, two died in infancy. Further notes on George Poole revealed he had a fruit and vegetable stall under the Brick Lane arches, exactly like the character of Mr Wilson, the father in the novel. He was also a heavy drinker and 'not a good husband. He visited local pubs while the children went hungry. ... He used to treat himself to fish and chips and give the children the left over fish skins.'

I also learnt on this website that Robert Poole had died at the age of just forty, from an accidental overdose of painkillers, only two years after his novel had been published.

How the novel was received on publication has been hard to gauge. After searching through the British Library's online newspaper catalogue for reviews of the book in 1961, I came across a single one-line reference to an article by the literary giant Anthony Burgess no less (best known for *A Clockwork Orange*). From 1961–63 Burgess worked as a fiction reviewer for *The Yorkshire Post*, mainly covering niche novels, most of which, much like *London E1*, are now long out of print. In a review dated 23rd February 1961, entitled 'Round the World in Five Novels', Burgess wrote about William Styron's *Set This House on Fire*, Jim Kirkwood's *There Must Be a Pony,* William Ash's *The Lotus in the Sky*, Katharine Sim's *The Jungle Ends* and Robert Poole's *London E1.*

The section of this article covering *London E1* is brief and disparaging in parts: 'the tale goes over ground already well trodden — "Probation Officer" stuff: what leads lads astray? ("...generation...We didn't believe anything real enough.")' However, Burgess enjoyed the scenes where Poole described 'authentic aromatic Stepney' in the first person and felt the novel to be 'promising enough for me to feel interested in seeing what Mr Robert Poole (he has vitality and flow) can produce next.'

I first read *London E1* about seven years ago, whilst writing my own book on the stories, memories and history of Brick Lane. The oral historian and long-time resident of Stepney, Alan Dein, had found a battered original copy at a jumble sale and thought it might interest me. It did. Immensely. I was astonished to discover the lost world within.

The novel is set in and around Brick Lane, both during and directly after the Blitz, and intimately describes the daily lives of a community who are so often overlooked in East London literature — white working-class cockneys. It also documents a period of flux in the history of the place — the war years — when the Jewish and white working class communities were still very present in the area and the first Asian migrants were beginning to settle there. The relationships and tensions between these different groups are, for the most part, well told, with an attention to detail that suggests true-to-life fiction.

The book prologues with the protagonist of the novel, Jimmy Wilson, imprisoned for murder, staring longingly through the tiny barred window of his cell at the distant silhouette of the two tall slender chimneys of Truman's Brewery on Brick Lane — the setting for most of the novel.

We next see Jimmy brawling on the streets with 'The Luxton Street Gang' and a group of local Jewish kids. 'You wait 'til I get you indoors — I'll tan the living daylights out of you,' screams Mrs Wilson, Jimmy's mother, as she pulls the boys apart. I expect Luxton Street refers to Buxton Street, a narrow turning just off Brick Lane. For my book on the area I interviewed an elderly Jewish lady called Sally Flood, who had grown up there in the 1930s. She described the street as 'a mixed place of Jews and gentiles.' She went to Buxton Street Junior School, where the majority of children were Jewish, 'but we didn't mix, the Jewish and the non-Jewish children.'

*London E1* accurately describes the way these two cultures lived side by side, sometimes coming into violent conflict, other times interacting amicably. The Luxton Street boys briefly befriend Wolfie (the leader of the Jewish gang) and become fascinated by his forthcoming Barmitzvah ceremony — a mysterious and dangerous-sounding rite of passage in their eyes. Jimmy's mother takes in washing for a Jewish neighbour. His older sister Janey works as a dressmaker for Jewesses. Jimmy earns extra cash as a *Shabbas Goy*, lighting fires and candles on the Sabbath for Orthodox families whose observance forbids it. His elder brother Billy, joins the Blackshirts before the war and Jimmy's classmates are clearly anti-semitic, chanting 'England for the English, down with the Jews' in the playground.

The novel also describes, sometimes in exotic terms, the emerging Asian community. The women with their 'swirls of colour' and the lascars, the seamen who had jumped ship at Limehouse and 'slept on bare mattresses on the floor, ten or twelve to a room.' Jimmy watched the first Indian café opening in Brick Lane, 'then suddenly they seemed to be everywhere... their spiced pungency mingling with the sweet syrupy odour from the brewery.' With the arrival of the curry houses he noticed painted emblems appearing on hoardings around Whitechapel

8

and Brick Lane, circles with lightning flashes and the words 'Vote Fascist' on them, which were soon painted over with slogans saying 'Vote Communism'.

The Wilsons live in a two-room run-down tenement block off Brick Lane. There are nine children in total (just like in the Poole family) but only Jimmy and his older sister Janey remain at home. The family live on the bread-line, the only real piece of furniture in the flat is the parents' bed but there is no mattress, old coats are stretched over the springs in an attempt to provide some comfort. Each week Jimmy's mother tries to stop 'the old man' spending the rent money down the pub, with the few pence she manages to save she buys their groceries: a sheep head if they are lucky and some bruised vegetables from the market.

There are many vivid and lively scenes in the first part of the book: Jimmy lifting apples from Spitalfields Market, playing Tarzan on the shafts of the empty drays around the brewery or interacting with some of the local characters, like Prussian Pete, a veteran of the Great War, who sells bootlaces and matchboxes, and Mad Mary, the meths drinker, who sings Irish ballads with her cronies near Christchurch.

*London E1* is comparable in many ways to Simon Blumenfeld's first novel *Jew Boy* (1930). The central characters are both bright, young, frustrated (sexually and otherwise) males, living in poverty in East London, desperate to escape. From the beginning of both of these stories it is clear this will never happen. When Jimmy manages to win a scholarship to attend the high school he is immediately beaten up at school for being a 'sissy'. On returning home his father gives him a black eye and he is told to never mention it again.

The only person who encourages him to better himself is Peggy, a well-spoken white woman who 'services' Indian seamen to pay for her mixed race child Jalani (commonly known as Pinkie) to attend private school, far away from Brick Lane. Her luxurious flat, with its carpet,

9

lampshades and divan, is so overwhelming for Jimmy the first time he visits that he is rendered speechless. Peggy tells Jimmy to work hard at school and improve his grammar or he'll be stuck in the East End with a 'dead end job in the brewery or a factory, you'll go nowhere, do nothing, see nothing.' With her assistance he begins his self-improvement. At school, he gets into trouble for using big words but, undeterred, he continues to visit Peggy, who gives him informal elocution lessons when she is free from paying customers.

In one of the most dramatic scenes in the book, Jimmy and his school friend Davey hitch a ride on the back of a brewery dray. Davey falls off and is run over by the cart behind and killed. In great distress, Jimmy goes to Peggy for comfort, where he meets Pinkie for the first time. He is instantly infatuated with the beautiful, brown-skinned, sophisticated twelve-year-old, who 'knows about classical music and has her own gramophone.'

Book Two opens to the backdrop of war; the East End has become a different place, with constant air raids, blackouts and bombsites. The market is no longer filled with 'swirling crowds and shouting vendors.... there was a feeling of tension... people still looking for food or clothing-bargains did so quickly and quietly, fluttering across the streets like distressed and nervous birds.' Jimmy has left school by this time but he is still living at home, working the stall with his father. His mother 'wishes 'e'd been able to go to the 'Igh School when 'e won the scholarship, but what was the good? They only got their 'eads full o' strange ideas.'

In the most memorable wartime pub scene in the book, the Wilsons visit their local, the Two Bakers, during an air raid. The pub is packed: 'the thick granite walls were believed to give more protection than the shelters.' A small group of 'Indians' nervously sipped brown ales in one corner. A group of Jewish women sit in another with Mrs Behan, wearing the 'fruit salad hat she had bought to celebrate the victory of 1918.' As the pub becomes busier and busier and the smoke haze grows thicker and thicker, Mr Wilson starts playing the piano, 'feet shuffled and a gradual stampeding was taken up by the whole crowd.' During the frenetic 'knees-up' the pub receives a direct hit — the room fills with acrid dust and smoke, women scream, glass shatters, debris falls and Mrs Behan is found slumped in a corner, with her fruit-salad hat sliding slowly to one side, temporarily hiding 'the bright red stream that pulsed and jetted beyond her shoulder.' Jimmy runs through the deserted, glass-glittered streets to find Peggy buried under a pile of wreckage, badly injured but alive.

Soon after, Jimmy begins scavenging the local bombsites for scrap metals to sell on the black market. He wants the cash to buy a new suit. His parents laugh out loud when he tells them. 'Why would received 'ya need a suit to work in the broory,' his father screams. After recognising how profitable the activity is Jimmy persuades his old school friend, Tommy Copper, to help him collect 'Blooey' from bombsites near St Paul's and sell directly to the dealers, cutting out Blind Billy, local gangster and head of the scrap-iron gang. As they enter the 'dead part of the great city' miles and miles of rubble make streets unrecognisable. Every night Jimmy and Tommy enter the dark basements of these precarious ruins to recover scrap, which is dangerous and highly illegal work.

When Pinkie returns to the East End to look after her mother (who is still gravely ill in hospital), the reader is fully aware she will be the downfall of Jimmy. This section of the novel is less successful than others. Pinkie uses Jimmy mercilessly, aware of his deep feelings for her. His hard-earned savings quickly evaporate. Peggy's money also dries up and, to make ends meet, Pinkie starts working for Blind Billy.

When Jimmy's handsome older brother, Boy-Boy, arrives home after years of no contact, with a young son and a heavily pregnant girlfriend (a plain Northern girl

11

called Maisie) the Wilsons plan a 'proper wedding party'. Crates of beer, bottles of spirits and 'two ferkins of ale' are delivered from the pub. Tables are erected in the court and covered with plates of curling corned beef and boiled bacon sandwiches. Jimmy proudly wears his brand new pin-striped suit and invites Pinkie to the party.

In the afternoon, after a long session in the Two Bakers, the wedding party returns to the court, but when Pinkie arrives the merriment abruptly stops. 'There was only the shrill blare of the gramophone as everyone stared.' Mrs Wilson, who doesn't like 'blackies' or 'Indians' begrudgingly allows her to stay. Soon after, Blind Billy turns up with a bottle of 'Shampain' and tries to recruit Jimmy as his field-officer in the East End, but Jimmy refuses. When Pinkie leaves the party in disgust, calling Jimmy's family 'animals', he drunkenly goes home with his sister's friend Rosie and loses his virginity. Depressed and exhausted, he seems to finally let go of all of his dreams: 'it was no good to want things you weren't born with. If you were born in Stepney you lived and died in Stepney.'

Two years later, the war is over and Jimmy is still living with his parents. He works for a brief time in an office but after fighting with a co-worker he is sacked. Slowly and manipulatively, Pinkie lures him into Blind Billy's dark underworld of Soho clubs, drug deals, black market spirits and prostitution. After being beaten close to death outside one of these clubs Jimmy buys some knuckledusters from Bethnal Green Market, 'he'd be ready next time. ...'

He temporarily manages to escape the East End by joining the Navy but after a few years at sea he returns. Desperate to get back in touch with Pinkie, he eventually tracks her down in the red light district of Cable Street. He follows her home, knuckledusters in his pocket, where the story reaches its inevitable dreadful end.

Curious to know how much of the novel had been based on Poole's own experiences, I followed some leads from the genealogical website and eventually managed to speak with his niece, Pam, who told me 'Uncle Bob' had grown up in Buxton Street, in a tenement block in a court. One of his childhood friends had been killed riding on the back of a dray. He had won a scholarship to the grammar school and his father did not let him go. As far as she knew he had not had an Asian girlfriend, but he did have one long-term girlfriend, called Midge. They were in a car accident together and she was killed: 'He had a lot of girlfriends but he never got over Midge, he never married.'

When he returned from a stint in naval prison in Portsmouth (for jumping ship in New Zealand) he lived with Pam's family in Stepney for about three years. 'He had loads of jobs, but he couldn't settle, he was always looking for something else. He lived life to the full at a great pace, but what he really wanted was to be a published author. He used to drive my mother mad. He would sleep a lot in the day and then type all night. All you could hear was this tap tap tapping. He was also a brilliant classical pianist, even though he couldn't read music, he was self-taught. He had so much talent but was never fully recognised within his lifetime. He travelled a great deal but always wanted to come back to the East End, it was home, he loved the people, the atmosphere.'

She told me he used to drink heavily and had been on anti-depressants when he had died. The inquest recorded an open verdict but Pam believed it had been an accident: 'He'd phoned me three weeks before and invited me to a party. He seemed happy.' Before she rang off she told me Robert had been writing another book when he died, a novel called 'Carnival for Shadows'. She did not know what it was about but said Secker & Warburg told the family they were going to hire a ghost writer to complete it. That was the last they heard about it.

Like Burgess, I would love to read this next work by Poole, but I doubt the manuscript even exists any more. For now, we are lucky to have this reprint of *London E1*.

In my opinion it is not a literary masterpiece, but the scenes based on incidents from Poole's own Stepney childhood are magical: the all-day wedding party in the court, children riding on the back of the brewery drays in Brick Lane, the destruction of 'the local' near Spitalfields Market during an air raid. These vivid and often humorous episodes really bring the novel to life and make this long-forgotten book a valuable and important document, both as a record of a bygone era and as a window into the closed world of a rapidly disappearing community.

***

Rachel Lichtenstein's books on the East End include *On Brick Lane* (Hamish Hamilton, 2007), *Keeping Pace: The Lives of Older Women of the East End* (The Women's Library, 2004), *Rodinsky's Whitechapel* (Artangel, 1999) and, with Iain Sinclair, *Rodinsky's Room* (Granta, 1999).

There is no cold like the cold of a prison cell.

In only a few days it eats into you, first your body, then your mind, then your spirit, and as it does so something in you dies. The others felt it too, but none of us knows exactly what it was; only that to each of us it was important, and now it is dead.

For the first day or two they leave you alone, for they know that during that time — unless you have been here before — you will break down. You will cry, you will scream, you won't eat, you can't sleep. ... These things they know. They know too that, without your being aware of it, Routine will plant itself at the back of your mind. The bells; the dead, hollow echo of heavy and hopeless feet; the sharp-called orders; the banging of enamel plates and mugs on wooden tables; the jeering, ribald remarks, dimly heard and so not fully understood. When they take you down you are already a part of Routine.

In this place we have everything — the con-men who sold one gold brick too many, the tank- or peter-men who blew one safe too many, the kite-flyers whose ink flowed too easily over other people's cheque books. There are the men who liked little boys and girls, there are the others who liked big boys and girls, there are the stair-dancers who could go through hotel bedrooms with the speed and efficiency of a heavy dose of salts. There are even two ex-policemen and these, of the eight hundred men the community has placed here, are the pariahs. Finally, there are those who, like myself, were suddenly and inexplicably involved with Death — those for whom the shattering and final knowledge of the intimacy of Death exploded into consciousness just an instant too late.

These are the people, the others tell you with pride and more than a little cruelty, upon whom you will draw for whatever stimulus or relief — mental, physical, spiritual, or sexual — you may need. You remember the way the

15

screw with the doll-face and the fat moist-red lips looked at you the first day, when you were in the shower, and you give full marks to the man, whoever it was, who said that the biggest criminals are those with the Law on their side.

I don't fully understand why it happened. I know only that the answer lies somewhere within myself, that I will find it if I think about it long enough and hard enough. Why, of the nine children in my family, did it have to be me? My older brothers went to the same school in Luxton Street that I went to; they played the same games in the same streets and the brewery-yard and stable was their forbidden — and therefore their favourite — playground, as it was mine. Yet they never carried knuckledusters and they never wore metal-tipped, pointed boots — though, like anyone else, they were not above putting the leather in if they thought they could get away with it. And they never made a shiny, steel-plated gift of Death.

The two north-country prostitutes who work for Blind Billy told the Court I loved Pinkie, that I would have done anything for her. They said that for a long time Pinkie had been lying to me, that they didn't tell me because they thought I'd either break my heart or their necks, so they weren't anxious either way. That was all lies — at least it was true, but they didn't know about it because they hardly knew me. They must have got their heads together with Johnny Burton, after it happened.

It is strange to think that even my old man helped me to get into trouble. The old man, with his skinny legs, with the big-buckled belt that was far more eloquent than he himself could ever hope to be; with his pale, watery blue eyes, with his stained and faded ginger moustache that trembled with fear when the old lady went for him, small as she was, and that trembled with ecstasy when faced with a free pint... it was the old man who told me to carry three pennies, and showed me how to clench them between my knuckles. He said three half-crowns were better, because the milled edges would slash their cheeks or ears to ribbons, but as I wasn't likely to have three half-crowns, three pennies would do.

That was soon after I got beaten up, when I learned about the pointed boots. Two of them held me, while the other kicked me four times, right where it hurt most. The gutter smelled of dry and musty cabbage water, there was blood in my nose and mouth, and I heard Pinkie's silvery laugh tinkling like an out-of-tune musical box. When I put my hand out for her to help me up she hissed "Get up yourself, you fool. You trying to make me look small?"

But even that wasn't where it all started. ...

When I first came to this cell I found two tattered books, left by the previous occupant. I put them on my cot and stood on tip-toe, looking out through the bars. Now I spend every minute looking out and dreaming — it's the first thing I do when I wake up in the morning, it's the last thing I do at night. I stay there until the muscles of my legs jump and I can no longer stand, then I take my clothes off and examine the mattress and pillow for signs of bed-bugs. Funny, I never did get used to those things even though they've shared most of my life... then I slide under the rough blankets.

I spend all my time looking out of the window because, only two blocks away, there is a large square building, five floors high, and a little to the right are two tall and slender chimneys. Day and night they pump pale and acrid throat-biting smoke up into the sky, and there is also the wonderful and comforting smell of hops and malt and barley and sugar.

I know this smell very well. A few miles away, in Stepney, I was born into the shadow of just such a brewery, and this smell was the background to my life.

# Book 1

# 1

They were the in-between years.

For the kids who surged daily into Luxton Street from the gates of Saint Mary's (Elementary) Church of England School, it was the time of new and exciting gyrations and shufflings known as the Jitterbug, the Big Apple, the Suzy-Q, and Trucking. After school they gathered in groups along the pavement and earnestly practised the strange kicks and heel-and-toe wriggles, holding their right hands up in the air and wagging the forefingers as though nothing would please them more than if they fell off. Some sang, some clapped, some stamped, all screamed encouragement. Jimmy Wilson, aged eleven, did his share of each. If you didn't you were either a cripple or ignored.

They had no music, and when they found out that in Grey Street, a Jewish boy was rehearsing a small band in the heavily-curtained front room of his home, naturally it became their custom to trail up there and perform in the road, watched by a crowd of admirers. The neighbours, mainly Jewish, were not so enthusiastic, and sometimes the kids' efforts were greeted with saucepans of water liberally laced with cabbage leaves, potato peel, and the naked bones of the beloved Jewish *schmaltz* herrings.

The kids didn't mind that so much because it was almost Easter, and Easter was also the Jewish holiday *Passover*. They knew they'd get their own back.

A day or two before *Passover* began the Jewish boys left home early in the morning and sorted themselves into pairs. Each pair carried a bucket suspended between them on a short length of wood; the buckets were all pierced at the sides and small fires were lit inside them. The Luxton Street kids knew when they were due to start, and on the appointed day they were ready and waiting.

The Jewish boys turned into Luxton Street, swinging their buckets and shouting '*chomats* — any *chomats*?' which was the signal for the Jewish people to empty their houses of all the unclean bread, which was then burned in the buckets, and left room for annual supplies of *matzos,* and the Luxton Street gang immediately started to drown their cries with jeering shouts of "Ikey Moses" and "Big-'ead".

For a while the Jewish boys ignored these insults, but gradually were taunted into retaliation. "*Yokkelehs,*" they shouted, "*yokkeleh schmerels!*"

"Big-'eads," was the screamed answer, "Moneylenders!"

The Luxton Street boys didn't mind being called stupid Englishmen, but for some reason their reference to what they regarded as one of the Jewish racial characteristics was always taken as the ultimate insult. With yells of fury the Jews dropped their buckets and rushed upon the Luxton gang like avenging angels, and the gang divided rapidly. The smaller boys ran for their lives to the nearest corner where, from safe vantage points, they continued to hurl insults, while Jimmy Wilson and his pal Tommy Cooper, with the other boys ranging in age from eleven to fourteen, formed into a straight but by no means solid line. Windows opened, doors slammed, and both Christian and Jewish friends and relatives added their encouragement or otherwise to the general confusion.

The leader of the Jew boys — a thick-set, beak-nosed boy of fourteen named Solly Levine — sped ahead of his group and was met head-on by Johnny Burton, also aged fourteen and leader of the Luxton gang; in a moment the street became a sea of writhing bodies and flailing arms and legs, from which came equally-mixed shouts of triumph and yells of anguish.

Jimmy heard his old lady's voice calling, "Jimmy, come out o' there," and at the same time came the voice of one of the neighbours, Mrs Yetta Plotsky, soaring above the noise like a destroyer breasting a rough sea: "Halp," she screamed, "Halp — they killink mine Volfie!"

If anyone was in danger of being killed it was Jimmy, not Mrs Plotsky's round and heavy son of just-thirteen years, Wolfie; at that moment Jimmy was being smothered. Wolfie's knees were going like pistons and he was doing his best to pull Jimmy's ears off and suffocate him, all at the same time. Jimmy managed to give him one in the eye, then someone wrenched him away and he was pulled to his feet by his hair.

"You wait till I get you indoors — I'll tan the daylights out o' you," grated Mrs Wilson. Jimmy knew she would too, but a quick glance at the fracas showed that Tommy Cooper was not doing too well. Jimmy tore himself away from his mother and dashed to Tommy's help, only to come to a sudden and spine-jarring stop.

A huge arm that felt like an inflated inner-tube encircled him and he was folded, kicking but helpless, into Mrs Plotsky's vast and agitated bosom. She waggled her wrinkled, sausage-like fingers an inch in front of his eyes and hoisted him so that his feet left the ground. "Vhy you fightink?" she demanded, "— is all *meshuggeh,* you boyss? Crinimalss!" She liked the sound of that so she said it again: "Crinimalss — is all crinimalss in Stapney!"

Mrs Wilson joined them, dragging both Tommy Cooper and Wolfie Plotsky by their hair. She let them go, thrust her hands on her hips and stood there glaring. "Shake 'ands," she commanded the two boys and, grinning sheepishly, they did so. "Now Jimmy an' all," they were ordered, and in turn they shook Jimmy's hand. "Big-'ead," Jimmy said quietly to Wolfie. "*Yokkeleh schmerel,*" Wolfie replied, and the boys laughed while Mrs Plotsky beamed on them and nodded her head.

"Is betteh," she said. "In Stapney should evvabody be frien's. Come inside," she added to Jimmy and Tommy,

"— I got horintches an' hepples."

Closely shepherded by Mrs Wilson they passed the still-writhing boys in the roadway, until they reached Mrs Plotsky's house, and when she had seen the three boys safely started on her oranges and apples, she and Mrs Wilson disappeared. When the fruits were all gone the boys sat back and stared at each other.

"In two weeks," said Wolfie, "is my Barmitzvah."

"Nice," said Tommy, squeezing orange-pips between his finger-tips. "What is it?"

Both Tommy and Jimmy knew that when Jewish boys became thirteen they had to go through some sort of ceremony in the synagogue, and that this was usually followed by a big party, but exactly what a barmitzvah was they didn't know. And they couldn't find out, because when they asked Wolfie he just picked his nose and became all mysterious.

"Is very important — for me," he said at last, and his words were digested in silence. Then:

"Does it... does it 'urt?" Jimmy breathed, with vague memories of painful tribal ceremonies gathered from library books, but Wolfie wouldn't say another word. Somehow it rankled; why did the Jewish boys get something special when they were thirteen, when all the English boys ever got was thirteen painful bumps from their pals at school, and the knowledge that in another year they'd be working for their living?

Jimmy was still thinking about it the next day when, after school, he went with Tommy and several schoolmates to the brewery and played Tarzan on the shafts of the empty drays that always lined the kerb. After a while they grew tired of the game because everyone wanted to be Tarzan and no one wanted to be the natives, who always got caught and left tied-up for the lions to eat, so they sat on the edge of the kerb. Johnny Burton was with them, and as he was fourteen and pink-faced and heavy and very strong, naturally he knew more about everything than anybody else. And naturally Jimmy asked his advice.

"'Ere, John," he said, "— next week is Wolfie Plotsky's barmitzvah!" He expected some strong reaction to this announcement, but Johnny was unimpressed.

"So what?" he said, "— all the Jews get one when they're about thirteen."

"I know that," Jimmy replied, "but what *is* it? What do they *do*?"

There was a brief silence, then Johnny said slowly and with great emphasis: "Don't you *know*?"

Jimmy felt the beginning of anger. He knew he was only eleven and just a kid, but he didn't like being made to look a fool, especially when he got higher marks in arithmetic than Johnny did.

"If I knew, I wouldn't bloody well be askin' you, would I?" he demanded angrily. "I bet you don't even know yourself."

Johnny's eyes traced the outlines of the brewery chimneys clawing at the faded-blue sky, and beside the brewery wall the air was warm and thick and moist and sweet, like syrup.

"You know what they do to Jew boys when they're thirteen, don't you?" Johnny asked the boys collectively, and they stared at him in wide-eyed silence. Johnny looked at the sky as though asking forgiveness for their ignorance. "Well," he said, "— you all know what they're famous for, don't you?" He studied the gang carefully, then added with enormous weight to his words, "The rabbi does it... with a knife. They call it their Covenant!"

So *that* was it!

"Does the rabbi give 'em injections, like when you 'ave your teeth out?" Tommy was very practical.

"'Course not," Johnny answered scornfully. "Injections are against their religion... 'less they're kosher."

Jimmy stared at Johnny without seeing him; his eyes were fixed on a vision of Wolfie, blood-drenched and writhing on the floor in agony. Would he scream? Suppose he died?

"I don't believe you," he said suddenly. "It's against the law."

"The law can't touch 'em, know-all," Johnny said aggressively. "It's their religion." So far as Johnny was concerned, that covered everything.

"Why don't they go to 'ospital an' 'ave doctors, like anyone else?" Jimmy asked, and Johnny's answer came back in a flash: "Because there's no kosher 'ospitals, Clever Dick!"

Jimmy still didn't know whether to believe it or not, but Johnny's next words convinced him: "All the Jews 'ave it done, then God looks after 'em an' gives 'em all factories an' workshops."

Now they all believed: they knew that even when Jewish families moved into the district without furniture, and slept on the floor, it was never long before they had English people, brothers and sisters and relatives and friends, all working for them; sewing and pressing and cutting the dresses and suits that followed in a steady stream from Stepney to the great stores in the West End. Some of the Jews even had cars... it was true all right.

Jimmy knew they'd done it to his elder brother Billy, but they did it while he was a baby. Did they have to? If they'd waited until Billy was thirteen would God have struck him dead for not being a Jew, or would Billy too have got a workshop? He was still wondering about it as he and Tommy trotted homewards.

As they turned into the street that led to Black's Court, where the Wilsons lived, they saw Jimmy's fourteen-year-old sister, Janey, peering into the window of the Indian house. The Indians never had any curtains and everything they did was done quite openly, without fear or embarrassment. Janey had been deeply struck by their brown skins which always looked so dry and dusty, as though they'd been left in the sun too long. She said they looked as if they were made of brown paper, and she wanted to touch one to see if he crackled. Jimmy told her of course not, because if they crackled they'd be able to hear it as they went past, but Janey said she'd find out for herself.

26

As the two boys came up Janey ran off to call for her friend Rosie Gates, and after a quick look in the window Tommy decided to go home because he was hungry. Jimmy stayed there alone, watching.

The Indians slept on bare mattresses on the floor, and there were often as many as ten or twelve in that one room. There were eight when Jimmy looked in, and one of them was just drawing an enamel bucket from beneath the plain and uncovered wooden table. The man stood over it with his back to the window, and Jimmy saw one of the others call out to him. The caller was answered by a stream of liquid from the one by the bucket, and immediately the room became a mass of brown, wriggling bodies. Jimmy was so frightened he couldn't have run if he'd tried. He heard a woman's angry voice, then he saw her for the first time.

She entered the room very slowly, yet immediately the noise stopped; Jimmy didn't see it because at that moment he couldn't see anything but the lady.

She was quite tall, and her piled-up hair was the strangest silver colour Jimmy had ever seen. Her face was beautiful and smooth and cool-looking and her full lips were a deep yet vivid crimson. Tiny pearls hung on thin golden chains from her ears, and a double row of pearls fitted tightly round her throat. A large jewelled brooch gathered the whole of the left side of her sleeveless dress into a narrow band running over her shoulder, and the dress itself, very tight at the top, swept out from the waist in a wide flare of brilliant flowers that seemed almost to have come to life.

She halted just inside the room-door, silhouetted against the light from the passage, and for the first time Jimmy saw a woman's body in clear outline. She spoke three sentences, her eyes flashing angrily and then, in a swirl of colour, she was gone.

Jimmy's house and the houses of his neighbours in the Court had only two rooms, one upstairs and one down, but the Indians had a big tenement of three floors, with

27

two rooms on each, and their street-door was never closed. There wasn't much to see as you went past — a length of bare passage, two doors on the right, and a flight of dirty stairs on the left. By the time Jimmy got to the street-door the lady was nowhere to be seen.

On Friday evenings and Saturdays both Jimmy and Tommy had a round of customers. These were middle-aged or elderly Jewish people who, being more orthodox in their religion than their children, refused to light candles or fires between the sunsets of Friday and Saturday, which period was called *Shabbas*. The boys lit the candles and fires for them, and on their last Saturday-afternoon visit each customer paid threepence. In this way they raised enough money to go to the pictures or to treat themselves to bags of sweets and chocolates.

One of Tommy's customers was the synagogue in Luxton Street, and when a couple of months earlier Tommy had been ill Jimmy had done his round for him; he remembered that in the rear wall of the synagogue was a wide, shallow window. It was dirty but uncovered, and Jimmy was certain that if they could climb over the wall from the barrow-yard and into the unused backyard of the synagogue, they would be able to watch the mysteries of Wolfie's barmitzvah. Tommy grew even more excited than Jimmy, and he said that they'd need something to stand on.

After school that evening they ran straight over to Spitalfields Market, where first of all they sorted through the piles of rejected fruit waiting to be collected by the dustmen. Almost immediately Tommy found a melon that was bad only on one side, then they found some specked apples and two lettuce-crates stuffed with rotten oranges, which they tipped out on to the pavement. They sat on the crates and ate the melon and the apples and then triumphantly, and smelling strongly of the sweet-heavy scent of decomposed oranges, they carried the crates homewards. That evening after dark they crept into the barrow-yard and hoisted the crates over the wall and into the backyard of the synagogue. They placed them one on top of the other by the window and when they were secure they did a little war dance to celebrate.

They were just astride the wall on the way home when they heard a deep rumbling sound and in panic they dropped back into the synagogue yard. It was later than they had thought, and the costers were arriving with their barrows from Bethnal Green, Whitechapel and Brick Lane. They knew that if the costers caught them in the barrow-yard, where they left their stalls and barrows for the night, they'd be accused of being after the stocks of fruit and vegetables, so with pumping hearts they waited. And waited, crouched silently down against the wall.

They heard barrow after barrow roll in up the inclined ramp from the street; they heard the costers calling good night to each other and then, just as it seemed clear for them to escape, there came the sound of yet another barrow being pushed into the yard.

Jimmy had never realised that so many people used the yard; his old man kept his barrow beside the blank wall of their house in the Court to save the five-bob-a-week rent, but the other fruit and vegetable vendors were not so lucky, and all their five-bobs went to swell the receipts of Solly Agishman, who owned the yard and also advanced money against watches and rings.

Jimmy heard a quiet, snuffling sound. "It's all right, Tommy," he said. "They'll all be gone 'ome soon."

Tommy leaned his head down on his arms and between snuffles asked: "S'pose Solly locks the gates an' we can't get out?"

"'Course we'll get out," Jimmy said, with a determination he didn't feel. "If the gate's locked we'll just 'ave to climb over the roof."

"I can't... I'm frightened."

Jimmy was frightened too; of the heavy and musk-like smell of the coster's stocks on their barrows, of the threatening rumbles of the barrows as they came in, and of the thought of climbing over the roof. Both boys climbed over roofs fairly often, but only when they were with Johnny Burton and the other kids, and even then only because they knew that if they didn't join in the other kids would make fun of them.

"Look, Tom," Jimmy whispered quietly and urgently, "— as soon as the next barrer comes in we'll jump over an' run like 'ell — we'll just 'ave to chance it. All right?"

"Mmmmmmmm." Tommy knuckled the tears from his eyes.

Jimmy hoisted Tommy up and told him to lie flat and quiet along the top of the wall, then slithered up beside him. Three more barrows came rapidly up the ramp and turned out of their view and into the stables.

"Now! Quick!" In his haste Jimmy misjudged the height and scrabbled noisily against the wall, while Tommy was already darting towards the street. Jimmy's ankle hurt. As he hobbled slowly down the ramp he heard the men inside calling to each other; a barrow turned in from the street and he was trapped.

He took a deep breath and walked carefully and without limping down the ramp; as the fruit-barrow passed only a few inches away from him he turned and said loudly: "G'night."

"G'night, son," the coster replied as he vanished round the corner into the stable.

Jimmy's ankle hurt worse than ever and as he turned into the street Tommy ran up.

"Thangawd," he breathed fervently. "I thought they'd got you — I nearly ran up fer your ole man."

Jimmy giggled weakly. "Bloody good job you never" he said, "'e'd 'ave killed the two of us."

When they reached the corner of the Court Tommy stopped.

"Jimmy," he said, "— I'm not comin' to see Wolfie's

barmitzvah. They can kill 'im for all I care," he added with deep conviction, "— but I'm not goin' in *there* again."

"Nor'm I," Jimmy said with equal conviction, and they laughed.

# 2

When Billy Wilson started work at the age of fourteen it became Jimmy's job, as the youngest boy — he was also the youngest in the family — to push the old man and the stall up to his position under the railway arch in Brick Lane, and he had to go back each evening just before dark to help him push it home. It was a job he hated, but somehow he never minded so much on Saturday, because that was always the best day of the week.

Once the old man was satisfied that he was exactly where the Council said he should be — he was terrified that one of the Council Inspectors would come round and, finding the stall an inch out of position, take his licence away — Jimmy ran off to start his fires. There were always four or five of these fire-customers, and once the fires were alight and well-stoked Jimmy always ran home. Today, as was her custom, the old lady had a cup of tea ready and waiting for him, and while he drank it she combed her thin, dull hair into a meticulous bun.

By the time Jimmy had finished his tea she was ready and wearing the long, close-fitting green coat that made Jimmy nervous, because it made her look as though she had suddenly changed into a caterpillar. Jimmy picked up the canvas shopping bag and then, holding hands, they went out into the Court on their way to Brick Lane.

Jimmy loved going down the Lane when it was crowded, as it always was on Saturday and Sunday mornings. People travelled miles to come and look at the brightly coloured fruit stalls, and to listen to the shouts of the vendors and the veiled insults of the run-out auctioneers. Often on Sunday the old lady hadn't enough food for the five of them — there were still three kids at home, as well as the old lady and the old man — and on such days she just said "'taters" or "fish" or whatever it was she wanted, and off the kids went: Jimmy, his sister Janey, and Billy, who was nearly seventeen. They never took any money with them, but they always came back with what they went for.

On this Saturday, the Lane was itself. The crowds swirled and bustled and shouted, never seeming to care that the overhead railway dripped slime on them, that somebody would probably lift something from their pockets, or that most of the goods they touched — particularly among the second-hand stalls — were almost certainly stolen.

The sun shone, although a little dimmed by the never-ending veil of smoke from the brewery chimneys, the vendors screamed their wares, the crowd met and parted and swept on and soon, a part of the pushing and struggling mob, Jimmy and his mother arrived at the old man's stall.

The old man wasn't there. Apple Jack, who had a face like a dried raisin and legs like matchsticks, came over.

"Jotch is in der market," he said.

The old lady looked him up and down and smiled. "You lyin' old bastard," she said pleasantly and Apple Jack, his job done, went back to his own stall, from which he sold all the fruit throw-outs from Spitalfields Market.

The old lady knew very well that George, the man she had married for better or worse, was with Tommy Cooper's father in the brewery. Mr Cooper worked there, much to Mr Wilson's envy, and had an allowance of two quarts of beer a day. On Saturdays it was Mr Wilson's habit to slip into the brewery and share the bottles of beer with his old crony.

Mrs Wilson reached under the box that did duty as a till and took out the ten-shilling note which was the old man's only contribution to the household expenses.

They went on up the Lane, pausing to poke at fish and cut-price groceries or at second-hand clothes stalls, with Jimmy just looking and taking it all in. Outside the pie-shop, near Bethnal Green Road, was a live-eel stall. They always stopped there for a few minutes so that Jimmy could watch the blue-black eels slithering round the pieces of ice in the shallow metal trays. You just picked out the eels you wanted and the vendor, dripping with blood and guts, chopped them on a wooden block into still-quivering two-inch sections.

Again they went on, and just after they turned into Bethnal Green, on their way to the rent office, the old lady staggered. Her face went grey and her lips turned blue; her hands fluttered to the left side of her chest, and she leaned against the wall.

"Mum..." Jimmy said, terrified, "— Mum. ..." Mrs Wilson struggled to force her face into an imitation smile, gradually the colour returned to her face and lips, and she took Jimmy's hand.

"Don't tell the old man," she said. "Don't tell no one. Understand?"

Jimmy didn't understand, but he nodded. Her word was law. Slowly they went on towards the rent office.

The Wilsons' house, like the others in the Court, had been condemned for years but that, as the old lady often said, didn't stop the thieving bastards from taking the rent, and she still had to pay nine and fourpence a week.

When at last they reached the office the old lady went in alone; the first and only time Jimmy went inside with her, he nearly got killed. ...

The little office was very dark and smelled of damp news-papers and cats. There was just a tiny piece of floor covered by a thread of worn and colourless coconut-matting, with on the right a counter so high that even the old lady had to reach upwards to push the rent-book across.

Above the counter floated a hairless white skull; the face looked grey, with two black recesses for eyes, and it had no lips. Without a word a talon-like hand took the rent-book, and Jimmy couldn't move his eyes from the face. The head moved slightly so that the sunken eyes reflected a gleam of light, and it was as though a dead man had come to life. Jimmy screamed in terror and bolted straight through the door and into the road.

There was a horse-and-cart; he saw it, but he couldn't stop running. The big rear wheel with its red and gold paint revolved slowly before his eyes, he saw fresh grease dripping from the axle-hub, then he hit it. He bounced back into the gutter and was still screaming when the old lady picked him up. She never took him in there again but, as now, he stood looking in the window of the baker's shop on the corner until she came out.

A little further along the road Mrs Wilson bought three cooked, cold sheeps' heads, then they turned and went back the way they had come. Mrs Wilson had made a mental note of the things she wanted, and now and then they stopped as she bought a half-o'-marge, a small loaf, a sixpenny packet of tea, and a pound of scrag-o'-mutton for dinner.

They had almost reached the railway arch in Brick Lane when, in spite of the crowd and the noise and the vivid colours, Jimmy spotted a patch of even-more-vivid colour. With a strange little feeling of excitement deep inside him he recognised the lady, and even at that distance he noticed that people seemed to make way for her, just as if she was a film star. She was better than a film star, he thought. He knew where she lived, he could wait in the street hoping for another glimpse of her and soon, although he didn't know how or why, he would speak to her.

He tried to urge the old lady to hurry, but she wouldn't; she seemed to go just as and where the crowd pushed, without herself making any effort. Jimmy kept darting forward and stopping, like an inquisitive puppy running ahead, then waiting for its mother. When the burnished hair and the vivid dress turned a corner and vanished he almost burst into tears.

As they gradually drew nearer the old man's stall Jimmy saw that he was back. He saw the dark and stained-grey of his peaked cap pulled well down over his eyes, which were watery-blue and smeared-looking. He was rocking backwards and forwards on his heels, and when his wife and youngest son joined him he just stared. There was nothing to say so they stared back, then the old lady stuck out her hand.

The old man reached into a lettuce-crate and pulled out a small bottle of stout which without a word the old lady placed on top of the shopping in her bag. She took Jimmy's hand again, then they turned and went on towards the street and Black's Court and home.

Janey and her friend Rosie Gates were there, and Janey was standing on tip-toe trying to see into the smoky and fly-specked looking-glass above the fireplace. She had a pair of curling tongs in her hand and was trying to put waves in her hair; the plain wooden table, under the gas-lamp in the centre of the room, was littered with bottles of lotion and small cream-jars.

The corners of the old lady's mouth drew downwards. "You'll drive yerself mad tryin' to put curls in them rats'-tails," she said, and Janey whirled round to face her.

"Why will I?" she demanded. "I'm fourteen. It's time I started tryin' to make meself up a bit."

"Just let yer father see yer," the old lady said dryly, "— 'e'll start knockin' yer down a bit."

"'E still thinks I'm a kid," Janey said scornfully. "I'm growin' up. Look!" Proudly she stroked her budding breasts, jutting up against a blue and faded blouse too old and too small to contain them.

"You remember you're still at school, my gel —"

"— Look at this blouse! Why can't I 'ave a new one, like other kids do?"

"— Other kids' mothers 'ave more money than I do."

"I know," Janey was almost shouting. "— an' other kids' mothers and fathers don't spend all their time an' money in the pub ev'ry Friday an' Sat'dy night."

The old lady straightened and her lips narrowed. Swift as lightning she darted across the room and her hands slammed against Janey's face. "You saucy bitch," she panted in fury, "— you talk to me like that, I'll break yer bloody neck!"

"Why don'cha then? It'd be better'n livin' like pigs —"

Janey was shaking and shouting and crying altogether and Jimmy, sitting on the edge of the old lady's double bed, was crying in fear and sympathy.

"Get out o' this 'ouse," screamed the old lady, "— get out!" She swept her arms over the table, knocking over the bottles and jars, then she grabbed them up and threw them into the fireplace. Most of them missed and spattered their contents all over the wall.

Drained by her temper the old lady collapsed into a chair while Janey, with a toss of her head, tied a scarf over the experiment at hair-curling. "C'mon, Rosie," she said, and as they went towards the door the old lady raised her head.

"You keep away from my Janey, Rosie Gates," she shrilled, "— I know all about your goin's on."

Rosie, an over-developed girl of fourteen, stared calmly at Mrs Wilson, then round the room. The bed was unmade, the chest-of-drawers at its foot was covered with unwashed dishes, the fireplace still had last night's ash strewn over it, and the glass globe of the gas-lamp was cracked. "Do you, Mrs Wilson? Do you reely?" There was something deadly and frightening in Rosie's quiet and level voice, and she added: "I can buy me own clothes — that's more'n what you can... look what you got for bein' so good — an 'usband 'oo tries to drink 'isself to death, an' kids who are glad to get away from you!" She nodded at Janey, and they swept through the door and out into the Court.

The old lady's mouth opened, then her face crumpled into tears and she began rocking herself backwards and forwards, the tears streaming down her face.

Jimmy knew his mother wasn't well, yet he could think of nothing to say or do because he knew Janey was right.

Every Friday and Saturday night, in spite of the rows and arguments that always followed, the old lady collected her weekly wages from Billy, the only one of the three children still at home and old enough to go to work. She went with the old man round to the Two Bakers and usually they came home rolling. Worse still, Jimmy knew that Rosie too was right; the six older children, most of them only vague memories to him, had left home as soon as they were able, and they had never been back. There were stories that this one or that had married, or had moved to Limehouse, but no one knew for certain.

"Peel some 'taters, Jimmy. I'll see about dinner." The old lady dried her eyes, put the sheeps' heads on a big plate, then opened her bottle of stout. After swallowing a couple of mouthfuls she went over to Jimmy and took the knife away from him. "I'll do 'em," she said. "Don't you ever talk to me like that, will yer?" Jimmy blinked and stared at the tear-marks on her face. He wanted to promise, to swear to be a good kid, but the words wouldn't come. Only more tears.

"I — I'll go an' do me fires, Mum."

He knew that the fires wouldn't need re-stoking yet but he wanted to get out, to do something, to stop himself thinking about something that was too big for him.

He left the house and wandered up to the street, calling in at the nearest of his fire-customers and putting on a little more coal and raking the ashes. He forced himself to call on each of them in turn, and when that was done there was nowhere to go; he walked aimlessly up and down kicking an empty cigarette packet. Brick Lane, only a short way away, was packed with people, but here the street was deserted. He was glad.

He came to the Indians' house and as usual he peered in the window.

There was a large enamel bowl and a saucepan on the table and the Indians were all crowded round dipping their hands into each and rolling the rice and fish-heads into a ball before sliding the lot into their mouths. They never used knives or forks or plates, and they wiped their fingers down their trousers or shirt-tails before diving in for another helping. Jimmy noticed that the bucket under the table was brimming over, so that a long stain trailed across the floor and under the dirty, torn mattresses.

He wandered to their street-door and looked in, and suddenly he heard Janey's voice raised in laughter. He crept up the passage to the far door and without knocking threw it open.

Rosie was sitting on the edge of one of the two single, dirty beds, with a young Indian stretched out behind her. Janey, her hands on her hips and her head thrown back in excitement and pleasure, was doing a wriggling little dance, and three other Indians, all with smiles fixed to their faces, sat like dark sparrows along the edge of the other bed. The room stank of sweat and curry and some strange but sweet Oriental smell, and it was sweltering hot. Behind Janey on a small table against the far wall two half-crowns glinted in the sunlight from the back window.

Janey's smile congealed like cold custard, but she didn't speak. Jimmy wanted to close his eyes, but they stayed open and he looked and looked and looked. Everything was frozen into perfectly clear and sharply-defined lines and colours.

"Janey," he said. "Janey... what did'ya come in 'ere for?"

"Nothin'," she said petulantly. "Come to that, what did *you* come in for?"

"The old lady'll kill you when she finds out." Janey moved across to her brother with an odd, sidling movement and her arms slid round his shoulders. "The old lady won't find out," she said, "— not if you don't tell 'er. An' if you do, I'll say we saw *you* come in first an' we follered."

Jimmy pushed himself away from her and backed out into the passage. The door closed quietly and he leaned against the stair-banisters, not knowing what to do, where to go, or what to think. A dozen houses away from home, yet he was lost.

"Don't you feel well, sonny?" The voice was soft and rich and cool and soothing, and he knew it was the beautiful lady.

She was half-way down the stairs and he glimpsed the wonderful fullness of her body; he wondered why, when the old lady washed at the cold-water tap in the yard at home, her breasts were like two shrivelled strawberries, where here was the smoothness, the richness of a luscious melon in which he could bury his teeth... bury himself... he knew without being able to define the words that if ever she took him up in her arms and held him close he would be warm and comfortable and safe. ...

"What's the matter — are you lost?"

He looked up at her, almost afraid.

"I — I'm all right," he said, and that was all he could think of. She came down the stairs and put a soft white hand on his shoulder. "I've seen you before," she said. "Do you live near here?"

She spoke so softly, so warmly, and so well that Jimmy didn't want to say anything in case he spoiled it. She spoke just like the announcers on the wireless and suddenly he was ashamed of himself; of the way he spoke, of his shabby clothes.

"Yes, miss," he said. "I live up the street, in Black's Court."

"That's wonderful — that means we're neighbours. If we're neighbours, we ought to be friends." She laughed; a soft, deep ripple of sound that made Jimmy feel warm and bright.

There was nothing he wanted more than to be friends with her, yet he remembered Janey and Rosie in the room along the passage, and he remembered the old lady warning them to keep away from the Indians and their houses. He didn't see why they should, because he knew the old lady herself wasn't above a quick peep whenever she thought no one was looking.

"Would you like a piece of cake — or a slice of pine-apple?" She put her foot on the first stair. "Come up, and tell me all about yourself."

She went up and Jimmy, feeling that he was dreaming, followed.

On the first landing there were two doors, the first painted pale green, the second deep red. She opened the green door then stepped to one side, waving him in.

"Home sweet home," she said.

Jimmy took one step into the room, then stopped dead. He had never seen anything like it, not even on the pictures.

A wide carpet, all in soft and gentle colours, covered the floor, with bright cushions scattered here and there, and in the centre of the room was a small, glass-topped table with white-painted legs. The curtains were of some soft but heavy-looking material, and the whole room smelled like Victoria Park did the day Jimmy was caught in the rain; the rain stopped, the sun came out, and the air was filled with a smell of many facets and colours so real that he knew he could touch them if he reached out, and he wanted to cry... it was like that, but now he didn't want to cry. He was quiet and at peace.

At an angle from the far corner of the room was a wide, deep-looking bed, and at first he thought there was something wrong with it. Then he realised that it had neither brass rails nor wooden head- or foot-boards. He had never seen a divan.

"Go and sit on the divan," the lady said, pointing to the bed; then she added before he could speak: "Which would you like — cake or pineapple? What's your name?"

The bed was like a soft, warm cloud, and Jimmy thought of the beds at home. They had no mattresses, but overcoats were stretched over the wire-mesh springs, with the linings facing upwards.

"Could I 'ave cake, please, miss? Me name's Jimmy. Jimmy Wilson." He was so shy he could hardly form the words.

"I'm pleased to meet you, Jimmy." They shook hands solemnly, in a way that suddenly made him feel grown-up. "My name's Peggy, and now we're friends," she said simply, then she smiled.

She went out of the room and with wide eyes Jimmy stared all round. The pale-blue washed walls and the soft-grey ceiling gave an impression of height and spaciousness, and he saw with surprise an electric-light fixture hanging from the centre of the ceiling, and two little wall-lamps with red shades. How did the Indians get houses with electric, when all the houses in the Court had only gas?

On the mantelpiece and on the little table were small Eastern images with slanted eyes and too many arms and legs, like rheumatic octopuses, all shining with a deep radiance. He was sure they were real silver, like the trays and tea-pots in the windows of the Jewish silversmiths and jewellers in Black Lion Yard.

The lady came back carrying two plates, which she placed on the table. On one was a slice of pineapple, with a tiny knife and fork, and on the other was a piece of cake with big red-glowing cherries set in it. Beside it was a small fork.

"There you are," she said, handing him the plate with the cake. "— Enjoy yourself."

The cake looked wonderful, but the fork made him nervous, It only had two prongs, one of them wide and flat, and he wasn't sure what it was for. Should he spear the cake and bite pieces off it, or should he hold the cake down with the fork and tear it to pieces with his other hand? Was there supposed to be a knife *and* fork, but had she forgotten the knife?

Furtively he slipped the fork off the plate and buried it in the soft bed-cover, breaking the cake with his fingers. For a moment Peggy looked puzzled, then she asked, "Didn't I give you a fork?" She rose and went to the door, and Jimmy was trapped and miserable.

"Miss..." he said. "Peggy... the fork's over 'ere. I — I

didn't know what to do with it."

He was afraid she would be annoyed, but she burst into a peal of laughter. The laughter stopped almost immediately and she looked troubled. "I'm sorry, Jimmy," she apologised, "— I should have known better." He could have hugged her.

She sat and watched in silence as he devoured the cake, then when he'd finished she said: "Tell me about your family — what do they say about me?"

Jimmy knew very well what his parents and the neighbours said about the white girl who lived with the Indians, but nothing would have made him tell her. He stared, then hurriedly looked away.

"You needn't be afraid," she said. "I know that the people round here don't think very much of me." She shrugged. "— As if I cared. ..." Her voice went on but in spite of the shrug and lightness of her tone Jimmy knew that she *did* care, that she was as alone as he was, and he wanted to bury his head in those soft and rounded breasts and laugh and cry and be happy with someone he understood. She stopped speaking and desperately he tried to think of something to say.

"Are you... are you married to one of the Indians?"

Her eyes flickered to him in surprise, then away to the walls. "No," she said quietly. "I nearly was, once... but it didn't work out like that. ..." Jimmy sensed that she was speaking defensively, forced on by some deep inner pressure. He didn't understand many of her words yet they stuck in his mind, so that when after school on Monday he ran to Whitechapel library and asked for a dictionary, he knew exactly what words to look for.

"I fell in love when I was at university," Peggy was saying. "He was an Indian student, the son of a rich diplomat. ... I was with him for nearly three months, and I didn't know until it was too late that they don't believe in contraceptives. As soon as the news got round his father took him away from college and sent him back to India...

43

before he went he introduced me to another Indian who was a doctor. ..." Her eyes focused on the curtains and she went on dreamily, "Do you know, Jimmy, there's nothing like a coloured man? Do you know why?" Jimmy shook his head in bewildered silence and without pausing she added: "White men are tired, they've no imagination... they make a woman feel that the whole thing's too bad, as though they ought to be wearing gloves... a woman wants strength and power and conviction... when you grow up and fall in love, Jimmy, love her and make love to your woman all the time. That way she won't run away and leave you for a coloured man."

She moved from the cushion and went and sat next to Jimmy on the divan. She was lost somewhere Jimmy couldn't go, and he tried to bring order to his confusion.

He knew about love. It was what they told you at school you should feel for your parents and relatives, though they never told you *why* you should feel it. Was *making love* the same? He didn't see just how the two things *could* mean the same, because all grown-ups spent their time going to bed, or hoping to go to bed, with other grown-ups. But that never had anything to do with love... did it?

There was a sharp rap on the door and Peggy called out in Urdu. The door opened and in came an Indian who looked to be about eighteen. He wore a brilliant-white turban with a jewelled pin in the centre above his nose, and a silver and red long-sleeved and tight-fitting coat. He also wore a deep blue skirtlike garment and there were open sandals on his feet.

Jimmy had learned the wrong words. Women are beautiful and men are handsome or good-looking, but those expressions no longer fitted. This Indian had broad shoulders — itself unusual, for most of them were slightly built — and this one looked very strong. Jimmy saw in one glance that this was a man, yet his lips and toe-nails were coral-tinted, and he was beautiful. He moved like a cat as he crossed the room.

44

"Excuse me, Peggy," he said, and Jimmy marvelled. The Indian's English was perfect — the English of the wireless, *posh* English. His speech was far better and more accurate than Jimmy's as he added: "I heard voices, and I couldn't *bear* the thought that I might be missing something."

Peggy suddenly looked quite different: there was a hardness on her face and in her voice that to Jimmy sounded strange.

"Don't worry yourself, Rajah," she said. "If it was something I didn't want, you know you'd have first refusal."

Rajah raised his eyebrows and laughed on a single, high note, then stared at Jimmy like Nitty Norah, the head-nurse at school who came round once a month.

The tinted lips split in a smile as he added: "Young, isn't he? I think I like your choice, Peggy, but *do* think of the neighbours."

His tone was light and mocking, and Jimmy knew that for some reason Peggy was afraid of him.

"Get out," she said venomously, "— and keep away from him. If I see you trying any of your tricks I'll... Blind Billy wouldn't like it." Again Rajah raised his eyebrows. "I'm not so sure," he said, "— he's a *great* friend of mine... he'd just increase your rent." He giggled and moved to the door as Peggy leaped to her feet.

Jimmy wasn't certain what Rajah's words had meant, yet there was something threatening and ugly in his tone... there was a blind man, who all the kids were frightened of, who was called Blind Billy. But what could Peggy and Rajah have to do with him? He began to realise that things are beautiful only so long as you remain at a distance, so that you don't see what's behind them, or underneath.

At the door Rajah stopped and turned. "Don't upset yourself, Peggy. I wouldn't spoil your fun for anything."

"I've warned you, Rajah. Keep away from him." Peggy's voice was quiet yet steel-edged, and a little pulse throbbed in her throat. Jimmy wanted to shout or cry or run, but he couldn't move.

Peggy sat down beside him and took his hands in her own. She looked into his eyes seriously, so that he could see a tiny reflection of himself in her pupils, and she said earnestly: "Listen, Jimmy. If Rajah ever tries to take you anywhere, or asks you up to his room, say No. Better still, run away as fast as you can. Will you promise me?"

"Yes, Peggy." He didn't know what Rajah might try to do, where Rajah might try to take him; he was frightened and bewildered. "I don't like 'im," he added.

Surprisingly she laughed. "You're safe then," she said, and let go of his hands.

"You don't like 'im, yerself?" Jimmy didn't want to know, yet the question formed itself without any effort.

"Oh... he's all right," Peggy replied. Her tone changed and she sounded tired and... yes, she sounded like an old woman.

"You could say we work together... comforts for land-based Indian seamen, and half the diplomatic staff." She laughed shortly, bitterly.

Jimmy knew nothing of the diplomatic staff, but he knew about seamen. Tommy Cooper had an uncle who was one.

"Are they all seamen?" he asked, "— all from India?"

"They were. But they're better off working here for thirty shillings a week than ever they were in India, or on the ships. When a ship with Indians comes into dock, half the crew walk off. Some of them get jobs, but most of them join the Labour Exchange." She added whimsically, "Rajah and I took after them, one way or another. ..." Again she smiled, leaving Jimmy more mystified than ever.

She rose and brought over the plate with the pineapple. "Can you eat this, too? It's quite fresh."

It was the first time Jimmy had ever tasted real pineapple; it was firm and cool, but with a sharp, pungent bitterness underlying the first sweetness. He couldn't manage the little knife and fork at all well, so he finished it off with his hands while Peggy looked on with amused admiration. "Have you any brothers and sisters, Jimmy?" He looked at her carefully. Did she know about Janey being downstairs — had Janey ever been there before, could Peggy have seen her? But Peggy's face was clear and there was no deep reason for her question.

"There used to be nine of us altogether," he said, "— four boys an' five girls, but the eldest ones've gone... left 'ome. I don't 'ardly remember 'em. There was a couple of others an' all, but they died when they was born." This brought no response, so he added, "There's on'y three of us left at 'ome now. I'm the youngest. Just turned eleven."

"That's quite a family," Peggy said dryly. "What does your father think he is — a rabbit?"

Jimmy giggled, for this too he knew something about. He told Peggy, with both of them laughing and giggling, about how on Saturday nights, when the old man and the old lady came back singing from the pub, he and Janey used to creep down the stairs and listen to the squeaks and groans of the old mattress, and sometimes to the old lady's refusal. ...

When their laughter died away, Peggy reached down behind the divan and brought out a large black handbag with a jewelled clasp. She opened the flat compartment at the back and took out a small photograph.

"I've a family, too," she said proudly, "— a family of one."

It was one of those old photographs, all in deep and bitter brown, and it was of a baby with huge dark eyes. The only thing that struck Jimmy was that the baby was not quite white; it was not black, nor even as brown as an Indian, but a sort of off-white colour. Apart from that it looked just like all babies.

"Well?" Peggy queried, and he didn't know what to say.

"It's nice," he found at last. "Is it a he or a she?" He tried to sound interested, although he would much rather have been offered some more pineapple, and he put the photo on the table.

"It's a she," Peggy replied, "the loveliest girl you've ever seen."

"Where is she? Where's 'er pram?"

Peggy threw back her head and laughed so heartily that Jimmy expected her to ooze out of the top of her dress.

"Pram?" Peggy gasped between gusts of laughter. "If she heard you say that she'd scratch your eyes out. She's twelve now — a year older than you."

The little interest Jimmy had felt evaporated completely. He knew enough about girls from Janey, and Rosie Gates.

"Why don't she ever go out an' play wi' the other kids? Do they take it out of 'er?" That was something he could understand, that white kids should take it out of coloured ones, and his question was simple and innocent, yet Peggy changed instantly.

"The children round here will never get the chance," she said vehemently. "I send her to an expensive convent in the country — like a public school."

Jimmy blinked in astonishment. "Why don't you bring 'er 'ome an' send 'er to Saint Mary's with us?" he demanded. "— It's a public school — anyone can go to it, an' you don't 'ave to pay. You could save the money."

Peggy stared at him briefly but sharply, then again she burst into laughter.

"You don't understand," she said. "Public schools are anything but public. You need to have money, and in return you hope they will give you knowledge and good taste. But you're too young to appreciate that."

Much as Jimmy liked her, he could have kicked her gleaming teeth in. "If I'm too young to 'preciate what you told me, what did you tell me it for," he said, unable to hide his rising temper. She looked at him seriously for a moment, then she said: "Because, Jimmy, you're intelligent, and before long what I've told you will make sense." She moved slowly and restlessly up and down the

48

room. "If you're not careful," she went on, "— you'll spend the rest of your life round here. You'll live in two rooms like your parents, and you'll have some stupid job in the brewery or a factory where you'll earn enough to make sure you don't starve... you'll go nowhere, you'll see nothing, you'll know nothing. The only way out for somebody like you is to work hard at school and learn and learn... the first thing is to start improving your speech and your grammar... you can start now by sounding your h's, and the g's on the ends of your words."

Much of the meaning of her words was lost on him, yet even as he listened to her speaking he decided to get some books on grammar from Whitechapel library. He felt a rising excitement.

"If I get books on it, will you 'elp — *help* me to learn, Peggy?" He was so earnest that she was taken by surprise.

"Of course I will. In any way I can. But there's one thing. Come up as often as you like, but always knock on the door, and don't open it until I tell you to. If I don't answer, I'm... working, and can't see you. Will that do?"

"Oh yes, Peggy," he said fervently. "If you don't answer I'll come back later on." He rose to his feet. "I'll 'ave — *have* — to go an' see to me fires an' get me wages... thanks for the pineapple an' cake, an' fer talkin' to me."

Almost absently she picked up the photograph and stared at it. "Beautiful," she murmured to herself.

Jimmy was almost at the door when he halted and turned. "By the way," he said, "— you didn't tell me 'er name."

Peggy smiled radiantly, softly. "Her name? It's Jalani, but most people call her Pinkie. Only her special friends call her Jalani."

Jimmy went down the stairs, pausing to listen for the sound of Janey's voice, but there was nothing. He went and did his fires.

# 3

Although it was only July, they were stifling.

There was no wind. The heat beat on the brewery chimneys and pressed the dark acrid smoke down through the stagnant air, so that the houses and alleys were filled with a throat-rasping, eye-watering mist; sunlight itself was glazed and remote, as though filtered through yellow water.

The great round dustbin at the bottom of the Court, which the council dustmen emptied on Tuesdays and Fridays, was blanketed by a shifting and buzzing cloud of flies and bluebottles; inside it fishbones and vegetables and other refuse lay exposed and rotting. The pink and bitter disinfectant the dustmen threw in after it had been emptied was as useless against the flies as it was against the rats, and the cats that fed on the rats, and the bedbugs that fed on the occupants of the old and crumbling houses. The world was filled with the warm moist smell from the brewery, but it was heat-soured and had the pungency of acid.

About a dozen boys and girls were playing cannon in the roadway. An empty cocoa-tin was placed in the centre of a manhole cover, with two small pieces of wood balanced on top in the shape of a cross. Janey stood on a chalk mark about twenty feet away, bouncing an old and ragged tennis ball as she waited for the tin to be set up. She had to throw the ball at the tin, and if she knocked it flying she then had to set it up again; meanwhile the others in the game tore down the street after the tennis ball and hurled it back. They also had to try to hit Janey with it, before she had replaced the tin and the pieces of wood. As some of the boys, like Johnny Burton, were fourteen and big and heavy, cannon was often a painful game to play.

They were not enjoying the game — it was just a way of passing the time until the water-cart arrived. The cart was simply a huge tank on wheels, driven by an old man called Prussian Pete. He had been severely injured in the Great War, so in summer the Council employed him as a driver, and in summer he always wore at least two filthy old raincoats and a peaked cap, so the kids called him the Admiral. In winter, when he really needed a job, the water cart was not needed, so the Admiral wandered up and down Whitechapel selling matches and bootlaces; he wrapped himself up in sheets of brown paper and slept under the railway arch.

Each day through the hot months the cart arrived just before dinner-time. The Admiral pressed a pedal with his foot and a curtain of water leaped from the perforated hose at the back of the cart and doused the pavement and half of the road, laying the dust and congealing the rutted, melting asphalt. The kids' favourite trick, for which the Admiral hated them, was to lie on the pavement and let the cool and sparkling water slide over them and then, shrieking and jumping in excitement, to run forward a few yards and do it again. Sometimes they did this all the way to Commercial Street, where the police usually chased them; it was why several of the gang wore only swimming costumes or trunks.

The game was slow and exhausting, and feeling hot and sticky Jimmy left it and went and sat on the kerb. He had saved enough from his fire-customers' wages to buy a small, soft-backed dictionary, and he found this far more interesting than cannon. He leaned his back against a lamp-post and began reading.

In the two weeks since he had bought the dictionary he had learned many new and long words, although he didn't always understand their meaning. 'Inchoate'... 'Definitely'... 'Magnanimous'... he picked words simply because of the way they looked, or the way they sounded, and when he went to Peggy's she helped him to fit them into phrases and to pronounce them properly. He didn't go up to Peggy's more than once a week, although he would have liked to; he knew that each visit brought closer the day when the old lady found out, and he knew that when she did he'd end up black and blue.

Thinking of the whacking to come made his hands tingle as he remembered the day, just before school broke up for the summer holidays, when his thirst for new words got him into trouble with Miss Bullock, his class-teacher at Saint Mary's.

She was marking her pupils' English Composition books, and Jimmy watched carefully while pretending to wrestle with sums. With a thrill of excitement he recognised his own exercise book as she lifted it from the pile on her desk. She began to read.

Her tailored costume was old and faded, as shapeless and colourless as Miss Bullock herself. She always wore pince-nez and flat-heeled brogues, and it was usually possible to judge her emotions by the writhing of her blubberous upper lip which tried, but failed, to hide her protruding, brown-stained horse's teeth. Her normal expression was that of a sufferer from acute indigestion, and as Jimmy watched he saw this change to startled disbelief, then to fury.

Jimmy had been proud of the new words he had written into his composition, but this time he had over-reached himself. Even before Miss Bullock spoke, he knew that it had been wrong to say that the hero of his story, Sir Walter Really — which he thought was a very clever name — always wore his carbohydrate back to front as a mark of distinction, and that he'd caught and trained a wild obsidian to attack on the word of command. But he didn't know exactly where he was wrong. Miss Bullock tried to purse her lips, then rapped on the desk. "Wilson," she called sharply, and Jimmy stood up. "— Come here." Her fingers still rapped on the desk and her upper lip slid up and down her teeth. Her cold blue eyes were riveted on him as he made his way to her desk, and she began fingering the cane that formed the most expressive part of her movements.

"What," she demanded, "is a carbohydrate, Master Wilson?"

Jimmy swallowed. "I... I've forgot, miss."

"You've forgot, have you?" Her finger-rapping grew harder and more insistent, like rain on corrugated iron. "You haven't forgot anything, Master Wilson," she went on. "You may have forgotten, but you have *not forgot*. Even you are not capable of that."

Her fingers stilled and her eyes flickered over the classroom. Her sprung-steel fingers shot out and grabbed Jimmy's shoulder. "Why did you copy those words?"

"Please, miss, I didn't copy 'em. I remembered 'em."

"You *what*?" Disbelief was written all over her face and her eyes were snapping. When she spoke again her voice was low, yet it cut into his senses like a knife. "I'll teach you to make a fool of me. Here!" She gave him a piece of chalk. "Write *carbohydrate* on the blackboard," she ordered.

Slowly, praying that he could still remember how to spell it, he crossed to the blackboard and began to write in large square letters; suddenly he was confident, certain; he moved to the right side of the blackboard and something jerked his foot. He pulled, and the blackboard swayed sideward on its easel. Frantically he tried to prevent it from falling, but with a crash board and easel hit the floor.

A sharp burst of laughter ran through the class and stopped suddenly, as though at a signal, then there was silence. Complete, utter silence.

In a long, controlled movement Miss Bullock leaned forward, pushed her chair back, and came towards him. Her face was dead-white, her eyes were glittering slits, and now she moved in jerks and spasms.

"Put... out... your... hands," she said.

"But, miss, I on'y wanted to —"

"— You only wanted to what, Master Wilson?"

"I... it was a nice word, miss. I..." But there was nothing more for him to say.

"You will now learn, Master Wilson, to use words you understand." Four times the cane floated up past his eyes and flashed downwards; tears ran down his face but he didn't make a sound.

"Go back to your seat. And in future use only those words — those *few* words — that you know and understand. ..."

"What you readin', Jimmy?" Janey's voice shattered his memories of that terrible day, and looking up he saw that because of Janey's mounting adolescence her old-fashioned swimming costume was too small for her. Johnny Burton had also noticed it, but he had known about it for some time; he and Janey were in the same class, and they sat together in the back row. Rosie Gates, standing next to Janey, was even more advanced for her age, and her mother had forced her to put on a button-up blouse over her swimming costume, but she undid it the moment her feet hit the pavement. Janey elbowed her brother away from the lamp-post and she and Rosie sat down in his place.

"Words," Jimmy said briefly. Janey looked at him in amazement.

"Words?" she said. "*Words*? What d'you wanta read *words* for? Don't you know enough already?"

Jimmy was aware that he did *not* know enough words already, and he was aware that he could never explain to Janey the urge that impelled him to absorb words, to understand them, to respect them. He slipped the dictionary to the pavement and in silence looked at the dreary game still halfheartedly going on. Some of the boys were bickering and he knew that, if the water-cart didn't arrive soon, there'd be a fight.

"Next summer I'm goin' away fer me 'olidays," Janey announced proudly. "— I'm goin' to save two bob a week,

54

an' I'm goin' to Soufend. P'raps Margate... y'know what?" she demanded suddenly. Jimmy looked at her in silence, not knowing what she expected him to say, and she added: "I'm goin'ta give you five bob out o' me first week's wages!"

Officially both Janey and Rosie had left school when school broke up for the summer. Janey had found herself a job with one of Mrs Plotsky's relatives who owned a dressmaking workshop, but she wasn't due to start work until after the August Bank-Holiday. Rosie hadn't even looked for work. Her father had a coffee stall in Whitechapel, and she said there were other ways of earning a living than by sweating on a sewing machine for six days a week.

"No use givin' me all that," Jimmy said to Janey. "You won't 'ave any wages left by the time you've give the old lady 'er twelve an' six a week."

"Won't I?" Janey looked at Rosie and they smiled secretly, knowingly.

"You're very..." Jimmy searched among his new words, and found the one he wanted: "*Magnanimous,*" he said proudly.

He had hoped for some effect, but he was surprised when Janey leaped to her feet. "I'm not," she cried, "— even if I look it, I'm not!" Then she burst into tears.

Johnny Burton, Janey's classroom hero, the boy with whom she tried various experiments during story-reading times, left the game and ran over. He was only a month younger than Janey, but because of the term dates he was not due to leave school until Christmas.

"Whassup, Janey? What'ya cryin' for?"

"Jimmy called 'er a terrible name," Rosie said vindictively. In a flash Johnny turned on Jimmy and pulled him to his feet by his hair. "Whaddidya call 'er? Tell me!"

Johnny had sandy hair, with the blue eyes and bright-pink face that so often go with it. Now his face was bloated and ugly and covered with glistening globules of sweat and his eyes bulged like those of a frog.

"Lemme go!" Jimmy yelled, "— I didn't call 'er a name!"

"Yes 'e did," said Rosie quickly, enjoying herself, "— I 'eard 'im."

The other kids were gathering round, heat dripped from the sky; Jimmy was shaken till his teeth rattled and his nose filled with the man-animal smell of Johnny's body. "What was it you called 'er?" Johnny demanded again.

"I... I said she was magnanimous," Jimmy said miserably.

"She's *what*? What's it mean?"

"It means she's kind —"

Johnny screamed with derisive laughter. "Janey's *kind*," he jeered. "Jimmy says Janey's kind. *Mag-nanny-mus!* Margawd!" A dutiful but doubtful titter ran through the gang, who were all uncertain of the meaning of the strange word, and Jimmy's face crimsoned.

Rosie, having started all the fuss, jumped to her feet; her eyes were bright and she was breathing heavily. Janey watched stupidly, sucking her shrunken thumb. She had sucked it ever since she was a baby, at all times and in all places, and it was a good inch shorter than the other. Rosie thrust her arms round Jimmy's shoulders and tried to prise the two boys apart. Jimmy began to struggle, and brought his knees up with a jerk; Johnny made a strange, voiceless sound, and Rosie and Jimmy fell backwards over Janey's feet. The air was forced from Jimmy's lungs in a great, painful explosion as Johnny landed on his back. "You little bastard," Johnny said. "I'll kill you for that."

"Leave 'im alone, Johnny. Wasn't nothin' to do wi' you," Janey shouted. Rosie was gasping and quivering and Jimmy felt that, in spite of the heat and the sweat and the fear, she was enjoying herself. But still she clung to him as they all sprawled on the ground.

Johnny tried to pull the smaller boy to his feet by his coat, then changed his mind and kicked him sharply on the side of his knee.

"You bloody bully!" With a shout of fury little Davey Clarke threw himself at Johnny and hit him so hard that he flew over Jimmy's head. Janey ran out and sat on Johnny's chest, doing her best to smother him, while Jimmy wriggled away from Rosie's clutching hands. With Davey helping he tried to get to his feet, but his leg was filled with red-hot razor blades.

Janey was pressing herself on to Johnny so that he couldn't move. "Let 'im alone, Johnny —"

"I'll rip 'im from ear'ole to breakfast," Johnny snarled, and Janey exerted herself even more. "I'll let you take me over the park tonight," she offered.

Johnny's eyes flickered greedily from Janey to Jimmy and Davey and back to Janey and his narrow pink tongue slid over his wet lips. "All right," he said, and with Janey still sitting on him he squirmed across to Jimmy and Davey. "I'll get you two later," he promised.

For a moment there was silence, then a train on the overhead goods line to Liverpool Street gave a weak, exhausted scream.

"Let's play cannon again," Janey said. "C'mon, Johnny."

The ball and the tin and the bits of wood were lying forgotten in the gutter, but the other kids joined in and soon the game was restarted, as droopily as before. Davey and Jimmy were left on the kerb.

"You shouldn't of gone for 'im, Davey," Jimmy said. "You know 'e'll wait for you."

Davey shrugged. "I'm not worried," he said, "'E won't touch me — 'e knows I'm not well."

Jimmy felt a sudden, deep stirring at the way Davey spoke. It wasn't envy, for although he knew he'd have no chance against Johnny in a stand-up fight, he still wasn't frightened, so he wasn't jealous of Davey's courage; and it wasn't shame, for he knew that he wasn't responsible for the way the gang treated Davey... he was wrong. He had helped the gang to make fun of Davey, and now there was a bitter taste in his mouth.

For years, until they were nine, Jimmy and Davey had

been pals, and even now he was one of the most decent kids in the neighbourhood.

He was always smiling and happy and the first to offer a share of anything he had, and together they used to race round the streets and pool their coppers and sweets and hang behind carts. ... Davey's yellow hair stood out all over his head, although his mother spent hours trying to control it with brilliantine, water, fish-oil, or spit, and his bright blue eyes always glinted with pleasure and excitement. But when he was nine Davey caught a disease, and he spent a whole year in hospitals. At first when he came home he didn't look very different, but gradually the kids noticed that he couldn't run very far or very fast. He began to stumble, then to fall over, and in the end the other kids abandoned him. It was a long time before Jimmy noticed Davey's peculiar top-heavy look and realised what was wrong; although his arms and head and body grew normally, his legs stayed almost as they were when he fell ill and now, with every month that passed and at a time when the other kids were growing fast, Davey looked more and more out of proportion.

The others formed gangs and cliques, both in school and outside, and gradually Davey was forced away from them; where once he and Jimmy had been at the front of everything, dodging past the stalls in Brick Lane and lifting apples and oranges and flying from bad-tempered vendors, knocking at doors and scooting for safety, Davey lagged behind and finally was left out altogether. Jimmy went on with the other kids of his own age, while Davey walked or trotted home alone. Now and then, as he had done today, he tried to join in the street games with the others who, if they were bored, jeered at his rolling walk.

After a while Jimmy teamed up with Tommy Cooper. Yet for all that, Davey had jumped up without thinking of himself, to help Jimmy against Johnny Burton. ...

"... The Admiral's late," Davey was saying. "P'raps 'e fell in 'is tank an' got drownded?" They giggled at the thought of it and suddenly it was as though Davey had never been ill. They were pals again and Jimmy couldn't speak because of the lump in his throat.

The game went on half-heartedly, there was the long musical jangling of a train being shunted. The kids ran for safety as a lorry honked its way through the street, and deliberately the driver ran over the cocoa-tin. He was followed by a stream of yells and curses, then slowly the kids began to drift away. Mad Mary, whose purple complexion matched her beloved methylated spirits, appeared at the far end of the street, already drunk. She clung to the wall for support, screamed an Irish ballad, and wet herself, all at the same time. The laboratories tinted the bottles of domestic meths in the hope of discouraging people like Mad Mary, but she thought the purple shade of the liquid was an improvement. She staggered off towards Brick Lane to find some of her cronies.

"Let's go an' jump a ride?" There was something doubtful yet hopeful in Davey's tone, but Jimmy hesitated. "— I c'n still run fast enough to jump on, 'specially if we get the cart when it comes out o' the yard," Davey urged.

There was a rapid patter of feet and Tommy Cooper ran up, wearing a pair of too-long khaki trousers and once-white plimsolls.

"I've bin runnin' errands," Tommy puffed. Turning, he added: "'Ow's goin', Davey?"

"We're goin'ta jump a ride," Davey replied proudly, and offered: "D'you want'ta come?"

"You try an' stop me," Tommy said with a grin, and Davey and Jimmy stood up. Jimmy's leg still hurt, but he wasn't hobbling.

Janey and Rosie were sitting on the kerb further up the street, with Johnny Burton and the usual admiring crowd of fourteen-year-old boys round them, and they didn't even notice as the three boys moved off on their way to the brewery.

They had only taken a few steps when without warning a taxi turned into the street and came to a sudden halt outside the Indian house. Automatically the whole gang moved towards it, wondering who was rich enough to afford such a luxury.

The taxi-man jumped down and carried two large and expensive-looking leather cases to the Indians' doorway, then he opened the rear door and brought out a neat black box which he placed beside the cases to a chorus of *oooohs* and *aaaahs* from the gang. It was a portable gramophone — there was one just like it in the record shop in Brick Lane, and it had a winding-handle that clipped on to one side. Jimmy watched enviously; the one in the shop cost fifteen pounds.

Next followed a long narrow box filled with records standing on edge, and this too was put beside the cases. Then the taxi door was pushed open from inside.

A tall and slender girl stepped down, enveloped in a pale — almost colourless — cloak-like blue dress that seemed to float on the air while it clung to her as she moved, and her feet were hidden in tiny Indian jewelled sandals. Her hair was parted in the centre and fell in two thick braids to her waist, black yet so glossy that it glowed with a blue radiance; her eyes were large and dark and soft, her brows so straight that they might have been ruled on.

She carried a little sequined handbag, and half-way to the door of the house she stopped and took out some silver for the taxi-man, who touched his cap and carried all the luggage into the passage. He drove away and all the time the gang stood watching, still and silent.

The girl looked at each of them in turn, slowly and carefully, her face completely expressionless; she looked up and down the street at the tall and dingy houses, then she turned and went inside the Indian house. The door closed softly but firmly, and Jimmy felt as though he had been cut off. He didn't know what from, only that he was cut off.

"Stuck-up bitch," said Rosie.

"Wonder 'oo she is?" came from Johnny Burton.

"That's a saree she was wearin'," said Janey with authority. "P'raps she's a princess."

Sunlight still filtered down, heat still dripped; Jimmy felt it on his skin yet he shivered. He felt Davey and Tommy pulling him towards the corner and the brewery, and as he passed he heard the others still talking about the girl, and deep inside he laughed. He was the only one of the whole gang who knew that she was Peggy's daughter Jalani, although only her special friends could call her by that name. Everyone else called her Pinkie.

"I hope we c'n get a ride all the way up to Whitechapel," said Davey as they turned the corner.

One of the most thrilling sights to be seen in Stepney was the brewery drays, each drawn by two well-groomed horses, as they pulled away from the loading-bays and went off to make their deliveries. When, as sometimes happened, their start was delayed, the drivers whipped the horses into a gallop as soon as they turned into the street, and they rushed down the road with a deep roar from the heavy, quivering barrels of beer that made up the load. The kids used to run along the pavement, then dart out and leap upwards to hang on the tailboard for a ride. When two or three of the carts formed a procession it was a point of honour always to hang on to the first in the line, no matter how fast they were going; the drivers of the second carts in the procession always screamed and shouted, which brought even greater excitement, but they could do nothing. The kids knew that their whips couldn't reach them, but sometimes the second drivers increased speed, so that their horses almost breathed down the necks of the kids hanging behind the first cart, and that could become too exciting. The best thing was to let go and dart for the pavement before the second cart came too close.

From the brewery came the hollow booming of empty barrels being rolled over the stone flags, and there was the thin high neighing of horses. Davey jumped up and down and grabbed Jimmy's arm in excitement. "There's some in!" he exulted, "— they'll be comin' out soon!"

"You jump on first, Davey," Jimmy said, "— as soon as it comes out."

"I'll be all right," Davey replied, adding almost gaily: "I've not 'ad a ride for munce."

"I'm not goin' past Whitechapel," Tommy said. "I've got to be back 'ome when me old man comes 'ome for dinner."

There was a fluttering feeling as Jimmy heard the hard metallic ring of approaching hoofs, then the horses appeared, drawing a half-filled cart.

"'Ooray!" Davey yelled. "'Ere it is. Get ready, boys!"

The cart reached the gate and as it turned into the street the driver, seeing the boys loitering on the kerb and knowing what they were going to do, immediately began whipping the horses.

"Quick, Davey," Jimmy urged, and in the same instant Davey leaped out and grabbed the tailboard and swung himself outwards hand over hand, towards the far side of the cart. Tommy followed, and by the time Jimmy was beside him they were moving at a good clip. The street was long and narrow and deserted; the driver was still using his whip.

The cart jolted and bumped over the rough surface, so that they had to grip with all their strength or they would have been shaken off. The grating of the metal-rimmed wheels with the continuous juddering of the barrels was almost deafening, but through it all Jimmy realised that Tommy was shouting.

"Whaaaaat?" he yelled back.

"... Underneath," came Tommy's faint voice, "... the axle."

The carts were not all of the same pattern, and on some of them the boys could put their feet on the rear axle. This made hanging-on much easier, and in no time Jimmy's feet were next to Tommy's.

There was a thin screeching and Jimmy realised that Davey was yelling in exhilaration; Davey glanced round and catching Jimmy's eye he mouthed some words which Jimmy lip-read: "*I* can't reach the axle."

The horses were galloping now, and the road surface flowed past their eyes in a long liquid stream. Jimmy put one foot down to measure how fast they were going; there was a sudden shock and a sharp slapping sound. They were moving so fast that his foot was hurled upwards and he knew that they would have to hang on until the cart reached the far corner and slowed down. He began to wish they were already there; his fingers and muscles and shoulders were taut with the strain of hanging on, as though they were on fire. Tommy wasn't looking very happy either, but Davey was still laughing and singing.

Gradually through the noise of the hoofs and the spinning wheels Jimmy's ears picked up another sound. He wanted to let go of the tailboard, to drop and run, but he was frozen. Looking over his shoulder he saw another cart rushing along, about twenty feet behind. From his angle the horses' heads reared black against the blue sky, and they were gigantic; he saw the sun glinting on their harness rings and the coloured ribbons flying from their streaming manes.

"Tommy!" Jimmy screamed, "— look out!"

Jimmy's terror was so great that Davey also heard his shout and looked back. Davey's laugh was still on his face but it was hollow, like a mask; Tommy was dead-white, with little sweat-beads all over his face and neck. "Get off," Tommy shouted, "— quick!"

Jimmy pulled himself as near to the gutter as he could; he swung his body like a pendulum, then let go. There was a sickening jolt and he stumbled, but recovering immediately he sped on after the cart. Tommy swung in hand-over-hand and did the same, and ran along beside the second cart, screaming to the driver to slow down. Davey, his face twisted with fear, was swinging in towards the kerb.

"Hang on, Davey," Jimmy screamed, "— wait till the corner!"

Davey may not have heard, for the horses were very close behind him. "Stay there, Davey!" Jimmy screamed again, "'Ang on!"

Jimmy was out of breath, the blood pounded in his ears, his legs felt like lumps of lead; Davey's short legs were swinging well clear of the road as he drew in towards the kerb, and just as he crossed one hand over the other the cart bumped. Davey's hand left the top of the tailboard and floated upwards with the fingers still curved into hooks; he seemed to pause in the air while his feet kicked frantically and then, turning slowly, he fell. There was a soft deep thunk as his head hit the kerb.

The near-side horse of the second cart screamed and reared with wide-flared nostrils, and Davey gave one weak, high-pitched wail. The narrow, steel-rimmed wheels passed over him and blood gushed from his mouth, and even as Jimmy stood shaking and screaming on the pavement he kept wishing that Davey would close his enormous blue eyes.

There was a great crowd; someone took their names and addresses, there was the warm feel of an arm placed round his shoulders. A soft voice said: "Let us through, please. I'll take them home."

Quickly Rajah walked Jimmy and Tommy back along the street, holding each of them by the hand, and although Jimmy still couldn't stop sobbing he noticed that Rajah was wearing an expensive-looking suit and smart brown shoes. He also wore his brilliant-white and jewelled turban, and the effect was more distinctive than strange. His eyes were large and brown and gentle, but he didn't say a word until he tapped on Peggy's door.

"Who is it?" Peggy was not expecting visitors.

"Rajah."

In a moment the door opened and Peggy's eyes widened in fear. She simply opened her arms and Jimmy ran to her and burst into a fresh storm of sobs. "There," she

64

crooned, stroking his hair and leading him across to the divan. Turning, she asked softly: "What was it, Rajah?"

"They were hanging on the back of a cart and one of their friends was run over. He's dead."

For a moment Peggy was rigid and motionless, then she led Tommy into the room and put him on the divan next to his pal, where they snuffled softly together. She went out and came back very quickly carrying two glasses which she held out to them. "Drink this, boys," she said.

They did as they were told; it was thick, like oil, and so sweet that Jimmy shuddered. But he felt better, and he saw that the portable gramophone was on the table.

"We tried to stop 'im, Peggy," he said suddenly, "— but the cart jumped and 'e fell off." He didn't know why he was talking about it: he didn't want to talk about it, but he couldn't help himself. Peggy moved and sat down between them, her nearness warm and comforting in itself. "Try not to think about it," she said. Then, as though at a cue, the door opened and Jalani stood there.

She hesitated, her eyes darting from Peggy to Rajah, and Jimmy noticed that beneath her long pale sari she wore a pink underslip; in the electric light it seemed to shimmer like sunlight on moving water. She rested with one foot pointed forward, like an animal poised for escape, but as she glanced at each of the boys in turn her eyes were level and cool.

She had a strange face; there seemed to be no curves in it. Just high cheekbones and flat bevelled-looking cheeks; a firm chin, and a smooth high forehead. Her nose was short and straight, and her mouth a little too wide. Something in her eyes made Jimmy stare.

She came into the room, carefully closing the door behind her, and again she glanced questioningly at Peggy. "What's wrong, mother?" she asked. Her movements were so smooth and graceful that Jimmy thought of the eels in their shallow ice-packed trays. She also had that same quality of coolness. The thought made Jimmy giggle, then abruptly he stopped. Nobody knew what to say, and the silence grew and grew.

"There was an accident," Peggy said at last, and Jimmy shot her a look of thanks. "This is Jimmy," Peggy pointed, "— and this is... ?" She faltered, but Tommy too was recovering.

"I'm Tommy Cooper," he said to Jalani, adding: "You're the one 'oo come 'ome in the taxi." He made it sound almost like an accusation.

"Yes," Jimmy said quickly. "We saw you get out. Welcome 'ome." He wanted to be pleasant, to talk to her, but her stare shut him up.

"Home?" she said icily. "This isn't home. This is —"

"— That's enough, Jalani," Peggy said quickly. In a softer tone she added: "Have you unpacked yet?"

"I've been unpacked for hours." Jalani was exaggerating; Jimmy knew she was bored. She moved further into the room and pushed a cushion with her feet towards Rajah, who was still standing, but he didn't notice. He was staring at Tommy, and Tommy was staring back.

"Shall we have some music, Mother?" Jimmy wondered at the curious formality in the way she spoke, at the stiffness in her that he could sense but could not define.

"What records 'ave you got, Jalani?" Jimmy felt an instinctive respect for her, for the way she spoke and moved, and he wanted to be friends. She stared at him for so long that he wondered what he'd done, then she said: "Only my best friends and my mother call me Jalani. To you and to everyone else my name is Pinkie." Her voice was so cutting that Jimmy's face flamed and he wanted to run and hide. Pinkie appeared not to notice and went on without a pause: "We'll have some Varg-ner. That will be perfect." Tommy and Jimmy grinned at each other for comfort; they knew she was showing off, but they knew nothing about Wagner.

"I don't think —" Peggy broke in, stopping immediately as Pinkie whirled on her. For a moment their eyes locked, then Peggy looked away. Rajah smiled gently to himself

66

as Pinkie went to the gramophone, raised the lid, and wound the handle. There was a faint scratching, then a soft high note that lasted too long. With a sound of trumpets it grew into a brassy blare which slowly faded and left only the note it started with. Then a strong marching rhythm took over and there were drums and a lot of noise.

Jimmy didn't like it. It sounded as if the orchestra were all playing different pieces at the same time, but Peggy was smiling gently to herself and watching with obvious pride as Pinkie began to move slowly and sinuously to the music. Her strange dance contrasted so strongly against the heavy music that Jimmy came out in goose-pimples.

At last the record ended, and Rajah came to life: "Why don't we all go to the zoo this afternoon? What do you say, Peggy?"

"Oh, yes please — I've never been." Pinkie clapped her hands and ran to his side.

"You can go if you like, Pinkie," Peggy said, "— but I've a couple of appointments this afternoon. We're leaving early tomorrow and —"

"You're leavin'? Where you goin' to?" Peggy's instructions about h's and g's were forgotten; Jimmy's fear that Peggy was going away, might never come back, brought his words in a sudden stream.

Peggy was puzzled, then amused as she realised how much he liked going up to visit her. She explained: "We're going to Devon — for two weeks. Then Pinkie is going on to join some friends in Paris, and I shall come back here."

Jimmy looked at Pinkie with respect. She was only twelve, yet she moved and spoke like a grown-up, she rode in taxis and paid for them herself; she had a gramophone and records and knew about music, and she was going to Paris. Jimmy had never travelled further than Hackney, and even then he got lost.

"Paris!" he said with all the scorn he could manage, "— that's... magnanimous!"

There was a brief and startled silence, then Pinkie

burst into laughter and again Jimmy's face flamed. Peggy had always been gentle and kind when he made mistakes, but now even she was laughing. Suddenly he hated them all.

"We'd better be goin' 'ome, Tommy," he said, standing up, but Tommy stayed on the divan. "I'm goin' to the zoo," he announced, looking at Rajah.

"I'm not going," Pinkie said, staring at Jimmy, "— not if the funny one's not going." Jimmy glared back at her until she looked away.

"I think you ought to go home with Jimmy, Tom," Peggy said. "Your parents will be worried about you. They'll know about the accident. ..."

It all flooded back into Jimmy's mind: the horses, the scream, the blood, the crowd and little Davey on the ground... he wanted to get away from these people he didn't understand. In spite of himself he felt the tears rolling down his cheeks.

"Don't cry, Jimmy," Pinkie said, taking his hands in her own. "I'm sorry I was rude to you. But I won't be rude again... ever. Please, Jimmy." She ran her fingers along his wrists and they were cool and firm. Jimmy was comforted.

"— I could tell my mum I'm goin' to the zoo after dinner," Tommy said hopefully, but Peggy didn't give Rajah a chance to speak.

"That wasn't a good idea at all," she said. "Besides, Rajah has some work to do."

Her face and voice were hard, as they had been the first time Jimmy went up to her room, the time Rajah had interrupted them. Instead of speaking Rajah rose to his feet and went to the door, where he paused.

"I'm sorry, Tommy," he said, and disappeared with his strange, cat-like walk. Pinkie went and began to wind the gramophone, but Jimmy couldn't stand it again.

"I'm goin' 'ome — *home* — now. I 'ope you 'ave — *have* — a nice time," he said. "Can I come an' see you when you come 'ome, Peggy?"

"You'd better," she said, smiling. "— I'll expect you."

Pinkie started the record then ran across. "You'll come and see me too, won't you, Jimmy?" For the first time he noticed a faint, tantalising perfume clinging to her; so thin and slight that he thought he imagined it. "I might do," he said, adding cuttingly: "I might give you somethin' else to laugh at."

For a moment he thought she was going to slap his face, but she turned and went back into the room. He went out through the door, with Tommy following, and as they went down the stairs they heard the music with the sound of trumpets.

# 4

It seemed to Jimmy that he had always been eleven, that he would be eleven forever, while Janey, in the three months since she started work, had suddenly become a young woman.

At first she used too much make-up, but with expert tuition from the young Jewesses she worked with — who at week-ends paraded up and down Whitechapel hoping to trap medical students from the London Hospital, and were known as the Whitechapel Walkers — she learned how to choose the colours, and the amounts, that most suited her. She spent hours at the plywood dressing-table upstairs, surrounded by pots and jars and tubes, putting-on and taking-off paint and powder and brightly coloured blouses and skirts; arranging, re-arranging and dis-arranging her hair. Meanwhile her long and thin face and body softened and swelled, became fuller and gracefully rounded.

She and Rosie Gates began to frequent the tiny dance-hall behind the skirt factory in Hanbury Street, which was used mainly by those girls who were anxious to learn too much too soon but who, in the general sense, still worked at ordinary jobs. The two of them became very popular, and also managed to cause several of the Saturday-night fights between rival gangs of boys who, drawn by the generosity of the local hostesses, came from all the nearby boroughs.

Billy Wilson, now over seventeen, also went there every week-end. He had fallen for a girl two years older than himself: blowsy, overblown, but aggressively pubescent and not too bright. Billy said there was no one like her, and Jimmy agreed.

One Saturday night Jimmy, feeling tired and miserable, went up to bed, taking his dictionary with him. The house was empty, the old man and the old lady having gone as usual to the Two Bakers, while Billy and Janey cavorted in the dance-hall. Jimmy lit the gas-mantle above the fireplace and then, wrestling with several new words, fell asleep almost immediately.

He woke up with a start as he felt himself being violently pushed across the bed, and looking up he saw that Billy was trying to slide in beside him. One of his eyes was puffed blue-and-green, and his breaths were short and gasping. His long hair was plastered down with the solid brilliantine he loved so much, although the smell of it was sweat-soured, and with his long nose and chin and his even longer underclothes, he looked so comical that Jimmy burst out laughing.

"It's not bloody funny," Billy growled. "If Janey starts any more fights she can look after 'erself — I'm not gettin' meself bashed-up again." He raised his vest and showed two wide bruised areas across his ribs, and as he crawled into bed beside Jimmy he said "Jeeeeeeesus."

"Someone done you up?" Jimmy asked. "Who was it?"

"'Arf a dozen o' the Cable Street yobbos," Billy answered. "Janey was leadin' 'em on an' Johnny Burton told 'er off, so the yobbo's went for 'im an' I joined in. Two of us against six of 'em."

Jimmy digested this in silence, then he asked: "Where's Janey gone to?"

"Johnny took 'er somewhere — 'e got a coupl'a shiners an' a busted nose an' I got Rosie Gates." Billy shook with laughter even as he groaned in pain.

"You wait till the old lady sees your black eye in the mornin'," Jimmy said, "— she'll black the other one for you."

"She won't get the chance. I'll be out that door quicker'n lightnin'. Don't you tell 'er anythin', either," Billy warned. He stretched out lazily, exhausted by his efforts on the dance floor and in the fight and then with Rosie; he took a deep breath, only to stop with a sharp yelp of pain. "They've broke me bloody ribs," he said.

"They did, or Rosie?" Jimmy asked boldly, and they giggled.

Billy turned on to his side, and when Janey crept upstairs half an hour later Jimmy thought he was asleep.

Janey, who slept on the far side of the room, was tiptoeing past her brothers' bed when Billy shot out his hand and grabbed her, giving her such a fright that she squealed.

"You wanna watch yer step, 'angin' round wi' that Cable Street mob," Billy said angrily, and Janey stuck her thumb in her mouth and stared at him.

"Nothin' to do wi' you," she said resentfully, "— you look after yourself."

"That's what I *am* doin'. I catch you wi' them 'ooligans again, I'll knock your teeth in. Don't forget it."

He released her and, knowing better than to argue with him when he was in a temper, Janey crossed to her bed and undressed.

The next morning Mrs Wilson called Jimmy just before eight to help the old man to push the stall up to Brick Lane, and he was back home and drinking a cup of tea when Billy came down. The old lady stared at him for a moment, then poured another cup. "There y'are," she said, slapping it down on the table and spilling most of it.

Jimmy guessed that her hangover had made her less observant than usual, for she said nothing about Billy's iridescent eye. Billy winked at his younger brother, swallowed his tea, then vanished towards the street.

The old lady looked at Jimmy and smiled. "'E didn't waste much time," she said, then went on to a different subject. "It's time you went an' joined Sunday School," she said, "— it's gettin' near Christmas."

It happened every year.

Saint Mary's was a church school, elementary grade, and both church and school occupied the whole of one block. Sunday School lessons were given in the ordinary classrooms, and throughout the summer they were rarely attended by more than a dozen kids, most of whom were sent so that their parents could have their Sunday-afternoon sleep. But during October and November the class attendance swelled to overflowing, and the vicar had to recruit additional teachers from among the more blatantly faithful of his parishioners. The reason for this yearly flux, as the vicar knew, was the party he gave every Christmas, and to this all the local children considered themselves entitled to go. The drawback was that at least six attendances had to be registered, but the boredom of the lessons could be overcome by marbles and wire puzzles. The vicar himself — a thin, pale man who appeared to carry all the sins of Stepney on his rapidly-rounding shoulders — had been heard to say that it was better to have the dear children go to Sunday School for the party alone than not to go at all.

"All right, Mum," Jimmy said, but he had no intention of going. He was weary of soggy custard and tired jelly, and there were other things to do. He went round and called for Tommy Cooper and together they wandered through the streets.

"There's some more Indians comin' soon," Tommy said suddenly, "— they've got the empty 'ouse in Luxton Street."

"Who told you?" Jimmy queried idly, and Tommy shot him a quick look. Then he looked at the sky and said simply: "Rajah." Jimmy didn't know that Tommy had seen Rajah, but somehow he wasn't surprised. "Let's go an' look," he said, and off they trotted.

The house was tall and narrow, and had been empty for weeks. The street-door had been forced open, and after a quick look up and down the street they went in. The windows were filthy, so that every room was gloomy, and the whole house smelled of cats and dampness. "Blimey," Tommy said, "— gives you the creeps, don't it?" Upstairs they found a pile of damp-rotted newspapers and books, and they were searching through in case there was anything worth keeping when they heard the street-door being flung back against the wall with a crash and there was the sound of raised voices calling in Urdu. They crept out of the room and watched over the banisters as five Indians carried several small marble-topped tables and a number of old wooden chairs into the room that looked out on Luxton Street. They heard the Indians chattering and laughing among themselves, then without warning two of them turned from the room and ran straight up the stairs.

The Indians were generally small and slender, but occasionally there appeared a different type; tall, wide-shouldered and able to move with surprising speed and agility; these all wore turbans and beards, often set-off by one ear-ring. Jimmy had asked Peggy about them one day, and she told him that they were Sikhs or Pathans from the northern provinces of India who took to the sea to avoid the police, whose interference in what they regarded as their private affairs — such as drug- and arms-smuggling and family feuds — was deeply resented.

Two of these were now rushing up the stairs like express trains, and in panic Tommy grabbed Jimmy's arm and they waited, wide-eyed. The Indians reached the landing, then stopped. Their smiles vanished and they appeared to be gigantic, threatening. Jimmy tried to swallow the lump in his throat.

"Hallo," he said in what he hoped was a friendly voice, as he tried desperately to think of something sensible to say. He thought the Indians looked as though they were going to wring his neck. Tommy's eyes opened even wider than his mouth. With the inspiration of fear Jimmy remembered one of the two Urdu phrases he'd learned to repeat parrot-fashion, from Peggy.

"Kittna baje?" he asked doubtfully.

Realising immediately that asking them the time was pointless, because even if they answered he wouldn't be able to understand them, he brought out the other half of his Urdu vocabulary and made everything worse.

"Ap-ka-nam-ka-hai?" he demanded, and he had the terrible feeling that, although Peggy had given him the two Urdu phrases, she had also given him the wrong meanings; the Indians stared at each other in consternation. Suddenly they leaped forward, and with a yelp of fear Tommy disappeared into the room the boys had just left; Jimmy too wanted to run, but his feet were glued to the floor. When the Indians reached him they began thumping him on the back and shoulders, each blow hard enough to knock a horse to its knees; they screamed Urdu at him, from which he gathered, in answer to his second question, that their names were Ahmed and Firoz. Jimmy realised that they were not going to wring his neck after all, and he caught sight of Tommy peering nervously from behind the room-door.

"Come out o' there!" he ordered bravely, "— they won't hurt you." There was a sneaking pride that he had remembered the 'H'.

"Coo," Tommy said as he joined them on the landing. "I thought you was done for."

"So did I," Jimmy said quickly. "Fine pal you turned out to be."

"I was scared," Tommy said with simple candour, then he too was swamped by hearty thumps and hand-pumping from the Indians.

They went downstairs in a bunch, into the room where the others were arranging the tables and chairs, and there were several bursts of rapid Urdu, with much eye-rolling and hand-waving. The floorboards were filthy and bare and the wallpaper, limp and flowered with great damp-stains, was peeling and torn.

With a big smile and expansive movements, big Ahmed indicated the whole room. "We... mek... eat-shop," he explained proudly, and demanded "You lak curri? Curri-fish, curri-mitt?"

Jimmy did not like curried fish or meat, or curried anything, and he said so. For a moment Ahmed stared at

75

him sadly, then he asked the usual question: "You got sista?"

Knowing that the neighbours rarely spoke to the Indians, and that it would be a long time before the Indians found out about Janey and her visits to the Indians in Peggy's house, Jimmy thought quickly as they stared at him intently. Tommy giggled weakly.

"No," Jimmy said, "I no got sista."

The Indians all looked suitably downhearted, so for a while the two boys helped them to push the tables and chairs into a series of too-cramped positions, then they went home for dinner.

That was the first Indian café they saw, but suddenly they seemed to be everywhere. At first the Indians had lived almost entirely near the docks, along Wapping and Shadwell, yet all at once they erupted like an over-ripe boil and spread through Limehouse and Poplar and Stepney and Bethnal Green, and the spiced pungency of their curry-cafés mingled with and sometimes defeated the heavy sweetness that poured day and night from the brewery.

As they went along the street Jimmy stopped, pulling Tommy also to a halt. They watched in silence as a group of strangers wandered past; most of them were short and stout and several of the men wore short leather or suede trousers. They all waved their hands and talked at the tops of their voices in Polish and Russian and German, languages unrecognisable to the boys. A surprising number of them wore thick bullet-proof glasses, and every now and then they would run and peer with anxious myopia at the painted emblems that appeared on the walls and hoardings of Brick Lane and Whitechapel and Bethnal Green: the emblems were circles with lightning-flashes in the centre with the words *Vote Fascist* painted beside them. Always within a few hours these were obliterated and somewhere close at hand blossomed the red-painted alternative, *Vote for Communism,* with the hammer and sickle design.

"Wonder why all these bleedin' foreigners are comin' over 'ere?" Jimmy said thoughtfully. They walked on and he soon forgot the problem; these things were part of the peculiarities of grown-ups, and they didn't impress or concern him any more than the facts that the Jews were usually Commies, while the English and Irish were almost always Fascist.

"Anythin' good 'appenin' this week?" Tommy asked as they paused before parting on the corner of the street.

"No... on'y the new vicar on Thursday."

"I wonder if 'is adam's-apple wobbles, like old Saunders' used to?" They giggled at the memory of poor Mr Saunders, and waited with patient curiosity.

Each Thursday morning it was the custom for the vicar of Saint Mary's to cross over to the school drill-hall to give a sermon-lecture to the boys of the senior classes. First of all they had to report to their various classrooms to be marked in the register by their teachers, then they filed across the playground to the drill-hall, which was also used for Drill, or physical training. It was simply a large bare glass-roofed hall where in summer they dripped and sweltered, and in winter turned blue; there was no equipment whatever for physical jerks, as Drill was known; Drill itself consisted mainly of the knees-bend-arms-stretch torture which the boys were told would make them better and fitter citizens. At the far end was a small wooden stage on which was a battered upright piano and a plain table, and on which year after year nativity plays which none of the boys understood were badly presented to an audience of vociferous and semi-alcoholic parents and relatives, who didn't understand them any more than did the boys.

In a small side-room were kept a number of long forms on which the boys sat during the sermon, which they usually ignored; someone would have marbles, or conkers or a new smutty story. In any case Mr Saunders, the old vicar, was so thin physically and vocally that he could rarely be seen or heard from where Jimmy and Tommy always tried to sit in the back row.

Worn out by years of struggling against people who resisted all his efforts to arrange their salvation, Mr Saunders had died a week earlier. His death left a gap in the local ecclesiastic ranks which was largely unnoticed or ignored by the population, but had now been filled by Mr Gapley, who was to give his first sermon that morning. Having reported to their classes the boys crossed with more than usual speed to the drill-hall. They didn't exactly rush, but at least they were curious.

As they went in there was no sign of Mr Gapley, but the headmaster, Mr Milson, stood behind the table on the stage. As a mark of respect and deference to Mr Gapley the table had been covered with a green baize cloth, topped by a vase of wilted flowers. Jimmy, with Tommy close behind, rushed for a seat in the back row, but they were beaten by Johnny Burton and a gang of bigger boys, so they sat in the row in front.

Jimmy noticed that Mr Milson sent him a vague and watery smile as he raised his hand for silence, and immediately there was a sharp jab on his spine. Johnny Burton had also noticed the smile.

"Please, sir…" he mimicked Jimmy's treble voice, then he growled: "Teacher's fav'rite!"

"You shut your 'ole up," Jimmy snapped back with quick resentment.

"I'll shut yours in a minnit!"

"You an'oo else?"

Since that day in summer when they'd all played cannon, the day little Davey got killed, Jimmy had tried to keep out of Johnny Burton's way. It wasn't easy, because since then Johnny had paid more and more attention to Janey and often hung round the street corner waiting for her to come home from work. Johnny didn't answer the question for at that moment Mr Milson's calls for silence were obeyed; nervously he cleared his throat and fixed his colourless eyes on the back wall.

78

"Ah... before the sermon..." he began hesitantly, "... the sermon from our new vicar who ah... I'm sure you'll all welcome. ..." He paused and waited hopefully for some sign of welcome, but there was a stony silence. "Er... I have something of ah,... great importance... one of our boys has won the Junior Scholarship. ..." His voice droned on but Jimmy didn't hear; his stomach was fluttering so much that he wanted to be sick. Several weeks earlier five girls and three boys from Saint Mary's, all aged between eleven and twelve, had sat for this scholarship, and Jimmy was one of them.

It seemed that Mr Milson spoke for hours, but Jimmy only caught odd phrases: "... a great honour for Saint Mary's... first time for three years... a half-holiday... James Wilson."

Jimmy heard his own name; it echoed and boomed in his brain like a raised voice in a cave; his face whitened and his knees turned to water. With a hard thump on his shoulder, Tommy led the boys in a great Hooray shout and then hands were pushing and prodding him towards the stage.

Again Mr Milson spoke, at what seemed to be unusual length, all about study and work and pride and privilege and colleges and opportunities available to a boy who *really made an effort,* but Jimmy was in a vacuum. At last Mr Milson gave him a long and closely-printed green form, and dazedly Jimmy went back to his place. Tommy told him later that although his face was dead-white his voice was clear and firm as he thanked Mr Milson and promised to study and learn all he could, and always to remember Saint Mary's.

He had only just sat down when there was a breath-taking stab of pain in the small of his back.

"Teacher's fav'rite," Johnny Burton grated between clenched teeth. "Goin' to 'Igh School! Sissy!"

Anyone who went to a High School was automatically a sissy, like people who wore pyjamas; Jimmy didn't know why — it was just one of those things, and he couldn't think of a reply.

There was a loud crash, and all eyes swerved to the door; for the first time the boys saw Mr Gapley, and it was as though the hall had gone cold. Jimmy's deepest impression was of the man's force; pulsing, real and living power. It radiated from him like heat from an electric fire.

Everything about Mr Gapley was big and strong and heavy; the large round head, nearly seven feet above the floor; the tremendous, ox-like shoulders; the thick red fingers with the little white pressure-points where he grasped his black-and-gold prayer book; the big feet visible beneath his flowing black cassock and white surplice. His hair was short and pure-white, his eyes a ferocious and snapping blue; his mouth was wide but thin-lipped, with little white lines at the corners.

"Blimey," Tommy muttered as Mr Gapley strode towards the stage, "— the 'Oly Ghost 'isself!"

With a few mumbled and incomprehensible words Mr Milson introduced Mr Gapley to the assembled boys, then with a whispered apology he left the stage and the drill-hall. In complete silence Mr Gapley watched him go and then, after the door closed, he began to speak.

He didn't shout. He didn't even raise his voice, yet there was so much sound it was almost frightening; deep and vibrant, his voice rushed and swept and swirled and battered the boys' ears and left them breathless and dizzy, and in a very short time they learned that Mr Gapley knew all about them and their families and the terrible things they all did; that they were corrupt and good-for-nothing but that he, Mr Gapley, was going to preserve them all in spite of themselves and whether they liked it or not.

"I will save and protect you..." he boomed, "and your families, and..." He paused and stared in startled disbelief, then went on immediately "— and if that boy in the back row doesn't stop playing with himself I'll come down there and pull his ears off one by one!"

It was the boys' turn for startled disbelief, and a cart outside in the street rumbled through the silence. Then there was a shattering roar as they broke into shouts and screams of rapturous applause, yelling and stamping their feet in approval.

Mr Gapley raised his hands in salute, like a victorious prizefighter, and the boys waited expectantly for other interesting threats. But Mr Gapley changed completely.

He told the boys he intended to visit all their homes, and that in a short time Stepney — or that part of it now under his guidance — would become a district in which even the pure and innocent could live without shame or fear. The sermon was followed by two hymns, after which the boys were marched row by row out into the playground, where they broke into a stampede.

It was now morning playtime and Tommy, rushing along behind Jimmy, was filled with excited anticipation. "I on'y 'ope me ole man's in when ole Gapley comes to *our* 'ouse," he puffed as they slowed down, "I bet 'e won't be frightened of 'im, even if 'e *is a* vicar." They looked at each other and smiled. It would be very interesting.

A group of boys came over to Jimmy and told him how glad they were that he'd got them a half-holiday by winning the scholarship, and he remembered the green form still in his pocket. He pulled it out and began to read the detailed information while the others talked about Mr Gapley and said he was a lot better than Mr Saunders had been, even if he was dead.

"I'm not frightened of any ole bible-basher," boasted Johnny Burton, who had caused Mr Gapley's interesting threat. "I don't care if 'e pulls me ears off an' I go blind as well — I c'n always sell matches." The boys laughed dutifully — all except Jimmy, who was busy reading the form and hadn't heard Johnny's words. Johnny's expression became a snarl; turning and muttering to some of his pals, he led them over to where Jimmy and Tommy were standing by the wall.

"Run, Jim," Tommy shouted, "— run, fagawsake!" He

gave Jimmy a sudden push and darted away in the opposite direction, but the push came as such a surprise that Jimmy stumbled. Then he was alone against the wall with the boys spread round him in a half-circle so that he couldn't escape. Johnny Burton was in the centre.

"'Allo," he said with false surprise, "— if it isn't the 'igh-school boy! 'Ow's it feel to be... *mag-nanny-mus?*" His memory was better than Jimmy had imagined.

"Roll up," Johnny shouted at the top of his voice, "come an' see the noo sissy-boy!"

"I'm no more a sissy-boy than you are," Jimmy said evenly.

"Ain'cha? We'll soon see about that." Johnny jabbed a fist towards Jimmy's face and instinctively he tried to shield himself. Johnny halted the jab and instead kicked swiftly and viciously, catching Jimmy on the shins. Helplessly he looked round as the rest of the gang closed in; several feet away a crowd of smaller boys watched silently, afraid to mix it with the Burton mob and so ashamed of themselves, yet unable to stop looking. Jimmy wanted to tell them it didn't matter, because he knew that if they interfered they'd get bashed up as well, but there was a lump in his throat. Tommy was near them, but there was nothing he could do alone; they'd wipe the floor with him.

Suddenly, with all his strength Jimmy kicked out and lunged with his fists and tried to break out; somebody tripped him and he ended up with his face on the ground and his arms twisted up behind his back. He struggled, but slowly his arms were forced higher and higher until he thought they would crack. The silence frightened him most; not one of the gang said a word.

Reaching down, Johnny grabbed a handful of hair and pushed hard, grinding Jimmy's face into the sharp, coke-like surface of the playground. Little white needles of fire shot through his head and eyes and he couldn't see, and with the rasping, searing pain he knew the skin was coming off in shreds. They forced his arms out at right-

82

angles to his body; two hands grasped each of his wrists and slowly, inexorably, began to twist in opposite directions; it was like having red-hot sand stamped into an open wound. Jimmy tried not to scream but the pain was too much, too big for him.

"Cry-baby," Johnny said, grinding again. "'Igh-school boys don't cry — why'ncha shout fer yer muvver?"

"Leave me alone," Jimmy shouted, "— bastard."

"I'll leave yer when I'm good an' ready." Johnny stood up and called to the onlookers: "'Ere 'e is — look at 'im! 'E's a sissy an' a Jew-lover!" He reached down and grabbed Jimmy's hair again, repeating: "Jew-lover, ain'cha? Like the yids an' the kanga's, don'cha?"

The Jews were also known as Yiddishers, and in rhyming slang as kangaroos, these words being used if and when the speaker wanted to be particularly spiteful.

"No I don't —" Jimmy began, but Johnny pushed his face down again shouting accusingly: "Yes you do — lightin' their fires an' waitin' on 'em like a servant!" He was working himself up into something approaching hysteria. "England for the English," he shouted, "— down wi' the Jews!"

Johnny's feverish excitement was catching, and gradually the others began to echo his shouts; his sandy hair stood on end, a stream of thick and sour-smelling saliva dripped from his wet lips and his bright-pink face was swollen and bloated. "Not on'y Jews," he went on shouting. "— 'E likes the spades an' blackies an' all." He twisted his hand so that Jimmy's face was raised for everyone to see. "'E creeps in the blackies' 'ouse!" Johnny was grinding Jimmy's face again, and he followed his new theme to the end: "Wot d'you go in there for, eh? After that little black bit o' stuff? Are you?"

There was a roaring in Jimmy's ears; he knew he'd had just about all he could stand.

"Look out —" came a warning cry, "— Bullock!"

There was a welter of kicks and twists and punches, and Jimmy was alone, his tears adding salt-tinged irony to his raw face. He was bitterly ashamed of his tears and of himself, yet in that same instant he was fiercely proud. Johnny Burton and his gang were strong, but Jimmy was intelligent. One day they would envy him: he would force their respect.

The boys who had been watching gathered round to shield him from Miss Bullock's sharp eyes while he tried to tidy himself up. His right eye was almost closed, his arms and face felt as though they were coated in biting acid. Tommy came over and stared.

"Christ," he said. "You better wash your face, Jim." As he spoke he bent down and picked up Jimmy's green scholarship-form, now crumpled and torn.

Jimmy was crying weakly, without force, and the playground was very quiet: no running or shouting. Johnny Burton was standing nearby, waiting to see whether Jimmy would split to Miss Bullock. Her thin, stick-like legs and her brogued feet approached, rising and falling, then they were gone. Gently, with Tommy's help, Jimmy levered himself to his feet.

"Cover me to the wash-'ouse," Jimmy said, and in a group they crossed to the washing block in the far corner of the playground.

"I... I couldn't 'elp you, Jim," Tommy apologised.

"— Good job you never tried," Jimmy answered, "— they'd have murdered you." With a surge of pride he realised that again he had remembered to pronounce the *h,* and he felt better.

As he rinsed the blood and dirt from his face Miss Bullock blew her military-sounding whistle to announce the end of playtime, and with nervous speed Tommy and the others disappeared. Jimmy couldn't move quickly — his arms and legs felt as though they were floating and independent, seeming to work by delayed-action.

When at last he reached the classroom Miss Bullock was facing the door, her cane tapping the side of her leg. Her long, protruding brown teeth were wet and shiny, and she and the whole class were waiting for him. With the cane she pointed to a spot three feet in front of her.

"Here," she said briefly, and Jimmy crossed the room. She stared at him for what seemed hours, her cane tapping all the time.

"Now, Wilson," she said, her voice cold and sharp, "— who was responsible?"

"What... what d'you mean, Miss?"

"You know perfectly well what I mean, Wilson. *Who... was... responsible*"? She was rocking backwards and forwards as she always did when she was disturbed or angry; her eyes flickered over the class.

"I — I was climbin' on the coke, Miss, an' I slipped." This, Jimmy felt, was pure inspiration. One corner of the playground was walled off into a small open-roofed space where the coke used to heat the hot-water pipes that ran through each classroom was kept, and the boys often climbed over it. Miss Bullock's blue eyes were fixed on Jimmy's face; she didn't move, she didn't blink. But she knew he was lying.

"Go to your seat, Wilson."

Jimmy hobbled through the class and Miss Bullock went and sat at her desk, then the arithmetic lesson began. Jimmy ached all over, yet for the first time he began to wonder about the scholarship, to realise what it might mean to him. High School... to learn strange things like chemistry and Latin and how to speak properly. A cold shiver ran through him as he realised that he might even learn all about music and Varg-ner, like Pinkie had done... He'd be able to get a good job when he left school, and that was what he wanted more than anything; he'd work in an office and wear clean clothes and nice suits all the time and live somewhere posh, like Palmers Green or Winchmore Hill. ...

Now came pride, so much pride that he was exhilarated beyond pain, and the sudden knowledge that Johnny Burton would never do more than work in the brewery or in one of the factories increased his satisfaction... why hadn't Miss Bullock said anything about winning the scholarship? And why hadn't she... time was passing, and suddenly he wasn't so pleased with himself. Supposing Johnny Burton and the gang waited for him at dinner-time? The whole school had been given a half-holiday, so Jimmy would be safe for the day if he could get away without being trapped... but how could he get out of school and away before the others? He wondered if he could jump out of the window and get sent to hospital.

Just before the class ended at twelve o'clock Miss Bullock looked up, her steel-grey, bobbed hair like a misty aureole in the weak sunlight from the window.

"Wilson," she said in a flat, expressionless voice. Jimmy wondered what else could come, why even Miss Bullock was picking on him. Yet her thick, rubbery upper lip was fairly steady, her face and voice calm and unruffled.

"You may go down and wash your face," she said. "And," she added, "— you will go home immediately. Go now — and congratulations."

Jimmy realised instantly that she knew who had attacked him, that she was making certain that he had enough time to get away and safely home before the others, yet he found it difficult to believe. She had never before shown any sign of mercy or understanding. He didn't know that she was fully aware of Johnny Burton's jealousy of him; Jimmy, because of his excellent marks in the yearly examinations, had jumped a class entirely, whereas Johnny, who was lazy and interested only in the experiments of adolescence, had been kept back for a year. Jimmy was proud of his ability, Johnny resentful. Jimmy began to stammer his thanks, but she cut him short: "Don't waste time," she warned. "Go now."

As Jimmy moved to the door her eyes swept past him to the back row. "When the class has ended, Burton, you will stay behind."

There was the coldness of her dislike, that she could make you feel, in her voice, and Jimmy just caught Johnny's incredulous answer: "Wot — at dinner-time, Miss?"

"Exactly, Burton. At dinner-time."

Jimmy didn't bother to wash his face, but half-way down the stairs he pulled out his precious green form and tried to read the small print with one eye. Then, knowing that the other kids would be out at any moment, he began to run. He ran all the way home without stopping.

The downstairs room was untidy, and from the yard came the metallic shriek of the big cast-iron wringer. The old lady was trying to finish the Jewish neighbours' washing that she took in each week, for delivery before *Shabbas* began the next afternoon. Two big black saucepans bubbled slowly over lowered jets on the gas-stove, and the coal fire sent a warm glow through the always-gloomy room.

The yard-door was open, and Jimmy stood and watched as his mother's thin little arms and body struggled against the weight of the big wheel which turned the rollers over the washing, wringing out the moisture. He crept forward, then pounced without warning.

"Gotcha," he shouted, and with an alarmed little scream she turned and faced him.

Her face was white, her eyes dull and heavy. She stared at him as if he were a ghost, and when she spoke her voice was a croak:

"Jimmy... what've they done to you?"

He had been so excited that he had forgotten about his face. Now he felt stupid, as though he'd been caught in the street with nothing on. "Nothin', Mum. Just got in a fight."

She reached out and grasped his shoulder. "You bin in fights before," she accused, "— but you've never come 'ome like that. 'Oo done it?"

"No one, Mum. Not anyone special... just fightin'."

Her eyes were glittering now and he half-expected a right-hander. "Look," he said quickly, before she could move.

Slowly and proudly he offered her the green scholarship form.

"Read that," he said.

"Wha... what is it? What's it for? What're you 'ome so early for?" Usually at dinner-time Jimmy played with the other kids on the way home but today, as he'd been let out before time and had run all the way home, he was early.

"It's somethin' special," Jimmy said, and then announced importantly: "I've won the scholarship."

Mrs Wilson sagged back against the wringer, doubt and pride fighting for her face. "Show me," she said thickly, and vaguely her eyes ran over the small print. She stared unseeing at this, her youngest child, then her eyes drifted away, across the vista of backyards to where the overhead railway-line ran to Liverpool Street. "Read it to me," she ordered briefly, "— I 'aven't got me glasses."

She had pretended all her life that she could read and often sat with newspapers or magazines on the table in front of her. But sometimes they were upside-down.

Slowly and with difficulty Jimmy read every word, deliberately softening his voice when he got to the part about staying at school until he was seventeen, and about the school uniform. He expected some heavy comment about these, but the old lady listened in silence and when he'd finished he looked up and saw that she was smiling all over her face. She pulled him to her and cradled him in her arms, crooning to herself. "Jimmy... my Jimmy... always knew you was clever —" She pushed him away suddenly, almost violently.

"Get me coat out o' the cupboard," she said. "We'll go straight up to the ole man."

She took off and carefully folded her white apron and went inside. She turned off the gas-jets under the saucepans, combed her hair into a bun just like it was Saturday and put on her long green caterpillar coat, and all the time Jimmy couldn't stop talking. "I might be doctor, Mum, or a teacher. ... Me, a teacher!" Teachers were among the chosen people. They lived in a strange world where everyone had been to university and talked

88

about books and plays and music and they lived, as Miss Bullock lived, in posh suburbs like Palmers Green, or in far-off Broxbourne, like Mr Milson, and they nearly all had little cars, or motor-bikes with side-cars stuck on one side.

"Teach yerself to fight better, first," the old lady said dryly. There was something bright and bird-like in her eyes as they stared at each other, and suddenly they were laughing.

Proudly, like royalty, they went out into the Court, and Jimmy couldn't help skipping and jumping, all the way up to Brick Lane and the old man's stall, but he wasn't there. For a moment Jimmy thought his mother was going to start crying, then she took his hand. "I bet 'e's down the Two Bakers," she said almost gaily. "Let's go an' give 'im a fright."

Jimmy pushed the door of the public bar open for her, and as she paused there he saw the old man at the counter, lifting a pint glass. The old lady went in quickly and quietly and slapped him on the back so that he spluttered and nearly choked.

Before he could recover she ordered a stout, then she turned and fixed the old man with her shining eyes. "Got some noos for you," she said. "Jimmy's won a n'examination. And," she added impressively, "— 'e's goin' to 'Igh School." She turned to the door and ordered: "Show 'im, Jimmy."

The other people in the bar were watching curiously, and importantly Jimmy left the door and went over to the old man, holding the green form in front of him like a shield.

"There y'are, Dad," he said. "I've won it, an' we've gotta n'arf — a *half* holiday."

The old man stared at his son, then at the form, and then threw his head back and shouted with laughter. "Christaw-mighty!" he said, "— an' I always said you was barmy!" Again he laughed, and the old lady waited until he quietened down.

"'E starts after Chrissmas," she said slowly and clearly.

"We've gotta get special clo'se for 'im, an' sign for 'im to stay there till 'e's seventeen."

Swiftly the humour died from the old man's face, and he turned away. He put his glass down on the counter and his eyes slid over the other customers.

"Like bloody 'ell," he said, then announced to the bar in general: "I was at work when I was eleven. What's the use o' keepin' a kid at school all them years, when 'e could be earnin' wages?" He turned back to his wife and his son, dismissing Jimmy with a nod. "Go on 'ome, an' less 'ave no more rubbish." He swallowed another mouthful of beer.

The proud smile was still on Jimmy's face, and it wouldn't move.

"Dad," he cried, "I gotta go — I wanta be —" Jimmy saw the fist coming, but his face was so frozen that it didn't hurt. There had been so much in this one day that again he was crying; deep, shuddering sobs. As he went with dragging feet to the door the old lady screamed, "You bastard! Yer own son —"

"Shut up, else you'll get a right-'ander an' all!" That was enough. With a screech Mrs Wilson threw her stout over the old man, then leaped up and raked his face with her finger-nails. They were still at it as Jimmy went out through the door.

The tears rolled slowly down his cheeks as dazedly he made his way homewards; people looked at him, some simply curious, some with sympathy. He was past caring.

When he arrived home the fire was out, the house was dead and lifeless. He went upstairs and lay on the bed he shared with Billy and prayed that something would happen, that something would change the old man's mind. He lay for a long time staring at the ceiling, his tears making grey stains on the crisp white pillow-case, and at last he heard their footsteps and their voices. They were both staggering, and singing in short snatches. For some time there was talking and screeching laughter, but gradually the sounds died away into silence; when Jimmy went down to rinse his face under the tap in the yard his eyes were dry, and he felt no pain as he rubbed his face on the towel. He went over to the street-door, and looked back; he was going away from this house.

His eyes took in the dirty dishes on top of the chest-of-drawers, and the whitened end of the broken chair leg the old lady used when she set about any of the children; the two black saucepans on the gas-stove, with the dinner congealed inside them; the mess in the fireplace. He looked carefully at the old lady, sprawled on her back on the bed, still wearing her green coat, at the old man snoring with his head on the table. Both their mouths were open, and there were flies.

He turned and went out.

He had no clear idea of where to go. Now he realised that there was only one place he *could* go; Peggy had a spare room, the room that had been used by Pinkie in the summer. That was where he could go.

There was a light veil of rain as he left the house and the Court and went to the Indians' house. The street-door was open as always, but the passage and stairway were shrouded in shadow. There was no sound, and he thought the house was empty.

As his eyes drew level with the landing he saw that there was no light showing under Peggy's door. But as he quietly went past he was surprised to hear her voice in soft laughter. And there was the voice of a man, a voice he knew and should remember, but it was so faint and diffused that he couldn't place it. Then he knew.

He crept downstairs again and hid in the cupboard under the stairs, leaving the door open. That way he could hear when the man went away.

He crouched there, miserable and cold. The rain dripped past the door from the guttering, the clock in Saint Mary's chimed again and again and the shadows deepened and became real, solid darkness. And still he waited.

He heard the door opening above his head; the light Goodbyes, the heavy uneven tread as the man came downstairs. He saw the big form go out into the street and he followed, wondering.

Why was Mr Gapley with Peggy, for so long? Why had she never said that she knew Mr Gapley?

He watched the great figure walking drunkenly down the street and he turned sadly back towards the Court. You could never depend on grown-ups, because they always hid something, they always had a reason they never talked about. Yet he knew that Peggy was not responsible; he knew that *Peggy* would not have approached Mr Gapley *first*.

The rain dripped from the black sky and he shivered. Yet it was not so bad as it seemed. Peggy had to live, and with her help, and with the help he knew he could count on from Miss Bullock at school, he would work and learn, and one day he would be *someone,* something. There was lots of time — he had his dictionary and his lessons, and there was the public library in Whitechapel... he would leave school in three years. It sounded a long time, but it would pass. Then he would have a job — an office job, of course — and then he would start to be one of those strange things, a grown-up.

# Book 2

# 1

The light that almost managed to spread through the room came in bubbling, sputtering surges, and did little more than emphasise the surrounding gloom. A tongue of violet flame curved through the hole in the gas-mantle and licked and flickered at the glass bowl hanging on uneven wires from the ceiling, and the same violet was repeated over by the far wall; the big black stew-pan, once used to make the scrag-o'-mutton stews that fed a clamouring family, but now used only to heat Jimmy's bath-water on Saturday nights, stood above the lowered jets of the gas-stove. It took both gas-rings to heat it, and it took a long time.

The fire glowed dully in the grate, and little blue-centred yellow flames leapt into being, struggled for life, then died with an exhausted popping sound. The fire and the gas-stove had been alight for hours, and the room was stifling. The windows were shuttered, and masked on the inside against splintered glass by a series of overcoats and blankets, and both the yard-door and street-door had a screen of coats and blankets to prevent the light surging into the court or out across the yard. The minute that happened you got shouted at by the air-raid wardens or some nervous neighbour.

The pillows on the rackety old bed behind the door gleamed white, as they had gleamed for years, and as the old lady pushed the zinc bath into position between the table and the fire she knew an instant of deep satisfaction; whatever the neighbours said about her and her family, they could never say her sheets and pillows were dirty... or the kids' underclothes. Never had been...

not like some people she could put a name to.

It seemed that all her life she had struggled against the wringer in the yard, wrenching and dragging whiteness from linen and clothes reluctant to yield their dust and grime; designed only for cheaper goods, and so not expected to achieve that eye-dazzling brilliance that Mrs Wilson twisted and cajoled and forced them to achieve. Of that she was proud.

The bath was ready, the water in the saucepans on the fire and on the gas-stove was hot, and... the light became even weaker and she realised that the gas was going out. Another penny! She crossed into the deeper gloom at the foot of the bed and quickly searched through the collection of odd dishes and broken cups on top of the chest-of-drawers, where she kept her change, but there were no pennies. She sighed, picked her way across the room, and flicked off the taps of the gas-stove. The lamp above the table flared into brief brilliance, then subsided into a soft blue-and-violet glow. She pulled a chair up to the table and sat down and stared at the fire.

Any minute now she would hear the rumble of the stall as the old man and Jimmy pushed it on its barrow past the door and round to the side of the house. There would just be time to bath Jimmy and nip round to the pub before Moaning Minnie went off again... reg'lar as clockwork, the bastards. You always knew they were on the way because the wireless went off, but when she was on her own she was frightened of the weird screams and whistles that came out of the wireless when she tried to make it go, so she sat in silence... silence that grew deeper, soft and gentle... her mind ran back through memories of the years and of her kids.

Ever since she'd been married she'd lived in this little two-roomed house, and every Saturday night through all those years the same zinc bath stood before the fire. First so that she and George could have their weekly bath, and then suddenly it was filled with splashing and shouting and fighting kids who grew up in next to no time; the house was filled with rushing and screams and laughter and sometimes the boys chased each other in childish fury, but there was pleasure in taking in washing and combing the boys' hair. Then came the time, as it came to all mothers, when as she leaned over her children she saw with fear, and with fierce pride, that they were growing into men and women, and as that happened, one by one they were sent to the Public Baths near Bethnal Green. There was only Billy and Janey and Jimmy left now. The others just went, and not one had ever come back.

She had been born on a farm in Cheshire, so she knew that as life grows it grows away from that which gave it life. Even so, it hurt. Not that she blamed them — it was just life — but for years she hoped and believed that her first-born, Boy-boy, would come back to see her. She imagined him standing framed in the doorway, with his big shoulders and his hairy forearms stretched out towards her — funny, the way he never would button his shirt-sleeves, but always wore them rolled up — and she saw his wide and friendly grin.

"'Lo, Mum," he would say, and she would drop whatever she was doing and run over to him... but it was no use. Boy-boy, and her second son Bert, would be in the army now. They might even be in a prisoners' camp, or bones lying on foreign sands... she was glad Billy had failed his medical — served him right for trying to volunteer. Just a kid... even though she knew that he knew as much about everything as she did, he was still only a kid. An obsternate kid, like when he joined the Blackshirts just before the war started and she had to knock sense into him — black-an'-blue sense at that — but he was a good kid, underneath...

*Boy-boy, where are yer?*

Just three kids left, Billy, Janey, and Jimmy. Janey was obsternate too — worse'n Billy, in a way. Quite the young lady now, with her high heels and make-up. Saucy bitch, too... Janey was harder to keep in her place than any of the others. Then there was Jimmy. ...

Funny bugger 'e was, with 'is nose always stuck in a book, an' listenin' so 'ard to the talks on the wireless you could almost see 'is ears flappin'. ... Once Jimmy'd made 'is mind up you could kick 'im, you could 'alf-kill 'im; you 'urt yourself, you 'urt 'im as well, but you couldn't change 'is mind... She wished 'e'd been able to go to the 'Igh School when 'e won the scholarship, but what was the good? They only got their 'eads full o' strange ideas, and got too big for their boots... It was after that time that 'e stopped rakin' round the streets with the other kids and glued 'is eyes on books an' dictionaries; sometimes 'e spoke in a different way and used strange words she couldn't always understand, like they did on the wireless, which confused 'er as much as the wireless itself. ... The worst thing was, 'e would never argue or shout; 'e just shut 'is mouth an' stared at you and you felt cold and your voice stopped, even when you didn't want it to...

She had begun to realise that Janey and Jimmy were growing beyond her control, and again she sighed.

*Boy-boy, where are yer?*

The kids had come, the kids had gone, and once she'd seen Jimmy safe at work and able to look after 'imself, her job would be ended. She would go to a doctor and see what caused the terrifying agony that brought her rigid from sleep, sweating and trembling; the deep bubbling cough that made her feel as though her lungs were being scraped with fish-scalers, like they used on the fish stall in Brick Lane. ... And on top of all that, night after night the bombers came and dropped their lot on poor old London. No use going down the shelters — if one 'ad your number, you got it... look what happened when the bomb got in the ventilator of the tube station... why'd they use lime... ?

It was warm, there was no gas... smiling gently to herself, the old lady reached up and pulled the string that worked the gaslight, turning it off altogether. When your face is yellow and waxy, when there are blue rims round your lips and eyes, darkness can be comforting. The old man and Jimmy would be back any minute. ...

*Boy-boy, where are yer?*

It seemed that her eyes had only just closed when she heard the faint bump of the barrow jumping up the kerb from the street; it ground its way through the court with agonised shrieks from wheels that had never been oiled since the day the old man found it abandoned — he thought — in a side street near Spitalfields Market. The old lady opened her eyes and gazed at the fire, waiting for her husband and her youngest child. The door opened, then closed a moment later, and there was the soft rustle of the blankets and coats being pushed back into position.

"Jeeeeesus Kerrist, Lizzie," the old man exploded, "— wotcha sittin' in the dark for?"

The room was in almost-complete darkness, but the dark was not so intense as in the blacked-out streets; there was no need to wait for the usual pause while eyes adjusted and re-focused.

There was a blur of movement, felt rather than seen, as the old lady's hands fluttered to the sides of the table. "Gas is gorn out," she said simply, "— I've got no pennies."

"Fine bloody 'ouse to come 'ome to, this is," grumbled the old man, "— never no one in, never no gas, never no anythink —"

"Don't start moanin' the minnit you get inside the door," said the old lady sharply, "put another penny in, fagawsake." Having organised her husband, the old lady turned to Jimmy. "Pour the water in the bath an' jump in, an' be quick about it," she said, "— the water's all 'ot."

From the coal-cupboard under the stairs came the metallic clink of a coin being fed into the gas-meter; the old lady tore a long strip from the newspaper-tablecloth, and moving carefully round the bath, poked it into the fire until it flamed. She shielded the flame as she came back to the table, and a moment later the room swam into depth and dimension and feeble colour.

Jimmy remained motionless, leaning against the door.

"Y'eard what I said," his mother shrilled, "— get yer water in."

The old man, having raked the fire into a brighter glow, sat down on the squeaky-backed chair, whistling soundlessly through stained teeth.

"I don't wanta bath. I wanta go round the Public." Jimmy meant to sound serious but his words were more comical than convincing, for his voice varied between a squeak and a dark-brown baritone. A soft flush spread over his face, but he added enticingly, "Why don't you an' Dad just go round the pub and let me go round the Public in the week?" The old lady ignored both his voice and his plea.

"I just toldya," she said quietly, with narrowed eyes. "Get the bath ready, an' jump in it." The old man still whistled, staring at the dark, smoky mirror above the fireplace, with the photographs of Billy's celluloid idols in a series of predicaments that threatened but never became fact. "'Urry up, Lizzie," he said. "They'll be over before long an' we won't get a seat."

It was funny, he thought, the way the pubs were full up nowadays. Before Dunkirk, before the air-raids, you could get a seat anytime o' day. But not now. Oh no... even the Jews had begun drinking in the bars... when the bombs dropped it didn't seem so bad if other people were with you... Some people drank because it was easier than trying to sleep, some people drank because they were frightened to sleep; some drank because soon they would be in the army, some drank even more because they were in it already. Still others drank because they'd seen their homes and their pals blown to bits, and because the sound of aeroplanes gave them the shakes... he didn't really know why everyone was drinking, but who cared? You only lived once, and the way things were going, it might not be long. ...

The old lady stalked across the room and stood in front of Jimmy, hands spread on her hips. "You gonna do as yer

100

told?" she demanded. "I won't tell yer agin." They stared at each other.

Didn't she *know*? Jimmy wondered. Couldn't she understand? How could anyone bring up a whole tribe of kids and still be so stupid? Words poured like lava into his brain but his throat was paralysed and he couldn't explain that he didn't want to bath here in this room as he had done in the past, in this room where he had stood naked and had his hair washed so often. He had a secret, and it made him proud yet self-conscious.

Like all boys of his age, Jimmy kept a record of his increasing height. It was on the wall upstairs, and when he had started, nearly six months earlier, his pencil-marks had been a good inch below the long smear of bug-blood. As the pencilled lines mounted so did Jimmy's pride and curiosity; the vague aches in his thighs and across his shoulders told him that he was growing up, and to help his body along he began to do exercises. He became more and more curious and excited as the months passed; two painful series of boils on his neck came and went and all the time, slowly yet inevitably, he grew. As he grew he also grew more and more impatient, for like all boys of his age he longed for evidence, for the sure knowledge that at last he was an adult, and like all boys of his age he sought this evidence of himself. He sought it, he demanded it; furtively, frequently, and on occasions painfully, he sought and insisted, and the most painful thing of all was that still it evaded him. It danced on the edge between his mind and his body and swayed and shimmered from one to the other and never became real. When he told Tommy Cooper, a bigger and heavier boy, his reply was a laugh heavy with the knowledge of one who has attained the unattainable: 'You're using the wrong muscles."

Jimmy realised that he and Tommy were no longer the friends they had been. Tommy was scared to go out at night in the raids, even though they got paid for it... and he kept combing his hair.

101

Jimmy determined not to make use of the muscles that throbbed and quivered and sometimes irritated him; he would save them. He would do more. He would develop them, every one, and he would grow tall and broad and strong... not that he believed all that stuff about going blind, and funny things happening to your hands... all the same, it was no good taking chances. Was that what had happened to Blind Billy?... couldn't be, because Blind Billy was no more blind than you were. ...

So each morning through the grey autumn made tender by the smoke and fire and rubble of the blitz, and into early winter, he crept upstairs and began the exercises that made aching and jumping muscles ache and jump even more. ... Bend, stretch, hup... bend, stretch, hup. ...

Now he knew, deeply and certainly, that at last it had happened. The soft, the beautiful softly-curled golden down on his skin was proof. From now on he would go to the Public Baths.

Jimmy gazed at his mother without seeing her. Without warning a hand flashed upwards and livid white streaks appeared on his cheek. Still Jimmy didn't move and still the old man whistled soundlessly, and they all heard the ticking of the clock.

The old lady darted across the room to the chest-of-drawers and savagely pulled down the broken chair-leg that was her final badge of authority. Her eyes glittered and her blue-tinged lips drew back from her teeth. "Get them clo'se off," she said.

Slowly, his face hard and set, Jimmy took off his jacket, then his shirt; he moved across to the old lady's bed and carefully laid his clothes on the edge. He went to the fire, lifted off the saucepans and poured the water into the bath. The old lady crossed to the bed.

"Look," she said scornfully, "Look at the state o' that shirt — a *schmutter*." It was an exaggeration to describe the shirt as an old rag, but angrily she pulled it from the bed and the jacket, as though suddenly come to life, slipped over the edge to the floor. There was a muted, metallic ring, and the old lady's eyes widened. Two long and narrow strips of metal lay on the floor, and a third was still half-inside the coat pocket.

"'Ere," she said. "What's this — what's them for?"

All three of them were staring at the floor, and the old man stopped whistling. "'Ack-saws," said the old lady sharply. "Look — 'e's got 'ack-saws." Jimmy stood motionless with the saucepans in his hands as the old lady whirled on him. "What're they for?" she demanded, "— what d'you do with 'em?" Slowly, stiffly, with eyes slitted in fury, she edged round the table. "You're one o' the gas-pipe kids," she accused, and the old man sat up with such a jerk that his greasy peaked cap fell off and showed his pale, vein-rippled skull. His tongue slid out and flicked gently at the ends of his frayed faded-ginger moustache. Jimmy still stared at the floor.

"Did'nch'ear me?" the old lady insisted, her voice rising and shrill.

"Well — s'pose I am?" Jimmy didn't want to lie, but he couldn't face the truth.

"Margawd... !" The old lady was unable to believe what she knew was true. "You dirty little toe-rag," she spat at him. "People get crippled an' killed in them 'ouses, an' all you can do is pinch their iron before they're cold!"

The old lady couldn't tell the difference between iron and lead and copper, and in any case it seemed to Jimmy that his crime lay not in taking the metals found in the bombed houses, but in doing it 'before they're cold'.

"You're gonna stop it," the old lady ordered, "— you're gonna stop it this minnit, an' if I 'ear —" she tried to swallow the lump in her throat but it was too strong for her, and as she finished her voice became thick and strangled-sounding: "— if I 'ear you're still at it, I'll — I'll put the Lor on yer meself."

The old man reached forward and pulled his wife round so that she faced him. "Nah nah, Lizzie," he said, "— don't upset yerself — 'e's not the on'y one. They sell all the lead

103

they get — don't yer?" he demanded, swerving on Jimmy.

The old man's blood-shot, watery eyes had come to life and his tongue-flicks were wet and incessant. "You sell it, don't yer?" He left his chair and stood over his youngest son, thumbs hooked into his brass-buckled belt.

"We don't sell it. We just cut it up and leave it where they tell us to. They collect it and leave the money."

"'Ow much d'ya get for it?" The old man's voice was quick and urgent and the old lady, knowing what was in his mind, shrugged and turned away. A bit more money wouldn't do any 'arm — 'specially as you didn't know when your lot was comin'... might even be tonight... she came back to the job in hand with a start, realising that already they were later than usual.

"Look 'ere, son." The old man was cajoling, whining, and in that instant the old lady despised him almost as much as Jimmy obviously did: "Look 'ere — I'll 'elp you. I'll — I'll cover up for yer, if there's any trouble. ... Yer muvver's brought you up all these years — doncha reckon she's entitled to a bit of what yer get — me an' all?"

"Fachrissake get them clo'se off an' 'ave yer bath," chipped-in the old lady, exasperated, "— the bloody siren'll go in a minnit."

"All right," Jimmy said coldly to his father. "I'll give you a pound every Monday. But I don't want no 'elp."

"Not everyone's 'ad a good 'ome like you," the old man said, slapping his son on the back in a demonstration of pleased affection that surprised himself even more than the others.

"George, fagawsake stop naggin' an' let 'im 'ave 'is bath." The old lady's voice was sharp-edged with temper, and the old man went back to his chair.

Jimmy kicked off his shoes and stepped out of his trousers, and as he wriggled out of his underclothes he turned away from his parents, determined to keep his new knowledge to himself. In one swift and elastic movement he was in the bath and crouched down.

The water was too hot and he hadn't got the soap or the

face-flannel, but he was too tired to ask and he didn't want any more talking or explaining. He just wanted to be left alone, to make his knowledge more absolute by one more quick look. ...

"What d'you do with the money you get?" The old man was not really curious, just talking for the sake of it, and as he spoke the old lady, in near-psychic intuition, handed Jimmy the saucer with the face-flannel and a piece of flabby soap. Jimmy lathered his arms and shoulders and pretended not to have heard the question. "I said, what d'you do with the money?" the old man repeated angrily.

Jimmy crouched lower in the water as the old lady took the face-flannel and began to wash his back.

"Nothing," he said dully. "I'm saving up."

The old man felt a light fluttering in his belly as he realised that somewhere in the house was a wad of notes. The old lady stiffened.

"What for?" she demanded, suspicion giving an edge to her voice. "You're not leavin' 'ome, are yer? What about yer rations?"

"I'm just savin' up," Jimmy repeated. "It's nothin' to do wi' you," he added, softening his voice in the hope of avoiding further questions.

With Peggy's tuition, and the reluctant assistance of Miss Bullock, he had achieved what he hoped was an effective control over his words and his native accent; he realised now, with surprise, that an unexpected or disturbing situation could destroy this control, and he felt a slow anger against his parents.

"You talk to yer mother like that again, you'll get my toe up yer arse," the old man threatened, adding for emphasis: "— Saucy bleeder." Satisfied with this dazzling display of authority, he started whistling again. Silently, between his teeth, looking forward to the time when he discovered Jimmy's hoard. Wouldn't take long to find. ... The old lady, her question still unanswered, prodded Jimmy sharply.

"You're up to no good," she stated in flat, even tones. "What're you goin' to do wi' the money?"

Knowing that his mother would keep on at him, that she could work herself up into a temper in almost no time at all, Jimmy sighed.

"I want a new suit for when I start work," he said wearily, but he couldn't prevent himself from adding "An' I'm goin' to Toynbee 'All night school when I've got a job."

"You're *what*?" Surprised to the point of stupefaction, the old lady could think of nothing else to say, while the old man's eyes and mouth formed three vague but near-perfect circles. The idea of anyone going to extra school of their own accord had never occurred to him.

It was useless to try to hide anything, Jimmy knew. He himself had opened the way to more questions, and now they would push and prod and pry until they knew all there was to know. He sighed and then explained slowly and clearly, with enormous seriousness: "I'm leavin' school at Christmas, so I've got to have a new suit. Then I'm going to Toynbee 'All — *Hall* — to learn music." (That's better, he heard Peggy's voice. Speak slowly, be careful.)

The effect of his words against his squeak-baritone voice was so strange that the old lady threw back her head and roared with laughter; Jimmy shrivelled while his father blinked.

"'E's mad," said the old lady when her breath came back, explaining in two words all Jimmy's thoughts and hopes and actions. "Besides," she went on, "you don't want a new suit to work in the broory."

"I'm not goin' in the brewery." (Careful, Jimmy, careful.) "I'm going to work in an office." He was calm and determined, but still the old lady wasn't satisfied.

"What'ya gointa learn music for?" she asked, "— so you can stand outside the pubs wi' yer 'at in yer 'and an' sing?" Again she burst into laughter, but noticing the dull flush that spread through Jimmy's neck and up into his face, she added pleasantly, "You always was a bit funny, wi' yer posh talk an' books."

106

Jimmy took a deep breath and held it for a moment before he spoke, and despite himself, to give greater emphasis to his words by less restricted movement of his hands, he stood up. His flesh turned to goose-pimples, something inside him was breaking, and his voice was thick and treacly. "Mum," he said, "I'm not posh. I don't want to be posh, and I never did... I just want to talk properly, to work and learn. ..." He swallowed convulsively, painfully. "... I want to get a good job where I can get on, with good wages... I don't want to live round here all my life in two rooms, like you and all the rest of the family. ..." Peggy and Miss Bullock between them had done a good job and now Jimmy and his parents were all confused and bewildered. Jimmy saw for the first time that he *did* want to be posh, because if he worked harder and learned more than those around him he would no longer be *with* them, which would make him posh. Or separate, or different. And he couldn't explain even to himself the strange urge he had to learn about music, to know something about what Pinkie called the Classic Composers... she would be pleased when she knew. ...

He might as well have remained silent, for his explanation made no impression whatever.

"Smack 'is arse," said the old man, "— make 'im talk sense."

The old lady, vaguely watching her son, suddenly bent her head and peered closer. "Why did'n'cha tell me?" she said, and stood back. "That's the last one." She spoke to the old man with relief and not a little pleasure in her tone. "Next week 'e can start goin' round the Public."

Between them the old lady and the old man had been close to breaking him, but now Jimmy stood there unashamed; as the old lady's meaning sank in his pride surged back and filled him; she had acknowledged that he had Grown Up. And she still didn't know about the photo in his trouser-pocket.

"Oh well," the old lady admitted grudgingly, "— if you wanta be posh, you wanta be posh —"

Three loud knocks startled the three of them, and in panic Jimmy sat down again as his mother, with a quick look at the doors and the window to make certain that the blackouts hadn't shifted, went to the street-door. Carefully moving the coats and blankets, she inched it open.

"'*Oo* is it?" Jimmy heard her nervous question clearly, and the reply came in a voice he dimly recognised.

"Boy-boy!" Mrs Wilson's scream of delight rang in Jimmy's ears and again the old man stopped whistling. At least, he didn't actually stop; it took him some time to realise that he couldn't really whistle with his mouth wide open, and by that time Mrs Wilson was excitedly trying to drag Boy-boy inside the room. Jimmy peered curiously between the legs of the table.

"'Ang on a minnit," Boy-boy said, almost as pleased and excited as his mother, "I've got someone wi' me." He came slowly into the room, pulling a wide-eyed and fair-haired little boy who was obviously about to burst into tears. "There y'are," Boy-boy said proudly, "— yer first grandson. Billy," he ordered the boy, "— come'n kiss yer gran'ma."

"Gawdelpus!" breathed the old lady reverently.

"Mum," Jimmy called, "— give me the towel."

Mrs Wilson ignored him, gazing proudly from her smiling Boy-boy to her grandson, who was trying to use his father's thick-sturdy legs as a shield. She bent down and tried to pull the boy farther into the room but he easily dodged her and ran round to the far side of the table, where he stood and stared at Mrs Wilson gravely, his fair hair standing up all over his head like pale broom-bristles. He addressed one word to his grandmother and immediately skipped back to his father's side, and after a moment of astonished silence the old lady threw back her head and roared her pleasure.

"You saucy cow-son," she said, enjoying the joke, and darting forward managed to snatch the boy up in her arms. She rocked gently backwards and forwards, her eyes closed, and she made little moaning sounds.

"I've got someone else outside, Mum." At Boy-boy's diffident, nervous voice the old lady's eyes opened again; the boy took advantage of her surprise and wriggled to the floor, where he stared at Jimmy still sitting in the bath.

"Mum," Jimmy called again, "Gimme the towel." He was beginning to feel cold, but again he was ignored.

The old man, tired of sitting unnoticed, came out with what for him was an inspired remark: "Course 'e's got someone else outside," he said, "'is wife."

"Your — your wife?" Dismayed, Mrs Wilson stepped back to the table. "Your wife?" she repeated dully, as though unable to understand.

"'Course, Mum," Boy-boy replied, "— that's why I've come."

"But — but where is she? Wyncha bring 'er in?" Mrs Wilson ran over to Boy-boy and began pulling him to the door. "Fetch 'er in, quick," she said.

"I... she..." Boy-boy stood short and thick-set and solid as a rock against her pulling and thrusting, yet still nervous. "She was frightened in case you didn't like 'er," he added.

"Not like 'er?" Mrs Wilson said incredulously, "what d'you mean, not like 'er? She's yer wife, ain't she?" Her voice made it clear that all mothers inevitably liked the wives of their sons, but she saw that Boy-boy was still uneasy. Looking more carefully she saw that his face was thinner, that his eyes no longer glowed with the warm friendliness she remembered so well; his smile, once so easy and generous, was now little more than a widening of his mouth.

"*Well,* Mum... y'see, we're not married yet." In Boy-boy's voice was the same quality he had as a child, when caught doing something wrong. The old lady was filled with a flood of love and tenderness.

"Yer — yer keepin' all right, aincha, Boy-boy? Where ya'bin all this time — whyncha come an' see us?" She was

109

worried and concerned for him.

"Well — I'll tell yer all that later-on," he said.

Jimmy splashed his hands loudly and yelled: "Mum, I've not got a towel," and in sudden irritation the old lady whirled on him. "Shut up," she said, "— first time you seen Boy-boy for years, an' all you can think of is —" here she mimicked Jimmy's unreliable voice — "'Mum, I wanna towel'. Fine relation *you* are to 'ave," she finished with deep scorn.

She was pleased with herself, particularly when Boy-boy and the old man laughed at her attempted mimicry, but their laughter caused Jimmy to call loudly: "Why must you keep takin' the mickey out of me — I on'y want the towel so I can get dry." But something else had occurred to his mother.

"Jeeeesus," she said to Boy-boy, "— you mean to say yer..." For a moment she faltered, unable to think of the correct word for a woman who was unmarried but was in every sense a wife; after only the briefest pause she added: "... yer lady-friend's waitin' outside in the dark on 'er own, an' the warnin' might go off any minnit? Y'orta be ashamed o' yerself," she finished in mock severity, darting towards the street door.

Without effort Boy-boy caught her and lifted her right up, so that she almost touched the ceiling, her knees pressed close to his deep, wide chest. She wanted to laugh and cry at the same time, and ended up in a great splutter and cough.

Holding her up towards the light with complete ease, Boy-boy laughed aloud. "She's more frightened o' you than the air-raids," he said, and explained, "— she's eight munce. ..."

The old lady gasped, then giggled. "You always was a one," she said proudly. The old man looked at his first-born with admiration, and with vague memories of a story about the return of a prodigal son. After all, he reflected, it's not ev'ry day a son comes 'ome, even if Boy-boy wasn't very prodigal. Whatever that was... an' a wife

110

who wasn't a wife... 'e'd always known that Boy-boy 'ad the right stuff in 'im. ...

The old lady's thin arms beat a tattoo on Boy-boy's wide shoulders. "Lemme go," she yelled, and this time she meant it, "— put me down... the pore thing must be frightened to death out there on 'er own."

"O.K., Mum," Boy-boy grinned, "'er name's Maisie."

He released his mother and as she carefully pushed aside the blackout blankets and edged out into the darkness of the Court he pulled off his jacket, to reveal that even now he always wore his shirt-sleeves rolled up.

"Wonder the air-raid siren's not gone off yet," said the old man almost to himself. "They're gen'rally over by this time."

"They're not comin' tonight. I sent a wire to 'Itler," Boy-boy grinned. He pulled a towel from the footrail of the bed and carried it across to Jimmy.

"Blimey!" he said, "— all skin an' bones, ain'cha? I know what'd fatten you up a bit," he said meaningly, staring critically at his youngest brother. Jimmy reddened, grabbed the towel, and furiously began drying himself.

Mrs Wilson, having carefully sidled through the screen of blankets and out into the Court, paused uncertainly. "Maisie," she called softly, "Maisie — where are yer?"

There were no stars, no moon, not even the cloud-glow of distant searchlights to relieve the darkness; no gleam of light from neighbours' windows, for those who were nervous or wise had already gone on their nightly journey to the deep shelters, or to their wire-mattressed bunks along the tube-station platforms. Those who stayed at home were hidden behind the veil of darkness that to Londoners was more comforting than batteries of searchlights, easier to believe in than any number of barrage balloons.

There was a slight, almost inaudible sound, and the old lady cautiously made her way along the wall towards it. Poor kid, she thought. I'd be nervous meself, standin' out

111

'ere on me own... eight munce, an' all. ...

She sensed rather than saw a deeper darkness and gently reached for it. "Maisie?" she queried gently, "— come on, love, it's Boy-boy's mum." She felt a trembling hand placed in her own; a quick search told her experienced fingers this was indeed Boy-boy's lady-friend. Her heart filled and overflowed with tenderness; if Boy-boy loved this woman, then she herself would love her just as much. More, because women know things that men never know. ...

"Maisie," she repeated softly and warmly, folding the shaking body in her arms, "— nothin' to be frightened of, love... come inside — we wanta 'ave a look atchu. Don'chu wanta 'ave a look at us...?" Gently but persuasively she drew the hesitant stranger along the wall; to the street-door, through the blankets, and into the room.

The old man watched like a hawk. He knew Boy-boy had an eye for a woman, and he was sure she'd be a real nice piece o' cracklin'. Jimmy yelped and quickly wrapped himself in the towel, and looked on dumbfounded. Even the old man looked a bit funny.

Feeling that something had gone wrong, the old lady pulled the girl into the centre of the room and then turned and faced her.

Her face registered surprise, then something close to disbelief. While Boy-boy stared at the fire, everyone else stared at Maisie.

She was short and thick-set, with wide blue eyes set in a blotched and bloated face; her hair was straw-yellow and brittle, with the colour and texture of corn dead and dried, and her mouth hung half-open and slack. She had no ankles. The flesh of her legs fell straight down from flaccid muscles and hung in bulges over the rims of her shoes, and she was so swollen that her bright-flowered skirt was six inches higher at the front than at the back.

The old lady's eyes took all this in, but she managed to transform her surprise into a cough.

"'Allo, Maisie," she said softly, "— it's — it's nice to see

112

yer. ..." Her voice stopped although she wanted to say something comforting, while Maisie looked all round the room and then fixed her eyes, as though fascinated, on the broken gas-mantle with its curling tongue of blue-tinted flame.

Boy-boy crossed the room and put his arms protectingly round her shoulders. "She gets nervous wi' strangers, Mum," he said. "That's why I've come back." Mrs Wilson realised with a pang that if it hadn't been for this woman, Boy-boy would still have stayed away — perhaps for years and years. "There's no need to be nervous 'ere, love," the old lady said. Her hands fluttered as she showed the room in an effort to be reassuring. "We're just ord'nary people."

"Aye." Maisie's voice was thick and bubbly, like heated syrup — or as if, the old lady thought, she had inflammation on her chest. And she spoke with a strong north-country accent.

"Why 'nchasiddown, gel?" said the old man, "— putcha weight where it orta be, like."

Maisie grinned faintly and looked up at Boy-boy, and Mrs Wilson saw something incredible; Maisie's wide eyes kindled into life, her facial contours seemed to firm-down and become finer and more regular and a tremulous, half-fearful smile drew her open lips closer together; her grossly-swollen body became all the women that are, that have ever been, in love.

"Aye," Maisie said again, this time vaguely in the direction of the old man.

"That's it," said the old lady, "— come an' siddown." She too put her arms round this strange girl from the north, and together she and Boy-boy led her carefully to the side of the bed. Maisie splodged herself down on the edge and went back to staring at the gas-mantle, and it was as though the wonderful thing Mrs Wilson had seen had never been. But she knew that this girl loved Boy-boy, and for that, if for nothing else, she would be welcomed into the family.

Jimmy, still wearing the towel, slipped round and picked up his jacket and the hack-saw blades and his trousers, furtively feeling into the hip-pocket to make certain that the photograph was still there. He smiled. They thought they knew everything, but they didn't. Not by a long way.

"Mum," said Boy-boy hesitantly, "we — we're gonna get married."

Mrs Wilson knew already that this was to be and she knew it was right, just as she knew that good looks were not everything, but the old man sat up with a jerk.

"You're gonna what?" he demanded. "Whaffor? You're doin' all right as you are, ain'cha?"

Once again Boy-boy looked like a small boy caught doing something wrong. "We *was* doin' all right," he said, "— till that Mr Gapley found out we wasn't married... that was a coupla years ago. 'E kept naggin', so we moved, but 'e found us again." He pulled a packet of cigarettes from his pocket and tossed one to Jimmy, who put it behind his ear. "'E kept on at Maisie about gettin' married, an' about women 'oo fall over an' get turned into salt, or somethin', an' —"

"If people are 'appier just bein' together, why don' 'e just let 'em alone?" said the old lady plaintively, "— they'll only move round the corner an' not be married to someone else... that there Mr Gapley orta mind 'is own bus'ness." She realised that for years Boy-boy and Maisie had been living nearby, without her knowing. But she knew too that it was the easiest thing in the world for people to do.

"An' then 'e said little Billy's not legal, an' Maisie started cryin', then the army sent me call-up papers an' we moved again... so we're gonna get married like old Gapley says, then I'll 'ave to give meself up. ..."

There was a brief silence, in which Mrs Wilson went and sat next to Maisie. "Ne'mind, love," she said, "We'll look after yer."

"Aye." Clearly Maisie had heard little of what had been said.

"But you don't know what it's like, Mum," Boy-boy went on, the doubts and worries of the past years showing in his words. "If I'm not there people take it out o' Maisie — 'cos she's quiet-like, an' don't talk much... Mum, if the Army puts me in the jug, will you 'elp 'er?"

The old lady took a deep breath and stood up. She was small and thin and faded, yet she spoke calmly, with something very close to dignity.

"'Course I will, son. We all will. If I 'ear anyone say anythin' out o' place, I'll tear 'em to pieces meself."

Boy-boy relaxed, and the old warm grin spread all over his face. "I knoo yer would, Mum," he said. He turned to Maisie and gently raised her to her feet. "Y'see, Maisie? I told yer it'd be all right." Tenderly they kissed, then parted, and again Boy-boy spoke to his mother. "Will you come with us tomorrer, Mum? We're goin' round to ole Gapley at Saint Mary's to put the banns up."

"'Course I'll come." The old lady was happy and fiercely proud as she added: "— just you try an' stop me!"

"It's funny," Boy-boy mused, "I went to Saint Mary's when I was a kid, but I never expected to get married there... we'll 'ave a party. A big party, like we 'ad in the old days wiv all the Court, an' the tables out... we got some money." The old man, temporarily paralysed by too many revelations in too little time, came to life. "Blimey," he said. "A party! Kerrrist! 'Aven't 'ad a real good party since the coronation... all the 'ouses in the Court empty, all the neighbours an' friends crowding the Court, crates an' crates o' beer along the wall an' shrimps an' cockles for 'igh tea. ... Old Tom Cooper an' 'is mouth-organ an' Mr Beggs an' 'is banjo, an' the spoons... mustn't forget the spoons. Long time since I played the spoons." Lost in a dream of a wonderful party, he began to sing softly, in a low gravel-voice, "There was me an' the missis an' the 'arf-a-dozen kids, a-kerlimbin' up the monniment so 'igh. ..."

Boy-boy and Mrs Wilson stared at each other amazed, then together they burst out laughing and the old man stopped. "Jist practisin'," he said. "I reckon we orta go roun' the pub an' 'ave one for old times' sake, an' one for the bride an' groom." At these words Maisie crimsoned, while Boy-boy grinned. "You always was a dry ole bastard," he said good-naturedly.

There was a sudden flurry of movement. Maisie stood and tugged at her badly-fitting skirt, the old man fidgeted with his cap, and Mrs Wilson dragged her coat from behind the door of the cupboard under the stairs. She turned to Jimmy.

"Nip upstairs an' get the mattresses — make yer own bed," she said. "We'll be back at closin' time, an' if the warning goes, or if you go to bed, don't forget to turn the gas off." She always had a fear that if the gas-mains were put out of action, as had happened on several occasions, houses where the gas was on might explode, or the gas might leak into the rooms and everyone would die in their sleep.

"Can't 'e come an' 'ave a pint?" Boy-boy asked.

"No thanks, Boy-boy. I'm tired." Jimmy was surprised to find that for once his voice stayed calm and even and in the low register, and Boy-boy too was surprised; not by Jimmy's words, but by the way they were spoken. Like a real posh geezer. "All right," Boy-boy said with a shrug, "I on'y arsked."

In a few minutes they were gone; the old lady and Boy-boy both holding on to Maisie, the old man and little Billy trailing behind, and as soon as the black-out blankets and coats were back in position Jimmy went and stood beneath the gaslight. Whipping off the towel he stared and stared. Was it real, was it imagination?... the gold a little deeper, almost brown, the curl a little more definite?...

Like many others in the East End, the Wilsons had stopped going to the shelters. Now they slept in the downstairs room, the old man and the old lady in their bed as usual, with the three remaining children stretched out on mattresses beneath it. As he dragged the extra

116

mattresses down from the beds upstairs, Jimmy wondered whether the bombers had found a new target — not that he wished them on any other city, but it would be nice to have a real good sleep. ...

When the mattresses and the coverings were ready he slipped into his clean underclothes, left ready for him on the old lady's bed, then slid into his place on the centre, with his head sticking out into the room, so that he could see. He reached up and into his trouser pocket and brought out the photograph. He didn't know why, but he could spend hours looking at it; she was a little taller than when he had first seen her three years ago, still slender, but filling out with early bloom. Her eyebrows were straight and narrow, the eyes themselves huge and dark. Two thick braids of glossy and raven-black hair curled gracefully down almost to her waist, and her slightly-parted lips showed a glimpse of perfect teeth. He remembered the last time he'd seen her, when she'd been ready to go out with Peggy to a Christmas party... he remembered the way she smiled when she handed him a small package, teasing him to guess what was in it... he remembered his pride and joy at the thought that she had bought him a Christmas present, and the sadness when at last she told him that Peggy had bought it, after all... but he didn't mind... not really. He just liked to listen to the cool way she spoke, the feeling she gave of knowing all about everything... *She* never had trouble with her *h*s and *g*s... he hoped she would be pleased when she knew that he was going to learn about music and *Varg-ner*... 'course she'll be pleased, he told himself. But he didn't know why.

It was nearly a year now since the night when Peggy, returning from a different party, had dropped her handbag on the stairs. A mass of letters and nail-stuff and face-powder had fallen out, and as Jimmy, who had been waiting for Tommy to come out of Rajah's room, bent down to pick them up, the photograph stared up at him. He reached down and slid it into his pocket... good thing

Peggy never noticed... The weird, two-note scream of the air-raid warning blasted into the ears of the waiting Londoners, and brought the small flutter of fear to insides already tense and expectant. It was a pity. They had hoped for a night off, but this wasn't it...

Mr Wilson, already well into his second pint, couldn't prevent the slight trembling of the hands that the siren always brought, but he knew that although he was frightened, it was better to stay here and be frightened than to run away and still be frightened. He was ashamed of his fear, so it never occurred to him that to stay, to be ready to run into the street the moment the cry 'Fire bombs' went up, could be bravery. Meanwhile, there was Boy-boy and the party to come. ...

"'Nother one, Maisie?" he asked brightly.

Mad Mary, tottering towards her new home in the unused surface-shelter in Luxton Street, broke into a doubtful run: she knew it was unwise to run for the protection of the railway arch because they always dropped their bombs along the railway, but the Luxton Street shelter was too far away, and she hadn't had a drink for a long time... It would have been better for her if she had gone on, for the first bomber dropped his H.E. bombs on the railway arch, and the next bomber dropped his fire-bombs on the fire that was already blazing. Mad Mary had as usual been drinking meth, and as always she had a bottle in her shopping bag. Somebody told Mrs Wilson next day that she had burned like a torch. ...

Peggy too felt the stirring of fear, but she was warm and comfortable, and protected by a strong right arm. Dark brown and dry-looking, as though left in the sun too long.

Jimmy got up and lowered the flame of the gas-light, listening to the sound of the anti-aircraft guns in the distance. Sounded like they were over Poplar, or East Ham... there was the wail of a big bomb, and an explosion that made the house jump and a tiny flake of the fabric of the gas-mantle drifted slowly down. That one was a bloody sight nearer than Poplar... he listened, but the sound of aircraft and guns receded into the distance and faded altogether... there came again the irregular grinding of German aircraft-engines but the guns remained silent, and this too faded.

He heard a flurry of footsteps, then Janey burst into the room. "For chrissake watch the light," Jimmy shouted, scrambling out to make certain that the blankets were in place. As he turned back into the room he noticed that the photograph was still in his hand, and he saw that Janey was crying.

"Whassup, Janey?" he asked, "someone been hit?"

Janey put her arms round him and cried and cried. "What's up?" Jimmy repeated irritably, feeling that there had been enough drama for one night. "It's Johnny Burton," Janey sobbed.

Jimmy's eyes widened. "What was it?" he asked, "— shrapnel?"

Janey's eyes widened in turn, and there was another flood of tears. "Whadd'ya mean, shrapnel?" she said.

"Well," Jimmy stumbled, "— what's happened?"

"What's happened? 'E's goin' to join the Army, that's what!"

Jimmy felt a strange sense of relief and anticlimax. "That all? So did Jackie Morris an' Dickie Turner —"

Janey shrugged. "I don' care about them," she said raspingly, "— this is Johnny — 'e might get killed, an' I won't ever see 'im again!"

Jimmy's lips curled. Having suffered at his hands on several occasions, he didn't care what happened to Johnny Burton. But he knew that Janey had always had a soft spot for him...

"You're mad worryin' about 'im," he said, and added with unmeaning cruelty, "— 'e never worries 'is 'ead about you." This was true, and Janey wailed louder than ever. Jimmy crawled back under the old lady's bed.

119

For generations the Two Bakers had supplied beers and spirits to those who worked and lived in or near Spitalfields Market, and had quenched the thirsts of many thousands of the people who came through the years to the Sunday Markets in Brick Lane and Club Row. Now, in the Blitz, unconsciously people realised that in an air raid the thick granite-block walls would give as much protection as any surface shelter, and so it was that although most of the nearby pubs emptied within a short time of the siren's scream, the Two Bakers filled up. There was nearly always someone handy to play the piano and make things lively and Fred Hunt, the landlord, was a genial round-faced man who never rushed you at closing time.

This particular night, just after the warning sounded, there'd been a big one dropped not far away — close enough to make the floor jump and set the electric lamps swinging like pendulums. By the railway, someone said... but that was all they'd had so far, except for an occasional flurry of gunfire. Perhaps tonight the bombs were falling on the docks farther east... the thought came to Fred that there might be more to come, but hurriedly he pushed it to the back of his mind and concentrated on those of his customers who could be seen through the veil of cigarette smoke.

In one corner a small knot of Indians nervously sipped at brown ales, with green-tinged glances when the door opened and the black-out screens leaped, and farthest away from the door sat Mrs Behan, still wearing the fruit-salad hat she had bought to celebrate the victory of 1918. She had wedged herself in next to the blubberous Mrs Plotsky, who with her friend Myra Rubens had started coming in after the raids began. It only took two or three port-wines to set all her flesh-folds a-quiver, and once they started they couldn't stop. ... Catching Fred's glance, Mrs Plotsky raised her glass in a toast. "Mid a good 'ealt'," she said, and added, "— again ve vill be shickeh!" She beamed and smiled and quivered.

The Wilsons had come in later than usual and had brought Boy-boy, whom Fred vaguely remembered, and what looked like his wife and son. They were a funny old pair. Been coming in every weekend for years, so reg'lar you could almost set your watch by them. Other people had been gradually slipping in through the screens, and suddenly Fred realised that the bar was filled; the chatter of many mixed voices rose and fell like waves on a pebbled shore, and the smoke haze grew thicker and thicker. There was no ventilation because the doors were screened to prevent light escaping; the big plate-glass windows were criss-crossed with strips of adhesive paper, then covered and re-covered with thick velvet curtains.

There was a light warning tap on the door, then with much puffing and shuffling Tom Cooper and his wife Adelaide pressed their way in. Mrs Wilson, delighted to see her friends and bursting with the news of the wedding-to-be, jumped up from her seat.

"Adda-laide," she called, "Addie — over 'ere." She waved her hands frantically and the Coopers saw her and laughed. Together they forced their way through the crowd and immediately their hands were seized and pumped in an orgy of greetings and introductions.

"Look 'oos come 'ome," said Mrs Wilson proudly, "— Boy-boy!" Adelaide sniffed. She knew all about Boy-boy and leaving home and not sending a penny to help out... she'd show 'im the door if it was 'er, not 'arf she wouldn't... and she knew something about 'im that Mrs Wilson didn't, though even wild 'orses wouldn't drag it out of 'er. ... 'E'd done six months for pinchin' cigarettes from a railway goods-truck. People said 'e was in the black market, an' all. ...

"An' this," Mrs Wilson went on, with a vague wave of her hands, "— is Boy-boy's Maisie. They're gointa get married at Saint Mary's an' we're gointa 'ave a real slap-up party in the Court!" Mrs Wilson waited for some pleased response, but Adelaide only smiled uncertainly. There came one of those moments when all tongues fall silent; the smoke streamers drifted and whirled and trembled, and the sound of anti-aircraft guns came clearly. Maisie grabbed Boy-boy's hand.

"Don't worry, love," said Mrs Wilson lightly. "When the railway gun goes off, that's when we know they're comin' this way. That's when we get ready to run." She laughed in attempted gaiety, trying to reassure her future daughter-in-law, but she failed. Boy-boy leaned over and gently stroked Maisie's yellow hair, then he bent right over and they kissed and Mrs Wilson thought it was lovely.

Mrs Behan's fruit-salad hat tossed indignantly at such behaviour in public and Mrs Wilson, seeing her frozen stare, pushed her way across the bar. "'Allo, Mrs Bean," she said, "'Ow are yer? Come an' meet me eldest boy — 'e's bin away…" She sought for an explanation for why he had been away, and found inspiration. "'E's been workin' in foreign parts, an' 'e's jist come 'ome to get married," she finished.

Mrs Behan sniffed again, so that the cherries on her hat threatened to fall off. Mrs Wilson brought her big guns to bear, well aware that Mrs Behan loved a drop of stout. "We're 'avin' a big party for 'em," she said, "— all the Court's goin', an' I'd like you to look in an' 'ave a drop o' somethin'… wouldn't you like to come over an' 'ave a stout now, Mrs Bean? Drink their 'ealth an' say 'allo, like?"

The cherries nodded joyously and Mrs Behan rose and crossed the bar with Mrs Wilson, to be drawn immediately into the Wilsons' circle. Everybody seemed to be shaking hands and smiling fixed smiles and Adelaide Cooper found it impossible to gossip with this strange yellow-haired woman who rarely spoke. But as there was to be a party, Adelaide was willing to be friendly.

Boy-boy quietly slipped three one-pound notes into his father's hand. "Push the boat out, old'n," he said, and turned to indicate his mother and Mrs Cooper and

122

Maisie. "Get the three wise virgins a drop o' gin, an' all," he added. Catching Mrs Behan's stare, Mr Wilson decided to include her too.

Gently, but with increasing insistence, came the sound of engines weaving through the sky and the rising challenge of the defensive guns; glass-lifting hands halted half-way to opened mouths and there was dead silence as the whole bar listened intently for the whine of falling bombs. There were four rapid explosions, some distance away, and the guns stopped as though surprised. The electric lights blinked twice, then steadied, and as though at a signal everyone began talking again; a little louder, a little faster, and glasses emptied more rapidly.

"Drink up," said Mr Wilson with a sly wink at Boy-boy, "— the next one's on me." He turned and pushed his way to the counter, followed by Boy-boy and Mr Cooper carrying the empty glasses.

"That's right, Maisie," encouraged Mrs Wilson, pointing at what she had already decided was to be another grandson. "Drink yer stout, an' keep the little bugger warm."

"Meester Lend-lott," shrilled Mrs Plotsky across the bar at the landlord, "— vhy izzen somevun playink der pee-anner? Sink abot der Siegfriet Lane." Mrs Plotsky thought the Siegfried Line was a German street-market, like London's Brick Lane.

Fred smiled and waved his hands. "How about a tune, George?" he said to Mr Wilson just as he arrived at the bar, and gladly the old man pushed over to the piano which willing hands had already opened. Mrs Plotsky, whose sense of rhythm was even worse than her English, began banging her feet, and it was catching.

Mr Wilson sat and pounded away, and voices raised nervously at first soon gained confidence; feet shuffled and a gradual stamping was taken up by the whole crowd. In no time at all they had hung out their washing, the troopships had all left Bombay, and Mr Cooper sang an interesting but impossible version of that song which describes the activities of soldiers when no young ladies are about. Faces ran with sweat, tongues short and fat or long and pointed poked from black-shadowed mouths, and even Mrs Behan's fruit-salad caught the rhythm. Feet and bodies moved in unison, voices cracked and screamed and the smoke grew denser and hung like drifting curtains of the northern lights. Again Boy-boy and Maisie kissed, but this time Mrs Behan's fruit-salad almost melted. Mrs Wilson and Addie Cooper jigged together on one spot, and the landlord sank a double and furtive whisky.

The piano sounded like a de-tuned harp but the old man, hands and feet going like hammers, was happy. Two pints on the piano-lid, and one on the table. Lovely.

There was a sudden, shattering crash, followed by an intense silence which was broken by a nerveless bass chord from Mr Wilson. "'S'all right," Fred shouted, "— it's only the railway gun."

"'Elp 'em on their bleedin' way 'ome," someone added, but nobody laughed.

Mr Wilson strummed his way into 'Coming Round The Mountain', an old and tried favourite, but few voices joined in, and even these were half-hearted and soon died away into nothing.

"Mum," Boy-boy said to Mrs Wilson, "— we'd better be gettin' 'ome. Maisie's gettin' excited."

"Go 'ome? Where to?" Mrs Wilson realised only then that she still didn't know where Boy-boy and Maisie were living.

"Vallance Road," he replied, "but don't you worry — we'll be all right."

"Gawdelpus! You can't go all that way with a raid on, an' Maisie like she is an' all. Stop 'ere a bit an' come 'ome with us — we'll fix you a bed downstairs."

"Whyncha come 'ome with us?" put in Addie Cooper. "We've got a spare room, since Joey went in the army."

Once again the hum of voices was rising as the sound of engines and guns faded, and Mrs Wilson thought quickly. Certainly the Coopers had Joey's room, which they kept ready for him in case he came home on leave. But on the other hand they lived up on the third floor.

The passageway was never lighted, and reeked of sour and unwashed milk-bottles and boiled cabbage. At least the Wilsons had a house to themselves.

"What — Maisie climb all them stairs in 'er condition?" Mrs Wilson demanded lightly but firmly. "Not while I'm alive an' kickin'. Besides, s'posin' somethink 'appens to 'er. ..." Seeing Maisie's scarlet face Mrs Wilson stopped and put her arm round her shoulders. "No thanks, Addalaide," she finished, "— you're a decent ole cow, but I wouldn't letcha do it."

"You all right, Maisie?" Boy-boy was quiet and surprisingly sober, willing and even anxious to do whatever Maisie decided. "Aye," Maisie answered, reverting to the monosyllabic conversation which had been overcome for a short time by stout and gin. She pulled Boy-boy down beside her, pushing little Billy further along the bench. He was half-asleep, and began to cry weakly. Mrs Wilson and Adelaide turned towards the bar to order another round of drinks, and Adelaide sniffed.

"No wonder she's eight munce again," she said, "if all she ever says is Aye," and she and Mrs Wilson roared with laughter. Mrs Behan, catching Addie's remark, joined in heartily, with rapturous nodding of fruit-salad.

The landlord was the first to hear the shrill descending whine, and sudden fear gripped then loosened his bowels. "Geddown" he screamed at the top of his voice, bringing immediate and intimate disaster upon himself, "— on the floor." He and most of his customers were just in the act of crouching when the first bomb exploded; not near enough to do any actual damage, but enough to make the heavy curtains flutter and jerk and to make heads feel as though they had been smashed by a sledge-hammer.

Several of the women screamed and Maisie's voice rose high and thin. *The lights,* Fred thought dazedly, *I must put the lights off,* and with the thought came the hollow roar of collapsing masonry.

He was reaching up for the light-switch when the second bomb exploded a little way down the street and across the road; three beautiful and delicate wineglasses displayed on a shelf chinked forward over the edge and smashed on the cash register, and Fred blinked in surprise at the long deep cut that spread across the back of his hand. "Never knew my hands had little bits of string and white stuff inside 'em," he thought, and it was uproariously funny; the cut filled with blood that flowed steadily to the floor and his middle fingers hung limp and slightly curled and he couldn't move them. He fainted.

Mrs Behan sat quite still, forgetting that she was no longer in her usual well-protected seat. She heard the ear-splitting *blam* of the bomb and saw the curtain lift and rip all along the top. She saw the myriad cracks appear in the glass, shattered by blast and flying debris, and she saw the long sliver that broke away from the restraining glued-paper strips and curved slowly and gracefully, spinning like a child's coloured toy, towards her. There was a sharp, biting agony just below her left ear.

Debris was still falling as Mrs Wilson sat up and blinked. The lights were still on, but it didn't matter because through the smashed windows came the red-and-yellow glare of incendiarised London. Another bomb smashed down but seemed no nearer than the first.

"Mrs Bean!" Mrs Wilson's face was grey and her eyes wide in horror. Mrs Behan's head nodded gently and the fruit-salad hat slid slowly and sadly to one side and hid the bright-red stream that pulsed and jetted beyond her shoulder. Mrs Wilson vomited quickly and urgently and as she struggled to her feet she kept saying Jeesus Gawdelpus and she thought that her words and Maisie's terrified screaming and little Billy's moaning sounded funny. She helped a few people to their feet and pushed over to where Maisie, in her efforts to protect little Billy, had half-slipped to the floor.

Boy-boy looked at his mother in silent agony, paralysed by Maisie's convulsive jerking and writhing; her nails bit deep into his flesh but he felt nothing.

"Mum," he said brokenly, as tears sprang to his eyes, "Mum, 'elp 'er, forgawsake 'elp 'er." Mrs Wilson and Addie, both trembling from shock but both making little soothing noises, prised Maisie's fingers loose and stretched her out on the floor, where gradually she quietened. "You take little Billy 'ome an' wait there," Mrs Wilson ordered Boy-boy firmly. "Maisie'll be all right in a minnit." She had no means of knowing whether Maisie would be all right or not, but it seemed the best thing to say. Someone turned the lights off, but it made no difference to the bright flickering glare that suffused the whole sky. Boy-boy lifted little Billy in his arms and walked slowly through the gap where the door had been.

There were several injuries but no deaths, other than Mrs Behan. Fred, now recovered and with a crimson handkerchief bound round his useless hand, told someone to ring through for the ambulances and rescue squads, then dispensed drinks on the house, to restore still-raw nerves. In less than ten minutes the squads appeared but by then Maisie was calmer. Adelaide tried to persuade her to go in the ambulance, and was reinforced by the medical orderly who urged Maisie to consider the benefits of evacuation to a safe area, but Maisie shook her head. "Boy-boy's mah man," she said gently but firmly. "Ah'm bidin' wi' Boy-boy." Mrs Wilson could have hugged her.

The whine of the first of the bombs sent Janey scrambling under the bed to lie next to Jimmy, afraid, expectant; knowing, as the people of all England's big cities knew, that death was close at hand; knowing that if this time they were spared they would go to work or to school, red-eyed and half asleep; knowing that tomorrow or the day after the sirens would sound again and again would come the roar of engines, the crashes of guns and of bombs; that more houses would collapse in clouds of dust to entomb friends and relatives and neighbours and enemies, for the bombs were not particular. Again there would be fires, and again the firemen, recruited from civilians as a wartime measure, would try to prevent the fires from spreading. And, if the water-circulation and pumping systems still functioned, they would succeed.

Trembling, holding on to each other for comfort, Jimmy and Janey heard the second bomb explode, but it was the third one which sent them cowering back against the far wall, that made the ground leap and deafened them and forced the air from their lungs and made their eyes bulge with intolerable pressure. The door crashed open and hit the headrail of the bed, the window was torn from its frame and hurled into the room, bringing with it the coats and blankets that had formed the black-out screen, and the already-broken gas-mantle flaked away and sifted slowly down through the dust like puzzled snowflakes. The weak blue flame grew fainter and disappeared altogether as the pressure died away from gas-pipes and gasometers that gave their warmth and light to red-glazed and unappreciative skies, and an echo of that red glaze now filled the Wilson home. Almost immediately came a rain of bricks and mortar that slammed against and penetrated the roof, and they heard the splintering as upstairs the old plywood wardrobe disintegrated. A dull throbbing filled their heads and their eyes saw only a red film; for an instant there was silence, then began the shouting and screaming of terrified neighbours, children, animals; the rush of scampering feet rose in a sudden crescendo then died away.

"Janey!" Jimmy shouted into the silence, "— the pub! The old lady's there, an' Boy-boy."

"Boy-boy? Boy-boy?" Janey was dull and trembling and unresponsive, and Jimmy remembered that she didn't even know Boy-boy had come home again.

"Boy-boy's back," he explained irritably. "'E's got some woman with 'im an' she's 'avin' a baby an' they're gettin' married at Saint Mary's."

Janey stared at him and then, her nerves and emotions overstrained, she rolled over on to her side and burst into deep and shuddering sobs. Jimmy reached out towards her, but stopped.

"Janey," he said hesitantly, "you gointa stop 'ere? I'll run round to the pub an' make sure the old lady's all right." Janey gave no sign that she had heard, and he shook her impatiently, "Janey," he said loudly and urgently, "*Janey!*"

"All right. ..." Her voice was a thin, moaning quaver and Jimmy simply looked, not knowing what to do for the best but feeling that she had neither heard nor understood his words. "Whyncha get up an' *do* somethin', 'stead o' layin' there snivellin'?" Jimmy too was at a high nervous pitch, and his anger made Janey cry louder than ever.

Jimmy wriggled out from under the bed, slipped into his clothes, and ran quickly up through the deserted, glass-glittered and tile-strewn Court. The red glare of the fires was heightened by the cold blue-silver beams of searchlights, and when he reached the street he stopped in surprise. It looked so different.

Flames and smoke wreathed through the top floors of the tall houses opposite him, most of the windows and doors were shattered, and neighbours were trying to save what remained of their homes and belongings. Down near the corner of Luxton Street what had been two houses now spilled into the road as rubble, with clouds of dust hovering like uneasy spirits, and more smoke curled lazily from the partly demolished houses next to them. He jerked into sudden motion, wondering whether Peggy had gone to one of the shelters... he knew that usually she stayed in her room.

An eye-searing flash lit the sky, he was hurled to the ground and along the surface for several feet; his hands and face and legs were torn and cut by splinters of glass and roof-slates and jagged-edged bricks, but he dragged himself to his feet and ran on, over or round piles of bricks and mounds of debris... he stopped, doubtful.

The blast of the bomb had spread upwards and outwards like a funnel so that the top floors of the houses next to the destroyed pair were more badly damaged than the lower levels. The top of the Indian house — the room where Pinkie slept when she visited her mother — had vanished entirely and part of the wall of the lower room, that had belonged to Rajah before he went back to India, had collapsed into the street. Even so, it was the first of the houses near the point of impact that still resembled a house.

The street door had been blown off its hinges and was halfway along the passage; somebody was shouting orders and there was a confused moaning and wailing of thin Indian voices. The wooden stairway sagged drunkenly, smashed through in two places, and over everything hung a pall of white dust from atomised plaster.

Peggy, who a little earlier had been warm and comfortable and aware of the comforting I-am-not-alone feeling given by the presence of another human being, had been alone when the bombs came down. She was still warm and comfortable but now she was tired, so that at first the meaning of the thin whistling made no impression on her. A moment later she almost fell from the divan in near panic, but she was too late.

She heard the first two explosions, but she could never recall the third, and she knew only an unbelievable pain that sheared through her eyes and ears; the left side of her face and body were twin flaming agonies that forced her to writhe and moan, but her movements were so feeble that they were barely visible, and her moans were little more than whispers. Blood oozed from her nose but poured steadily from her left cheek; ripped open by the splintered end of a rafter which now crushed the whole of her left side and was in turn buried under other rafters and tiles and bricks, her cheek was opened and her molars and part of her jawbone exposed. She began sobbing weakly, not knowing that she did so.

Poor Pinkie... it wouldn't be easy for her now... not much money, now that so many of the Indians had gone back to sea or to their own country... the richer clients had all disappeared into the safe countryside...

The darkness swirled momentarily away from her eyes and for the first time Peggy realised that she was trapped under a mass of rubble... she was warm and... wet?... blood?... do something... Peggy, *try. Try* Peggy, try hard. ...

Her mouth opened and she tried to scream and she tried for a long time, but there was nobody there, no one to hear... the darkness closed in on her again and, exhausted, she fell silent.

Somebody was calling her name and shaking her but she couldn't open her eyes... she was so tired... and they still wouldn't open... a scream bubbled in the back of her throat as she realised she was blinded.

"Peggy... Peggy"... it was a voice she knew from a long time ago... ages... the little boy who liked pineapple but was frightened by the fork and the knife... everyone should have dessert cutlery. ... She giggled when she thought of him winning the scholarship and she wished the pain in her head and body would stop... why was he crying? No good crying... too late now. ... "Jimmy?" Her voice was just a sigh. Her fingers fluttered, but she could do no more to help him.

"Peggy!" His sudden relief was disturbing, startling...

"Peggy, listen. I'm gointa try to get some o' that stuff off... the rescue men'll be up in a minnit. I'll try not to 'urt. ..." His voice faded and became lost in the roaring that filled her head and all the world, then she was being lifted and she knew Jimmy was crying again.

"Jimmy. ..."

"Y'mustn't talk, Peggy. Just keep still." Strange... his voice had suddenly gone deep and calm, even stern... something had happened to him tonight... he had grown up...

"Jimmy," she pleaded, "... handbag... letters from Pinkie... send a telegram..." Her voice faded entirely, but Jimmy understood. She heard a faint rustle of movement and then of paper, and his voice came cool and quiet: "'S all right, Peggy, I've got the letter an' the address an' I'll send a telegram tomorrer. Now, keep quiet." His hand, still immature but firm, pressed her own comfortingly. There was a small pain in her arm and once again the darkness swirled down...

Sadly Jimmy watched as Peggy was lifted gently into the ambulance that not long ago was a fashion-house delivery truck. He asked where she would be taken, and as tears rolled down his cheeks the ambulance drew away, bumping over the rubble, and turned the corner.

Much later dawn lifted over Stepney, pointless and futile, for the smoke and dust swirled and were beyond penetration, but as it lifted, Blind Billy, without his dark glasses and without his blind-aid walking stick, left his home and walked quickly and purposefully down Luxton Street and along Whitechapel and Aldgate. He was trying to estimate how much metal he could expect from the kids during the next few days, but he soon gave up the effort. There was too much.

# 2

The day was well advanced and the pall of smoke less dense when at last, weary and red-eyed, the Wilsons and the Coopers left the Two Bakers and went home. Mrs Wilson, confident that Boy-boy would now stay in the family fold, was already looking forward to the wedding; she seemed undismayed, even unaffected, by the sight of the debris-strewn Court and of her own damaged house, and quickly began putting things to rights. Janey, who had eventually cried herself to sleep, was hauled out from under the big bed, given a hand-broom and shovel, and told to start clearing up the mess. Then the old lady turned on her husband and Jimmy, who were soon hard at work sawing and hammering lengths of timber into boards and shutters for the downstairs window, for the blackout-screens had to be fixed before dark came again to London. The old lady knew that an Inspector would come to examine the house, and she knew too that as many thousands of homes had been damaged beyond repair, her own home would be made livable; until then they would all have to manage in the downstairs room.

She stripped the old dishes and cracked cups from the top of the chest-of-drawers, and as she began to dust them she suddenly stopped. It had just occurred to her that she would have to put in a war-damage claim, and she smiled. As with other people she knew, the value of the damaged or destroyed furniture would be increased, inflated; she would invent a fur coat for herself and suits and coats that the family had never possessed, so that they would all come out of it better-off. "After all," neighbours told her, "— they always try to knock you down a bit, an' why shu'n't we make a few quid? 'S'our own money they took away from us wi' taxes an' ev'rythin'. Why shu'n't we 'ave it back?"

The old lady began to feel a sense of injury, a grievance against a possible War Damage Claims' man who would doubt that she'd ever had a fur coat..." Don't see why I shu'n't" she echoed aloud the general attitude, justifying herself as she went on with the dusting — "we're on'y tryin' to get some o' the money the Govamment takes off us every time they put prices up"... 'S'all right, for them... they live in the country in big 'ouses an' they 'ave special air-raid shelters built under the Thames, where the bombs can't reach 'em. Mrs Cohen said that when the German invasion was expected, the Govamment was all packed an' ready to go to America or Australia or somewhere... "Govamment!" As she said the word her lips curled scornfully, and a cracked cup in her hand broke; "The Govamment don't know nothin' about us... if they do they don't care, an' that's worse. ..."

As she carried on cleaning up her spirits rose at the thought of the money to come from the War Damage claim... it was a shame she wouldn't be able to get it in time for Boy-boy's weddin' present, but she'd buy something for him an' Maisie later on... she hoped they found their room still all right when they got home...

Mr Wilson and Jimmy fixed their boards into the window-frame, but even with the street- and yard-doors open the room was so dark that the old lady sent Jimmy out to get a new gas-mantle, and soon after he went off the old man, whistling to himself, slid upstairs. He said he wanted to see if he could do anything to fix the roof, and for some time he could be heard moving about. He didn't stay up there very long, and when he came downstairs again he unfastened his belt and stretched himself out on the big bed, while Janey and Mrs Wilson went upstairs to straighten the room.

By the time Jimmy returned with the gas-mantle the old man was asleep. It was Sunday, so Brick Lane could do without him for once... 'specially after last night...

Tired, but with his mind filled with the memory of Peggy's bloodied face, and thinking about the telegram he had promised to send to Pinkie, Jimmy realised he would have to keep himself awake until the afternoon. After the telegram had gone he would go to St. Michael's Hospital, near Whitechapel, in the hope of being able to see Peggy herself. He would need some money for the telegram, so with studied carelessness he went upstairs and helped his mother and Janey by pushing the naked bedsteads from one side of the room to the other, and piling the remains of the collapsed wardrobe against the far wall. There was a surprising amount of pulverised plaster dust; everything in the room was filmed with a patina of it from the ceiling, part of which was now distributed over the floor. A great lump of still-cement-bound brick-wall had smashed right through the roof and ceiling and now lay near the top of the stairs, and Janey found a six-inch piece of bomb-casing which she put on the mantelpiece as a souvenir.

Jimmy filled a couple of buckets with bits of rubble, with glass from the gaping windows, and emptied them into the great round dustbin at the bottom of the Court, as several of the neighbours were doing. When he returned his mother was wiping the dust from the top of the mantelpiece and Janey, stepping carelessly out of her skirt and furling her slip round her thighs, began washing the floor down. Going to the battered plywood dressing-table Jimmy opened the bottom drawer and took out the heavy, well-fingered dictionary he had bought a year ago. He opened the back cover... then stared, hearing nothing, seeing nothing but the blank white lining and the grimed-finger marks. In a frenzy he tore the shirts and socks and underclothes from the drawer and strewed them over the floor, then sat back on his heels, breath hissing between his teeth.

"Mum," he said, "Mum, you been over this drawer?"

Mrs Wilson, still thinking about the War Damage claim

and about her arrangement to go later on with Boy-boy and Maisie to see Mr Gapley and arrange the wedding banns, didn't hear his question. The sharpness of his tone when he repeated it broke into her thoughts and she stared at him in irritated surprise.

"Me?" she said. "What for? I put the clean washing in there last Friday... why?" Janey watched curiously.

"'Ave you, Janey?" he said, rounding on her suddenly. "There's somethin' missin' — some money."

Janey's face was so innocent that her denial was unnecessary.

"I've not touched it. Didn't even know you 'ad any money. Besides," she couldn't resist the boast, "— I've got enough o' me own." They stared at each other with the same thought in their minds, which Janey put into words. "The ole man," she said simply. "— I bet 'e's got it."

Mrs Wilson watched her son uncertainly. She knew without question that Janey was right, as she knew that somehow she would force the old man to return the money — or part of it, anyway. She would defend the old man against strangers with tooth and nail, and had often done so, although well aware that he was not above short-changing his customers at the stall, particularly the more overbearing or condescending of the Jews. But this was different. This was his own family, his own son.

"The ole bastard..." she said softly. "— 'Ow much was it?" Only last night Jimmy had told them why he was saving up, and she saw from his pale and stricken face how deeply he was upset. 'E's a funny kid, she thought — wastin' 'is money on suits an' lessons... but still —

"Nine pound." Into Jimmy's mind flashed the idea of going to the police, but he rejected it immediately. Splitting to the Law was an admission of weakness, and he would make himself the butt and laughing-stock of the whole neighbourhood.

This was family business, and must be kept in the family.

The old lady's eyes widened. Nine pound! Even 'alf that would be enough to get Boy-boy an' Maisie a nice weddin' present. An' there was all the stuff to get for the party. ...

She had never used the Black Market — had even despised such activities, but what could you do? Everything was rationed, officially or otherwise. Whisky and gin and rum, essential to a good party, had jumped up in price and were practically unobtainable, like decent cigarettes. They had all gone under the counter, and you could only get them if you knew someone... even then you had to pay over the odds. She could save and sell or exchange some of the family ration coupons, for they never had things like butter, or tinned salmon or fruits... but even then there wouldn't be enough to get the meat to make sandwiches for about thirty people, and you couldn't invite people to a wedding party and ask them to bring their own ration books... Boy-boy had said he had some money, but he wouldn't have very much... they said the blind man who lived round the corner sometimes had legs of pork or lamb to sell... she'd have a talk to him. ... Some of Jimmy's money would help, an' all.

Janey too was surprised. "Nine pound? Where'd you get all that from?"

"I saved it." Jimmy's voice was defensive, flat, rejecting any further questions. "— An' I want it back."

"You've got some 'opes," Janey said cynically, and she went on with her floor-washing.

"For chrissake don't go near the ole man now," Mrs Wilson warned, "'e's asleep. I'll get it back for you later on — even if I 'ave to go down 'is pockets meself."

Jimmy knew that for the moment he could do nothing. If he woke the old man up there'd be murders, yet he needed several shillings for Pinkie's telegram. He wandered undecidedly downstairs while his mother, wondering where the old man would have hidden the money, replaced the shirts and socks, then went on with the cleaning up.

Downstairs, Jimmy glared at the old man's indifferent, slightly-vibrating moustache, at the stained teeth... bloody old crook. But money. He must get hold of some money.

He sat in the squeaky, loose-backed chair and stared morosely at the gas-stove, and the dull paint with the row of brass taps became a malicious and derisive grin.

It was no use, he saw. It was wrong to pinch piping and metals from the blasted houses, although he'd intended to stop as soon as he'd saved enough for his suit and the lessons. He'd been lucky so far — the police were always on the lookout for looters... now he'd have to start all over again and his luck might not hold. But in the face of this setback his determination to achieve a way of life other and different from the life he knew grew stronger.

Yet at the back of his mind came for the first time a tiny but bright spark of doubt, painful but undefinable. Was there something wrong with him? Why couldn't he be like Boy-boy and Billy, and just accept things as they were? What was it in him that even his own family could not or would not understand and found it easier to ridicule? Was he trying too hard? If the old man had let him go to the High School when he was eleven, when he won the scholarship, it would have been a lot easier... but he was young and he knew he would be a hard worker, that he was intelligent and would get on... so his small doubt faded as gradually his belief in himself was re-established. For the first time he set his mind to examine his problems, to find a way out. ...

In the bombed houses were lead pipes, fire-irons, sometimes ornaments or saucepans of copper, brass taps... all were worth money. It was useless, he saw, to go out with two or three of the boys from school, creeping over the ruins and digging furtively, sawing like mad to make the lengths of tubing portable, afraid all the time that someone would come along... Who passed the orders about where the metal was to be hidden? Who collected it, and who left the money in the hole in the wall in Luxton Street?...

There were several scrap-iron dealers in the area. Could he come to a private arrangement with one of them, and collect the metals himself?... there'd be more money in it... He could, he decided, and he would. There was a war on, he told himself, and metals were needed for ships and tanks and planes... he would need someone to help him. One person only, someone he knew and trusted. Then, when he had twenty pounds, he would give it all up. He nodded his head. There was a way to kill two birds with one stone; borrow the money for the telegram, and arrange an assistant.

He stared at the room; at his snoring father, at the old bed with the door-dented head-rail and the mattresses beneath it. He rose, frowning, and as he went out into the Court there was a cold feeling in the pit of his stomach. Yet there was a subdued but nervous excitement in him as he went round towards and then beyond the Two Bakers.

People with puffy and red-rimmed eyes were dipping into blitzed homes like hens picking into a heap of corn, a gang of council employees were salvaging bits of furniture and shovelling rubble from the roadway to the pavement. The gloom was lifting slowly, but the twin brewery chimneys still poured their dark sweetness up to the low-lying, ash-darkened clouds. A chill and spasmic late-autumn wind soughed through the streets and the gaunt, hollow-eyed tenements seemed taller and closer than ever. Jimmy wondered if they were huddling closer for warmth or because they were frightened of the bombs.

A few minutes later and he was holding his breath against the sour darkness of the passage, then running up the narrow twisting stairs to the top floor, where four doors opened on to the landing. He tapped on what he knew to be the Coopers' kitchen door, and Adelaide opened it immediately. When she saw Jimmy she took a little step backwards, her hands flying to her cheeks in quick alarm. "Omargawd!" she said, almost gasping. "— Whatsamatta?"

Jimmy smiled reassuringly. "Nothing wrong, Mrs Cooper," he said, "— except the Court got blasted a bit." He would remember Peggy's instructions to sound his g's and h's all the time. Perhaps that would help her to get better... "I've — I've come to see if Tommy's home yet."

"Oh. Thangawd for that. I thought someone'd caught a packet..." Her voice tailed away uncertainly, but she pointed to Tommy's room door. "'E's asleep — on'y come 'ome from the shelter a couple of 'ours ago. Give 'im a call an' I'll put the kettle on for a cuppa." Jimmy crossed the landing, and Adelaide went back inside the kitchen.

Adelaide and Tom Cooper were fortunate, for they and their children shared a four-roomed flat. Tom earned good money at the brewery, and until he went into the Army a few weeks earlier young Joey too had brought home three pounds a week. Their furniture was comfortable although far from luxurious, and included one of the few three-piece suites in the whole neighbourhood. It was oversprung and overstuffed and damp-streaked, but it was more than most people had, and Adelaide was proud of it. She often boasted too of the fact that each of her sons had his own room, even if Tommy's *wasn't* big enough to swing a cat round in. She said it so over-modestly that you immediately thought Tommy's room was as big as a dance-hall.

There was no reply to Jimmy's knock, so after waiting a moment he opened the door and went in. Tommy was lying on his back with one arm crooked over his head, and even when asleep his hair looked as though it had just been combed. His long lashes curled down on his cheek, and with adolescence his features had softened so that... Jimmy shied from a thought that flowered swiftly in his mind. They were growing up, and Tommy had changed. They were no longer the friends they had been, and they were steadily growing farther apart. There was a strange regret for the years of whispered confidences, of running behind carts, of sharing sweets and money-for-the-pictures. Jimmy realised that being aware of Growing Up meant a remoteness from the established order of boyhood, from the familiarity of things-that-were. When he spoke his voice was harsh and grating.

"Tom," he said. "Tommy, wake up."

Tommy's arm came down and plucked at the blanket covering his shoulders, then with a low sigh he turned away to the wall. Jimmy leaned over and rapped on the headboard of the bed. "Tommy, wake up," he repeated, and Tommy groaned and slid round on to his back. His eyes opened and blinked vaguely and he sat up with a start, only to relax immediately back upon the pillow.

"Hi, Jim," he said, and that was all. There was no expression in his face or in his voice, and for no reason at all Jimmy felt the same small self-doubt he thought he had overcome. His family and his friends were against him, he had taken on too much. And there was that strange feeling of regret.

"'Lo, Tom. How was the shelter?"

"How was the shelter?" Tommy repeated the question in exactly the same tone and with the same attention to pronunciation that Jimmy himself had used in asking it, but with a gentle irony that made Jimmy squirm. "I never expected you to come round an' ask that," Tommy went on in his ordinary voice, and added as though thinking aloud, "— never expected you to come round at all, if it comes to that. ... What's up?"

Tommy's bluntness had the quality of the electric shock that comes from chewing silver paper with dentalised teeth, and Jimmy felt exposed and ridiculous. With Tommy, at least, pretence was useless. They knew each other too well. His resolve to speak and to behave as he himself determined vanished and in its place was the realisation of his own weakness. Jimmy decided to put his proposition baldly, without frills.

"I'm — I'm stuck," he said. "I want you to 'elp me. First of all, can you lend me a few bob, or a quid?"

Tommy looked at him for an elastic moment, then reached under the chair beside the bed for his cigarettes and matches.

As he tossed one to Jimmy, then struck a match, Tommy knew a brief feeling of pleasure, almost of triumph. Jimmy had come to him for help, and he knew he would do whatever he could, whatever was possible.

"You c'n 'ave a coupla quid, if you like."

Jimmy's eyes widened. "Someone died an' left you a fortune?" he asked, and Tommy's face split in a grin. Jimmy grinned too, then together they burst into laughter, warm and easy.

"I bin usin' me loaf," Tommy said as they quietened. "— I thought you was doin' all right in the scrap-iron game. You broke?"

"Busted wide open," said Jimmy, sitting on the edge of the bed. "I 'ad nine quid saved, an' the old man's pinched it." Tommy whistled, but before he could speak Jimmy added: "Peggy's 'ouse got a near-miss last night, an' they took 'er to Saint Michael's 'Ospital."

"Jeeeeeezus," Tommy breathed. "I didn't know nothin' about it. She 'urt bad?"

"'Course you didn't know — you was in the shelter. She got knocked up good an' proper... face all split open. The first-aid bloke said 'e thought she 'ad a fractured pelvis an' all. That's why I've got to borrer some cash — she asked me to send Pinkie a telegram. Then I'm goin' roun' to Saint Michael's, to see 'ow she's doin'."

Tommy took a long drag on his cigarette. "So pore ole Peggy copped it, eh?" As he finished speaking he threw the bedclothes aside and in his underclothes crossed to the clothes' cupboard.

"Mmmmmm," Jimmy agreed, "— but that's not all I come round for."

Tommy raised his eyebrows quizzically as he stepped into what Jimmy noticed were new silver-grey flannels. When Tommy spoke it was at an oblique angle, almost careless-sounding.

"Why 'aven't you bin round for so long, Jim?"

They stared at each other until at last Tommy turned away and pulled on a clean shirt.

"You already know why," Jimmy said, his voice veiled and defensive. "— Peggy always said you'd get into trouble, but —"

"— But I didn't get into trouble, did I?" Tommy tucked his shirt inside his trousers in angry jerks. "Rajah made me laugh, an' 'e took me to places no one else'd ever take me to..." Now Tommy spoke sadly, desperately; he was trying to show that Jimmy and Peggy were wrong, but he was without sufficient command of his words or of himself. "Anyway," he went on with a change of tone, "Rajah's been gone back nearly a year. An' if anyone gets into trouble it'll be you an' that bloody scrap-iron."

Jimmy was grateful for the swerve back to his own problem. "That's what I want to talk about," he said quickly, rising to his feet. "I'm not goin' on wi' that scrap-iron stuff. I've got to 'ave twenty quid by Chrissmas, so I'm goin'ta collect the scrap an' flog it meself." Jimmy looked at Tommy's startled face for a moment, then added. "Will you 'elp me?"

Tommy breathed out explosively. "Jeeeeesus," he said. "What's Blind Billy goin'to say?"

"Blind Billy? What's 'e got to do with it?" Jimmy was more startled than Tommy had been a moment earlier.

"Kerrrrist! Din'cha know 'e's in charge o' the kids an' the scrap-iron? Din'cha know Blind Billy gives the orders about where to collect it an' where to leave it, an' puts the money in the 'ole in the wall for you?"

For a moment Jimmy thought he was being kidded, but a glance at Tommy's face convinced him. "'Ow d'you know all this?" he demanded. "I didn't know it meself!"

"Use yer loaf," Tommy said scathingly. "You know what'll 'appen if you get caught — Borstal. Blind Billy's got it all worked out so 'e won't take the can back. ... 'E gives the word to a coupla contack-men, an' they pass it on. The less everyone knows, the more Billy likes it."

"But 'ow d'*you* know all about it?" Jimmy insisted, and after a pause to sort out his words Tommy slowly told him. "Rajah put me on to it first — 'e used to get packets o' stuff from the Indians off the boats, an' take 'em to a club in the West End. I went with 'im a coupla times an' sat in a back room, an' Blind Billy was there. P'raps 'e owns it. But —" Tommy's voice was soft, puzzled, as though he doubted his own eyes. "— but 'e didn't wear 'is glasses or 'ave 'is walkin' stick. Real posh, 'e was."

Jimmy digested all this in silence, with frowning eyes and puckered mouth. "— Still," he said after rapidly thinking it out, "Blind Billy can't *make* me do anythin' I don't wanta do. 'S'far as 'e knows, I'm just goin'ta stop gettin' the scrap-iron. 'E can't kill me for that."

"I'm not so sure," Tommy put in ominously. "Y'never know what can 'appen when you get mixed up with that crowd."

"I'm mixed up with 'em already. I'm goin'ta get out of it now."

Jimmy paced quickly across the room and back, with the same feeling of nervous excitement that the air-raid siren gave him when it sounded.

"Look, Tom," he went on, speaking in rapid jerks, "Blind Billy gets all the scrap-iron an' sells it to the dealers. 'E gets all the profit, an' we on'y get the change. ... I'm goin'ta get it meself, an' I'll sell it meself somewhere else, where 'e won't know about." In his need to convince he grabbed Tommy's arm. "Where's a big bomb-site? One that goes for blocks an' blocks. Where?" Jimmy was getting worked up, and it was catching. Before Tommy could speak, Jimmy answered his own question. "I'll tell yer. In the city — round by Saint Paul's, the Barbican — where all the offices an' ware'ouses was smashed and blown to bits. There's tons o' scrap round there, an' Blind Billy never does anythin' over that way, does 'e? An' there's no people lives there," he added, remembering that his mother had objected to his taking metals from bombed houses. "I on'y want to get twenty quid, then I'll stop altogether. I never did like doin' it, but —"

"But why must you 'ave twenty quid?" Tommy thought that was a strange sum, and his curiosity brought

Jimmy's rapid words to a stop; he licked his lips.

"Because... well, I want a new suit for when I start lookin' for a job. Y'know I've always wanted to get an office job," he added miserably. "— I don't know why, Tom. I've just got to... an' now the old man's pinched what I'd saved, I've gotta start all over again."

Tommy reached under his pillow and pulled out a small leather wallet, drawing two one-pound notes from the pouch in one long and smooth movement. "'Ere y'are," he said. "That should do you for a day or two." He sat down in the spot on the bed-side that Jimmy had left a little earlier. "What... what do you want me to do? I'll 'elp you if I can... y'know that," he added wistfully.

"I want you to keep lookout for me. It'll be all right." Jimmy felt a surge of pride as he realised that he had won, that Tommy would help. "We'll 'ave to go late at night... I'll tell the old lady I've got fed up wi' tryin' to sleep at 'ome, an' I'm goin' down the shelter at night while the raids are on. I just want you to watch in case the law or someone comes past. There's blocks an' blocks o' ruins, an' 'undreds o' places to 'ide... it'll be over in a coupla weeks, Tommy, an' we'll 'ave plenty o' money — we'll split even. Will you 'elp me, Tom?" He was pleading now, and even as he spoke he was ashamed. He had been honest when he said that he had never liked taking the scrap-iron, and he had never expected to be so cold, so deliberate in his planning, in making use of his old pal... but he must have his suit... It didn't matter all that much, he told himself. Everyone's doin' somethin' to get some extra cash — floggin' fags an' ration books an' clothin' coupons. ...

Tommy, anxious to help, was nervous; there was the feeling, the taste of fear in him, although he knew that the chances of being caught were small. Jimmy, the more intelligent of the two, was nervous and excited.

Tommy crossed the room and put an arm round Jimmy's shoulders. "All right, Jim," he said, "— when do we start?"

Jimmy was grateful, yet unable to speak; he was suffused with the wish to help Tommy in return... "It — it won't be for more'n a coupla weeks... you see if I'm wrong."

Tommy was suddenly so happy that he wouldn't have cared if Jimmy *was* wrong, just so long as they were pals again. "Shall we go an' get a cuppa tea?" he asked brightly.

"I won't — I've got to get to the post office an' send the telegram to Pinkie — Gawd knows what she'll say when she gets it."

"It's what she does that'll count," Tommy replied curtly, and his comment brought an idea that hadn't even occurred to Jimmy. Yet after a moment's consideration he shrugged and dismissed it.

"What can she do?" he said. "She's got to stay at school till she's eighteen. An' Peggy told 'er she's to keep out o' London while the raids are on... you wanta come wi' me?" Jimmy asked, moving towards the door.

"No, I won't come. Tell Peggy I asked after 'er," Tommy replied, following Jimmy out on to the landing.

Tommy had never taken to Peggy in the way Jimmy had. Peggy's bright hair and vivid dresses and sometimes garish make-up worried him, although he didn't know why. And he resented her, for she had become important to Jimmy, and in a slow process had changed him...

"I'll 'ave your money before long, Tom," Jimmy said, halting at the top of the stairs.

"When you reckon to start on yer own?" Again Tommy felt that sense of fear, and it showed in his voice.

"Don't know yet. After I've seen Peggy I'll go for a walk roun' the City an' see what's doin'." Jimmy was so tired that his eyes began to close against his will and he fought to keep them open. But he *had* to go on, to get organised.

He took several steps down then stopped again. "Didya mother tell yer — Boy-boy's 'ome. Gettin' married at Saint Mary's, an' we're 'avin' a big booze-up. All the Court's goin'. You comin'?"

Tommy's face broke into a smile. "You try an' stop me," he said.

"O.K., Tom. I'll see you later — an' thanks for the cash."

Jimmy went quickly down the stairs while Tommy stood, sadly staring after him.

The Main Post Office in Whitechapel was jammed with people trying to make telephone calls or send telegrams to reassure friends and relatives, as usually happened after a severe raid. As Jimmy stood wedged in the queue for the telegram section he suddenly felt giddy, nauseated, then almost immediately he was deathly tired. He staggered a little, and a fat Jewish woman next to him clicked her tongue sympathetically.

"Oh," she said, "— is soch a beezniz, mid all der bomps." Again she clicked her tongue, and she looked and sounded so tragic that Jimmy couldn't prevent a smile. The woman smiled too, and they both felt better. "Put ot de tunk," she commanded, and as though hypnotised Jimmy slid his tongue forward. "Dere," she said with satisfaction, placing a boiled sweet in his mouth, "— Kinehorreh."

"An' good luck to you, Missis." They turned and faced the clerk.

Nearly half-an-hour later Jimmy passed through the ugly pillared entrance and into the reception and inquiry hall of Saint Michael's. There was an air of urgency, and the smell of disinfectant and scrubbed floors mingled oddly with the smell of burning and the disturbed dust of centuries that pervaded all London. An elderly man in a white coat and peaked cap beckoned to him.

"Can — can I see Peggy... ?" Jimmy, awed by the lofty entrance hall and the feeling of being inside a hospital, couldn't remember Peggy's surname, and realised for the first time that although he had known her for three years, she had never actually told it to him; if it had not been for Pinkie's letter, he still would not know it. Again he took the letter from his pocket. "... Peggy Harcourt." That's a nice name, he thought, as the old man rapidly

147

scanned several lists of names.

The man looked up, pushing his cap to the back of his head. "Sorry, son. There's no one o' that name come in last night —"

"She *must* be 'ere," Jimmy said desperately, terrified that Peggy had died and been taken away. "The amb'lance man *said* they would bring 'er to St. Michael's —"

"'Ave you tried the Cambridge Clinic in Stepney Green? We was so busy last night we 'ad to send some of 'em further on. Know where it is?"

Jimmy nodded dumbly, then thanked his informant and walked slowly back into Whitechapel Road. Peggy wasn't at Saint Michael's, and she wouldn't be at the Cambridge either. They'd taken her away — out to the country hospitals like they did sometimes, and he might never find her again. And she wouldn't be able to tell them, with her face all stitched and bandaged. ... He broke into a run and was gasping when he reached the Cambridge. But she was there.

She was seriously injured and had already been twice to the operating theatre. Besides the twenty stitches in her cheek, she had a fractured pelvis and a smashed knee-cap. No, she was still unconscious, and you couldn't see her. The young lady in the inquiry desk was quite firm, and it would be several days before visitors could be allowed. When Jimmy explained that he was a neighbour, that Peggy had no friends and no relatives apart from a daughter in the country, the young lady looked up with sharp-drawn lips. "A daughter? She is on the list as *Miss* Harcourt." Jimmy gulped and fidgeted, then the lady's face relaxed slightly. "I suppose," she said with mild reproof, "I suppose the orderly misunderstood."

"'Course 'e did," Jimmy said stoutly. "'E must've done. When will she be able to see anyone — I want to tell 'er I've sent the telegram to 'er daughter... she might be worried about it, if I can't see 'er an' tell 'er."

The prim-thin face seemed to regret its bad manners and a hand beckoned Jimmy into the space next to the desk and a small writing-pad was pushed into his hand. "Can you leave a message? I'll see that it is given to her as soon as she wakes up... I'm sorry, but as soon as she is able to stand the journey, she will be sent to the hospital Annexe near Saint Albans. I shouldn't tell you this, as you are not a relative, but it might be later today — we're so short of beds."

At first Jimmy stared at the note-pad, unable to think of the words he wanted. Yet once he started he couldn't stop, and went on to fill three sheets with regards — fictitious — from his family, and best wishes, and the hope that she would soon be up on her feet and back where Jimmy could see her again, that he had sent the telegram to Pinkie, that he would try to help the Indians who were left, that he missed her, but would come to Saint Albans as soon as he could... it all came out in a long unpunctuated stream, and when Jimmy had finished he knew that Peggy would tell him off because he hadn't used any commas or full-stops. He wished she could do so now.

Sadly he folded the sheets, slid them inside the envelope, sealed and addressed it, and handed it up to the receptionist. "You won't forget, will you? As soon as she comes round?"

The young woman nodded. "I won't forget it. By the way," she added, "— how old is the daughter?"

"— Just fifteen — still at school."

"Will you leave her address? We will write to her."

With a feeling of regret Jimmy gave her Pinkie's letter with the long handwriting and the school address, then once again he was walking slowly back towards Whitechapel Road. It was Sunday, but Sunday was no longer the day of swirling crowds and shouting street-vendors in Brick Lane and Bethnal Green; there was a feeling of tension, of brooding silence, of waiting and of sadness. Those people still looking for food or clothing-bargains did so quickly and quietly, fluttering across the streets like distressed and nervous birds.

149

... Fancy Blind Billy being behind the scrap-iron gang, and having a club in the West End?... he wasn't really surprised — there'd often been hints and whispers. ...

Neither Jimmy nor any of his friends or relatives knew that Blind Billy also ran an expensive flat and a low, powerful sports-car.

When Jimmy came to Aldgate he was surprised to see that several of the over-painted, doll-faced women who patrolled up and down day and night were still there; despite fires and bombs and death the ships still came in, and where there were ships there were seamen who, if they had just finished a long voyage, would have thick wads of notes to spend. They would need someone to share their bottles and the lonely hours as they sought to forget mines and torpedoes. And seamen, when they woke up and found their girls and their wallets gone, rarely made a fuss. They seldom had enough time.

Jimmy wandered past the centuries-old Aldgate Pump, where once horse-carriages had stopped to water the horses as they progressed towards the hamlets of Stratford and Ilford, then turned to the right along Leadenhall Street, the street of the great shipping companies, towards Cornhill and the City of London. Carefully noting the bomb-sites as he passed, he went through to that area close to Saint Paul's that storms of incendiary and high-explosive bombs had pulverised and melted. The gleaming premises of the great banks, the big stockbrokers' offices, the little textile warehouses that had remained almost unchanged since the time of Dickens; all were amorphous, without identity. All were rubble.

As Jimmy went into that dead and weird and uncanny expanse of ruin, he was suddenly afraid. Great mountains of rubble, pierced here and there by cracked and drunken up-rearing walls, by bent and agony-twisted girders pointing sadly and accusingly at the sky, were all round him; in only a few seconds he had passed from the London that lived to the London that had died suddenly and swiftly. The hum of traffic from the distant roads was barely audible, seeming to deepen and magnify the silence that surrounded him, that seemed to be pressing him away from this dead part of the great city. He felt that he was moving through a fantastic cemetery of brick and steel and concrete and mortar, and he shivered. But he went on, searching carefully for glimpses of metal — of brass or chromium-plated taps and faucets, of copper or steel, or pieces of lead... it wouldn't be difficult — there was more than enough to keep him and Tommy busy. ...

At the thought of coming back to this place in the middle of the night, when perhaps an air-raid might start, he faltered and almost panicked. But he owed money to Tommy, and he *had* to have a new made-to-measure suit so he could get a good job... he cheered up. He had never had a tailored suit before...

# 3

When Jimmy arrived home again he found Janey alone, washing imitation-silk stockings in an enamel bowl. A pair already washed were draped over the back of a chair, drying before the fire.

"Where you bin?" she demanded almost before he was inside the door. "Yer dinner's in the oven stone cold," she went on in a rush, "— an' the old man an' the old lady've gone wi' Boy-boy an' Maisie. They 'ad murders with old Gapley." She smirked, then laughed outright. "'E's not goin'ta marry 'em after all — says it'll be blasphemious, or suthink!"

"— It'll be what?" Jimmy asked with a puzzled frown.

"Blasphemious," Janey repeated with satisfaction. "'E took one look at Maisie an' nearly fainted —"

"— It was all through old Gapley they wanted to get married in the first place, wasn't it?"

"Mmm," said Janey wisely, "— but 'e 'adn't seen Maisie since a coupla munce ago. She didn' look so bad then. ..." She rubbed the stockings as though she hated them.

"Where's everyone gone?"

"Back to Boy-boy's... they're goin'ta get married in the Register Office down Mile End... could you see Maisie dancin' up the altar in a white weddin' dress?"

Tired out, irritated by Janey's casual comments, Jimmy snapped "No, I couldn't. Any more'n I can see you —"

"Sorry," Janey sneered. "— S'matter wi' you — still worryin' about yer money?"

"I'll get some more."

"No one said anythink about it. But the old lady said she wants'ta try an' get a weddin' present for Boy-boy,"

Janey warned him.

"I s'pose she does. But she won't get it wi' *my* money."

Jimmy was suddenly aware, with a sharp and incisive pain, that he could no more control his words and the way he said them than he could ever go to university. He *could,* he amended, thinking deliberately of Peggy; *speak slowly. Speak carefully.*

"What've we got for... what have we got for..." He stopped, confused. He wanted his words to be clear, precise, but Janey made him self-conscious. "Bloody'ell." He sighed exhaustedly, then finished what he wanted to say "What's for dinner?"

"Faggits." Janey, having already eaten, was no longer interested in the meal although Jimmy's mouth watered at the thought of what was to come. Faggots were the large cubes of shredded and cooked meat that could be bought at any butcher-shop along Brick Lane or Bethnal Green. Dome-topped, spiced, seasoned with herbs and half-submerged in golden gravy, they were delicious. And all they needed to make a meal was a few mashed potatoes.

Delicious as they were, Jimmy didn't like them cold.

"Warm 'em up for me, will you, Janey? I'm dog-tired." He sat on the edge of the bed and watched lazily as Janey lit the gas-oven and put a knife and fork on the table. "There y'are," she said. "They'll on'y take a coupla minnits." She went back to her stockings.

"You goin' out tonight?" Jimmy didn't really want to know, but he wanted an opening to pass some casual comment about being fed up with trying to sleep at home, and going down the public shelters at night instead.

"Mmmmm." In an excited burst the words streamed across the room, as Janey wriggled in the contortions of the Jitterbug dance. "I'm goin' up West wi' Rosie Gates. Everyone goes up there now. There's soldiers an' sailors an' airmen. Sometimes even officers talk to you... real posh ones."

"Billy was up there last night, wasn't 'e? Wonder where

'e's got to?"... A new idea occurred to Jimmy and he spoke without thinking: "— Why're *you* goin' up there? Thought you was so keen on Johnny Burton?"

"Well, I am —" Janey defended, "— always 'ave bin. But Johnny don't get much wages. ..." She shrugged helplessly, then to hide her flushed face she leaned over and hung up the second pair of stockings. Jimmy shrugged too, but for him it was without meaning. "There's even some special Volunteer Yanks," Janey added. "Real good jivers, they are. Rosie says they're smashin', an' they don't argue even if you 'ave two or three gins —"

"As long as that's all you 'ave," Jimmy said dryly. Her brother, he was now her adviser.

"You look after yourself," Janey said shortly, and re-arranged the stockings. She stopped almost immediately and looked up.

"D'you know ole Gapley's startin' a club round Saint Mary's?" she asked, to change the subject. Jimmy was not impressed.

"What for?" he asked, turning off the gas-stove and taking out the plate with the faggots and mash.

"Dunno. Rosie said it's somethin' to do wi' givin' the kids somewhere to go at night. They're goin'ta 'ave a radiogram an' dancin'!"

"'E'll get the Band of 'Ope an' no one else. Besides, why d'you always listen to Rosie Gates? Y'know what they say. ..."

"— I don't care what they say. She don't do anythin' I don't do. ..." Jimmy's sardonic smile made her realise the ambiguity of her words and she stopped speaking. Suddenly they both burst into laughter, so that Jimmy almost choked.

"You better not tell the old lady where you're goin'," Jimmy advised, "— she'll 'ave yer guts for garters."

"You won't tell 'er, will you?" Janey was anxious, wondering if she had said too much.

"*Me*? I don't tell tales. Besides, Billy goes up West. Don't see why you shouldn't."

Several times lately Jimmy had heard about the West End, and he wondered what made people go there... even Tommy'd been to a club. ... I've never been anywhere, he thought. But I will, soon. ...

"I'm goin'ta start goin' down the shelters," he said abruptly. "It gets on your nerves indoors, with all the raids an' everythin'."

Janey smiled, and stared knowingly.

"You don't get so much sleep in the shelters, either," she said, still smiling. "As long as you watch yer step, an' don't get caught."

Again they smiled at each other, Jimmy with a feeling of gratitude. Janey wasn't a bad girl, 'specially for a sister... he raised the plate and noisily swallowed the rich gravy. It was time to get moving. He pushed the plate away and rose, moving towards the door. "I'm goin' round Tommy Cooper's," he said, and just as he reached the door Janey put in her parting shot. "'Ow's Peggy?" she asked.

Jimmy halted, one foot raised, as though suddenly paralysed; for a sharp, unforgettable moment he stood like a statue. Then he put his foot down and opened the door. "She's 'urt," he said. "She's 'urt bad."

As he shut the door he heard Janey's snicker and as he walked up the Court there was cold, muted fury in his mind. Tommy could make him feel stupid, Janey could make him feel stupid, his mother... everyone. It was his own fault, he'd have to struggle all the time against himself. ... What chance is there, he wondered wearily. School lasts for six hours a day — when school was open — but even there you couldn't try to speak properly, because everyone laughed and made fun of you... I'll show 'em, he vowed. One o' these days. ...

At the Coopers he was just in time for one of Adelaide's never-ending cups of tea, during which he suggested that he and Tommy should go to the pictures. Tommy, who seemed unusually quiet, agreed immediately, and off they went.

The film was all about a faded actress who tried for over an hour to get back on the stage, but never quite made it. Three times she threatened suicide, but never quite made that either. Jimmy hardly remembered any of it, for most of the time he and Tommy were whispering, deciding that the next night was to be their first night of independent operations, whether there was a raid on or not. Their minds were so filled — Jimmy's with excitement, and with the longing to get it over and done with, Tommy's with an anxiety that amounted almost to fear — that they were incapable of absorbing any other impression.

When they had seen the programme through they walked slowly along Whitechapel, towards Aldgate.

"Why don't you come down the shelter tonight, Jim?"

"I can't — not right off. I've got to get the old lady used to the idea first — stop 'er gettin' all excited. But I will tomorrow."

Tommy grinned. "Sharp bugger, ain'cha?" he said admiringly. But he saw the wisdom behind Jimmy's words, so as they parted they agreed to finalise their plan of operation the next day at school, during lessons. Tommy suggested taking a day off, but Jimmy shook his head. "We've lost a lot o' time already, since the raids started," he said. "If we stay away again they might give us a bad report when it's Chrissmas." That could happen, and a bad school-leaving report would make sure that he never got a good office job.

With a grin and a cheery wave of the hand Tommy went home and then down to the shelter while Jimmy, finding his own home deserted, lit the gaslight and straightened the bedclothes on the mattresses beneath his parents' bed. He stripped off to the waist and had a cold wash under the tap in the yard and then, returning inside, he undressed. He couldn't resist standing on a chair to gaze at his slowly-developing body in the misty mirror above the fireplace; as he did so, flexing his muscles, he realised with an intense pleasure that since

156

last night — was it only *one* day ago? — his voice had remained deep and even-pitched. His mind switched to the adventure of going for the first time to the Public Baths, and he decided not to put stones in his pockets as Billy, one sleepless night last summer, had advised. The stones were to throw at the old men who stayed for hours in the plywood cubicles and looked over the top, but Jimmy thought, mistakenly, that Billy had been exaggerating.

Finally, with a hurried glance at the photograph of Pinkie, he slipped his underclothes on and slid on to his mattress, with the wire springs of his parents' bed only a few inches above his face. He was asleep almost before his head touched the pillow.

Some time later the eerie rise-and-fall of the air-raid warning brought him back to consciousness, and as he squirmed out into the room to douse the gaslight he felt the same old tightening in his belly. Yet he wasn't scared; just nervously excited. He was asleep again before the guns began their rumbling, but they remained distant and he slept on. When his parents eventually came home they were light-hearted and noisy and he crawled out of his bed for long enough to be told again that the wedding would be at the Mile End registry office; that Fred, from the Two Bakers, had been kept in hospital; and to tell his mother in a round-about way that he was tired of sleeping — or trying to sleep — at home, and intended going back down the shelters at night. His words aroused no comment or reaction beyond a sharp stare from his father, and soon once again the house was in total darkness. Billy and Janey disturbed nobody when they came home in the small hours, and even the all-clear, when at last it sounded, brought only indistinct muttering.

"Janey... Janey! Come on — put the kettle on." Janey stirred and groaned, then everyone was awake and so began another Monday. Yet it wasn't like other Mondays for Jimmy; it became the most important Monday of his life.

The first surprise came from Billy who, as he sat at the table drinking his tea, riveted his eyes on the battery-driven wireless and made his announcement.

"Mum," he said carefully. "I might be goin' away in a week or two." Three pairs of eyes stared at him as firmly as his own stared at the wireless, and with a strangled, thick voice he added: "I've bin told I c'n get a good job in the govamment factories — the powder works — near Enfield. ..." His voice faded and he waited nervously for the expected tirade from his mother, who stared at him blankly. "Go 'way?" she asked, as though her ears had heard the impossible. "Powder works? What for?"

"Want yer brains tested, yer scatty bastard," said the old man scathingly. "One bomb, an' you'll be deader'n doornails."

"We c'n get killed 'ere just as easy," Billy defended. "— I'm fed up wi' pressin' shirts an' uniforms, I can't go in the forces, an' I never 'ave enough money. I c'n be earnin' twice as much as I do at Plotsky's an' besides, they don't 'ave as many bombs out there as we do 'ere."

"You don't want many," the old man countered. "Jist one'd be enough."

Billy played his trump card.

"I could send you a coupla quid 'ome every week," he said, "I c'n earn nine or ten a week on war work!"

The old man licked his lips. "Nine or ten? Bloody for-choon!" For a moment he considered giving up the stall and himself going to work in the gunpowder factory, but he shrugged. 'E'd done 'is whack already, an' all 'e got for 'is trouble was a big depression an' no work... munce an' munce lining up for the dole. ... He swallowed his tea, hitched up his trousers, and belched. "Come on, Jimmy," he ordered, pulling on his faded old overcoat, "The bloody market'll be shut be the time I get there at this rate. An' putcher coat on — 's'bloody cold out." He waited just inside the door for his youngest son to help him with the stall.

158

Sullenly Jimmy did as he was told, and wordlessly once again the stall was pushed over gritty, dust-laden street surfaces, the agonised shrieks from the rusty axle setting Jimmy's teeth on edge. When the old man was satisfied that he was not encroaching on his neighbouring stall-holder's territory, he looked up. "All right," he said. "'Oppit."

Jimmy hopped it, and when he arrived home Billy had already left for work. Janey, having lit the fire, was also ready to leave, quietly exulting that there had been no questions about last night's activities.

"By the way, me gel," the old lady demanded, as though by divination, "— where'd you get to last night?"

Disconcerted, Janey showed no trace of emotion, even when she caught Jimmy's wink. She would have preferred not to lie, but she knew beyond doubt that old people — especially mothers — have funny ideas about dances; that they always regard their children as infants, and only get upset when they're told the truth. Taking the question calmly, she produced her alibi.

"I went to pictures wi' Rosie, then we went to 'elp 'er dad in the coffee-shop."

Despite Rosie's frequent incursions into the takings in the till, Mr Gates' coffee-stall had prospered so well that he had sold it, on condition that the new owner set up his pitch far enough away to avoid creating any opposition, and had blossomed out with a little coffee-shop near Aldgate. Rosie now spent a great deal of her time there, for soldiers and seamen travelling to and from Liverpool Street Station made it a rendezvous and where these came, came also the hard-faced, enamel-painted women who made such interesting comments and conversation. Rosie learned quickly and well.

"That don't take all night, do it?" The old lady was showing signs of working herself up into a temper, and Janey knew it was time to go. "When the warnin' went I went 'ome wi' Rosie. I was goin'ta stay all night, but when the all-clear went I come back 'cos I couldn't sleep."

Mrs Wilson stared suspiciously, then turned away. She herself had only vaguely heard the all-clear sounding, and as she had had no idea of the time there was nothing more she could say. Kids these days always 'ad their answers ready. ...

Janey went, with a brief "G'mawnin'," and Jimmy began his Monday-job of chopping wood in the yard, to heat the water in the copper for the neighbours' washing his mother always started as soon as he went off to school. Mrs Wilson thought over the events of the morning.

I don't want Billy to go away from 'ome, but if 'e c'n get a good job an' send 'ome a coupla quid a week... useful! There was a twinge of sadness that yet another of her family was leaving home, but it always happened, one way or another. Soon there'd be on'y Janey an' Jimmy, an' in a year or two Jimmy'd 'ave to go in the Army... she hated the war, and everything it stood for.

She went into the yard and watched as Jimmy thrust pieces of wood into the maw of the firegrate, immediately below the boiler of the copper.

"I've got somethin' for you, Jimmy," she said, and Jimmy looked up warily. He thought she was in a temper, but he was wrong. His heart leaped as he saw the finger-clutched wad of notes being drawn from the pocket of his mother's apron. "There's seven poun'," she explained. "— 'E must've spent the rest."

She knew that when the old man found the money was gone there'd be a real up-an'-downer, but she was prepared for it — wouldn't be the first time she'd put *'im* in 'is place. She couldn't understand or sympathise with Jimmy's hopes and plans, but she knew they were important to him. Strange as they were, they came first.

With difficulty Jimmy thanked her, swallowing the lump in his throat, and Mrs Wilson asked gently: "Will... will'ya lend me some, to 'elp wi' the weddin'?"

There it was. Janey'd told 'im that was comin', but *no one* was goin' to use Jimmy's money... "There y'are," he said, holding four of the pound-notes out for his mother.

"— It's not borrowed — I've give it to yer." And he meant it. There was a deep, vibrant humming within him that filled the yard and the house and the world, and Jimmy knew it was going to be *his* day. He had three pounds left, plus what remained of the money he'd borrowed from Tommy... in a couple of weeks, by selling the lead and the chrome taps and the copper he was going to start collecting from the ruins that very night, he'd have more money than he'd ever had in his life, per'aps even enough for *two* suits. He'd buy a present for the old lady, an' a bottle o' scent for Janey. And somethin' for the old man, even if 'e was a cunnin' old bastard. ...

His exhilaration was so great that he suddenly hugged his mother and did a little dance in the yard, all over the remains of the lettuce-crate he'd been chopping for firewood. Mrs Wilson was breathless, but happy, and she joined in with gusto, laughing like a schoolgirl. The poor kids didn't 'ave much enjoyment these days... she went into a violent spasm of coughing, her heartbeats drumming in her ears. Round her lips appeared the blue rims Jimmy had first seen three years earlier, one Saturday when she had taken him shopping in Bethnal Green. He patted her back and waited anxiously as she clung to the great cast-iron wringer and slowly recovered.

"Mum, why'cha go down the London 'Ospital?"

"I will," she gasped, "— later on."

Jimmy stood and waited uncertainly, but as the clock at Saint Mary's began striking the hour he hugged her again. "I'll 'ave to get off to school now, Mum."

She wiped the beads of sweat away from her forehead and smiled, although it seemed to be the most difficult thing she had ever attempted. "All right, boy. Don't get up to no mischief."

Jimmy soon forgot the episode, for Tommy was waiting on the corner of the street even though he too would be late. But somehow, for these last remaining weeks of school-time, Miss Bullock seemed of less importance, despite her still-acid tongue.

The morning passed quickly; Jimmy got full marks in the Arithmetic test, and was top in Dictation. Just before they broke for dinner Miss Bullock read out a notice about the school club, sent by Mr Gapley. It would be open each evening, there would be a radiogram, table-tennis, darts and lemonade. The girls in the class greeted the news with wondering ooh's and ah's, while the boys snorted. There were other and better things to do.

As they walked home for dinner Tommy suggested that each should take a tissue-paper-dimmed torch with them that night. You never knew what was goin' to 'appen, or what you might find. ...

Jimmy agreed. Tommy would stand near to where Jimmy was at work with the saw or the soft-headed hammer (lead was easily beaten away from rusted-in clips and fastenings), keeping look-out, ready to run or give a warning whistle if anyone should approach. In plimsolls Tommy was confident that he could outrun any pursuit, and his being chased would also allow Jimmy to sneak off with the loot. Jimmy said it was a good arrangement, but only for emergency; he was certain there would be no interruption. Tommy was not so certain, but remained silent.

They parted cheerfully at the top of the Court and Jimmy, suddenly remembering his mother's spasm of that morning, was glad to see her looking her usual self, and with fish-an'-chips waiting for him on the table. Two margarine-spread slices of bread perched on the side of the plate, and the kettle chirped happily over a red-and-white and cheerful fire. Jimmy's happiness-feeling spread all through him, and he knew that his mother too was still happy.

"Whatcha goin'ta buy me for Chrissmas, Lizzie?" Jimmy was being saucy and flippant in the way that was never allowed unless Mrs Wilson was in exceptional spirits, and instead of sending her hands flashing across his cheeks she chuckled.

"Time the weddin's over," she said, "I won't be able to

buy anythink. Might even 'ave to sell the bedstead." The idea was so incongruous that they screamed huge gusts of laughter. When they recovered Mrs Wilson poured the boiling water into the tea-pot.

"When you've ate your dinner, run round the shop an' get fourteen pounda' coal in the pail, will yer? An' 'alf a pound'a margarine for tea."

Jimmy had intended to run round to the scrap-iron dealers near Whitechapel, to find out about prices for metals and to try to come to an arrangement with one of them, but running a couple of errands for coal and marge wouldn't make much difference. "Don't forget to take the ration book," his mother reminded him. She looked up in startled surprise as a sudden sound of running footsteps ended in a flurried tattoo on the street-door. Tommy burst in.

His hair for once was dishevelled, there were dirt-smears all over his hands and face, and his eyes danced with excitement.

"What's up? The Lor after yer?" Mrs Wilson knew that something important had happened, but she knew that Tommy was not the sort of boy to get himself in trouble, so she smiled. Tommy was a nice boy — always so clean an' neat; she hadn't seen him looking so untidy for years.

"I got somethin' to tell you, Jim. Quick."

One look was enough. Jimmy was already bolting the last of his fish-and-chips, his mother watching with amusement as he slid the skate-bones through his teeth to make certain he had missed none of the flesh.

"You bloody little 'og," she said with admiring censure. "That was a fourpenny wing an' two pennorth!" Even fish-an'-chips was gettin' expensive. ...

Jimmy rose and looked anxiously at his mother. "Can I get the coal an' stuff later on, Mum? I won't be long."

"I spose I'll 'ave to get it meself," she grumbled, but it was a light, almost pleasant grumble. Jimmy squeezed her hand, there was the patter of feet, and she was alone. These kids. ...

As soon as they were away from the house Tommy pulled Jimmy to a halt. "She's 'ome!" he said.

"Who is?" Jimmy asked, puzzled. "Peggy?" She couldn't be —

"— For Gawsake wake up. Not Peggy. Pinkie!" Tommy gave his words the tone and importance of a patriarch announcing a new revelation. Before his meaning had sunk in he went on: "She's walkin' up an' down by the Indians' 'ouse, cryin' 'er eyes out."

Jimmy stared open-mouthed, then he sped off up the Court and disappeared round the corner. In the instant that followed, Tommy knew that he was no longer happy or excited. It was like a nice sunny day, when a great black cloud suddenly blots out the light and warmth; everything goes quiet and waits.

The moment Jimmy turned into the street he saw her, and he stopped running. Her attaché-cases were by the doorway, as they had been on that day three years ago when he saw her for the first time, when Janey guessed in an awestruck voice that she might be an Indian princess.

She was wearing a dark, long-sleeved coat and a little upturned hat. Her eyes were as large and dark and her hair just as glossy and blue-black as he remembered, and although she had grown and filled out in the year since he last saw her, her face still seemed to be all angles and planes, as though carved. The only suggestion of curves was in her slightly rounded chin and the gentle swell beneath her coat. When she saw Jimmy she began to run towards him and for one paralysing, inexplicable instant he too wanted to run. But he wanted to run away.

He walked slowly forward, closely followed by the hesitant Tommy and then, without knowing how, she was in his arms, crying as though she would never stop. She made him nervous. He said nothing and he thought nothing; he was incapable of either. There was a great bewilderment that she was here, in this street; there was a fear that one of the neighbours would see and gladly tell his mother; there was a strange pride that she had turned to him in her trouble and distress. He had forgotten that his telegram had said that Peggy had been taken to Saint Michael's Hospital, as he himself believed at that time. He could not know that Pinkie had already made inquiries there, that she had spoken to another of the reception staff who knew nothing whatever of Peggy Harcourt. Least of all did he know that only a few hours earlier, as she left the convent, Pinkie had been dry-eyed, laughing, exultant. The convent had become a prison which prevented her from going to the Saturday-night dances at the airfield nearby; she had had two narrow escapes, but she knew it couldn't last. ...

When Jimmy's telegram arrived she cried bitterly and sincerely, although she learned only that Peggy had been seriously injured. But in a few minutes Pinkie realised that here was a perfect excuse to leave the convent. And, she determined, she would never go back.

Learning on arrival there that Peggy had never been admitted to Saint Michael's had come as a great shock, for Pinkie had intended living in Peggy's room until Peggy came home again. But she didn't know the extent of the bomb-damage. In something like panic she took a taxi from the hospital to Peggy's home address, to find only ruin. She sat on the sagging stairs and cried... she knew that Jimmy Wilson lived somewhere nearby, but she didn't know exactly where. That was how Tommy had found her.

Gently Jimmy eased away from her clinging fingers, trying to put his sympathy into words. "Don't cry, Pinkie," he said. "It'll be all right soon."

She wiped her eyes and looked at him tremulously. "When they said she wasn't at Saint Michael's, I thought she might've died... I didn't know what to do."

For a moment her words defeated him, before he realised his error. "I'm sorry, Pinkie." He was miserable and contrite, thinking he was responsible: "When I sent the telegram, I didn't know Peggy'd been sent to another 'ospit

— *hospital.* She's at the Cambridge Clinic, near Mile End. At least," he amended quickly, "— she was. They said they'd shift 'er to the country as quick as they could."

Pinkie forgot her tears and broke away from him. "Why didn't you send another telegram?" she demanded. "I've been running all over the East End, thinking she was dead! How did you expect me to know where she was?"

"Jeeeeesus," said Tommy, the word long-drawn, critical. "You can't blame Jimmy — 'e didn't know they'd sent 'er to the Cambridge, any more'n 'e knew you was comin' 'ome. An' 'is own 'ouse got blasted, without worryin' about *your* troubles!"

Pinkie spun round on him, so that Jimmy saw only the rippling dark hair. When she spoke her voice was casual and almost pleasant, as though making light conversation, but her eyes were sharp and vindictive. "Still here, Tommy?" she asked. "Have you had any letters from Rajah lately?"

A dull flush spread slowly over Tommy's face; his mouth opened, but instead of speaking he swallowed. He stared at Pinkie as though fascinated, but when he spoke his words were for Jimmy. "I'll — I'll go on to school, Jim," he said, adding hopefully, "— you comin'?"

Jimmy was uncertain of what had happened between them, and the feeling that he had had a chance to do something for Pinkie, to help her, and that he had made a mess of it, confused him even more... he couldn't even send a telegram without making a mess of it. He'd make it up to her, somehow.

"In a minute, Tom. I'll catch you up." Tommy turned and walked slowly away, and as he went Pinkie said softly, scornfully, "Schoolboy!"

"I'm a schoolboy myself," Jimmy reproved her coolly. "— there wasn't any need to go for 'im like that."

"I'm sorry, Jimmy, I didn't mean to upset him. It's... it's... I couldn't help myself. ..." Jimmy saw that again her eyes were glistening.

"I didn't mean to tell you off, either," he said quickly,

hoping to avoid more tears, and Pinkie smiled.

"Is the hospital far from here?" she asked. "I must try to see Peggy. Will you take me there?"

"Me? I've got to get to school. I'm leavin' at Chrissmas, an' — *and* — if I stop away I'll get a bad report." Pinkie didn't know how important it was that the report should be a good one.

Aware of Peggy's lessons and Jimmy's ambitions, Pinkie imitated her mother. "There should be a *g* on the end of *leaving*," she said evenly. Jimmy, crimson-faced, looked at the pavement.

"What can we do with your cases?" he said suddenly. "I couldn't manage more'n two, an' it's a long way to walk."

"Walk?" For the first time she laughed aloud. Tinkling, clear, and bell-like, then she asked: "Where can you get a taxi?" Seeing the startled look on Jimmy's face she added, "— I'll pay for it."

A taxi! Jimmy Wilson in a taxi!

"I — I might be able to get one in Bethnal Green."

"All right then. I'll wait here for you," she said, not realising that the taxi rank was five blocks away. "Don't be long," she ordered, but Jimmy, moving on flying feet, was already out of range.

A moment later Johnny Burton, on his way home for dinner from the sugar factory where he worked, saw Pinkie and whistled in soft admiration. He lounged on the corner with his hands in his pockets, whistling louder and rocking with a faint air of suggestion in his movements. Pinkie stared at him with expressionless eyes and the whistle faded away to nothing. Johnny's pink face reddened and he slunk away round the corner. Pinkie smiled gently.

The taxi rank was empty when Jimmy arrived, and exhausted from his run he clung to a lamp-post and waited. Half an hour passed before he rejoined Pinkie and her face, as he left the taxi, was composed and cold-looking. Wordlessly she took the seat Jimmy had just left, and stared stonily at the other side of the street as Jimmy lifted her cases on to the luggage platform beside the driver.

"Cambridge Clinic, driver," he ordered, and couldn't resist adding impressively, "— Mile End." Despite himself he felt big and important. One day he'd ride round in taxis all day, just for the fun of it.

"Pinkie," he said softly, "I couldn't 'elp it. I 'ad — *had* — to wait for a cab to come back... I ran all the way there," he ended, almost pleading.

She shrugged petulantly. "I might just as well have gone myself."

The words 'Well, why didn't you?' formed hotly in his brain, yet he remained silent. Only half an hour ago he had hoped for another chance to help her, but instead he was upsetting her again.

"Pinkie — what will you do if they've already sent Peggy on to Saint Albans?" The question jolted her.

"I'll have to go there — wherever it is. I've left the convent, there's nowhere for me to stay, and I've got about four pounds left —"

"You've left the convent?" Jimmy demanded, astounded. "— What for? What'll Peggy say?"

Pinkie thought for a moment before she replied: "She won't know. I'll just —"

"But she'll *'ave 'ta* know," Jimmy interrupted. "She said —"

Rudely, vehemently, Pinkie in her turn interrupted: "She *won't* know. I *can't* go back. ..." At Jimmy's unconscious withdrawal from her, Pinkie's tone softened. "I can't go back while Peggy's in hospital, can I? Who would look after her when she comes home? Where will she live?"

This appeal to Jimmy's emotions was effective, yet he was still doubtful. "But what can you do, even if you stay in London?"

"I'll find a job, and save every penny. I'll find a room, and try to get it ready for her. ..." She sounded so frail, so girlish, yet so earnest, that Jimmy admired her all over again. But still he hoped she would change her mind.

"She'll *have'ta* know sometime!" Jimmy insisted. "She won't *half* be mad." *That's it, Jimmy. Speak slowly, carefully. You can do it.*

Pinkie began to regret telling him that she had no intention of returning to the convent. "You won't tell her, will you, Jimmy?" she pleaded. "Promise? I'll tell her myself, when she's well enough. Promise me?"

"I..." Jimmy knew there was something wrong, that in helping to deceive Peggy he was helping nobody, least of all himself, for Peggy would never forget, even if she still tried to help him. And even that was doubtful... Could he tell her the truth, seriously injured, in great pain as she was? If he did, Pinkie would hate him...

"I'll tell her, Jimmy, honestly," Pinkie begged, "— but not just yet. You see — she'll be pleased when she knows I've come home to look after her."

That did the trick. Jimmy knew that for Peggy there was nobody like Pinkie, he knew something of the plans Peggy had once had... the war had altered things a bit, but even the war couldn't last for ever. Nor could the air-raids.

"Where will you sleep — down the air-raid shelters?"

"With everybody eating fish-and-chips and scratching all the time? No thank you." Pinkie's prejudice against the East End was very clear.

"Well... where *will* you sleep, then?" As an afterthought Jimmy added, "They don't scratch all the time, anyway," but this was ignored.

"I don't know. I'll wait until I've seen Peggy. ... But it'll be all right." She didn't know who needed the reassurance most — Jimmy or herself, for while Jimmy felt his admiration growing, Pinkie was beginning to regret the finality of her actions. Suppose her plan didn't work? But it *would* work, she told herself. She'd *make* it work.

The taxi came to a halt beneath the portico of the Clinic.

Jimmy paid, and grandiosely added two shillings to the

fare. Yet at the same time he hoped Pinkie would remember that it was *her* idea to go in a taxi, that *she* had promised to pay the fare. But Pinkie, seeing the notes and the silver in his hand, conveniently forgot.

Together, carrying the cases between them, they walked to the inquiry desk and Pinkie, in the cool, educated and superior voice that impressed Jimmy so deeply, asked if she could possibly see her mother, Miss Peggy Harcourt.

The porter — different from the one Jimmy had spoken to a day earlier, scanned his list of patients, then looked up. "I'm sorry, miss. No visitors allowed. Miss Harcourt's on the serious list."

Pinkie breathed sharply and audibly, staring at him.

"Please," she said. "She's my mother. I *must* see her — I've come all the way from Brighton."

He smiled. This girl was coloured — part coloured, at least, and if Miss Harcourt was coloured that information would be shown on the list by an initial beside her name. The girl was lying.

"Sure she's your mother, young lady?" he asked caustically. "It says here *Miss* Harcourt."

Pinkie's cream-caramel face darkened and Jimmy thought she would smack the porter's face. But she smiled.

"She happens to be an actress," she said coldly. "That's her stage name. I must see her, even —" and a small threat crept into her voice, "— even if I have to go to the matron. ... I've come all this way, and I have to go back this afternoon. It's the only chance I have... please?"

The porter gaped, then with a hurried "Just a minute, miss," he scuttled away down a tiled, bathroom-like corridor. Jimmy wondered how it was possible for a girl to be so cool, so superior, yet to smile so sweetly that people found themselves doing what she wanted. He knew that the actress-touch was a lie, and his respect deepened as he realised sadly: That's what education does for you.

His nails bit into the palms of his hands; he determined, as never before, to control himself and his speech, to appear sure, confident. ...

Pinkie turned to him, laughing. "You see?" she said lightly. She took off her hat and coat and laid them on a chair; her hands flashed to the back of her head and in a moment the dark braids of her glorious hair joined and then fell in one thick and lustrous coil over her left shoulder, almost to her waist.

Jimmy's mouth opened. This wasn't a fifteen-year-old girl. She looked... eighteen? nineteen? Again Pinkie laughed, pleased at his stupefaction.

She had seen the hair-style in a book of ancient civilisations and had taken and adjusted it to suit herself. Helen Mandeville, her silly English-rose rival for class leadership at the convent, had been furious. Poor Helen — she looked terrible when she tried to copy it. ...

The porter, when he returned with an attractive young nurse, was so surprised at the transformation that he immediately lost all his doubts about Pinkie's statements. If this girl could change so completely in such a short time, what wouldn't the mother, a real actress, be able to do?

"I'm sorry, Miss Harcourt," said the nurse, her voice tinged with the softest Irish brogue. "Your mother is too ill to see anybody —"

"Please, nurse, just let me see her. I won't even *say* anything. ... I've come all the way from Brighton, and I have to go back this evening... I *know* she'd like to see me!"

Jimmy could only gape, dazed by the repetition of this lie, while the nurse hesitated. "Well," she said finally, "only for a minute — no more. And you mustn't disturb her... oh," she added, looking at Jimmy, "— I'm sorry, but only one of you can go —"

"That's all right," Pinkie dismissed him easily, "— he's not a relative." To Jimmy it was like a kick in the belly.

As Pinkie and the nurse walked up the corridor, Jimmy went slowly out into Mile End. There had been so many lies, so many changes, that he couldn't think straight. He had stayed away from school to try to help, but it was a

171

waste of time. *Why* did she tell such lies? Which was the truth? Was she going back to the convent that night, or not? He was lost, but he sensed in Pinkie a determination that was stronger than his own, and this irritated him. It was only because she'd been to a convent, he told himself. If *I'd* gone to the High School *I'd* be able to give orders, and make people do as I wanted them to. ...

The only clear idea hanging loose in his mind was that he had intended to call on one or two of the scrap-metal dealers in the Mile End and Whitechapel areas, and now he was in Mile End. He shrugged and determined to stop thinking about Pinkie. Metal would help him get his suit, and that was more important.

The first dealer he approached wasn't interested, but the second was all smiles and co-operation. In a few minutes Jimmy knew where and how to dispose of the metals he and Tommy would collect — "Try'n get lead, boy. Very val'ble," — and as he noted the prices he whistled. If he couldn't make twenty quid — *forty* quid, splitting with Tommy — in a fortnight, his name wasn't Jimmy Wilson. He'd soon have his new suit, but he decided not to worry so much about music lessons and Varg-ner. He'd take proper English lessons instead. He was happy.

He was so full of plans and ideas that he would have walked straight past the Clinic if Pinkie's hands hadn't pulled him to a stop. She was pale, almost the colour of old ivory, and she stared and stared. Jimmy's happy-feeling evaporated.

"What... how is she?" It was all he could think of.

Pinkie's face crumbled and tears streamed down her face.

Peggy had been lost in the dark detachment of morphia, she had given no sign of recognition, of life; even Pinkie could not reach her. Her long, full body was protected from the weight of the bedclothes by a wire cage over which the blankets were spread, and not even the

172

comforting sign of her breathing was visible. The only part of her that could be seen was her right eye, which was partly opened but blank, empty. For one horrifying instant Pinkie was frozen by the fear of death, then with the Irish nurse she tip-toed to the bedside. "Peggy," she said, almost inaudibly. "Mother... Peggy, it's me, Pinkie." There was no response, not the smallest sign, and the other patients in the long shadowy ward held their breath and watched in pity as the tears began to roll down her cheeks and the nurse gently pulled her away.

"She's in great pain," the nurse whispered, her Irish lilt sounding out of place yet oddly comforting. "She'll be under drugs for a good while yet."

Pinkie stopped dead, dazed, bewildered. A good while?... But she couldn't, she mustn't. ... Pinkie was almost defeated.

How could Peggy sign a cheque when she was unconscious, couldn't lift a finger?... How long would four pounds last? "Nurse," she asked, "— I've spent all my money on the fare here... could I look in her handbag, to see if there's any loose change?"

The nurse was horrified, as only the Irish can be horrified when their sense of propriety is upset; she refused absolutely. She would be dismissed in disgrace... the only thing she could suggest was that perhaps the Matron could. ...

"I... I think I'll be able to manage, thank you," Pinkie smiled sweetly through her tears.

She had remembered that Jimmy had several pounds. If she could persuade him to loan them to her. ... Of course she could persuade him. Again she smiled, again sweetly. "Thank you for your trouble, nurse. When she comes round again, would you tell her that Jalani called? I'll be back again tomorrow. You'll tell her? Thank you."

When she looked round the cases were still there by the desk, but Jimmy had vanished. "Excuse me," she said to the porter, "— do you know —"

"He went out the front door, miss," he smiled, and

173

Pinkie, gathering her hat and coat, went to the entrance.

There was no sign of him. There were a few people, buses. ... A double funeral passed. Hurriedly Pinkie looked away. For a while she would need Jimmy — he knew the neighbourhood, he could be useful... she would have to make a fuss of him. But where was he? Restlessly, filled with doubts, she walked slowly up and down the pavement. The dark sky glowered on grimy buildings and dark and ugly lengths of brick-wall, with not far away an expanse of bright-smashed bricks forming a contrast, like a livid sore on dark skin. She wished she had never left the convent.

She saw Jimmy the moment he rounded the corner of the Clinic, walking slowly, almost dreamily. Her face took on a look of misery and then, realising that Jimmy hadn't even noticed, she ran forward, her hands pulling him to a stop.

"She didn't even recognise me," Pinkie replied, sobbing. "I thought she was dead."

"She didn't... ?" Jimmy was dumbfounded. He knew Peggy was very ill, yet somehow he had expected her to be better today, at least able to see and speak. Brought back so suddenly from his world of new suits and money he couldn't think what to say or do. He knew only that Pinkie was in trouble. Deep trouble.

"Well... what're you goin' — *going* — to do?"

"I don't know, Jimmy." The misery in her voice was real, alive, and Jimmy was filled with pity. "Can we... can we go somewhere and sit down. For a cup of tea?" she asked.

"You'd better put yer 'at an' coat on," he said practically, "— you'll catch your death o' cold." Again her sweet-winsome smile just managed to struggle through her tears, and fondly she pressed his arm. "You're a real pal," she said. When she went in to the Clinic again he followed.

"Could you watch the cases while we go for a cup o' tea?" he asked the porter.

"Of course. Just push them over against the wall." The porter, seeing Pinkie's tear-stained face and Jimmy's serious look, and thinking they had had bad news of the patient, spoke sympathetically.

They walked silently along the road, looking at but not seeing the houses and shops, and Jimmy was aware that people — especially the men — were staring at Pinkie. Timidly she slipped an arm through his and when, a moment later, a window-cleaner whistled his admiration Jimmy's pleasure was so intense that he almost forgot to breathe.

They soon found a small but reasonably clean tea-shop, and as Jimmy joined her, carrying two cups of tea, at one of the marble-topped tables, she smiled. Jimmy sat down on one of the chairs facing her across the table, but she waved him to the chair beside her. "Come and sit here," she said, "— next to me."

As he sat down beside her she took from her pocket a packet of cigarettes and a small jewelled lighter. Offering Jimmy a cigarette and taking one herself, she noticed the way his eyes followed the lighter. On the flat surface was picked out in small red brilliants the name *Jalani.* ...

... As he watched the lighter Jimmy had the strange sensation of being drawn into a whirlpool without knowing how he got there, or why. But he tried to find out.

"Pinkie," he said, choosing his words, "why did you tell all them lies about Peggy being an actress? And about going back to the convent, if you're not goin' back at all?"

Pinkie stared, her astonishment clear to all the world. Her dark, glowing eyes were so soft, so large, that Jimmy swam in her love and compassion. "If I hadn't, they wouldn't have let me see her, would they? Wouldn't you have told lies if it was *your* mother?"

She was right. Jimmy knew that if his own mother was lying in hospital, then he too would tell lies — any lies, in the hope of seeing her. Pinkie's reply was so loyally pure, so dazzlingly simple, that Jimmy's doubts evaporated and were replaced by an overwhelming sense of shame. He had doubted her when she was beyond doubt, and as she regarded him steadily, quizzically, his regret was deep and bitter. Silent, ashamed, he sat and waited.

# 4

As they waited outside the tea-shop for another taxi, Jimmy wondered dully why everything he decided to do went straight into reverse. ... He had hoarded his money, but it had been stolen; he wasn't going to give or lend any of it, yet he had given his mother four pounds of the seven she herself had stolen back from the old man; he was going to save what was left, and increase it, but he had just lent it — all of it — to Pinkie; and he had wanted to give up taking scrap-metal from the bombed houses, yet he would have to go on because he had no more money and because, whatever happened, he had to have a new suit to wear when he started work. ...

There was a dull, empty awareness that things — big, vague things that could be felt but never touched — were working against him, forcing him to do things he hadn't wanted to do. Now, having loaned Pinkie his money, and promised to help her in any way he could until Peggy was well enough to sign Pinkie's allowance cheque, he was committed even more to creeping through the shells of houses and office-blocks, to trying to sell clothing coupons, and any other black-market deal that came his way. Worse, he had also involved Tommy Cooper. Oh well, if Tommy backed out Jimmy would have to go on alone... he couldn't stop now. But the ache, his help-lessness, made him want to hit out at something, someone, to hurt. But there was only Pinkie, and as he looked at her gently smiling face his misery deepened to a great, intense sadness. Yet in his pocket his fingers gripped the small cigarette lighter with the name *Jalani* picked out in small red stones; his fingers slid over the

177

stones until the tips were sore, and the soreness was almost a pleasure. His grip tightened.

Pinkie smiled thinly, managing to hide her elation. Jimmy was so easily led... if she couldn't find a reasonable room she could now afford to stay at a small hotel. Only for a day or two, because it might be several days before Peggy was able to write a cheque... but as she smiled her confidence grew. Jimmy looks as though he's going to start crying... he's a funny boy, but likeable enough. Why didn't he try to press his leg against hers when they were in the taxi, or try to kiss her, as any other boy would have done? Bet he hasn't even kissed a girl yet. Not *really* kissed one. ... She remembered her dates with David, the air cadet, and she grasped Jimmy's arm.

"Don't look so sad, Jimmy," she said softly. "If you're worried about the money, I'd rather not borrow it. ..."

"It's not that. I'm just... fed up."

Pinkie urged him along the pavement, back towards the Clinic. They'd have more chance there of picking up a taxi.

"Fed up? Why? *I'm* not fed up. ... I'm all excited. In a day or two I'll have a nice room — perhaps a flat. Then I'll get a job, and save up and buy nice curtains, and I'll paint it and —"

Jimmy's vision of Pinkie, smothered in strips of well-pasted wallpaper, brought a grin to his face, but she appeared not to notice, going on without pause: "— for when Peggy comes home. You can help me if you like, Jimmy. Will you?" Glancing at him, seeing his now smiling face, she said unexpectedly: "You ought to laugh more. You look a lot better." Jimmy blushed.

Slowly, with subtle control of his thoughts and ideas, with stories of her visits to Paris, of life at the convent-school, she led him out of his depression. They walked along arm in arm, and when suddenly she let him go and gave an imitation of an organ-grinder, and then of his monkey, Jimmy nearly had a fit. His misery and bewilderment flowed away in tears of laughter, and there

178

was a lump in his throat. When, shortly afterwards, Pinkie told him of her dates with David, he was unaffected. Girls always liked boys. As Janey would have said, it was only natch'ral.

By the time Jimmy had carried Pinkie's luggage from the Clinic to the pavement she was already waiting in a taxi, and he joined her with a swift and lithe, surprising movement. "Well," he said, "off we go... but where are we going?"

"Back to the brewery first. Do you know anybody with a spare room?"

"Me?" Jimmy's smile vanished. "Blimey! Rooms are 'ard — *hard* — to get, what with everywhere bein' bombed. I don't. ..." His voice tailed away as he remembered that Addie Cooper had Joey's room, with the bed made... he said nothing. Tommy wouldn't stand for it, even if Addie was willing. And even that was doubtful.

He directed the driver, and as they drew away Pinkie shrugged. "Oh well," she said. "— I'll just have to look round. If I can't find a room I'll have to go to a hostel — I might be able to get into a Y.W.C.A." She had no intention of even attempting such a thing.

"Pinkie? What'll you do if the air-raid warning goes?"

"— Be frightened to death. But I'd rather stay on the ground and take a chance than go down the shelters." Again her voice had that faint touch of scorn.

"Well... what're you goin' to do about Peggy? How will I know how you're getting on?" The suspicion that perhaps Pinkie might go away was unexpectedly disturbing, and again his fingers slid across the surface of the lighter and felt the stones setting out her real name, the name that sometimes crept without cause into his mind.

"I'll go to the Clinic every day, until Peggy's through the worst of it. Can you come too?"

"No — I can't. I can't stay away from school again. I'll get the stick as it is, I s'pose, an' they might give me a bad leaving-certificate, an' that'll make it 'ard — *hard* — to

179

get a job. But I can come straight on after school — get there just before five o'clock."

"All right then. I'll wait for you in the tea-shop, where we went before."

She held her breath as he reached towards her, and she didn't know whether she was pleased or disappointed when his fingers uncurled and revealed her lighter.

"Thank you for this. ... I'll look after it." They smiled, and they were still smiling when the taxi drew up across from the brewery. The faint, almost-indistinguishable fragrance of the perfume she always used mingled oddly with the hot, lazy smell of the brewery; somehow they clashed, yet they combined and left a sensation at the back of his throat that remained for hours. He couldn't decide if it was really a smell or a taste.

When he left the taxi he shook her hand almost formally, then as she drew away again he saw only her dark eyes, smiling and friendly.

After tea he took his mother's biggest leather shopping-bag and furtively slipped inside it his spanner, hack-saw, a small rag-padded hammer, and the dimmed-down torch. These were covered and completely hidden by the army blanket from his mattress.

His mother was busy at the oven beside the fire, cooking soused herrings for Janey and the old man when they came home later in the evening.

"Ta-ta, Mum," he said from the door, "— I'm goin'ta put these in the shelter, to get a place."

Mrs Wilson looked up with a quick frown. "Don't you get up to no mischief. An' put yer coat on, else you'll get froze." As he turned to go out she added: "An' don't go up an' push the stall 'ome tonight." Jimmy stared at her in surprise, and realised that she was protecting him from the old man; she knew that when he found Jimmy's money gone from where he'd put it, there'd be a real ruckus; Mrs Wilson knew it, and she knew she could handle it. But she wanted it to be in her own home, with Jimmy out of the way. That was why, although she didn't like the idea of Jimmy going down the shelters, she didn't object. It was better that way.

When Jimmy arrived at the Coopers' flat Tommy was ready and waiting, with blankets and light plimsolls in a canvas grip, and lightly they said cheerio to Addie, who gave them some brown-paper-wrapped sandwiches and an apple each.

To be within easy reach of the acres of rubble, they had decided to stay in one of the City tube-station shelters, and as they walked they told each other of the afternoon's events. To cover-up for Jimmy's absence from school, Tommy had told Miss Bullock that he had had a bilious attack. Jimmy told his pal of the visit to the Clinic with Pinkie, but couldn't bring himself to tell of his loan, or of his promise to help her even more than he had already. Tommy wasn't any too happy as it was, without making it worse.

As they went along, the early, swiftly-deepening gloom of another winter softened the outlines of still-whole rows of tenements and blocks of flats, and the frequent jagged walls, and gaping windows of blasted houses seemed to have been there forever, just waiting for not-forgotten occupants to come back from work and turn the lights on, to put bright curtains up, to turn them once again into homes.

As the gloom thickened into darkness, so the sounds of the great city died away to a throbbing, waiting hush. Cars and buses with hooded, barely-visible headlamps glided quickly into the shadows, and workpeople scurried anxiously homewards, to begin almost immediately their nightly journey to the deep shelters. Millions of people shared the same unlikely hope: Perhaps they'll leave us alone tonight.

The tube shelter when they arrived was not too crowded, and together they unrolled their blankets and reserved their sleeping-places. Already the noise, amplified by the long dark tunnels with the gleaming rails, and rippled and distorted by the low curved roof, was deafening. Mothers screamed for lost children who screamed for their lost mothers, and there were rapid and violent searches in cases and bags and bundles, with the unending question: Have I got... ? There were one or two portable radios, the owners with their ears glued to pick up the first fading of the BBC programme, which meant that bombers were approaching the coast.

Time dragged. Slowly and gradually a feeling of hope, then of relief surged through the now-jammed shelter and through the whole of the capital. The bombers were not coming.

By eleven o'clock most of the shelterers were asleep; grateful, warm, and asleep. The air attack had switched to and almost obliterated a small provincial city, but London was unaware. Yet even now Jimmy saw here and there eyes that stared vacantly, sometimes fearfully, at the walls or at the ceiling, as taut nerves refused to relax.

Jimmy took the non-arrival of the bombers as an omen: "Come on, Tom. No excitement tonight. Let's 'ave a san'-widge, then we'll start."

When the sandwiches were eaten they picked up their bags with the tools and torches, and buttoned up their overcoats. The atmosphere was sweat-tainted and thick and warm, while up in the streets it would be snapping with cold. Jimmy wished he'd remembered to bring Billy's woollen mittens.

They threaded their way over or round the sprawled or crouching sleepers, arousing no comment from the air-raid warden on duty at the entrance, and as they set out Jimmy knew once again the feeling of heightened nervous tension, as if the warning had already sounded. Tommy was simply afraid, although he would never have admitted it.

Jimmy reached out into the darkness and gave Tommy a warning nudge: "Keep your torch 'andy. We'll 'ave to keep off the main streets, in case the Law spots us wi' these bags. 'Spesh'ly on the way back." Jimmy was confident that on the return journey the bags would be so filled with lengths of lead or copper tubing that they would hardly be able to carry them, and they knew that to be caught struggling with heavy bags, in the middle of the night, would mean trouble. Jimmy's words, meant only as a precaution, made Tommy more frightened than ever.

The night was heavy and overcast, and only twice did they spot the glow of dimmed torches. As they passed into the ruined acres of the City there was only darkness; darkness which, as they neared Saint Paul's, intensified, threatened, dried their throats. The surrounding hills and ridges of rubble were invisible, yet they had an eerie, menacing power that was almost tangible. They were alone, alone in a world of blackness which retained and exuded memories of fear and violence and death.

"Jim," Tommy whispered, "— what're we goin' to do if the warnin' goes?"

Jimmy swallowed, but managed to sound casual. "Do?" he said. "We'll just carry on. Might even be a good thing, if it keeps the cops away."

"Where... where we goin' to start?"

Despite himself, Jimmy's confidence was fading, speeded on by Tommy's fearful, whispered words. He put his hand on Tommy's shoulder.

"Not far now. I know where we are," he said, trying to reassure him. "— You can put your torch on if you like. But for chrissake don't wave it about. Shine it on the ground."

A light, hardly more than an aura, gleamed on kerbstones and shattered debris, and they both felt better. Glancing ahead, Jimmy sensed rather than saw a deeper darkness soaring upwards, and sighed in relief. Dead on target. He grinned, remembering these words from a film about the Air Force. Yet it was true; he was dead on target. Part of a concrete wall reared upwards for about thirty feet. Fractured, with gaping holes where once had been doors and windows, it was still a landmark. To one side and right at the base, in what had

183

once been a cellar or basement, Jimmy had noticed and remembered a faint gleam that he thought was from metal. It had been a good idea, he congratulated himself, to walk round the City yesterday, after he'd left the hospital. He halted.

"This is it, Tom. There's a cellar down there, an' that's where I start. If you see or 'ear anythin' close, shout like 'ell an' run for your life. Gimme yer bag, an' turn your torch off."

The gleam of light ended abruptly and Tommy handed over his bag; he tried to say something light and cheerful, but the words wouldn't come. His arm was gripped strongly, almost painfully; he heard the faint sound of a body slithering over stones, the near-explosion as a cascade of rubble slipped down into the roofless cellar, then there was silence. Absolute, stifling, black. Forgetting Jimmy's instructions, Tommy edged closer against the wall and pressed the button of his torch.

He didn't know what time it was, how long he'd been standing there, when from far to the east came the faint, undulating wail of the siren. When, a moment later, the London sirens knifed into and shattered the silence, his bladder emptied without volition, at first even without his knowledge; he crept away from the wall and over the heaped rubble, and scrabbled down into the cellar.

Jimmy, sawing through a length of gas-piping, did not hear the first sirens, but when the local siren screamed from only a few blocks away he burst into a prickly sweat. Swearing gently he picked up his torch and went back towards the road and Tommy. He moved quickly and quietly along the brick-strewn passage of what had been the basement of an office-block and then, as he turned to face the road, he faltered, the hair rising on the back of his neck. Someone was there. He had heard nothing, seen nothing, but he knew. Someone was there. It might be the Law, it might be someone after lead, like himself, it might be... his relief was so great as he realised who it might be, who it *was,* that he giggled. "Tommy," he called hoarsely, "Tom. Over 'ere."

The gleams of the two torches mingled, and thankful, Tommy gulped. Jimmy, recovering quickly from his fright, said: "Down there, on the left. There's a sort o' room, wi' the roof on."

"We — we goin'ta stay 'ere till the all-clear goes?" Tommy was almost in tears.

"'Course we are. There's some lead pipin' further up. Besides, we're as safe 'ere as anywhere else." Jimmy was tense, but no longer afraid, and Tommy's dependence brought his confidence surging back. In a couple of weeks he'd have his suit...

They sat in the darkness listening for the sound of gunfire or of bombs falling, but there was nothing; even the searchlights did nothing to relieve the blackness.

"Tommy," Jimmy said suddenly, "— seein' as 'ow you're down 'ere, why not gimme a 'and, eh? It'll save time."

Tommy, glad of the chance to *do* something, to avoid being alone, agreed immediately, and together they crept back to where Jimmy had left his tools. Shortly afterwards, the raiders having passed over the coast well to the north, the all-clear sounded.

"Thangawd for that," Jimmy said briefly; quietly, determinedly, they worked on. ...

It was nearly four in the morning when they made their way back to the shelter; cold, dispirited, exhausted. Certainly there was lead-piping for the taking, but it was slow work raking through the piles of bricks, shifting chunks of masonry... they had to go careful too, to avoid moving any lumps acting as supports, in case they started a rubble-slip. They could be crushed, if they did. ... And after the piping was uncovered, the real work started; hacking, sawing, hammering, with fingers numbed with cold, with sweat-blinded eyes. ...

They had taken several lengths of lead gas-pipe and a couple of brass taps; they were heavy, and would be worth money, but Jimmy knew they'd have to do a lot

185

better. Suppose Peggy died... quickly he avoided the thought and instead wondered how he could manage if Pinkie needed any more money... Gradually his disappointment wore off, and he grew calm and contented. At last he was working actively towards the things he wanted.

Stretched out in the shelter, wrapped in blankets and warming slowly, Tommy fell asleep after a few whispered words. Jimmy lay on his back, staring at the ceiling.

He knew suddenly that he would be caught, and his imagination, stirred by the events of that whole day and by his tiredness, grew more and more vivid. He was not certain what the Law could do to him, as he was only fourteen, but he saw himself in prison clothes, being sentenced to Dartmoor... and he decided, his mind swerving off at a tangent, that he'd have to change his underwear more than once a week. He might get injured in a raid, or he might be caught under a pile of rubble, and be taken to hospital and undressed. The thought that his underwear might be soiled, or that there might be holes in his socks, was unbearable.

... Wonder where the bombers went tonight?... where's Janey, an' the old lady?... Jalani... that's a funny name. But it's a nice name... makes you think of foreign countries and mountains an' jungles... if I stand by Pinkie an' 'elp all I can, will she let me call 'er *Jalani*? Instead o' Pinkie?... that'd be nice. Real nice...

He slept, and it seemed that his eyes had only just closed when the yawns and grumbles of fellow-shelterers raised his unwilling eyelids. Tommy was already awake.

"You was snorin' like a bleedin' pig."

"Christ. I don't feel like school, d'you?"

Tommy grinned in response and brought his hand down on Jimmy's shoulder in a sharp slap. "Wakey-wakey," he said, "— an' put your socks on." They smiled at the omission from the traditional Naval reveille, but Jimmy had to grumble a bit more: "I never took me bloody socks off."

Carefully they folded their blankets so that the tools and the lead and the taps were hidden at the bottom of their bags, and went back to Tommy's home, where the metals were slipped into the cupboard-wardrobe. Jimmy turned with a smile.

"Not so bad, Tom," he said. "We ought to do better, but —"

Tommy leaned down, dug at the bottom of the cupboard and brought out a fat envelope. "Could you flog these?" he asked. He shook the envelope on to his bed, and there were dozens of clothing coupons. Jimmy stared.

"Where'd you get 'em?" He already knew, but he didn't want to believe. Tommy grinned. "We collected 'em from the 'ouses — before the ARP and the AFS got there. They'd on'y keep 'em theirselves."

Jimmy stepped back, horrified. The men of the Air Raid Precautions and the Auxiliary Fire Services had the highest reputation for kindness and humanity, and he couldn't accept Tommy's words. It was bad enough taking the lead and the taps, but they were just built-in things, they had never belonged personally to people who might now be in hospital, or even dead. He pushed the coupons away, dazedly shaking his head.

"Whassamatter? They're worth a few quid, I bet. ..." Tommy frowned. Seeing Jimmy's bewilderment he added: "You're not scared o' the black market, are you? Everyone's in it. My mum, an' your mum — everyone who wants anythink that's rationed, they get it on the black... what else can they do?"

In a way Tommy was right. Jimmy tried to think of the words to explain the immense difference between scrap-metal and stolen coupons, but it was useless; to Tommy, frightened of crawling over the ruins in the night, the one was neither better nor worse than the other. And, if it came to it, what *was* the difference? Jimmy knew he could sell the coupons on Sunday down the Lane, and they *were* worth money... he took the envelope.

"Jim. If — when we go back down the ruins, can I come

an' 'elp you, instead o' waitin' up top?" Tommy was diffident, and Jimmy thought about it again. It would be a help if they worked together, yet it would be dangerous; no matter how careful you were, you couldn't stop the rasping of the hacksaw or the thudding of the hammer. And you never could tell — there was the cops, or there might just be someone going past, taking a short cut to or from the shelters.

"Tell you what, Tom." Deliberately he spoke softly, encouragingly, for the result of their work was more important than Tommy knew; "You stay up top on lookout, 'till I find some o' the *real* stuff. Then I'll come up for you an' we'll cut it together. O.K.?"

"O.K." Tommy crossed to the small mirror and combed his hair. "But 'urry up, ferchrissake. If I stay up there on me own for long, I'll start doin' me bonkers."

They grinned, and Jimmy turned to the door.

"Jim... you seein' Pinkie any more?"

"Later on — after school. Why?"

"I... you oughta be careful. I don't wanta talk out o' place, but —"

"But what?" Jimmy's voice was sharp, incisive.

"But... well, you're always talkin' about 'er, an' she's... she's funny."

"'Ow d'you mean, *funny?*" Jimmy was getting wild. Tommy wished he hadn't said anything, but now he had to go on: "She's trouble," he said. "If you 'ang round 'er, you'll be in trouble yourself."

Jimmy's face showed his surprise, his disgust. "What's that mean?" he demanded. "I'm not 'angin' round. I'm just tryin' to 'elp, that's all. Why shouldn't I? Wouldn't you try to 'elp someone stuck 'ere all on their own, wi' their mother in 'ospital?"

"'Course I would. But she's..." Tommy knew what he wanted to say but he couldn't say it. And Jimmy's voice was rising: "She's a good kid — tryin' to get a job, an' a room for when Peggy comes out of 'ospital —"

Tommy's lips curled derisively. "Look, Jim, Rajah told

188

me about 'er, an' 'er tricks, an' bein' too bloody good for Stepney. ..." As he saw Jimmy's frozen face, Tommy faltered.

Slowly Jimmy crossed the room to Tommy's side. "You're *jeal*ous," he said, incredulously. "— That's all. Just jealous, because she's bin to a convent an' talks nice. ..."

Tommy turned away and when he spoke his voice was soft and sad and terribly earnest. "Look, Jim," he said. "If you wanted me to, I'd 'elp you to rob a bank, or... or..." Whatever Jimmy wanted, Tommy would help. But his affection was dried, inarticulate.

"But you're not 'elpin' at all —" Jimmy began but Tommy broke in: "If you like 'er a lot, I'll do what you say —"

"I *don't* like 'er a lot — not the way you mean," Jimmy exploded. "It's just that Pinkie an' Peggy've 'elped me a lot, an' now I c'n 'elp them. Is that what's upset you? Wouldn't *you* do it?"

Jimmy's voice was high because even as he spoke he doubted: he hadn't been upset when he'd heard about David, the air-cadet, so how *could* he like Pinkie in the way Tommy meant? But why did having her lighter please him so much? Why did he want to be one of those she allowed to call her *Jalani* instead of Pinkie?

Tommy put his hand on his pal's shoulder, but Jimmy wrenched himself away. "I just want to 'elp 'er, that's all, Tom." The edge of Jimmy's anger was blunted and he spoke almost to himself; "She talks nice and she's educated an' clever, like I wish I was... is that wrong?" He shrugged hopelessly and sat on the edge of the bed. "Sometimes I can't make you out at all, Tom. One minnit you want to 'elp, then you start makin' a fuss about nothin' at all."

Tommy replied softly, intensely: "I'll 'elp *you*, Jim. You know that — that's why you asked me to go on the ruins wi' you. I just don't wanta see you get in any trouble, that's all."

189

There was a moment of painful silence, then Jimmy rose from the bed. "O.K., Tom. Just — don't worry yerself." To avoid any further discussion he went to the door. "See you later," he said, and managed a weak smile. Tommy did not smile, but simply waved his hand.

When they met later, on the corner of the street, they were cool and reserved, like distant relatives gathered for the funeral of another distant relative, but as the day wore on and they ploughed through geography and arithmetic their constraint broke down. They were both very tired and for the first time in over a year Jimmy came only fourth in the daily test. Miss Bullock stared but made no comment, for which Jimmy was grateful. When finally school was over for the day and they parted on the same street corner, Jimmy arranged to call for Tommy later on with tools and bag, as on the night before, but he said nothing about going to meet Pinkie near the hospital. Tommy seemed to be his usual self.

Pinkie was already waiting when he arrived, at the same table, and she looked very smart and very... Jimmy didn't know what it was, but it made you look twice. Her eyes were warm and friendly, and she half-smiled as Jimmy carried the two cups of tea.

"Hallo, Pinkie. How's Peggy?" Funny — he'd sounded his h's without even thinking about them! Pinkie pretended not to notice.

"They said she's a little stronger, but I couldn't see any difference. She looked just the same as yesterday."

"Oh... well, what're they goin'ta do? Will they send 'er — *her* — to Saint Albans right away, or will they wait?"

For Jimmy the evening took on a quality of unreality, almost dreamlike. He had tried for so long to sound his h's and g's, and for so long they had defeated him; it was all right while he just *thought* the words, but when he *said* them something slipped. Now it was like standing next to himself, and as he listened with growing excitement he knew that his words sounded different. His pronunciation was getting better and better. Even Peggy

190

would have been pleased, yet it took no — or *almost* no — conscious effort. It was as though the pieces of a difficult jigsaw puzzle had fallen into place of their own accord and this, he thought, was because of Pinkie. Even so, he knew that with his family and his other friends he would have to speak as usual, as they did.

He listened as Pinkie told him of her fear when the air-raid warning sounded in the night, and his replies were slow and careful. When Pinkie told him that she'd found a flat down near Aldgate he didn't know whether he was pleased or sorry, and his feelings were so mixed that he didn't notice how skilfully she evaded his questions about how she had managed it. Instead she described it to him; it had two large rooms and a tiny kitchen, with a front door all of its own. The house had railings in front with a gate in them, and you went down iron fire-escape stairs from the pavement. There was a tiny space, and a tiny front window, and a tiny —

"Oh," Jimmy said. "You mean it's in one of the '*areas*'?"

Pinkie stared at him, as though he had slapped her face.

"No," she said edgily. "It's nothing to do with areas. It's the *basement* — a *base*ment *flat*."

Jimmy grinned happily. "Call it what you like," he smiled, "it's still in one of the *areas*."

He was right, and he knew it. The little spaces in front of houses that had cellars — or basements, as Pinkie preferred to call them — were called *areas*. Always had been... but he felt so happy that he refused to argue.

"I've paid two weeks' rent, and the people are lending me a bed and some saucepans and things — just till I've saved up enough to buy my own —" Jimmy responded quickly to her growing excitement and enthusiasm, and he soon learned that the flat was terribly dirty. It would have to be cleaned and scrubbed and painted from top to bottom, but Pinkie didn't mind that... Jimmy immediately promised to borrow buckets and brushes and scrapers, and to go round there each evening after school. He could even do the wall-papering —

"No wallpaper, thank you. Not in *my* flat." The idea of having her flat papered, as was so usual in the little houses she detested, was unthinkable. "— I'm going to colour-wash the walls. Like Peggy's old room used to be. Then when she comes out of hospital, it'll be just like coming home again and she'll be happy."

Jimmy agreed that it was a good idea... he would gladly have tried to wall-paper the ceiling if Pinkie had asked him, but after all, colour-washing — or distempering, as Jimmy knew it — was much easier... he wanted to see the flat right away, but firmly yet gently Pinkie refused, saying that she wanted to do some tidying up, to get her things sorted out a bit first. She gave him the address and asked him to go there after school the following day.

Again he had his vision of Pinkie trying to do redecorations, and he burst out laughing. When he told her why he was laughing so much she joined in, and he was deeply impressed by her high, Indian-thin voice: bright, young, bubbling, with a tinkling sound that reminded him of a music-box... he liked it.

Pinkie finished her tea, but Jimmy lingered. He wanted this meeting to go on and on... he had never seen Pinkie so light-hearted, so happy, but the proprietor stared stonily at them, so at last they left.

"There's one thing, Jimmy," Pinkie said hesitantly as they stood outside on the pavement. "If you see Mrs Rubens — that's the woman who lives upstairs... well, if she says anything, will you tell her I'm seventeen? She's a bit old-fashioned, and she might think it's funny, me being only fifteen." Jimmy agreed wholeheartedly, knowing very well that for some strange reason a year or two in age seemed to have an enormous effect on grown-ups.

They shook hands formally, like self-conscious courtiers, and as they did so Jimmy said diffidently: "Pinkie... how's the money lasting? Will you want any more?"

Again Pinkie laughed, light and cool, as she grasped Jimmy's arm. "You're a good friend, Jimmy... about the best I've ever had. But I've paid two weeks' rent — only eighteen-and-six a week — and I hope Peggy'll be well enough to give me my allowance cheque before I run out altogether. But thank you. Very much."

Her thanks and her refusal made Jimmy doubly glad. She had been warm and kind, and she would not need the money Jimmy hoped to have made on the scrap metal and by flogging the clothing coupons. Which meant in turn that after splitting with Tommy, all his own share could be put as deposit on his new suit. His first new suit. ...

Jimmy waited with Pinkie at the bus-stop until her bus came and then, remembering that he had had nothing to eat since dinner-time, he trotted home to the Court.

Already dusk was falling, and he realised that it had suddenly turned much colder. From the open manhole-covers in the road little whisps of sweet, cloying steam from the sewers rose and crept along the surface, then disintegrated in the cold, restless air. Jimmy shivered and ran faster.

That night he and Tommy went to the City ruins earlier and, as the raid warning had already gone, they scrambled together from the roadway to the rubble-choked cellars. The raid was not severe, but the sudden whirring of a lump of shrapnel made Tommy duck to one side. He lost his footing and scrabbled at the pile of debris and as his dimmed torch fell from his hand he caught the gleam of jagged but buried metal.

Quickly he called Jimmy over and working side by side they dug away at the hillock of smashed bricks. A huge segment of the roofing of what had been an office building was laid bare, and they stared silently.

"Jeeeesus!" Jimmy breathed softly. "Blooey! Miles of it. Must be worth a forchoon." Excitedly they shook hands, then began digging more urgently than ever. "Lucky, eh?" Tommy asked proudly, but Jimmy was too engrossed to reply.

Frantically they pushed and heaved and banged and sawed; sweat ran down their faces and now and then came the deep roar of exploding bombs and the defiant bark of gunfire. A soft pink glow spread through the sky to the south, and several times Tommy paused to look up at the sky and listen. Jimmy worked frantically, exhilarated, beyond Tommy's fear. Blooey!... something he'd thought about but never hoped to find. Blooey... the wide strips of lead used by builders to provide extra insulation, now worth its weight in gold. ... They worked fiercely and without stopping right through the all-clear, until shortly before dawn, prising the lead away from its backing material, hacking with cut and bleeding finger-tips, then jumping on the sawn strips to force them into rolls small enough to fit inside the bags, which at last they could hardly lift. ...

Tired to the point of exhaustion, Jimmy lay on his back staring at the curving roof, listening to the sleep-noises of the other shelterers. He had expected to drop off to sleep immediately his head touched the pillow, as Tommy had done, but for some reason his brain kept going back to the conversation of the day before, in Tommy's room. ...

... *Did* he like Pinkie? He'd never said he didn't like her, but Tommy meant in the way that Johnny Burton liked Janey, or Boy-boy liked Maisie... Jimmy slid over on to his side. In contrast to the cold outside, the air in the shelter was moist and clammy, and the rough army blanket prickled and irritated his skin.

... Tommy only meant about kissing, and doing it with a girl, but that was just rubbish. Jimmy'd known for years that Peggy had special hopes and plans for Pinkie. ... How was Peggy?... Would her plans come off now?... What did Boy-boy see in Maisie?... Was it the same old thing that grown-ups always had on their minds, next to eating and drinking? And fighting?... What would it be like, the first time?...

He was hot and fretful and he squirmed; the blanket was rough and hot and stifling, sweat trickled down his neck, and angrily he rolled over on to his belly. There was a strange tingling, a lifting, a dizzying writhing and jerking... it had happened, he knew with a soaring exaltation. And he wouldn't go blind because... well, because it was an accident, like. He thought again of Pinkie and then, in his last moment of smiling wakefulness, of the Blooey. Miles of it... he slept.

That night, with the finding of the Blooey, began the happiest and busiest weeks he ever remembered. Happy, exciting, exhausting. He drove Tommy to the point of staggering, and he drove himself beyond it. There was the Blooey each night, there was school in the daytime, and in the early evening there was Pinkie and the flat; scrubbing, sweeping, painting, scraping at paint. He ate and slept where and when he could, and allowed nothing to deter him.

Most of all he liked the time spent at Pinkie's. He worked with her, laughed and joked with her, he heard her stories of life at the convent, and gradually the flat began to look like a home. During one of the evenings there Pinkie, who went each afternoon to the Clinic, told him that at last Peggy had shown signs of coming out of her long coma, that they were decreasing the drugs. She hadn't spoken yet — just moved and sighed. But it was wonderful, exciting news.

In only a week Jimmy's face tautened and he grew paler, but he was lucky; his mother was so preoccupied with her efforts to provide food and drink for Boy-boy's wedding party that she hardly noticed him as he slipped into and out of the house. He bolted all his food as quickly as he could; he made his first Saturday visit to the Public Baths in Bethnal Green and fell asleep in the beautiful hot water; he worked day and night despite the cold and the rain and the raids and he told nobody — not even Janey. He traded his metal-lengths and taps, he flogged the clothing coupons on Sunday down the Lane, and he went round to Mr Jacobs, the tailor who lived in Luxton

Street. There he paid the deposit on and was measured for his first made-to-measure suit. He hoped things could go on like this for months. But they stopped on the following Friday. The night before Boy-boy's wedding.

Jimmy ran home from school, gulped the stew his mother had left simmering on the gas-stove, then reached into the coal-cupboard under the stairs. He brought out a cocoa-tin and gloatingly, lovingly, counted the banknotes hidden inside. He had just replaced the tin and the money when the street-door slammed and his mother came in, carrying a paper-wrapped parcel. She put the parcel on the table and tore off the wrapping, as Jimmy put on his overcoat.

"My Gawd," she said, staring at him briefly. "You goin' out again? Never stop still a minnit, you don't." Her mouth widened into a smile as she tore away the last of the paper.

"Look at this," she said proudly. "An 'ole legga' bacon. Black Market." She laid the bacon on the table and began pounding it with the flat of her hand. She stopped and asked, surprisingly: "You ever 'ad anythin' to do wi' that bloke, Blind Billy?"

It was Jimmy's turn to stare.

"Me? No. ... I've seen 'im in the street, that's all."

"Oh." The old lady's relief was evident as she pointed to the leg of bacon. "I got that off'n 'im. No coupons." She pursed her lips. "'E asked 'ow you was, an' when you was leavin' school, an' what you was goin'ta work at... I just thought you might've bin talkin' to 'im."

"I know 'e's in the Black Market," said Jimmy, edging towards the door, "— an' 'e's always walkin' up an' down Aldgate, but tha'sall." Deliberately changing the subject he asked: "When's Boy-boy comin', tomorrer?"

"Tomorrer?" The old lady chuckled. "Im'n Maisie's comin' round tonight. We're goin'ta start doin' the san'widges an' ev'rythin'. Janey's stayin' 'ome to 'elp, as well."

She put the bacon into a wide, flat baking dish, then asked: "You comin' 'ome tonight?"

"Not 'less you want me. I'll be down the shelter." He wanted to get away and round to Pinkie's, but he didn't want to make his mother suspicious. "You'll be best off down there," she said. "You'd on'y get under our feet if you come 'ome."

"O.K., Mum. I'm goin' round for Tommy now. ... See you in the mornin'."

"G'night, son. Don't get up to no mischief."

Seeing that the old lady was in a good mood and pleased with herself, Jimmy answered cheekily: "Well, look after yerself, Lizzie. An' don't 'ave too much stout." He guessed that Boy-boy was coming round to help the old man to ferry the two barrels, and the crates of beer, from the pub to the house.

"You saucy little sod," his mother muttered as he opened the door, then at last he was on his way.

He hurried down the fire-alarm steps, tapped his usual two-and-one signal on the window, then stood there whistling. When Pinkie opened the door he saw that her face was pinched and drawn, and that she had been crying. His questions came even before he stepped in.

"What... ? Is it Peggy?" He stopped in the centre of the transformed room and took off his coat. The fresh paint sparkled and gleamed, the plain colours made the room look spacious and light, and although Pinkie was still using the furniture loaned by her landlady, Jimmy thought it was wonderful. He knew that by the time Pinkie had done all the things she wanted to do, with her flair for colour and design, the little flat would look even better than Peggy's old room in the Indian house.

"They — they're moving her away tomorrow," she said, her voice flat and emotionless. "She said she'd like to see you, but they wouldn't let you in, anyway. She's still on the danger list."

"She's on the gate, you mean." Jimmy nodded in understanding. "But still," he added, "at least she's talking now." His eyes shone with his pleasure and he took Pinkie's hands in his own.

197

Pinkie half-smiled, but shook her head. "No. It'll be a long time before she can speak. But she can move her right arm, and she writes messages on a little pad. That's not so bad, but —"

Without warning she burst into tears, and Jimmy felt uncomfortable. He wanted to put his arms round her, to ease her tears as he had so often eased Janey's tears, but he was afraid.

In the last weeks he had seen her moods — the little flash of temper when she caught her dress on a protruding nail, the light-hearted way she had of impersonating someone — a teacher, perhaps, or a market vendor, and he had seen her in her rare quiet and reflective periods, when she told him of her hopes for her future, but he had never seen her like this. Not knowing what to do he stared silently, without moving. Pinkie added between choked sobs: "She doesn't know what's wrong with her, but the doctor told me today... her face will always be scarred, and she'll be crippled for the rest of her life. ..."

Jimmy breathed out noisily, a long aaaah of sympathy and concern, as Pinkie threw herself on to the sofa. It was loaned to her, a battered and torn old thing, but she had made it look much better simply by throwing a second-hand chenille tablecloth, the colour of port-wine, and with a faint design of flowers running through it, over the whole ancient piece.

"Per'aps... *perhaps* it might not be as bad as that. If —"

"— Don't try to make it easier. D'you think the doctors don't know what they're talking about?"

"But..." He crossed the room and sat beside her, and without thinking he was stroking her thick, glossy black hair in long, soothing movements. Her crying eased, then stopped, and at last she sat up and looked at him.

"I'm sorry, Jimmy. ... It's not only that... it's everything else. This place, all the work we've done to it... and I'm still not working yet. It's all hit me, all together. ..."

"You mean — are you short of cash? I'll get some —"

"Again she shook her head. "No — that's all right. Peggy signed my cheque for me. ... Oh, I don't know. I never go anywhere, never meet anyone... I'm depressed, that's all."

Jimmy reached forward and took her hands. He swallowed.

"Pinkie," he said tentatively. "Would you like to go to a party tomorrow — tomorrow night?"

Her face brightened. "A party? Where?"

"Well. ... I didn't say anything before — I didn't think you'd like it..." He could see the stares from Janey and his mother as Pinkie went into the house... The old lady'll kill me... he stifled the thought and went on: "— It's my brother's wedding, and we're 'avin' — *having* — a party." He knew he had gone mad, that it was the last thing he should have suggested, but he couldn't stop: "I would've asked you before, but I didn't think you'd go. We — we're on'y ord'nary people," he added diffidently, "— but we've got a wireless, an' Boy-boy — that's the brother who's gettin' married — he's hired someone's gramophone an' some records. ..." He couldn't keep the pride from creeping into his voice as he mentioned these last items. Pinkie's eyes widened, and she smiled. Then the smile vanished. "But I've got nothing to wear," she said, then burst into a peal of laughter at Jimmy's look of blank astonishment.

"Nothing to wear?" he demanded, knowing that the whole idea of Pinkie erupting into Boy-boy's party was stupid, ridiculous, but knowing too that he no longer cared. "You've got more clothes than Janey — that's my sister," he explained, "— you'll remember 'er, you've seen 'er in the street — you've got more clothes than she's ever 'ad in all 'er — *her* — life!"

(*Watch your words, Jimmy Wilson. Speak slower!*)

Pinkie frowned as she stood up, then went to the door. "Wait there," she said, vanishing along the passage.

He heard the sounds of doors and drawers being opened and pulled and slammed, then there was a brief silence. When she reappeared she was wearing a dress of lacy white material, and her arms were filled with a riot of colour, which she dropped on the sofa. Then she stood back.

The white dress was very tight across the bodice, but from her tiny waist it swelled into a knee-length flare. Jimmy swallowed. She looked very young, very gay, and... beautiful?

That's it, he decided with surprise. She's beautiful!

"D'you like it?" she asked lightly, pivoting on one foot so that the skirt ballooned and shimmered over her blue slip.

"Mmmmm — s'lovely." Join in the game and cheer her up... but she pouted.

"What about this one?" she said, darting to the sofa and pulling out a misty-blue, silver-trimmed sari. Only two feet away from him, and completely without fear or embarrassment, she slipped out of the white dress and in a few moments became a wonderful, smiling Indian doll. She moved her head, without moving her shoulders, from side to side, and wreathed her arms in front of her in what must have been an Indian dance. He stared fascinated, and triumphant. So much for Tommy! Jimmy might like Pinkie, but if she'd liked *him* that way she'd never stand in front of him and change her clothes and not blink an eye! He knew for certain that Tommy was wrong, and there was a strange feeling of disappointment in the knowledge. He stared, almost afraid to breathe and then, before his silence became noticeable, he said: "*That* one. It's *smashin'*!"

He watched her try on the dresses one by one, and in the end he couldn't remember which one she decided on. There was a wild feeling, as though he was flying, yet choking; he was suddenly restless. He remembered the night in the shelter, the night he couldn't get to sleep. ...

When he left her he felt very pleased, very sure of himself. No matter what the old lady thought, she wouldn't cause any trouble and spoil Boy-boy's wedding party, and who could help liking Pinkie? There might be a row *afterwards,* but who cared? That's it, he thought, who cares? I'll worry about what happens afterwards... afterwards.

Tommy was ready when he arrived at the Coopers' house, looking a bit down in the mouth. "You're late," he said, before Jimmy could say a word. "I thought you wasn't comin'. You might of gone down the pub wi' Boy-boy an' yer ole man."

"Tom... I've asked Pinkie to come to the party tomorrow. She 'ad some bad news about Peggy an' she was cryin', so I asked 'er. Just to cheer 'er up, like."

"Oh." Tommy's face fell.

He didn't refer to it again, but as he waited in the shelter of the wall, listening to the rasping of Jimmy's hacksaw and trying to define the far end of the rubble-strewn street, he couldn't stop thinking about it. He sensed trouble, but he couldn't face another argument, or Jimmy's accusations, again.

"Tom, Tommy! Come an' gi'me a 'and? I've found some more Blooey!"

Jimmy's voice was soft yet urgent, excited. Tommy was unaffected, but dutifully he groped away from the wall and slid down the rubble into the basement, where Jimmy pulled him along a series of passages.

The Blooey this time was not such a big find, nevertheless it was worth more to them than the cut lengths of lead piping, so once again they pushed and scraped and dug and swore at the obstinate lead strips. Jimmy passed a light comment once or twice, but Tommy did not respond, and eventually they settled into a grim, silent but determined effort.

Jimmy's mind was full of Pinkie-at-the-party, and although his movements were quick and accurate, he was oblivious of his surroundings.

There was a sudden grip on his arm, and Tommy's torch went out.

"Jim. Someone's down there — quick." Tommy's nervousness had returned, and he couldn't help his shaking voice.

"Jeeeesus!" Jimmy's torch blinked out and together they listened. After a moment they could just discern a faint glow, silhouetting a jagged edge of rubble some way away, but there was no sound. Jimmy shivered and there was an icy feeling, like the first touch of a barber's clammy-cold steel clippers, on the back of his neck. He reached down and felt for a lump of brick.

"Tom. I'm goin'ta take a look. Keep just be'ind me."

Silently Jimmy moved away, careful as a stalking cat. Tommy would have given anything to follow, but he was trembling, paralysed. In his panic he slipped and the roar of cascading rubble exploded into the silence. The faint glow ahead of Jimmy disappeared, and he drew a sharp, hissing breath.

... Kerrrist... is it the Law?... Another metal-grabber?...

Jimmy heard only the thick thudding of his own pulses as he slid forward: then froze as there came a faint rasping sound from over on his left. His fingers grasped the half-brick as he slid from the narrow, fairly clear gully between the piles of rubble. Now there was no sound whatever, and he could see only the blasted wall rising dimly against the sky. There was the sudden sound of flying feet just in front of him and without thinking he lashed out with all his strength. There was a sharp, agonised grunt, then a vicious white pain seared his shoulder and down his arm. The breath screamed from his throat and his shout for Tommy died as a heavy body landed squarely on him. A hand pulled his head upwards, then thrust it back hard against the bricks, and there was a sweat-thick man-smell he knew he ought to recognise. The soaring wall circled crazily, then seemed to collapse on him. ...

The fingers tormented him. He tried to push them away but he had no strength, no will. Only a great aching... he was blinded by a dim torch.

"Jim... Jimmy. ..." Tommy was sobbing and muttering to himself as he scrambled on the rubble, trying to find a firm footing against which he could raise Jimmy to his feet. "Jim... you're not dead, are you? You're not —"

The words had more effect than the futile tugging and pulling, and Jimmy sat up.

"'Course I'm not bloody dead. But I might of bin, for all the use *you* are. What'd'you run away for?" he demanded.

"I... I was frightened. ... I'm no good at all this, Jimmy. I just get scared. ... I knew somethink like this'd 'appen."

Tenderly Jimmy ran his fingers over the back of his head, wincing as they touched a bump that felt as big as a duck's egg. There was some blood, a drumming in his head. Could've been worse... shame about Tommy... he's a good pal, but he's got no guts. ...

"Ne'mind, Tom... at least it wasn't the Law. Did you see who it was?"

"I didn't see anythink... when you shouted I started runnin' — backwards, an' 'ooever it was run the other way."

"Mmmm — I've got an idea who it was. We'll see tomorrer night."

"Tomorrer?... What...?" Tommy was floundering.

"We'll see."

Moving gingerly they went back to where they had been working, gathered their tools and bags and the lead, then set off for the shelter. They moved slowly and silently, Tommy already with the knowledge that for him, at least, the lead-cutting was over. Jimmy, with his still-pounding head, also realised it.

... But with all of it, they'd done well. He'd made enough to pay for his suit, and he still had a few quid left over, besides which Pinkie wouldn't need any more, as Peggy had given her her allowance. ... Tomorrow was the day of the wedding, tomorrow he would spring his surprise. Thinking of Pinkie at the party made him reflect wryly that tomorrow he'd spring *two* surprises...

As he stretched out in the rough army blanket again he was almost glad the metal-taking was over, and his aches changed gradually to a feeling of intense, soaring exaltation.

It had all been worth it.

# 5

Even though she had been up half the night sawing loaves, spreading marge on slices that varied in thickness from wafers to doorsteps, depending on who had cut them; cutting and hacking at the tinned meat, at the corned beef and at the boiled bacon, Mrs Wilson was awake again at daybreak. Beside her in the big bed Janey and Maisie, her swollen body huge and grotesque in the semi-darkness, slept soundly while underneath, on the mattresses, the old man and Boy-boy snored with great enthusiasm and even greater discord. Little Billy, snuggled against his father for warmth, was both invisible and inaudible. Like Janey, he slept with one thumb in his mouth.

Boy-boy and Maisie were supposed to have gone home last night, but as the evening wore on it became clear that they'd never make it. While Maisie and Janey and Addie Cooper and Mrs Wilson between them cut and scraped at the food or scrubbed the floor and table with carbolic, Boy-boy and the old man and Tom Cooper went backwards and forwards to the Two Bakers ferrying the crates of beer and the bottles of spirits and the two ferkins of ale. Each time they arrived back at the pub they had to have a quick one, or two or three; the old man, anxious that Boy-boy should enjoy his last night as a bachelor, fed him with whisky-and-chasers, turning each visit into a minor stag party. So, by the time Tom and Addie went home, Boy-boy was already asleep, a wide grin all over his face.

Addie would be back again at nine o'clock, and while the Wilsons changed and got ready for the ceremony,

Addie and Jimmy — who was not going — would spread the mattresses over the floor upstairs — they'll be needed, before the day's done, the old lady reflected happily — and they'd dismantle the big bed and carry it too upstairs. About half of the beer would be stacked out in the yard, as a reserve for the evening's schemozzle, and the rest would be divided between the small tables in the room downstairs and the big table which would be out in the Court, against the wall. Neighbours had lent glasses and plates and chairs and Mrs Wilson, knowing of the unfortunate tendency of the guests to make straight for the short drinks if any were about, had hidden most of the bottles of spirits upstairs, or in the cupboard. During the afternoon they could make do with port wine and such stuff, which nobody drank if they could help it.

The afternoon party, she thought, would be a sort of drifting-in-and-out turnout, when friends and neighbours and probably distant cousins would turn up to wish the couple well, as they said, but really to see what the bride looked like, and to see whether they had more food and beer than Cousin Ted had when *he* got married.

The real party would be indoors, in the evening, and to this only special friends and cronies were invited.

The old lady was supremely content as she lay and watched the slow brightening of that Saturday morning. Boy-boy'd spent nearly thirty quid on beer and stuff, and she herself had added another eight. On top of which, surprisingly enough, the blind man had given her — free, no coupons or money — a dozen tins of corned beef and sardines. ... It would be a day of happiness. Nothing, she determined, would spoil it. Not even the bombers, not even if she had to stand on the roof and throw the bombs back at the bastards. ... This day belonged to Boy-boy and Maisie.

Gently she reached across Maisie and tugged Janey's hair. "Come on," she said. "Up you get. Time for a cuppa."

Janey stirred lazily and opened her eyes and immediately, as she realised that at last the great day

205

had come, she slid out of bed and across to the gas-stove. She even sang as she shivered at the tap in the yard, waiting for the kettle to fill.

As the house slowly gathered itself for the coming events, Jimmy, in the shelter, woke up and lay staring across at Tommy, who lay with one arm crooked over his head and his long lashes curled down on his cheeks. It still looked as though he'd just combed his hair. Jimmy sighed, then reached across and pushed. Hard.

"Oy! Come on. It's *Shabbas*." His voice was soft yet urgent as he repeated their early morning ritual. "Come on, Tom, 'ands off... on socks."

Tommy leaped up, as though electrified.

"Christ!" he said. "Whassamarrer? It's still the middle o' the bloody night."

"Round things," Jimmy suggested briefly. "— You forgot what day it is?"

Tommy knuckled the sleep from his eyes and reluctantly pulled on his trousers. "'Ow's yer 'ead?" he asked.

"Orrable..." Jimmy grinned. "Not so bad, 'cept I'll 'ave to buy a bigger 'at to fit this bump. ..." Together they laughed, but carefully, so as not to disturb the other shelterers.

Once again, but now for the last time, they packed their blankets on top of the tools and the lead, then went home to Tommy's for a cuppa which Addie, also rising early, had just made, and they hung about the house until almost half-past eight, at which time the scrap-metal dealer opened his yard. They watched him as he weighed the lead and assessed the value of the taps, and as he gave them their money he looked round carefully.

"Seen any o' the Law about? They bin askin' questions these last coupl'a days." Jimmy's eyes widened innocently. "Us? The Law? Nah — even if we did, they couldn't do anythink — we ain't done nothin' wrong."

The dealer smiled. "That's all right, then... by the way, is one o' you named Wilson? If it is, you better watch yer

206

step. A blind man's bin askin' about a boy name o' Wilson — I said I never 'eard of 'im."

For an instant the boys stared at each other, and Jimmy felt his insides tighten.

"Ne'mind, mister," he said. "Our name's not Wilson, anyway. But I was goin'ta tell yer — we're layin' quiet for a bit."

"Thassa good idea, son. Don't forget me when you get some more — lead's good fer trade."

As they walked homewards Tommy's face was pale and set, but at least he had the sense not to say: I told you so, and Jimmy was grateful.

"— Not scared, are you, Tommy? Blind Billy don't know anythin', an' even if e' did, what could e' do?"

"I dunno. 'E's got people workin' for 'im all over the place, an' —"

"— So what? What we do's got nothin' to do with 'im. ... Come'n, I'll race you to the brewery."

They ran, and at the brewery they parted. Jimmy knew that the parting went deeper than just saying cheerio to each other, but he felt helpless. As he watched Tommy walking slowly up the street his eyes lifted to where the twin needles of the brewery chimneys soared and seemed to scrape the clouds, each one with a long flat plume of dense white, sour-smelling smoke at its head. Apart from his little spasm of fear at hearing of Blind Billy's inquiries, he was quite happy. Exuberant, almost. Blind Billy was jealous because Jimmy had started getting the lead-piping and stuff for himself, instead of for Blind Billy, that was all... on'y natural. ...

By the time he arrived home Boy-boy and Maisie and Little Billy had gone home to get washed and changed. They were due at the Registry Office at 12.15, but they'd be back down the Court by eleven. Jimmy's parents and Janey were washing and fussing with buttons and blouses and coats, so Jimmy sat on the edge of the bed and watched.

At the foot of the bed was Addie's best coat, which after

207

much heart-searching she had lent to her old pal Lizzie. It was too big, but the fur collar gave the old lady a rare and exciting feeling of dignity. Addie herself had already taken charge of the house, with quiet but rigid determination. The old man realised this when, half-way through shaving, he stopped and said he'd drop down dead if he didn't 'ave a drop o' whisky. He made as though to open a bottle, but there was a blur of colour-movement and the bottle was snatched from his hands.

"You leave that alone," Addie snapped. "— Yer like a bloody yooman drain, swelpme Gawd you are. You c'n 'ave as much as you like after it's all over an' they're good an' married, but yer not touchin' a drop before. So there."

Almost immediately the old man began a series of visits to the backyard, and Addie thought he was having an attack of nerves. Mrs Wilson and Janey grinned at each other, knowing that he had a quarter-bottle in his back pocket, and Jimmy smiled too. He knew his father.

Janey, who was going to the Registry Office to see the couple married, began rehearsing her tears of happiness, but decided reluctantly that she'd have to miss the pleasure of dramatic weeping. It made her mascara run all over her face. Still an' all, she knew as she primped and prodded herself in the mirror, she'd never looked prettier. She had to be sure of this, because Johnny Burton was coming to the party in the evening.

Even Mrs Wilson used some of Janey's make-up, but her lack of experience made her use too much. Jimmy thought she looked like a wax doll suddenly come to life, although the blue rings round her eyes looked worse than ever.

"Hey, Dad," he said, using an unusual form of address and nodding at his mother, "— you better watch out, else she'll be gettin' off wi' someone if you're not careful."

"Saucy bleeder." Mrs Wilson sniffed happily and put on even more make-up. She was wearing a long grey dress she'd bought second-hand at the Institute sale and it fitted real nice, except that she had to clutch one side all the time to stop it sweeping the floor.

At last Mr Wilson stood resplendent in his one and only suit, a navy-blue serge he'd had since the depression, and a collarless white shirt. At his throat was a dotted scarf, and he also wore his old peaked cap.

While this was going on Addie pottered about, sorting out and placing on trays and plates the piles of sandwiches, already dry and curling at the edges, and faintly tainted with the smell of carbolic. If the Law comes an' sees all this Black Market stuff, she thought, we'll all get six munce. ... She sighed. Why did the laws always work so that you'd get in trouble, just through 'elpin' your own flesh an' blood? Lizzie Wilson was as straight as a die, she knew, but she'd get put inside for all this. But if Lizzie was rich, she could give the party in an 'otel, an' no one would worry. It wasn't right, that's what it was... not right. Addie knew too that when her Joey got married, if the war was still on — Godfabid — she'd do the same as Lizzie. War always made what was right wrong, an' vice verchoo, or whatever it was. ...

She edged away from her thoughts and concentrated on the sandwiches, with Jimmy helping.

Then, suddenly, they were all ready and waiting, fingers twiddling with buttons or patting already-tidy hair, and growing nervous. Addie offered to make a quick cuppa tea, but gruffly the old man refused. "Tea?" he said scornfully. "Oo wants a drink tea on a weddin' day?"

Addie was more than equal to this: "You carry on combin' yer whiskers," she rebuked him, "— an' don't get uppity wi' me, else I'll soon spit in your eye." The gleam in her own eye softened her words and with a grin the old man, pushing Janey aside from the looking-glass, began trying to stiffen the ends of his drooping moustache. Mrs Wilson sighed thankfully. It was good to 'ave a real old pal like Addie to rely on. ...

The street-door crashed open and Little Billy erupted into the room, his eyes blazing with excitement and the remains of Boy-boy's glass of whisky that he'd quietly drunk. Boy-boy was in such a state of nerves that he hadn't even noticed, and had simply poured himself another.

"Bless 'is little 'eart," the old lady murmured. "— like a hangel."

Certainly Little Billy looked a picture, with his curly hair and bright eyes, with his pale blue satin blouse and dark-blue velvet trousers. He surveyed everyone in the room, then threw himself at Mrs Wilson, trying to jump up into her arms. "They're comin'," he said. "Mum'n Dad's nearly 'ere. All dressed up, they are, like —"

There was a series of slow, painful squeaks, and Boy-boy, followed by Maisie, limped in and sagged on the bed. "Christ-amighty!" he breathed fervently, waving his feet in the air, "— me feet's red 'ot. These shoes are killin' me."

Jimmy laughed aloud at the expressions of consternation, which became near-panic as Boy-boy tore savagely at the stiff white collar that threatened to choke him.

His new off-the-peg suit, while it cost eight pounds, was too long in the sleeves and the legs, and too tight; although he was of average height Boy-boy was so broad, so deep-chested, that no stock suit would fit him. He hadn't worried about a tailored suit because through the multiple tailors they took so long, and they were more expensive. As he said to Maisie, "— What's the use o' payin' a lot for a suit I'll on'y wear once in me lifetime?" He disliked suits almost as much as he disliked stiff collars.

"Doan tek off tha collar, Boy. Tha'll not get it on agen." Maisie was quiet and composed yet firm. Boy-boy abandoned his collar and began to untie his shoe-laces.

"Doan tek off tha shoes, Boy. Tha'll never get them on.

Boy-boy gazed plaintively at the ceiling. "Jeeeeeesus!" he said. "If I'd known it was goin'ta be like this I wouldn't of started it."

Mrs Wilson and Addie grinned happily at each other. The groom was nervous, which was as it should be.

"Take your shoes off, Boy-boy. Just nick 'em inside the

toes, an' they'll be easier. Jimmy —" Mrs Wilson ordered, "— find the scissors."

Maisie opened her mouth to object, but remained silent as the new shoes were prised off from Boy-boy's sore and swollen feet, as small incisions were made on the inner-sides of the toe caps, and Boy-boy wriggled his feet back inside them.

The old man sighed. "Runed 'em," he said. "That's what you've done. Runed 'em." He stared anxiously at his oldest son, and when at length Boy-boy stood up again he grinned and hugged his mother. "You're a clever ole girl, ain'cha?" She smiled fondly up into his clear, grey-green eyes, and said sternly: "Put your tie straight. An' comb yer 'air." She had never seen Boy-boy so smart, so spruced-up looking. New suit, new shoes, curly hair, fine bold eyes... 'ansome 'e was. Real 'ansome."

Boy-boy looked round. "You comin', Jimmy?"

Jimmy forced himself to reply evenly, hiding his growing excitement. "I've got a coupla jobs to do," he said. "— But I'll be changed and ready by the time you get back."

Mr Wilson cleared his throat noisily. "Well..." he said. "We all ready?" As he spoke he glanced at the clock. The Two Bakers had been open for nearly an hour. ...

As Maisie stood up and began to fasten her coat Janey didn't know whether to laugh or cry. The yellow hair was as dead-looking and brittle as ever and her mouth was a crimson gash, yet clearly she was happy. What upset Janey was the green swagger-style coat Maisie had bought in a vain attempt to hide her condition, and the ice-blue, sagging dress... she looked like a tent with arms and legs stuck on.

"Maisie," Janey said, "I've got some new lipstick. Why don't you try it? I... it'll be better than the colour you've got on." Janey faltered, then stopped altogether. Maisie was such a funny one, you never knew how to take her. But Maisie, who knew only too well that her make-up was bad, was grateful.

"If... if tha'll do't for me, Janey. I doan' know..."

Quickly and efficiently, to a chorus of do's and don'ts from almost everybody, Janey sat Maisie in a chair and set to work. A clean rag, a damp face-flannel. Janey's powder and lipstick, and some mascara... comb the hair, push it into waves... won't stay in? Put clips in it. ...

When Maisie stood up she looked for a long time into the mirror. She smiled softly, then turned to face the others.

Boy-boy looked as though he didn't believe it, Jimmy blinked, and the old man wished he hadn't finished his whisky.

"Maisie!" Boy-boy whispered. "You're like... like 'Edy Lamarr." This was his highest compliment, and Maisie smiled proudly, serenely.

They all felt something strange, close to reverence. Maisie's blue eyes were emphasised by mascara and were large and clear and direct; her hair had never looked better, and the eruptions on her skin, so raw when she first met the Wilson family, had dispersed. But it was her look that brought the strange feeling; a look of radiance deep within her. Mrs Wilson thought she looked like the Virgin Mary must have looked... she crossed the room and kissed Boy-boy's woman, and was content.

"Ta, Janey," Boy-boy said, squeezing his sister's arm, and Janey too was happy.

The old man had grown impatient. "Come on then," he said with a touch of irritation. "The register office'll be shut by the time we get there, at this rate." He wished they'd had the sense to go by taxi. With Maisie's slow, rolling walk, it would take ages even to get to the bus stop in Whitechapel. Why don't we put 'er in a wheelbarrow an' push 'er, or lay 'er down an' roll 'er along like a barrel? Be a bloody sight quicker... he too smiled.

There was a last-minute pulling-on of gloves, of trying to loosen Boy-boy's too-stiff collar, of seeing that hats were on straight, of listening critically to new shoes that still squeaked but were at least easier to wear, and as a

212

surprise Mrs Wilson brought from the chest-of-drawers a white button-hole for Boy-boy and the old man and a bunch of red imitation roses for Maisie. Both she and Janey had roses to be pinned to the lapels of their coats.

As they moved towards the door Little Billy, his voice a shrill squeak, rushed out ahead of them, and up to the street.

"Me mum'n dad's gettin' married," he shouted to several indifferent passers-by, then invited them: "Come'n watch."

Back in the house Addie and Jimmy started to get things ready. The fire was stoked, the big table was carried out into the Court and laden with plates of sandwiches and two crates of bottled beer; the mattresses were all ferried upstairs and laid out on the floor, the old lady's big iron bedstead was dismantled. The spring, a wire-mesh base stretched on a wood frame beloved by bed-bugs, was too big to go up the stairs too, so they pushed it out into the yard and left it standing against the broken fence.

"I 'ope it don't rain," Addie said doubtfully, "— it'll go rusty."

Jimmy shrugged, smiling. "A few more squeaks won't make any difference."

"You saucy young bugger," Addie laughed, cuffing him lightly.

When everything was ready Jimmy collected one of his mother's spotless white towels and a piece of soap, wrapped his clean underclothes and socks in the towel, and set off for the Public. He also, when Addie wasn't looking, dug into the coal cupboard and took his money from the cocoa tin, with several loose clothing coupons. He ran along Brick Lane, going quickly along from one shop to another, and bought a new shirt with a semi-stiff attached collar, and a port-wine-coloured tie. He dried himself thoroughly after his bath and did some exercises, studying himself carefully in the small inset wall-mirror, and as he slipped into his underwear, then felt the crispness of the new shirt against his skin, he began to grow elated, to tremble. Taking the shirt off again he did more exercises and examined himself again in the mirror. He flexed his biceps, he breathed in, he breathed out… and once again he couldn't resist a quick look; stronger, more definite, darker, more of it… good.

From the Public Baths he ran straight to the home of Solly Jacobs, who with his son Isaac worked for one of the big multiple tailoring companies. Solly was an expert cutter and Isaac was a presser, and in their home was a full range of the company's samples and patterns. They made excellent suits at home, without charging too much and without the formality of clothing coupons, and their profits were very high. The company was generous to its workers but was unaware of the fact that besides supplying Solly's patterns, it also supplied the materials he used for his private work.

When Jimmy arrived, breathless, Isaac took him straight into the workroom at the back of the house.

"'Mornin', Solly. Is it ready?" Jimmy was so anxious that Solly smiled. "Ve chost finish. Vhy soch a hurry by you?"

"It's special. My brother's gettin' married today, an' I want it for when I start work, as well. I'm goin'ta work in an office."

Jimmy made it sound terribly important and Solly, who had known him since he was a kid, was quite impressed by his earnestness. Mrs Wilson had done the Jacobs family's washing for years, and they were good people, so Solly had decided to do his best for the boy. Together he and Isaac had advised Jimmy on costs, on patterns and types of cloth, and when Jimmy paid his deposit they worked hard and quickly and put into the suit all their considerable experience and technique. Now, as Solly took the suit from the cupboard where it was hung to air after Isaac had worked on it with his favourite steam-iron, he was pleased. It was a pity the boy couldn't afford better material, but still…

"You wouldn't get it soch a soot in Sevel Row," he said.

"Not even for fifty pun'." Isaac grinned and nodded. "Is a good soot," he confirmed.

"Can I put it on right away, Solly?"

"Ufkawss. Right avay, in der badroom." Solly pointed to a door, and going through Jimmy found himself in the Jacobs' bedroom. Everything seemed to be brand-new — the heavy curtains, the gleaming lino, the walnut wardrobe and tallboy and dressing-table. Changing quickly Jimmy looked into the mirror and knew a deep, solid satisfaction.

The deep blue, pinstriped suit, single-breasted, both suited and fitted him perfectly, as Solly had assured him it would, and his nails bit into the palms of his hands. At last things were beginning to go right. ... *This* was what it felt like to be well-dressed. ... This intense pleasure, focused like a deep light somewhere inside you... if you was rich and had two or three suits you could feel like this every day. ...

When, fully dressed, he went back into the workroom, Solly clucked his tongue and stroked his cheeks. "Movvellous," he said. "You lookink like a million dollar." Jimmy smiled shyly and held out the rest of the money. Solly took it, counted it, then gave him back two pounds. "Is a veddink prazent," he said. "— Fromm me an' Isaac." He beamed, they all shook hands, then Jimmy left them, carrying his old clothes wrapped in paper under his arm. He felt dizzy, light-headed; he wanted to run, to shout, and he knew that if he took a deep breath and held it he would float above the ground, above the houses... he made himself slow down and walk calmly, his head up and shoulders thrust back. *This* was living. ...

Back in the Court a few neighbours stood drinking and talking idly, with occasional toasts to the bride and groom, whom few of them knew. Others were inside the house drinking and taking cautious bites at the sandwiches, making the most of the Wilsons' hospitality, several asking Addie if there wasn't something short and

215

stronger... as they said, it was the sort of weather to make even a gorilla squeak like Minnie Mouse. Addie however had decided that generosity had gone far enough, and began taking the beer bottles back from the Court inside the house. Bloody pigs, she thought resentfully... 'aven't even brought any presents... one or two of the visitors had brought a bottle of something or other, but they drank them themselves. Apart from Addie's own gift, now hidden in the coal-cupboard awaiting the propitious moment, the happy couple hadn't received a single thing.

As Jimmy entered the house Addie was just putting on her second-best coat, shooing the fire-huddled guests round to the Two Bakers. "They'll all be round the pub now," she kept saying. "They won't be back 'ome till closin' time." Drinking slowly and moving reluctantly away from the fire, the drinkers gradually dispersed. Good riddance, Addie thought... won't see any o' *them* round the pub... too bloody mean... they're so mean, if they was ghosts they wouldn't even give you a fright. ... She saw Jimmy, and her mouth opened in surprise.

"Blimey!" she said, "— Look 'oo's 'ere. Little Lord Faunkelroy!"

Jimmy smiled uncertainly; pleased at her tone but doubtful of her words, knowing that she had mis-pronounced the name. He could have said it better. Addie went on quickly: "D'you want a quick nip o' somethin'? I'm just goin' roun' The Bakers — that's where they'll be. And," she added as an afterthought, "You look real nice, Jimmy. A real torff."

Jimmy's pleasure mounted, although he refused the offer of a drink. Addie quickly plucked the dead cinders from the fire, heaped fresh coal on top, then looked round with a sigh. "You comin' round, Jim? Tommy'll be there an' all."

"Mmmmm." Jimmy wasn't keen on going — there'd be just a lot of grown-ups singing and shouting and dancing and making quiet but pointed comments about Maisie...

216

but he'd expected a crowd to be in the Court and in the house, and he didn't want to stay there on his own. ...

Together he and Addie stood the emptied beer bottles on the floor and put the used glasses down by the yard door, then they went out, Addie carefully locking the street-door behind her. This was the first time in Jimmy's memory that it had been locked.

When they reached the Bakers they had to force their way in. There were porters from Spitalfields Market, traders from Brick Lane, various friends and acquaintances of Mr and Mrs Wilson, none of them more than vaguely-known to Jimmy, all come to pay their respects. Maisie sat happily tearful in one corner, next to the old lady, Boy-boy was at the counter. Janey and Tommy Cooper were jigging together to the old man's thumping on the piano, which sounded more harp-like than ever, and they were the only two who appeared to be enjoying themselves. Mrs Wilson kept repeating, with immense satisfaction but to no one in particular: "Man an' wife, tha's what they are." She swallowed her stout and pointed at Maisie. "Drink up, love," she said. "A little drop o' stout'll put lead in 'is pencil." She crowed with laughter and her hat fell off, and Maisie gave a watery smile.

Addie pushed her way across to where her husband was talking to one of his fellow brewery-workers and someone pushed a glass into her hand. Jimmy stood just inside the door and watched as a tall thin woman, rattling a collection box, came in. Spotting Boy-boy at the counter she elbowed her way over to him and shook the box almost in his ear. Boy-boy glared at her.

"Would you care to give something for the Mayor's Trust Fund?" she asked sweetly. Boy-boy was nonplussed.

"Mayor's truss fund?" he repeated. "What's 'e done — ruptured hisself?" Two red spots appeared on the lady's cheeks and her smile congealed on her face. Without another word she crept away and out into the street. Jimmy smiled, then wandered sadly over to the piano. They hadn't noticed him.

For a while he watched the old man's horny, black-nailed fingers clicking on the beer-stained ivories, and gradually he realised that there was a sequence in the movement of those fingers. Hesitantly, with the old man crashing away with hands and feet and oblivious, Jimmy began picking out the tune on the higher octaves. At first it wasn't very good; sometimes he missed the note he wanted and the old man did the same lower down, with a weird and jangling result, but he got better, and began to enjoy himself.

"I never knew you could play the pianner, Jimmy," Rosie Gates screamed in his ear. "Cor — look at 'im. Dressed up to the nines an' all posh an' grown up."

"I can't play it," Jimmy answered her with sudden shyness, but showing that in fact he could play almost as well as the old man.

Rosie as usual wore a brilliant but too-flimsy blouse and a loosely flared skirt and too much make-up, but still Jimmy could have hugged her. She rammed a chair behind his knees so that he practically collapsed into it.

"Gor'n, Jimmy boy. Show 'em 'ow it's done," she urged.

The old man, mouth wide open in pleasure and surprise at the noise he and his son were kicking up, pounded louder than ever, and Jimmy was swallowed in the rhythm and excitement. As he played, now and then Rosie fed him sips of her gin-an'-orange. Intensely happy, Jimmy banged and sang at the top of his voice, urging the old man to go faster, louder. Then, when the old man slipped outside, Jimmy slid into his chair and played with both hands at once. He knew that his left hand ought to do something else than just crash down anywhere, yet he felt himself uplifted, soaring; it was ecstasy, and when the old man returned he stared in open disbelief then turned and shouted across the bar: "Lizzie! We've got anuvver pianner-player in the fam'ly, Liz!"

"I always knew there was somethin' clever abaht you," Rosie said several times as she held her glass to his lips. "Fancy not tellin' anyone!"

Jimmy simply smiled, loving the whole world. He thought his head would burst with the noise and with pride as he heard his mother: "That's 'im. That's our Jimmy!" Glancing round quickly, afraid to move his eyes away from the keys in case he went all wrong, he saw that his family had come over to the piano. Boy-boy and Janey were dancing, and Tommy stared with wondering, worshipping eyes.

Without warning Rosie pulled his hands away from the keyboard and tugged him to his feet. "Come'n, Mr Wilson," she screamed, "— bang a tchoon an' let Jimmy 'ave a darnce."

The old man immediately slipped back into the chair and with a flurry of feet and fingers the piano twanged again and Jimmy was drawn against Rosie, shuffling and rubbing and warm and soft. A wide smile was fixed on her face and she danced with her eyes almost closed. "Quicker, Jimmy," she urged, holding him even tighter, so that he could hardly move. The bar seemed to expand and then contract, there was a slow revolving inside his head... the piano stopped.

"Nah, come on, ev'ryone," the old man shouted, standing on his chair. "Altogevver nah. ... Shoul-dol-dacquaintance-beeeeforgot." His arms waved so violently that he knocked himself off of the chair, then the piano picked up the tune and the whole bar fused into a static, compressed, hand-clasping circle, just as the bell rang for closing time. Jimmy was glad when it was all over, and he kept away from Rosie as the whole crowd made for the Court. There was shouting and singing, and even dancing in the street, and Jimmy's head began to ache.

Soon after they reached the house and everyone was drinking and the wireless screeched its songs unheard, Jimmy crept quietly upstairs, carefully took off his new suit and laid it on the mattress beside him, then slid under the blankets and overcoats. The noise from below formed a pleasant cushion, so real that he could almost lean on it, rocking him gently as it came and went in waves, and he fell asleep.

The roof and the windows had been repaired by the men from the Council a week earlier, but the windows had no black-out screens. When he woke up dusk was falling.

On one of the other mattresses Boy-boy slept peacefully, and Jimmy grinned as he saw that the hated stiff collar was gone, as were the squeaky shoes. He stared enviously at the thick, muscly forearms, at the dark hairs that stood out like bristles from the unfastened throat of the shirt, at the strong yet good-natured features. He slid away from the mattress and furtively did some more exercises before putting his new suit on again. Then refreshed, full of life and eager, he went downstairs.

"Where ya bin?" Rosie Gates collared him with a hoarse scream. "I bin lookin' all over for ya." She must have been looking for him in the streets, because, he noticed, sometime during the afternoon she'd been home and changed her blouse and skirt. "Asleep," he said briefly, fending her off. He crossed over to where his mother and Janey and Maisie were standing round one of the small tables. Things were a lot quieter than he'd expected, and looking round he saw that there were only a few strange faces and one or two neighbours, drinking and talking half-heartedly. They were all friends or acquaintances of his parents, hardly known to Jimmy, and he thought of them as grey people.

Mrs Wilson too was surprised that the afternoon had brought so few visitors, but at least some of them had done the decent thing and given the newly-weds presents, which were being displayed on the table and caressed by Maisie. They didn't amount to much — the usual cups and saucers, cheap knives and forks, a water-jug and some glasses. Maisie, who was completely unknown to most of the Wilsons' friends and relatives, was overwhelmed by such generosity, but Mrs Wilson knew that some of the well-wishers who would and could have brought gifts had brought a bottle of something instead. They were aware that Boy-boy and Maisie had been together for some time, so obviously they would have all the essentials — such as towels and pillow-cases and ornaments, that were needed. So they brought bottles, which they drank themselves. Disappointing, but it could have been worse.

Jimmy stood near them, then helped himself to a sandwich and a glass of beer. "Whatsamatter?" he suddenly asked Janey. "— You all dyin' or somethin'? Where's the records?"

"We're all restin'," Janey replied. "We bin up all day, not snorin' like pigs. We're savin' it up for tonight." Brother and sister grinned contentedly, but Janey crossed to the gramophone, wound it up, and put on the loudest record she'd been able to find. She and Rosie automatically drifted together and began a lazy dance, accompanied by the old man's tuneless whistle. He was sitting by the fire, a plate of sandwiches in one hand and a half-empty beer-bottle in the other, and he was warm and half asleep. ... About eight or nine o'clock they'd all be goin' back round the Two Bakers again, an' then, when they got back, the party'd *really* get goin'... pity to go, in a way, seein' as 'ow there was so much beer left, but you couldn't 'ave a party without goin' round the pub first — puts everyone in the right spirits. Tonight his own special cronies would be droppin' in, an' they'd 'ave a right ole time... he swallowed the rest of his beer.

Mrs Wilson suddenly noticed Jimmy and her face lit up.

"Lor — look at 'im!" She hurried over and hugged him, calling to Maisie: "Hey, Maisie, look 'ere. If you get tired o' Boy-boy, you c'n 'ave Jimmy instead — 'e's the spitten' image of 'im." Jimmy smiled happily and Maisie blushed. Jimmy folded his tiny mother in his arms and walked her slowly round the floor in time to the music. "You're bigger'n me already! An' you look real smart!" Jimmy hugged his mother and her words in his brain were warm

221

and comforting. He kissed her lightly on the forehead. "You all right for cash, Mum?"

She looked up into his eyes and laughed. "Mmmm. I won't want any more money tonight. Boy-boy an' the ole man might go round the pub later on, but me'n Maisie's stayin' 'ome in case anyone special comes." She thought for a moment, then asked: "You goin' round with 'em?"

"No. I've got a surprise."

"Who for — me? What?"

Jimmy wanted to tell her now, before it happened, but the words wouldn't come; he managed to say only: "I'm bringin' someone special — a friend o' mine."

"Tell me." She smiled and tried to sound light and casual, but there was a trace of anxiety in her tone. "Not courtin' already, are yer?" she added. Jimmy laughed.

"'Course not — you're me best girl. It — it's just a girl I know who's had some trouble over the raids, an' I thought it'd cheer 'er up, like." He tried desperately to tell his mother that Pinkie was part-Indian, but he faltered and the moment was gone.

"Oh... well. ..." Reassured, Mrs Wilson leaned her head against him and then, growing conscious of a pain in her chest, she slowed and finally stopped. "You go an' dance wi' Janey, or Rosie," she said. "You don' wanta waste your time on an ole gel like me." Already the pain had etched a network of thin lines round her eyes and mouth, and she looked away so that Jimmy wouldn't see her face. Jimmy understood, but the last thing he wanted was to dance with Rosie. He walked his mother to a chair. "'Ere y'are, Mum. Siddown. Shall I get you a drink?"

"No, son. Just let me sit quiet for a bit. I'll be all right."

Jimmy sauntered over to the fireplace and looked at the smoked, cracked-glass clock. Only half-past five. Two hours before he went round for Pinkie. ...

"Come on, Maisie," he called across the room. "Come an' dance wi' your new brother."

Confused and embarrassed, Maisie shook her head, at the same time smiling at his consideration. "The boy

222

wants some rest," she said shyly, pointing at herself, and still she smiled.

The gramophone ground to a halt and Jimmy re-wound it and put on another record. He saw that his father had fallen asleep, head back and mouth gaping, and he saw too that Janey also had changed, and had done her hair differently. He moved over to her and elbowed Rosie aside. "Come'n, Janey," he said. "Let's jive a bit an' liven 'em all up — they're all dyin'."

Gradually things came to life as time wore on and others joined in the dancing, the youngsters jiving and jitterbugging, the older folk jigging in the only step they knew. The old man woke up and immediately began his whistling again; Boy-boy came downstairs still without collar or shoes, smiling all over his face. He went straight over to Maisie and kissed her, gently and tenderly.

"How you feelin', Mrs Wilson?" Maisie blushed again. She put her head on his shoulder and began to cry, softly.

"Ah'm... just so 'appy, Boy." She wiped her tears on his open shirt-front. "Why doan' you put on tha collar? You're half nekked." Always acutely conscious of her thick accent, Maisie often tried to soften it by using the sort of words Boy-boy would have used. It didn't work very well.

Boy-boy burst into laughter. "No fear," he said, "I'm all right like this. Siddown, love."

"Look at these," Maisie said proudly, pointing at the presents, "all for us." Mrs Wilson, noticing Maisie's gesture, and moving very slowly, joined them.

"Kerrrist," Boy-boy admired them. "— I c'n start runnin' another 'ome now, can't I?" Maisie's face fell. "Aye," she said. "If tha wanted."

For a moment Boy-boy stared, puzzled. "Oh, Maisie," he said, dismayed. "Y'know I didn't mean it. I wouldn't leave you. Not ever. I —"

"— But thee'll be goan awa' soon. ..."

It was a moment before Boy-boy realised what she meant.

"But, Maisie, I've *got* to. We can't keep movin' from one

room to another all over London, can we? An' the Army's bound to catch up wi' me before long, then it'll be worse... they'll put me in clink, anyway."

Mrs Wilson, listening anxiously, pushed him away.

"Leave 'er wi' me, Boy," she said. "— She don't mean it — she's just a bit excited." Turning to Maisie she added: "Sit quiet wi' me, Maisie. You'll be all right." They sat down and Boy-boy wandered over to the fireplace, where Jimmy was standing near his father.

"Watcher, tosh," Boy-boy said, then added in a man-to-man way: "Tried it yet?"

Jimmy looked at his oldest brother calmly. "Reckon one bloody ram in the fam'ly's enough," he said evenly, and Mr Wilson, awake again, threw his head back and hooted with laughter, slapping himself on the thigh so heartily that his beer slopped over.

"Saucy bastard," Boy-boy grinned, then started talking to his father about the war. Jimmy listened but their words made no impression on him. He was willing the hands of the clock to go faster. The three Coopers came back shortly after seven o'clock and after a while Addie dug in the coal cupboard and brought out her wedding present and offered it to Maisie, who immediately shouted for Boy-boy. Together they stammered their thanks, then opened the box and stared at the shining electric iron. It was by far the best present anyone had given them, and Maisie loved it on sight. It was an omen, and it meant that one day they'd live in a house where they had electric instead of gas, and she'd be able to use it. ...

Gradually the room filled with newcomers; the beer and spirits, now brought out from the hiding places, flowed more easily and were drunk more quickly; the gramophone blared above the rising voices, and at last it was half-past seven. Shrugging himself into his overcoat, Jimmy said to Tommy: "I'm goin' round for Pinkie now, Tom. Don't say anything to anyone. ..." He paused, uncertain what to add, then said: "I want it to be a surprise."

Tommy pursed his lips. "Might be more of a shock to *some* people," he said pointedly, and with a quick flare of temper Jimmy whirled round and went. He had an uneasy feeling that Tommy was right.

The night was bitterly cold, and a cloud-veil diffused the faint moonlight so that it was just bright enough to see without using the dimmed torch. Wondering if the bombers would come again, Jimmy turned the collar of his coat up and hurried on.

Pinkie's door opened as soon as he tapped his usual signal and he stepped into the dark living-room. There was no passage at the front, and whenever the door was opened after dark the light had to be switched off.

He heard the door being closed behind him and then, for a moment as the light came on again, he was dazzled. When his eyes re-focused he could only stare.

Pinkie stood beside the door, leaning against the wall, lips parted in a half-smile. She wore a vivid electric-blue dress that slid down over her small, pointed breasts, and at her waist was a deep belt of black velvet, with a jewelled clasp. From the waist the dress flared, almost as though spread over hoops, and the lower part was patterned in raised pink flowers, connected by black stalks and leaves. At each wrist was a narrow Indian bangle with miniature animals hanging on thread-like silver chains, and they tinkled faintly as she moved. Her lustrous hair was piled high on her head, and on her feet were jewelled Indian sandals.

"If you keep staring like that," she said, "— your eyes will come out."

With fumbling fingers he unbuttoned his coat, then Pinkie was surprised. She had never seen him looking so... what? He moved lightly and quickly, like an animal. She could feel his excitement, and he... he smiled as he spoke.

"Madam," he said with a courtly bow, "your escort awaits."

"Sir," she joined in the game, "— I shall be delighted."

There was a moment of understanding, of intuition, as she saw Jimmy not only as he was, but as he might become... she crossed the room and stared him full in the face.

"Jimmy," she said, with slight hesitation, "— I used to think you were stupid, with your English lessons and your dictionaries, but... I don't any more. I just hope you'll get a good job to start off with."

Jimmy sat down on the chenille-covered sofa, and she sat beside him.

"I will." He smiled. "I don't expect I'll be lucky first time, but it won't be long. If I work 'ard — *hard* — and keep learning... well, you'll see."

His words and his manner impressed her as much as his new and, as she saw, well-tailored suit. Did clothes make a man? she wondered. In this case it was not much more than a boy, but he'd be a man before long. She smiled secretly, wondering if he was a man already.

Casually but deliberately he pulled a packet of expensive cigarettes from his pocket and lit two together, using the lighter she had given him. He gave her one of them, then sat back and relaxed. She stared at him silently for an instant, then rose and danced lightly into the centre of the room. "I feel so happy," she said. "On top of the world. D'you know that feeling?"

Jimmy smiled his content. Certainly he knew that feeling; it was something deep and warm and comforting, something they shared between them.

"Pinkie..." he said, then paused, hoping that perhaps now, this night, she would tell him he could call her Jalani instead, but she simply stared.

"I — well, Pinkie. ..." He struggled, knowing what he wanted to say but not how to say it: "It's just... will you try an' be nice tonight? We're just ordin'ry people, not clever or anythin', an' we don't know about books or music or things like that. Just people. ..." His words dried in his throat and he swallowed.

"Me?" She was astonished, indignant at the suggestion

that she might be anything other than nice. "Of course I will... sometimes I say things I don't mean, without thinking. ..." She smiled: "But tonight I'll be all sunshine and joy. I'm so happy I couldn't be anything else."

Her bangles tinkled and she laughed aloud and Jimmy caught her laughter and magnified it until somehow they were giggling and screaming in near-hysteria. Slowly they quietened, and at length Pinkie pointed along the passage. "There's a bottle of beer in the kitchen," she said. "As we're going to a party, I thought we could have a drink before we go. Just the two of us, eh?"

Jimmy was so pleased that he ran, and when he returned with the beer and glasses on a tray Pinkie was sitting on the sofa, smiling. "You'd make a good waiter," she said, "— as well as being a good painter and a good friend," and she patted the sofa beside her. Feeling almost dizzy with happiness Jimmy sat down, and although acutely aware of her every movement as he toyed with her lighter — *his* lighter — her easy conversation seemed to be directed at somebody else. He didn't care about the party, he didn't want to go; he wanted to stay here, wrapped in a warm and happy companionship.

"— and in a few weeks, when they take the bandages off, she said she'd like to see you again. But not yet. ..."

Quickly Jimmy came back from his dream and caught the meaning of Pinkie's words.

"— 'Course I'll go," he said. "I'd like to see her before they send her out to the country, but —"

"— But she doesn't want *anyone* to visit her until the bandages are all off." Pinkie smiled, glancing at her wrist-watch. "If we're going, we'd better leave right away. It's getting on for nine o'clock."

It was impossible, but it was true. Nine o'clock... they had to go to the party, the happy time was ended. He held the brilliant-red coat for her and then, regretfully, he followed her up the steps to the street.

The cloud had thickened and it was so dark that he had

to use his torch to pick out the edge of the pavement. Pinkie slipped her arm through his and together they walked through the silent, deserted streets.

They had just turned into Luxton Street when the sky was shredded by a flurry of gun-flashes, with the rumbling following a moment later; to the east, and far-off. Perhaps Romford way. A split-second later came the scream of the London sirens, and feeling Pinkie's quick tremor Jimmy slipped his arm round her waist. It was the first time he had ever done such a thing, and although it made him tingle with excitement, Pinkie seemed not to have noticed. They walked faster, making straight for the Court, and the gun-flashes and rumbles and the sirens died away together, leaving a dazed, exhausted silence.

As they moved down the Court they ran into a small group of people who had abandoned the party and were now running back to their own homes or to the shelters, and over the rapid thudding of their feet Jimmy could hear the twanging of old Pete Begg's banjo, and his father's voice raised in what was a ritual, a feature of all the Wilson parties:

*'I ain-tarf-praa-aah-dof-my-yol-mum*
*An'-she-ain-tarf-praah-dof-meee-ah —'*

The street-door, with its specially made double blackout-screens, was still ajar when they reached it. Jimmy pushed Pinkie through, closing the street-door behind him, and then, fumbling with the inner blankets, they were suddenly inside the room.

The old man had finished his song and someone had started the gramophone. Directly beneath the gas-lamp Janey and Boy-boy were dancing, Janey showing her brother the kicks and jerks of the jitterbug. Being nearly thirty, he was too old to know much about it, but he jumped and kicked with such energy and enthusiasm that the other dancers kept respectfully away. Pinkie gasped and felt a strange, rising excitement.

Boy-boy was still without shoes, still without collar or tie; his shirt was unbuttoned and the sleeves rolled up. His head was thrown back and he danced with one arm raised, his mouth open in a happy grin and showing his gleaming teeth. Pinkie thought they looked as strong and white as sugar-cubes.

Janey, although enjoying the dancing, kept staring towards the yard-door with an unhappy look on her face, and glancing across, Jimmy saw Johnny Burton talking to Rosie Gates. There was a little fluttering in his belly as he saw the long strip of sticking-plaster just in front of Johnny's right ear. So it *was* Johnny Burton after all... but what was he doing in the City ruins in the middle of the night? Jimmy shrugged the problem away, and led Pinkie into the middle of the room.

She moved easily and coolly after him with a faint smile on her face, and the chatter and the dancing stopped. There was only the shrill blare of the gramophone as everyone stared, and again there was the quivering in Jimmy's belly. Why hadn't they stayed in Pinkie's flat? Automatically he saw Johnny Burton's eyes flicker with interest; the intense, tight-lipped stare from the old lady; Maisie's pink, open mouth; Tommy Cooper within touching distance but staring from a great way away, remote and cold; he heard his father's muttered "Gawdelpus. Tar brushes!"

Serene and still composed Pinkie held out her hand to the old man. "Mr Wilson? How do you do."

The old man's eyes blinked as though dazzled, then he remembered to shake the proffered hand. He gulped, and Jimmy's words fell into the silence:

"Dad — this is Pinkie. Pinkie Harcourt."

Mr Wilson's straggly moustache shook as he replied: "Pleasetermeetcha... 'ave a drink?" His pale blue eyes watering in excitement, unable to take his eyes from this talking kaleidoscope of black and brown and red and deep-blue-green-pink, he fumbled on the table behind him for a glass. But Jimmy had taken Pinkie across the room, to where his mother sat beside Maisie.

"'Lo, Mum. I said I 'ad — *had* — a surprise. This is —"

Pinkie was pulled away from his grasp as Boy-boy swept her, still wearing her red coat, into a quick, shuffling dance. Pinkie smiled over his shoulder at Jimmy and raised her eyes to the ceiling, just to show that she didn't mind. Not really. ... The chattering and dancing picked up again, and Jimmy felt his mother's rigid, unblinking stare.

"— That's who I was talking about, Mum," he said defensively. "Her mother caught a packet in a raid an' she's on 'er own, so I asked 'er. ..." His voice ended uncertainly and Mrs Wilson pointedly turned away and spoke to Maisie. There was a helpless, uncomfortable pause as Jimmy waited hopefully for her to speak to him, then slowly he moved over to Johnny Burton and Rosie Gates. He stared at Johnny's sticking-plaster.

"How's things, Johnny?" he queried lightly. "Been fighting again?" He couldn't help smiling. Did Johnny know who'd hit him? Did it still hurt?

Johnny replied softly, casually, as though discussing the weather. "You laugh now, sonny boy. You'll be laughin' on the other side o' yer face before long."

So he knew... he must have been spying...

"Who — me? What've I done?" As an expression of innocence it was a complete failure, but Jimmy couldn't think of anything else to say. Rosie didn't understand what was going on, but she had problems of her own. "— Don't see why you brought *'er,*" she said with injured pride. "White girls not good enough for yer?"

The record ended and immediately Pinkie came over. "Jimmy, I'd like to meet your mother." Pinkie spoke so loudly that Mrs Wilson couldn't help but hear, and something inside her coiled, like a spring.

"Mum," Jimmy said again, turning, "— this is Pinkie."

Pinkie offered her hand but Mrs Wilson ignored it.

"Shake 'ands — *hands* — Mum," Jimmy urged.

The old lady's stare fixed on her youngest son, and she

was surprised to see that his eyes were moist. Slowly she raised her hand and Pinkie took it.

"Jimmy's told me so much about you... and congratulations. It's a wonderful party." Pinkie smiled, and despite herself the old lady's frozen expression began to relax. "Thank you, I'm sure," she said. "Take your coat off. Jimmy," she added, "— why don'cha get your friend a drink, or a san' widge?"

"Okay, Mum." Turning to Pinkie and smiling again he asked: "Beer, whisky, or gin?"

"Just a glass of beer, please, Jimmy. Thank you." She took off her coat and gave it to him and he hung it on a nail near the door. Pinkie turned to Maisie.

"Hallo," she smiled. "How does it feel to be the new Mrs Wilson?" Her voice was so warm and friendly that Maisie took to her immediately, and even the old lady wondered why she had been so willing to dislike this vivid, unusual girl... she wasn't white, but she wasn't black, either. She was a mixture... it's gettin' harder an' harder to tell who's which, these days... first of all there was just the whites, an' then, just before the war started, there was the Indians. Mrs Wilson didn't really mind them: they had long, smooth black hair, and although they even went in the pubs, they never did anything more than smile and nod their heads if someone spoke to them.

But now there was a different sort of darkie — Blackies, most people called 'em. These had short, crinkled hair, they got in the pubs an' drunk all the port an' stuff, an' when they was drunk they usually ended up fightin'. At any rate, there was three different sorts of people, the whites, the Indians, and the Blackies. And Mrs Wilson didn't like the Blackies, or the way the young girls seemed to run after 'em. ...

She glanced round quickly, noting with satisfaction that Boy-boy was talking to the old man and guzzling some beer. She was glad Boy-boy wasn't on the spirits. ... Jimmy was dancing with the girl Pinkie, although Jimmy wasn't a very good dancer, while Janey and Johnny

Burton were jumping and clapping hands and enjoying themselves. She turned to Maisie.

"All right, Maisie? 'Ave a little drop o' somethin' to keep the cold out —"

There was a rising crescendo of gunfire and some not-too-distant bomb-bursts, climaxed by the ear-cracking bark of the railway gun. The room darkened into a purple-yellow glow as yet another gas-mantle shivered into fragments and snow-flaked to the floor, and Rosie gave a little scream.

The bloody, bloody bastards, the old lady thought. Why can't they leave us alone, just so's we c'n 'ave a weddin' party in peace?

Angrily she darted to the chest-of-drawers and took out a new mantle from the reserve she had wisely built up. She'd spent a bloody forchoon in gas-mantles these last few munce. She'd 'arf a mind to sue the Govvament for gas-mantle money... fat lot she'd get out o' them. Bet they didn't even know what a gas-mantle *was*. ...

She gave the new mantle to Boy-boy who quickly stood on a chair and fixed it, and the room swam back into golden-yellow focus. She saw with relief that the explosions had had no effect; the dancers still danced, the gramophone still blared.

Boy-boy went back to the old man and his cronies by the fire.

The noise suddenly increased and became deafening as Tom Cooper started blowing his mouth-organ, and old Pete Beggs twanged his banjo. They didn't 'old with all these crooners an' such rubbish. They liked the good old songs.

"Lizzie," the old man shouted, his words a little slurred, "— put that bloody thing off, an' let's 'ave some o' the old 'uns."

The gramophone ground wailing to a stop and Pete and Tom, with the old man clicking his beloved spoons, went into a series of old-time songs. The youngsters stopped dancing and watched as the older folk took over, with their usual jigging and knee-lifting. Mr Wilson sang some solos at the top of his gravel voice.

At first Jimmy, standing near the door with Pinkie, thought he was hearing things, then he realised that someone was hammering on the door. Leaving Pinkie he pushed through the inner screen and opened it.

"Mrs Wilson? Can I come in for a minute?"

*That voice?... Did he know it?*

"Well. ..." he hesitated, "she's indoors. Come in."

He felt someone brush past him, then he closed the door and followed the new visitor back inside. One glance, and he halted. Blind Billy, carrying a box and a tissue-wrapped bottle, was already speaking to the old lady.

Feeling oddly tense, and aware of Tommy Cooper's stare, Jimmy leaned against the wall and watched. He saw Blind Billy speak to Maisie and give her the box, then speak again to the old lady and give her the bottle; he saw her flush of pleasure as she looked at the label, and watched her lips as she said, "shampain?" He saw Blind Billy swallow some quickly then look round the room, and he noted the way his glance rested on Pinkie and on Johnny Burton. Then Jimmy knew that those eyes, supposed to be blind, or part-blind, were fixed on him.

It was like being in a vacuum; he saw the dancing, the drinking, the mouths opening and closing, but was aware of no sound. He knew only that something was going to happen, that something was wrong.

Where was Blind Billy's white walking stick? How was it that he stood upright and walked easily, when time and again Jimmy had seen him in Whitechapel, shuffling and tapping along the kerb, his unshaven face hidden beneath a filthy cap and a knotted choker, head down as though he had no neck, as though his head went straight into his shoulders? Where was the dirty, ragged old suit? Jimmy felt that an invisible wire had been drawn from himself to Pinkie and to his parents; Boy-boy was threaded too, and Janey and Johnny Burton. They were

233

all on it, dancing like puppets, and Blind Billy was the one who jerked the string. Jimmy didn't move as Blind Billy shook hands with Maisie and the old lady and then pushed his way across to the door, but he felt the staring eyes, despite the tinted glasses.

Blind Billy was pleased that Johnny Burton had given no sign of recognition; it was wise not to advertise their connection. And he had almost gone up to Jalani to ask after Peggy, but her blank stare had warned him against it. He quickly realised that in this she was wise; the fewer people who knew or guessed at his association with Peggy the better. The seamen, white or coloured, who brought the little packages that were so vital delivered them via Peggy, who in turn passed them on... so profitable. ... So Blind Billy in turn gave no sign of recognition to either Johnny Burton or Pinkie, deciding instead that he must go and visit Peggy again. Her injuries had left a serious gap in his supply chain... it was strange that Peggy had been so influenced, so affected by a kid named Jimmy Wilson, yet he had to admit that she was right. The kid was clever, able to think for himself and to act independently. And that, after all, was what Blind Billy wanted. Someone he could rely on, quick, shrewd, and not afraid... Johnny Burton was a good lieutenant, but he was only capable of doing exactly as he was told, in minute detail. He couldn't think for himself. ... Blind Billy saw himself as a general, moving pieces up and down on a map in a big war game. But at the moment the pieces were ordinary people, and ordinary people were not very reliable. They got caught, but in a way that wasn't a bad thing: they learned more tricks and dodges in six months in the 'Ville than they could learn in six years outside of it. You made sure that their families didn't starve, you sent them cigarettes to their residence in Pentonville, and when they came out they served you better than ever. But now the general required a lieutenant — someone not quite ordinary. A youngster like Jimmy Wilson would do very well; able to think, and act on his own, someone who wasn't afraid to take a chance. There weren't many kids who'd dig in the ruins in the middle of the night for metal, defying the Law and the bombers... This kid could be trained, and no one would ever be suspicious of him. ...

Blind Billy stopped just by the door, next to Jimmy, who stared up at him, waiting.

"Evening, Jimmy. How's the lead game and the clothes coupons? Doing well?"

"I — I don't know what you're talking about." Jimmy's voice was hoarse and cracked, and Blind Billy smiled.

"Don't worry," he said, his smile widening, "— I've got secrets too. By the way," he went on with a brief nod towards Johnny Burton, "If anyone works for me, I don't like 'em getting knocked about. I always look after 'em. You'll be all right this time, but you'd better watch your step." He looked away, still smiling pleasantly, and the old lady wondered that he and Jimmy seemed to be getting on so well. Blind Billy spoke again in the same short-sentenced, staccato manner: "Leaving school, eh? Got a job yet? What're you going in for?"

Jimmy shrugged with affected carelessness. "I'm not fixed up yet. I'm going in for office work."

"Office work?" Blind Billy's smile faded and his voice filled with scorn. "I thought you wanted a *good* job, with good money?"

"I do. I'll —"

"You'll spend all your life shut up in some office, and at the end you'll be a clerk — if you're lucky. You'll work all your life like a donkey, and you'll get nothing for it, except five quid a week and a wife and kids you can't afford. ..."

"I c'n learn. I can go to night school —"

Unexpectedly Blind Billy leaned down and his voice was intense, concentrated. "Look, Jimmy. I know you've got brains, and you're not frightened to use them. ... I can get you a job — a *good* job, with *real* money. Nothing dangerous —"

"You mean like Johnny Burton, collectin' lead from the

kids at school, and flogging bottles o' whisky in the sugar fact'ry?" Jimmy was no longer nervous; as he realised that Blind Billy hoped to make use of him he laughed outright. "No thanks," he said. "I'll earn my money straight. I'll get on all right."

"Will you?" There was a faint threat now in Blind Billy's tone, and Jimmy knew they'd come to the point. "Will you? Suppose someone put the squeak in to the Law about the lead and the clothes coupons?" He nodded at Tommy Cooper, "— Your pal'd rabbit in no time." Now the smile was wide, almost affable. "— I wouldn't do it myself," he went on virtuously, "but someone might..."

Jimmy stared coolly, insolently. "I'll worry about that when it 'appens," he replied with a mocking smile. "I know a thing or two meself." In spite of his tone and manner Jimmy was trembling, wanting suddenly to be sick.

Now Blind Billy laughed aloud. Clever? Shrewd? This boy was one in a hundred... one in a thousand. Blind Billy became more convinced than ever that this would be his field-officer in the East End... he'd need to be persuaded somehow, or pushed, even, but it would be done... didn't scare easily, either. ...

He pushed a small card into Jimmy's top pocket. "When you're tired of flogging yourself to death, and want a *real* job, come and see me." He turned to the door and added, "I'm leaving here in a few days, but you can always reach me there. Don't be too long."

As Blind Billy pushed his way into the Court Jimmy took out the card. It said Wm. Andrews, Esq., and gave the name and address of a billiards saloon in Soho.

"I didn't know *he* was a friend of yours," Pinkie said as she came up immediately, but Jimmy missed the significance of the remark.

"He's not," he replied. He shrugged Blind Billy's proposition aside. There would be no more lead or black market for Jimmy Wilson. All he wanted was a job, to work hard and learn, to keep straight. ... "Let's find some beer."

The old man was now singing one of the old Cockney patter songs. His eyes were screwed tight and he swayed slightly, like a palm tree in a high wind:

*Muvvergettheammer, there's a fly on baby's 'ead,*
*Muvvergettheammer sister Susie's got in bed.*
*She's on a rodger wi' the lodger who. ...*

The words came with the speed of a machine-gun, and the last line, which everyone but Pinkie knew, was drowned in screams of laughter. When the words were finished the old man began his favourite spoon dance, with Tom Cooper and Pete Beggs blowing and twanging like mad; in accelerated time the two spoons, held in one hand, flashed up and down his arms and legs, while his body jerked and spun; they paused and hovered like butterflies at his elbows, at his wrists and knees, on his bald head, on the soles of his feet, and the metallic clicking never faltered. When he had finished, dripping with sweat, there were shouts and yells and clapping for more, and caught up in the applause he raised his hands in salute, like a boxer. Laughing with pleasure he took up the chorus again, and everyone clapped and stamped in time with him.

Then he noticed the coloured girl with Jimmy. She wasn't laughing or clapping. She looked, he thought, as though she was going to be sick. His pleasure faded, and he was angry.

"Whassamarrer wi' you, stuck-up?" he demanded thickly, "— ain't we good enough for yer?"

Everything stopped, as though cut off. Jimmy felt the blood rushing to his face.

"Go easy, Dad." He was embarrassed, and didn't realise that he was shouting. "She's not used to it — she couldn't understand —"

"*She* couldn't understand? There's a few things I don't understand. *You,* wi' yer dicshonerries an' yer posh talk —"

It was frightening, dreadful. It had to be stopped.

"I on'y wanta get on —"

"Gerron? The on'y thing you ever get on is my bleedin' nerves." Swaying, turning to the onlookers, the old man waved his hands expansively. "Look at 'im," he shouted, "— my son. Saves all 'is money in a tin, an' wouldn't lend no one a penny —"

"You didn't ask me. You found it and pinched it —"

Appalled, feeling sick, Jimmy stopped. He saw Boy-boy's white, furious face; he saw the thick wrist and the veil of dark hair rise and fall in a slow curve, but he couldn't move. There was an explosion on the side of his head and he was hurled across the floor, and then everything happened in a confused rush. He saw Johnny Burton's stare, as vindictive as Pinkie's was cold; he saw Janey run across and put the gramophone on; he felt his mother help him up into a chair beside her. His face was white and his head ached, and the sudden scream of the gramophone made it worse.

Addie Cooper, who had seen and heard everything, and who knew from Mrs Wilson about Jimmy's money, was furious. She strode with blazing eyes across the room and stood before the old man. "What'd'ya pick on 'im like that for, George?" she demanded, "— 'E's on'y a kid! Jeeesus... if you was my ole man, I'd bloody-well give you a glass o' poison!"

The old man eyed her with beery malevolence, swaying slightly, his moustache quivering. "Would'ya? Would'ya *just*? Y'know what, Addie Cooper? If you was my ole woman an' you gave me a glass o' poison, I'd bloody-well drink it!" Satisfied with this rejoinder, the old man collapsed against the table. Boy-boy grinned, and Addie looked as though she was going to crown him with a bottle. Instead she marched across the room, found her best fur-collared coat among those hung behind the door, threw her second-best coat over her arm, and left without another word.

"Ne'mind, George," Tom Cooper winked, "— she'll get over it. 'Ave another drink."

Sadly Mrs Wilson had watched, unable to move. Her arm was laid carefully but firmly across Jimmy's shoulders, forcing his head down into her lap, and she almost crooned her words: "Sit quiet, Jimmy. They're a bit boozed."

She felt each silent but convulsive sob as it racked him, and his unshed tears were her own. Tiredly she pushed back a strand of long, dull hair...

"Feel better now, son? 'Ave a drink."

Jimmy sat up, and again felt Johnny Burton's malicious stare; when he saw Pinkie and Boy-boy dancing together he had to turn his head away and look at the wall. They were laughing and chatting as though nothing had happened, and he couldn't bear it.

The old lady noticed them, how close they were, and her mouth drew down at the corners. She saw that Maisie too was watching, happiness gone from her face and her big blue eyes tear-clouded. Mrs Wilson rose to her feet and then, with a quick glance round the room, she went swiftly into action.

"Now come on, my gel," she said pleasantly but pointedly, prising Pinkie's hand from Boy-boy's grasp, "— No use dancin' with 'im, 'e's old enough to be yer father. Y'wanta dance wi' someone yer own age." Smoothly, irresistibly, she drew Pinkie away, leaving Boy-boy standing with one arm raised and his mouth open. Mrs Wilson turned and pulled Johnny Burton away from Janey. "'Ere y'are, Johnny," she said with great satisfaction. "Let's see some o' that fancy dancin' o' yourn." She knew that she had made Janey wild, but that couldn't be helped. She turned to Maisie, and ordered her quietly: "Go over to Boy-boy. Tell 'im you're tired, an' wanta go upstairs an' lay down for a bit. *An'* keep 'im up there with yer."

Maisie nodded and moved away, and a moment later, with even greater satisfaction, the old lady saw them go upstairs. Again the old lady turned.

"Jimmy, why don'cha 'ave a dance wi' Janey? Get lively an' cheer yerself up a bit." If she didn't think o' somethin' to get 'em all movin', they'd all end up fightin'. She could feel it in the air... funny, the way everyone seemed to get wound up all of a sudden.

Johnny Burton, only too pleased to obey Mrs Wilson, smiled all over his face. The smile was at once smug and malicious, and wherever he moved he turned his head so that he could stare at Jimmy. Jimmy returned the stare calmly, knowing as he did so that he hated Johnny, so much that he was trembling.

Trying to appear unconcerned he went over and pulled Janey up and into a dance, and it soon became a competition in which Jimmy and Janey and Johnny Burton and Pinkie were the only entrants. Everyone else watched, clapping and stamping, as they kicked and trucked, Lindy'd and pecked. Jimmy was not a good dancer, but he was inspired, and Janey felt it; brother and sister danced as they had never danced before, yet Johnny and Pinkie were better. Despite Johnny's heavy build he could move as lightly and quickly as a snake, and Pinkie seemed no more than a feather; they rocked back on their heels, they leaped and cavorted, and even the old man had to admit that the stuck-up little bitch certainly could dance... the record ended and Jimmy and Janey gave up. Their place was taken by Tommy Cooper and Rosie Gates, and as the gramophone blared again the dancing became general.

Jimmy, obstinately concentrating on talking to Janey and ignoring his enemy, saw nothing but heard the sharp slapping sound. Looking round he saw the grin congealing on Johnny's face and the livid white marks on his cheek, and he saw Pinkie hurriedly grab her coat and move to the street-door. He ran across and pulled her arm.

"Pinkie," he said. "Pinkie, I —"

Her face was set, like stone, but her eyes were blazing. Turning, she glared at him. "There's only one difference between your family's party and the zoo," she said loudly. "— I didn't have to pay to get in."

240

The blackout screens rustled and she was gone, and sadly Jimmy plucked at the sleeve of his new suit. He felt empty, drained, exhausted.

"Don't worry, Jim," Tommy Cooper said softly, "— it's all for the best."

Jimmy stared at his pal of so many years; his lips curled viciously and he turned away. As he moved slowly back to the chair beside his mother he saw Janey, her eyes filled with tears, run past him to the door. She knew she was going to burst into tears and she wanted to be on her own, but there was nowhere to go, except out into the Court, so she ran.

Johnny followed her. In the blind end of the Court, near the dustbin, a heated cat writhed on the ground, oblivious of the narrowing circle of belly-crawling, growling Toms with night-gleamed eyes. They all paused momentarily as Johnny called softly: "Janey?"

She was just a little way along the wall, beyond the table left outside, and he heard her snuffling.

"Janey... Janey."

Quickly he found her and suddenly, violently, without knowing how, they were kissing.

Johnny — Johnny. ...

His hands were doing funny things. She wanted him to stop, but if he did she'd break her heart.

"Johnny, what'd you do to 'er?" Janey was still sobbing quietly, almost to herself, and Johnny's hands were drawing her, compelling.

"I did'n' do nothin', Janey. 'Onist I did'n'... just a crack, like I 'eard on the pickchas. Thassall."

Johnnyjohnnyjohnny. ...

"Why'd she —" Her words were drowned by his lips.

"I don' want anythin' to do with 'er — you suit me, Janey. No one else. Never was anyone else, you know that. You're fresh an' sweet," Johnny went on with a note of wonderment in his voice, "— like when I used to work in Spitalfields, an' I used to open a new crate of oranges... like Victoria Park, when they cut the grass. ..."

Johnnyjohnnyjohnny. ...

His hands, which at first had been gentle and pleading, now insisted, demanded. There was the fraction of an instant when Janey drew a quick, hissing breath, then again she was crying softly. And as she cried Johnny was happy, happier than he had ever been before.

From round the corner came the sudden shriek of the heated cat, conquered yet triumphant, and one by one the other Toms slunk away into the blackness. Johnny and Janey didn't hear. ...

It was funny, Jimmy thought, the way the room seemed empty. One minute there was Pinkie and your family and their friends, then it was empty, except for a few grey people still trying to enjoy themselves. Addie's place as filler-of-glasses had been taken by a tall, harsh-voiced woman named Mrs Clarke, and her husband, a shrunken, weedy little man, hovered anxiously in her rear. "Now, Gladys, that's enough," he kept saying, but she ignored him. It wasn't often you got a chance of free drinks, so she made the most of it. Mrs Wilson, watching tiredly from her chair, wondered how *they* came to be at the party — *she* certainly hadn't asked them. As Mrs Clarke filled the glasses, and her own more often than anybody else's, with her little husband trotting behind her, Mrs Wilson's lips curled. No need to wonder 'oo wears the trousis in 'er 'ouse, she thought savagely.

Jimmy sat down and watched critically. The grey people were trying to enjoy themselves, and trying to get drunk, and he knew they weren't managing to do either. His head throbbed and his throat felt as if it was lined with sandpaper... he wanted a drink, and within a short time he had several.

Tommy Cooper and Rosie Gates were dancing again, then there was another spasm as the old man sang some more of the old songs, then once again the gramophone blared.

Janey and Johnny Burton came in again, and Janey's mascara was all over her face. Johnny was all puffed up about something, and intuitively Jimmy knew what had happened. As did his mother, who stared suspiciously.

"You all right, Janey?"

"'Course I'm all right, Mum. Guess what?" Janey smiled happily, taking Johnny's hand. "We're goin'ta get married, before Johnny goes in the Army."

"Gawdelpuss!" Mrs Wilson's gasp brought Mrs Clarke to her side. "Jeeeesuschrist!" the old lady said, "— now we're goin'to 'ave another weddin'. They're on'y kids, an' all."

"Best thing for 'em," said Mrs Clarke. "It's best when they start off young an' legal, like."

Jimmy noticed Rosie Gates, looking as though her gin had turned to poison. Poor Rosie... she wasn't so bad, not when you knew 'er. On 'er own too, like him... well, that made 'em a pair. ... He stood up and, lurching slightly, pulled Rosie to her feet.

"Come'n, Rosie," he shouted, "— let's go mad an' 'ave a dance."

"Woooops!" Rosie dropped her glass as he pulled her round. They kicked the pieces to the wall and it was funny. It was so funny that they shook and screamed with laughter.

"'Ere, Jimmy, you better not 'ave no more. You've 'ad enough." Mrs Wilson regretted her words as soon as she said them, but luckily Jimmy hadn't heard. Be the best thing for 'im, to 'ave a'nangover... give 'im somethin' to think about for a coupla days... she smiled.

Jimmy and Rosie danced several times, often drinking from the same glass, and Jimmy had the pleasant feeling that somehow he was defying Johnny Burton. Again the old man fell asleep, with his bald head gleaming, his mouth open, his hands dangling towards the floor. Pete Beggs and Tom Cooper put away their instruments and prepared to go home, with some of the grey people. The gramophone played on and Jimmy drifted, lost in Rosie's moist warmth, the smell of her cheap scent, the soft but firm pressure of her. She kept leading him into cross-steps, managing to push her thigh between his legs. He noticed her shiny-wet lips, with even her teeth stained by her lipstick. Her harsh laugh rang loud and often in his ears, and sometimes he joined in. But at the back of his head was a soft, insistent warning.

Mrs Wilson leaned limply against the wall, beside Maisie's presents, finishing the last of the blind man's champagne. Jimmy looked about ready to drop, and Rosie looked as though she'd just got out of bed... the room was littered with plates, bottles, glasses broken and unbroken, with half-eaten sandwiches; the air was filled with swirling cigarette smoke, with the damp smell of the dying coal fire. Her head ached with a dull pounding that rose and fell and she felt dizzy. It was a shame the warning had gone and sent some of the people scurrying home, but after all, the undrunk beer could be finished in a day or two, and the meat in the sandwiches still left could be used to make a cottage-pie, or somethin'... she saw with sudden anger that the spigot of one of the ale-barrels was dripping steadily, that a long stream of beer ran along the wall and left pieces of smashed plates and glasses and sandwich-crusts sticking up like little islands from a thick brown sea. She called good night to Tom Cooper and the others, who left in a bunch.

"Janey," she called briefly. "You an' Jimmy gimme a 'and wi' the clearin' up. Come on." She left her chair, dug beneath the chest-of-drawers and pulled out a wad of rags. She went slowly down on her knees and began mopping up the beer, remembering after she'd started that the spigot was still on. As Rosie reached for her coat the old man started to snore.

"You goin' 'ome, Rosie? With a raid on?" Suddenly Jimmy was once more just a Stepney boy; hurt and bewildered, with at the back of his mind the knowledge that his h's and g's had gone, too weary to do anything about them. Balls to 'em. Balls to Johnny Burton and Pinkie... balls to the whole bloody world. He'd get by on his own...

"'Course I'm not," Rosie answered with a false, coy smile.

244

"It's not safe for little gels to be out on their own... I might get lost, an' I'm frightened o' the dark... you'll see me 'ome, woncha, Jimmy?" she ended anxiously. She and Jimmy smiled in understanding. He'd expected it, he'd *known* it would come. He didn't want to go, but he didn't want *not* to go... he was supremely indifferent.

"Mum," he called, "— you don't want me to 'elp, do yer? I'm goin'ta see Rosie 'ome." An idea struck him and he added with sharp satisfaction: "Janey an' Johnny'll 'elp you — 'e's good at washin' up." He watched carefully, expecting some quick reply or threatening gesture, but Johnny simply stared at him icily before saying: "I'll give you a 'and, Mrs Wilson."

Janey pulled Jimmy aside. "Jim, why doncha try'n' get on wi' Johnny?" She was almost whispering, alive to the dislike that flared between her brother and her husband-to-be, unable to understand it.

"*Me* get on with '*im*?" Jimmy's reply was equally soft and guarded, but filled with scorn. "You could've raked in any dustbin an' dragged out somethin' better than '*im*."

Janey ignored her brother's anger, becoming aware of the depth of his dislike for Johnny, aware of a premonition of trouble. "Don't start any trouble with 'im, Jim," she pleaded, "— 'e'll kill you."

"Will 'e?" Jimmy smiled sardonically.

"— Why doncha try'n get to know 'im better? 'E'll be one o' the fam'ly soon —"

Unconsciously Jimmy's voice grew louder. "The family's so low already, it can't get any lower. Not even with '*im* in it. Besides," he went on, his growing resentment making his words viciously pointed, "— you know 'im well enough for both of us... don't you, Janey?"

His voice and his stare were icy as he taunted her, making it clear that he knew what had happened in the Court. ... Janey's shoulders slumped and her eyes misted as Jimmy slipped into his overcoat.

"I can't 'elp it, Jimmy. I like 'im. ..." She stiffened and said with painful accuracy: "You wouldn't be like this if it

245

wasn't for that Pinkie an' Peggy an' their funny ideas. They make you think you're too good for us, don't they? You always did think so. ..." Janey's voice too was rising with anger. "— But you know what? That black gel's no good. She's —"

Her shoulders whipped as Jimmy's fingers bit into her arms and he shook her, trembling with fury.

"She's a bloody sight better than you are," he shouted, and suddenly Janey screamed. The scream was echoed by the old lady.

"Jimmy! Jimmy! Stop it." Both she and Johnny rushed over as Rosie watched with wide and frightened eyes.

Johnny pulled Janey away, his pink face working for words that wouldn't come. Janey and the old lady smothered him with their bodies. "Jimmy, get out of 'ere, quick," Mrs Wilson shouted, struggling to hold the smouldering, powerful writhings of Johnny, "— Get out, forgawsake!"

"Johnny, leave 'im alone... Johnny, leave 'im alone. ..." Terrified of even more trouble, Janey was pleading and crying: "'E didn't mean it, Johnny... 'e's just upset. ..."

Johnny breathed heavily but didn't move as without another word Jimmy and Rosie went out into the Court. Then he said simply: "On'y for you, Janey... on'y for you. ..." Still crying, Janey leaned down and kissed him.

It was freezing, and a fine, misty rain drifted down from the wind-raped clouds; the all-clear still had not sounded, but the streets were silent, absolutely deserted. Jimmy leaned against the wall with a long, shuddering sigh.

"Whassup, Jimmy? What started all that?"

"Oh... I dunno. I'm just fed up, Rosie. Fed up wi' meself, fed up wi' the 'ole bloody world." He breathed deeply, trying to bring some order into his thoughts, and went on as though musing aloud: "Everythin' I do goes wrong, Rosie. An' I don't want much. Just decent clothes, an' a good job... I thought I was goin' to enjoy meself tonight. ..." His voice failed and he almost choked.

"But you've got decent clo'se already," Rosie asserted. "You was smarter'n anyone else was. 'Onist. You was real sharp."

Jimmy smiled doubtfully, but he felt better; he also wondered why he'd always felt a faint dislike for Rosie.

They walked slowly up the Court and turned into the street, and as they went Rosie put his arm round her waist. His hand was ice-cold; she pushed it up, almost into her armpit, then gradually increased pressure on it. Jimmy was intensely aware of her and the drumming at the back of his head speeded up. Their breath hung on the air in little clouds and streamers, and Rosie leaned her head on his shoulder.

"D'you like me, Jim?"

He considered the question before answering briefly: "Not much."

"— At least you're 'onist." They walked a few more steps, then Rosie said, "— That's the trouble. None o' the boys like me. They all say they do, for a while, but they don't really. You c'n never tell about boys... not till they get busy wi' the ole nasty... if you let 'em you're no good, an' if you don't let 'em you're even worse. So. ..." she explained sadly, "— you might as well let 'em. It makes *them* feel better, anyway. ..."

Jimmy didn't see the tears in her eyes; he knew he was staring through a dark, lonely door, and there was nothing he could say. But of his own accord he tightened his arm round her, and in response she slid her own arm round him. Huddled close, stumbling occasionally, they came at last to Rosie's door,

Rosie leaned against the wall, then slowly turned and faced him. She unfastened her coat and slid his arms underneath.

"Keep yer 'ands warm," she said lightly, but Jimmy didn't hear. The drumming in his head had become a rising crescendo; the muscles of his arms and legs were trembling.

The whitewashed wall across the road was ghostly in

the weak moonlight, and its pale glow was reflected in Rosie's eyes. Pinkie would be in bed by now... dreaming of the rich bloke she was going to marry... to obliterate the thought he pressed forward and covered Rosie's wet-gleamed lips with his own. She seemed to have the power and effect of a vacuum and held him there while his head pounded and his trembling increased. Rosie wondered if he was excited, or just frightened. As though from a great distance he heard her say: "Come in, Jimmy? No one's in." And then, enticingly, "We've got some drinks. ..."

He wanted suddenly to run; this wasn't the way he wanted it to be. There were things he had to do, to think about... but the trembling stopped and he was calm again.

Taking his silence for agreement Rosie reached behind her and opened the door, pulling him unresisting after her. In the pitch darkness of the passage she drew him to her and kissed him.

Again he trembled, and again he thought of Pinkie. This time he saw her as she was in the moment before she swept out of the house: the glittering eyes, the flared nostrils, the metallic blue-green dress with the pink flowers, her furiously drawn eyebrows... she was lovely... he leaned down and bit the base of Rosie's throat and was pleased when he heard her little scream, felt her convulsive jump. Breathlessly she pushed past him and almost dragged him into the front room. It was a nice room, with a soft pink light glowing warm in one corner. There was a three-piece suite and a radiogram, with next to it an open cabinet showing an assortment of bottles and glasses. Rosie clicked the radiogram, there was the whirring of automatic machinery, then there was a flood of violin music, slow and sentimental.

Throwing her coat on to one of the armchairs, Rosie opened her arms wide and began to dance. "Take your coat off an' let's 'ave a dance. Or would'ya like a drink instead?" She took Jimmy's coat and threw it on top of her own, then pushed the armchairs back, leaving a small cleared space. Again she danced on her own. "That's a nice suit, Jim. Real nice."

He sighed again, wishing she wouldn't keep reminding him of the suit because it made him remember all the things that went with it. Rosie went to him and they danced all on one spot, without moving. They held each other tighter and tighter; she spun round and put his fingers on the zip-fastener running up the back of her blouse. "Undo it," she whispered hoarsely.

Fumbling, filled with a wild, screaming emptiness, he pulled. She turned to him again and the pressure of her breasts seemed to constrict his lungs, so that he couldn't breathe.

Again he wanted to run; he was terrified and ashamed and appalled but his limbs and muscles had taken control and instead of moving to the door he moved with Rosie to the settee. She reached up and pulled his head down and he caught the faint woman-musk of her armpits. Again there was the wet-shiny mouth and the red lips, and there was the musk and there was the red glow warming pale flesh and the screaming and pounding inside him. He'd show 'em — the whole bloody world. ...

"Jimmy! Jimmy!" Her hands were beating at him and her eyes were big with fear. "— Whassamatter — you wanta kill me?"

A little of the tension flowed away from him and in that instant Rosie realised; when he said he didn't like her much he had told only a half-truth. She knew now that he hated her; she could feel it in the terrible urgency of his body, in the wrenching grasp of his hands, in the frenzied way his teeth bit her lips. She had never been treated so savagely, yet she was grateful and she was filled with pity for him. ...

Twisting her head she stared at him. His eyes were open and dark and he breathed softly and evenly, and he was drained of all emotion and energy and fear. She knew with complete certainty that it had been good for him and she smiled. She knew that no boy ever forgets the first time, that he will always try to go back. And she knew that when Jimmy went back to her she would be glad. ...

He was walking along slowly and aimlessly, without knowing how he came to be in the street. He was exhausted and he knew that it was no use trying to do anything, that it was no good to want things you weren't born with. If you were born in Stepney you lived and died in Stepney, and no one would be sorry. No one would even be glad. ... Funny, he thought, that of all the people at the party only Janey and Johnny were any better off... a deep silent sob caught in his throat.

He began to hurry, then he was running. He ran until the breath came in great agonising gulps, he ran until he reached the ever-open Barmy Park. He ran across several winter-naked flower beds, then threw himself face down on the damp, icy ground. His fingers scrabbled violently in the soil, frantically destroying the blades of stiff but still-living grass, and inside him was a great open space which reached deep into the earth. Then, from this great void, with irresistible force, came the lonely, bitter tears of growing. And the tears flowed back into the earth.

# 6

Jimmy sat at his desk, staring vacantly through the strips of adhesive paper on the window panes. In the square outside the wispy trees were in the first moment of breaking into greenery, and the greenness was little more than an aura wafting round the black branches and stems. The Council dustmen were wearily emptying the waste of several days into their van, and there was something almost laughable in their peaked caps and their thick leather shoulder-capes. Jimmy was restless, dissatisfied.

More than two years had crawled past, and he knew that he had accomplished nothing beyond being promoted from his first position as office-boy to that of post-boy and then to that of junior filing clerk. Of the three he preferred that of office-boy; at least he had been able to get out from the office with its whispered requests and instructions, the scratching zur-zur of pen-nibs, and wander round to the post office with his arms full of bundles and packages and with smaller packages sticking out all over him. Now he had only to file the letters that were received each day and filtered slowly through the various departments to the records room, and later to file the replies sent to these letters, typed on blue or pink or yellow flimsies according to the department concerned. Besides these accomplishments he had also learned a curiously imitative but definitely improved way of speaking, which he used only at the office.

He had started work filled with enthusiasm, arriving early each morning and often offering to stay late at night, and as soon as he got the hang of the office routine he had begun to ask questions — questions which he thought were intelligent, which showed his need and desire to learn. His questions were rarely more than half-answered, and were more frequently side-stepped completely, and after a few months he realised why. The men of military age had gone into the Forces, like dust drawn into a vacuum cleaner; those left were those not considered fit to drown in icy seas, to bleed in desert or jungle, or to soar like birds through the air. These men were afraid of someone young and fit, who might one day take their cherished positions.

With a faint but real nervousness, Jimmy saw that he wouldn't be able to make much progress in the office, so he tried to learn something about the machines in the factory, only to find that there was a deep and active hostility between the office-staff, who thought themselves superior to the factory hands, and the factory hands themselves, who took home much fatter wage-packets.

Jimmy was becoming disillusioned.

His new suit, which had once meant so much to him, was now shabby and too small; despite frequent pressings it was permanently creased and shiny and a little frayed at the cuffs and, although his wages were now twenty-five shillings a week, it would be a long time before he could afford another. He thought sometimes of going back to the scrap-metal game, of flogging more coupons, and though he told himself he was determined to keep away from everything connected with looting and the black market, at the back of his mind was the suspicion that Blind Billy, who had so strangely become Wm. Andrews Esq., had been right; he saw himself working for the rest of his life in the records room and getting nothing for it but a few pounds a week. ...

He thought yet again of Pinkie, as she looked when she swept out of the door; his old photograph of her was torn and cracked, but he still looked at it and often found himself going off into a reverie in which he had a lot of money and was able to take her out to clubs, to hotels for posh meals. Sometimes, telling himself he was going to the pictures or just for a walk, he walked past the house where she lived. He always walked quickly and on the other side of the road, swinging his arms and whistling with careful carelessness, but there was no sign of her; he wasn't even certain that she still lived there and he hadn't the courage to knock and ask Mrs Rubens. Now and then, when he could no longer bear the strange thoughts that came to him, or his feeling of aloneness, he went back to Rosie. He wondered if he loved Rosie, and he thought he must. Else why did he sometimes take her to the pictures, not even kissing her, but feeling happier when her hand touched his leg or rested on his arm? Why did he buy her that little brooch? But Rosie, without ever complaining, knew that for Jimmy she was a last resort, a substitute, and she hoped simply that somehow things would straighten themselves out for him. ...

"You dreaming again, Wilson? Some mothers *do* 'ave 'em — *and* they live, what's more." Mr Martin, the office-junior immediately senior to Jimmy, delighted in prods and caustic comments and in using an imitation-cockney accent. Jimmy detested him, and privately and justifiably called him Pimples.

"Your mother's got nothing to be proud of, at any rate," he snarled back, and Pimples smiled in his superior way.

"She isn't a washer-woman for Jews, either." And the smile was bigger and more superior than ever.

In a boyish and unprotected moment, soon after he started work and when Pimples appeared to be friendly, Jimmy had told him something of his home life, and had regretted it ever since. Pimples never missed an opportunity of referring to it.

"Clever bastard. You —"

Pimples' fist landing square on the tip of his shoulder took him by surprise, sending a sharp and exquisite pain all down his arm. Without thinking Jimmy leaped up, then they were on the floor and the typists were screaming and Mr Lyons, the manager, and one of the clerks, were pulling them apart.

Walking home slowly, shortly afterwards, with his employment cards in his pocket, Jimmy wondered what and how to tell his mother. He wondered too whether it would give him any satisfaction to go back to the office at closing time and wait for Pimples, who was tall and skinny and didn't have a pennorth-o'-go in him, whereas Jimmy was proud and sure of his firm and still-developing muscles. ... He knew that in a straight fight he could take Pimples apart piece by piece. But what was the good of that? Only mean more trouble. ... The knowledge that for several months his mother had been unable to take in any more washing made it worse.

In an unconscious attempt to delay having to tell his mother that he'd been sacked he walked well out of his usual way home, but when at last he arrived she was sitting with her arms resting limply on the table, staring hollow-eyed at the wall. She seemed neither surprised nor curious that he was home so soon, and simply went on staring at the wall.

"'Lo, Mum."

Her eyes flickered to him and away again, back to the wall.

"I've got a present for you, Mum. My cards." He laid his employment cards on the table and watched hesitantly and then, as a faint smile played with her lips, he moved to her side.

"Mum, whatsamatter?" He still tried to sound light and cheerful, as though there was nothing really wrong, but he felt suddenly cold. He put his arms round her shoulders.

"Mum... you bin coughin' again?" Her blank, glazed eyes stared at him for ages and then, gathering her strength, she smiled.

"Whassup, Jimmy? You're early."

"You've bin coughin' again," he accused. He went down on his knees and her hand caressed his hair. "Mum, why don'cha go to the London 'Ospital, like you said you was goin'?" His voice was fear-chilled and he stared upwards at her drawn, waxen face.

"Not bin coughin' much... why've you come 'ome so early?" Jimmy was frightened, and she didn't want him to be frightened. It was just sometimes she got so tired she couldn't move, couldn't think. ...

"Mum, I've... got the sack." His voice faded, expecting some sign of surprise, even of anger, but again she smiled.

"Good," she said. "P'raps now you'll get a job doin' war work, wi' more money." She paused, exhaustedly brushing back her thin, lustreless hair. "People like us never do any good in offices. You oughta do a good day's work wi' yer 'ands, then you feel 'appy." She remembered George when he was young, a porter in Spitalfields Market; the pride in him as he carried a stand of seven or eight crates of lettuces on his head, as he hurled the heavy bulging sacks of potatoes to the top of the pyramid. ... George was old now, a sweeper-up in a factory. Still an' all, it was better than standing by the stall in Brick Lane. He got twice as much wages, as well. ... "Besides," she went on, drifting away again, "— there's nothing wrong wi' me'. I'll just 'ave a rest, after I've bin round Janey's. Don't say anythin' to the old man." Her eyes went back to the wall and stayed there, and Jimmy rose. The house was still and quiet, and it gave him the creeps.

What could he do? The old lady was smiling gently to herself, lost in memories, somewhere on her own. ... His legs moved slowly, of their own accord, and he wandered along the streets hunched and miserable.

Mrs Wilson sighed, her thoughts drifting to Janey and Boy-boy. ...

Janey was lucky, being married to Johnny Burton, even if 'e was unfit for the Army... of course, the old man didn't like 'im, seein' as 'ow 'e was too mean to give a party when they got married, like Boy-boy did, but still

255

an' all, Janey'd done well. She'd looked so nice in 'er white wedding dress, even if she *was* five munce, and Mr Gapley at Saint Mary's didn't like it very much. ... They'd got a flat in one o' the Council blocks put up just before the war, an' it was full of all the things you couldn't get. They always 'ad tinned salmon and stuff, but no one knew where it all came from... they 'ad polished lino and bright carpets, there was a cabinet with bottles of gin an' whisky an' a special shelf for fat little glasses... there was even a television, and that was best of all. Mrs Wilson knew no one else who had a television, and although it wasn't working she could sit and stare at it for hours. ... They said it made pictures and noises, just like the wireless did, but she didn't really believe it. How could pictures come out of the air? Or even over wires, like voices in the telephone? She was annoyed with the Govvamment for stopping the television while the war was on, and she knew it was just another one of their tricks; how could television guide the bombers to London? In any case, when the Germans had wanted to bomb London they'd bombed it, television or not... it would be wonderful to see it working. ...

She sighed again and shifted restlessly, her thoughts centring sadly on Maisie and Boy-boy... she thought of all those munce in the Glass 'Ouse, and the happiness when at last 'e'd been released and put into the anti-aircraft unit... just as well, she thought proudly, that the Germans 'ad given up the raids on London before Boy-boy got on the end of 'is four-point-five or five-point-four or whatever the gun was 'e was always talking about. Wasn't 'e lucky, bein' sent to defend the Docks? 'E seemed to be at 'ome more than 'e was on the gun... but it wasn't so lucky after all, because that's when the trouble started. At first she didn't believe it when Maisie told her that Boy-boy'd started playin' up, and stayin' out all night. Not always, but now an' then, and poor Maisie didn't know what to do. There wasn't anythin' anyone *could* do, because as soon as you said anything to 'im 'e just flew into a temper and stormed out... who ever thought 'e'd turn out like that? She shuddered suddenly, and again pushed back her hair. It was all through the war, and for a long time now she'd known that for her the war would last for ever. ... She would welcome the end. It would bring release from the shocking, searing pain... no one ever saw the tiny pin-points and flecks of blood that sometimes appeared, as though by magic, on her handkerchiefs and her snowy sheets and pillow cases, and she had no intention of telling anybody about them... her children were all over the place — she didn't even know where most of them were, or how... she'd done her best and now, with Jimmy at work and able to look after himself, it didn't matter any more... she wished Jimmy wasn't so quiet, so... she couldn't think of the word, but still she was disturbed over Jimmy. He had always avoided Boy-boy since the night of the wedding-party, and when Boy-boy and Maisie came Jimmy just walked out and usually slept in the shelters... he still read dictionaries and strange books, and his head was still full of dreams and funny ideas... yet he was so like Boy-boy! Every day Jimmy grew more and more like his brother, but where Boy-boy was so thick and powerful you could actually *feel* him, with Jimmy you felt... funny, like. ... But she hoped the two of them would be friends after she'd gone. ...

The numbness crept up, through her chest and along her arms, but she fought and beat it. The old man'd be home soon, and he'd want his tea. He often came home with stories of girls and women who worked shiny great machines, and things called welders, but she didn't believe him. She thought he made them up, just to amuse her... she needed something to drink, to perk her up a bit — a little drop o' brandy'd be nice. She wished that the blind man hadn't gone away. He'd always had a bottle of short he could bring out, and a drop o' short was just what she needed. She wondered where he'd gone to as slowly, wearily, she began to prepare the old man's tea. The blind

257

man, Wm. Andrews Esq., was only a few blocks away. He was sitting in his sports car, waiting for the new and highly efficient addition to his field staff, Miss Jalani Harcourt.

What a girl! What a cool head, how quick she was at figures and percentages! She was a good worker, a natural learner, and she was the best checker he'd ever had. And, when she wasn't visiting his various depots and arranging deliveries or collecting rents, she was an added attraction at the club. If only he'd been able to get young Jimmy Wilson and train him, he could have made him into a highly successful businessman... Wm. Andrews Esq. smiled happily, thinking of the events that had put him where he was. ...

... Name? Wm. Andrews Esq. Age? 37. Profession?... That was awkward. Say, Purveyor of Pleasure and Entertainment. Income? Better not go into that — the Income Tax people would have a fit if only they knew. ...

Still smiling, he lit a cigarette and blew a long stream of expensive smoke through the open window.

... It was funny, the way it all started. Accidental, really. Just step off the kerb, on one of those Hore-Belisha pedestrian crossings, and there you are. A year later the insurance company pays up nearly two thousand quidlets. Marvellous!

Of course, your right eye is damaged, but what the hell. You've got *two* eyes, haven't you?... so you develop a nice case of what they call Compensationitis, and you lay it on real thick. You use your head and you get past all the specialists and their tests... damn fools, they are... and then your plans begin to take shape. You know there's a war coming and you know that the money's made by those who manage to play it safe and keep out of the Forces. Then, to set you really on your feet, the doctors give you a little card declaring to all and sundry that Wm. Andrews Esq. is a Disabled Person. Lovely!

In the hospital you couldn't be bothered to shave; when you leave there, with your beard and your white stick and the dark glasses, you're on your way to your gold-mine. Pull your head down, hunch your shoulders, wear a filthy old suit, and you're an old man. An old man people pity, because you're blind. Simple!

You don't waste your cash. You move to Stepney, where things are cheap, and you buy the leases of three little properties. You live in one, and gradually you buy the things you know will be hard to get once the war starts... cigarettes, tinned foods, all the bottles of spirits you can lay hands on. You pay the right price and you never ask where the stuff comes from. And so you build up your stocks. Perfect!

But there's more yet.

Nobody takes any notice of an old blind man, so you watch the prossies working in Aldgate and Whitechapel. Slowly, carefully, you find out where they live, what they earn... surprising! As Johnny Burton says, every woman could be a walking goldmine, but Johnny Burton's a cynic. He's worked well, but he has to be told exactly what to do, what to say... what's the idea of giving him another medical examination, with a view to what the official letter calls *reclassification*? They rejected him once... but if they take him away and put him in the Army or somewhere, there's going to be a gap, and that gap will have to be filled by somebody. How was it that the Wilson boy had never tried to contact you? There was a likely one if ever there was... but he'd gone straight, wasting himself in an office. A few months' training... imagine him and Jalani Harcourt working as a team! What a pair they'd make! But how can you get a kid like that? He's not frightened of you, he's not frightened of the Law — if he had been, he'd never have gone into the lead game. You'd have thought that an intelligent, ambitious youngster like him would never be satisfied with an office-boy's wages, but you'd been wrong. But how do you *get* a kid like that?... there must *be* a way. ...

Peggy, perhaps?... no. Don't tell Peggy — she'd always had a soft spot for the kid, she wouldn't like it. ...

Jalani?... Maybe, but be careful. What was Jalani doing at the Wilsons when the son got married? Why did she always change the subject when you tried to talk to her about it? Why does she dislike Johnny Burton so much?

Jalani is due to collect some rents tomorrow. ... Funny, the way it all worked out. ... Rosie Gates's father has a teashop in Aldgate, and Rosie knows some of the prossies. One day she tells her friend Janey Wilson — Janey Burton, that is — that some of the prossies have got together and rented a house and started an unofficial club. Naturally, Johnny Burton hears about it and tells Wm. Andrews Esq... Very interesting, but you don't do anything. Not yet. If *you* know, the Law knows, and before long they'll step in and liven things up. And it wasn't long, either, although it was a bit of a surprise, the way it happened. The papers certainly played it up. ...

It was a shame the airman got himself stabbed... they never found who did it, but the poor airman got a lot of publicity. Johnny Burton said they should have reported him as Killed In Action, but Johnny Burton's a cynic. ...

Two of the prossies got three years each, the others were fined. You got in touch with them, you paid the fines... you chose the best ones and you got them organised. Somewhere decent to live, good clothes, but no pimps, no ponces. Definitely not.

So there you are. Arrived. The two best girls, both from the north-country, are in love with their work, and they're good for the club... Geordie and Sheila... smart, brittle — just what the Forces ordered. They come from all over the world; Kiwis, Aussies, Yanks, Africans — everything, from everywhere. The Yanks bring a special invention called the Almighty Dollar, which is their religion. You are doubtful at first, until you learn just what the Almighty Dollar can do, but soon you too learn to worship, with even greater devotion.

Johnny Burton says it's funny that all the Governments spend all their time and money giving the Forces health and strength, while Geordie and Sheila spend all their time doing the reverse, but Johnny Burton's a cynic. ...

His head turned as Jalani ran up the steps from her basement flat, and in the driving mirror he saw someone turn the corner into the street, then stop dead. It was Jimmy Wilson. He stood and watched her move to the car, and you could see him trying to make out who was inside it. Lucky, it's getting dark. Why did he suddenly turn and run back round the corner?

The brain of Wm. Andrews Esq. slid into gear as quickly and smoothly as did his car and Jalani, who had noticed nothing beyond the frown of concentration on his face, played gently, with long and slender and crimson-tipped fingers, with her ear-rings.


From the Labour Exchange Jimmy wandered slowly, aimlessly, down to Whitechapel Road. *Why* were the people behind the counters in Labour Exchanges so stupid? Again and again you said 'Office work', and again and again they said brightly 'Factories? War-work?'

Why was it that, no matter what time you got there, it was always tea-time? As though a secret signal had been given they all vanished behind the glass-topped Government screens and you heard the rattle and chink of Government cups and saucers and you could see them all clustered together and chattering and twittering like a lot of sparrows. And when they came out again they said brightly 'Factories? War-work?' They were useless.

He was sick of them, he was sick of the whole bloody world. If they wouldn't help him, he'd find a job on his own.

As he approached Aldgate he wondered: Should he go into Mr Gates's tea-shop? He didn't want to spend any money, but if Rosie was serving she wouldn't charge him.

The light touch on his arm made him jump, and the light and mocking voice made him feel stupid: "Hallo, Jimmy. You looked so worried..."

261

She stood there, smiling, and she was a real young lady. You could see it in the way she glanced at passers-by, in the smart little fur cape she wore, in the ear-rings, the trim shoes and handbag. Jimmy swallowed.

"Hallo, Pinkie," he said coldly. "— How's the animals in the zoo these days?"

He meant it to be sarcastic, crushing, but she brushed it aside with the gay, tinkling laugh he remembered only too well. She looked straight into his eyes and realised for the first time that she had to look upwards. She saw that the look in his eyes denied the coldness of his voice, and she knew that she hadn't lost him. Mr Andrews — or Billy, as she called him in the oddly familiar moments that happen occasionally when you work closely with a particular person — was more shrewd than she had thought.

"Believe me, Jimmy," she said softly, with all her persuasion and her hand again on his arm, "— I didn't mean to hurt you, and I didn't mean what I said. You know I didn't —"

He stared her up and down, his eyes alight but his face still cold and set. "Not much you didn't mean it. For once you told the truth... I s'pose they were like animals, to you. ..." Again he swallowed, knowing already that he was weakening.

"It was your fault," she accused him. "You shouldn't have let me go so easily."

Her attack was so simple, so naked, that for a moment he was speechless. He realised that people were staring at them. "Let's walk along a bit," he said, then, bitterly: "*My* fault! I s'pose I told you to make fun of my old man, and to flirt with Boy-boy and Johnny Burton." His voice was flat and dull, as though he were tired.

"Jimmy, I didn't make fun of your father. It was just that his words came out so fast, I couldn't understand them. Everybody was laughing and clapping, but I didn't know what at." He was walking smoothly and firmly along, his expression unchanged. She added: "As for

262

Johnny Burton, I wasn't flirting at all. I *detest* him... it was your mother who made me dance with him and then he... insulted me, only a few minutes after your father had made me feel such a fool. ..."

Jimmy smiled. Hesitant, uncertain, but he smiled. "I looked a bleed'n' fool too, after Boy-boy swiped me."

She eyed him narrowly, but there was no sarcasm in his remark.

"I waited at the top of the Court for you," she lied. "I hoped you'd follow me... we could have gone back to the flat and had a cup of tea or something. ..."

Truly she despised Johnny Burton but now, in spite of Mr Andrews and his instructions, and because Jimmy was so willing to believe her, she began to despise herself.

"If you meant that, you could've called for me, or sent a message, some way." He thought of the slow misery of the weeks following Boy-boy's wedding, when he kept himself apart from Tommy Cooper and Rosie Gates, and did nothing but read his dictionary.

"I walked up and down Luxton Street several times hoping to see you. I almost knocked for you, but I was too frightened of meeting your father. He terrified me that night, honestly. Then as the days went past, I thought you didn't really care about me anyway."

"Not care? Me?" His indignation was so intense, so sharp, that his words came in jerky rushes: "— but I *do*, Pinkie. I 'ave done ever since the first time you come 'ome in a taxi, when you was eleven —" Now he was confused. He hadn't known how much he cared until the rushing words spoke for him, crystallising his feelings with startling clarity. And he was afraid that now, having spoken without thinking, he had said too much.

"You shouldn't get so excited, Jimmy," she said lightly, with brilliant perception. "You forget all your h's and g's. I was surprised just now. You spoke... well, as though you'd had a good education. ..."

With that remark she won him; he was still nervous, without confidence, but she knew that the fight was over.

And she was sorry.

He laughed, deeply and with a strange sincerity, and she joined in. "I always do when I get upset," he said ruefully, still chuckling. "I s'pose I always will, even if I live to be a n'undred — a *hundred*."

They smiled warmly, and glancing round he realised how far they had walked. They were outside Barmy Park … Was it an accident? This was where he'd run after the humiliations of the wedding party, where he'd cried… did things like that happen to other people? He thought they must, but you never knew. These were the secret things, the things you never told anyone… but he was finished with Rosie Gates. He saw that in a way Rosie had helped him, but it was all over now. He was Jimmy Wilson, and there were big things, important things, for him to do.

"… asks after you," Pinkie was saying. "I always tell her you're well, and want to be remembered to her. I've never told her about that night."

"— Peggy? I'm sorry. I ought to've asked before. How is she?" As he thought of Peggy he heard her voice: Speak *slowly,* carefully. He would, always, even if it killed him…

"Did you know she was in hospital for a whole year, and then wouldn't come back to London, although the big raids were over?"

"Why not? Where'd she go?"

"Shall we walk to that tea-shop — our tea-shop? There's so much to tell you, I don't know where to start."

They turned and retraced their steps towards Whitechapel and the tea-shop where they had gone the first day Pinkie had come home from the convent, the first time Jimmy ever rode in a taxi.

"Well," Pinkie took up the conversation again, "— It wasn't because of the raids… not even because of her hip — she'll always be a cripple, you know?"

Jimmy nodded sadly: "You told me, a long time ago."

"It was the scar on her face… oh, Jimmy, it was terrible." She held his arm tightly, her eyes swimming with tears. She was being honest with him. "— It was all

264

red and blue, all over her cheek, and the stitches pulled her eyelid down... when she left the hospital she took a room in a village near St. Albans. She wouldn't go out anywhere, and she wouldn't let anyone go near her. Not even me."

"Ohhhh. I'm sorry about it, Pinkie. ..."

Why is he always so kind, so *good*? she wondered irritably. Why couldn't he be hard and selfish, so that it would be easier to do what she had to do?...

"But you don't know the rest of it," she went on in lightened tones. "A week or two ago she read about a new way of doing operations, called plastic surgery, I think... I don't know much about it, but they can change the shape of your face, or your nose, and they can even make scars disappear."

"Is that what she's goin' to 'ave — *have* — done? Jeeeeesus!" He was so excited, so happy for Peggy, that he almost choked.

"She's seeing the specialist this week — she'll find out what they can do... it's terribly expensive, but it's worth it. ..."

For a moment she wanted to tell him the truth: that Mr Andrews was going to pay for it all. But she couldn't do it. It was worth it, she tried to convince herself. No matter how much it cost, how much it hurt Jimmy or Pinkie herself or anyone else, it was worth it. The price Mr Andrews demanded was that she should get in touch with Jimmy again; to pretend that she really liked him and, whenever the chance came, to suggest that he was too clever to waste himself working in an office... and later, when Jimmy had got used to the idea, Mr Andrews himself would offer the bait. ... Pinkie had tried to make him change his mind, to suggest other people who would gladly join Mr Andrews' field staff, but he refused any alternative. At last, for Peggy's sake, Pinkie had agreed. But she hadn't known it would be like this... the thought flashed into her mind that perhaps Jimmy was in love with her, but she dismissed it. That would have made everything impossible. She told herself that he just had a crush on her, and even that was bad enough.

"— And then, when it's all over, she'll come back and stay in the flat with me."

They turned the corner, into Whitechapel and ran into a group of youths and boys. Two of them had been with Jimmy in Miss Bullock's class at Saint Mary's. They eyed Jimmy and Pinkie belligerently, and immediately came the first taunt: "Hey, Jimmy — what's that you've got — a blackbird, or a Black Bird?"

Feeling the sudden stiffening in him, seeing his blazing eyes, Pinkie pulled him sharply away. "Take no notice, Jimmy. They're just looking for trouble."

She literally dragged him along but still he managed to face them, bristling, waiting for the first stone. "I'll wait for you, Knocker," he grated, and Knocker Williams, the leader, laughed scornfully. He was quite safe — there were five of them.

"Oh, yeah? You an' 'oo else?" He rocked backwards and forwards on his heels, grinning.

The rest of the gang, seeing that Jimmy wasn't going to stand and fight, lost interest. Jimmy turned and went on with Pinkie still holding his arm.

"I mean it, Pinkie. I'll wait for 'im — *him*."

"What's the use, Jimmy? It'll only mean more trouble."

"They'll be in trouble before long, anyway." And though he didn't really know why, he was right. The grown-ups were all involved in the war, in the almost-tangible tension of working up for the great events to come. As England filled with fighting men of all colours and creeds and of many nations, the young people of Jimmy's age grew more and more bored. The war would be important soon enough, when you were eighteen and had to go in the Forces, so why worry about it now? But nothing ever happened, there wasn't even the excitement of air-raids... they formed small groups that wandered about, playing like monkeys on the rubble and in the blasted houses, and if the Law interfered they simply leaped on to a peak or a pinnacle and jeered and threw stones... it was when two of the groups met in the streets or in the clubs that were spreading through the East End that things got lively. Jimmy had seen it several times... there was the pause, the tightening of formation, the   weighing each other up; there were the first tentative insults — sarcastic, then obscene, then both; soon there was the first flying stone, and then came the mixing. Usually it ended with bleeding noses and a few black eyes, but sometimes it was worse. ... Jimmy, who apart from Rosie Gates had lived so much in himself, kept away from all these goings-on.

Outside the tea-shop Pinkie pulled him to a stop. "You don't want to get upset by things like that," she said. "I get it all the time," she added sadly.

"You let me 'ear 'em —" he began aggressively, then seeing Pinkie's smile at his slipped accent he too smiled. Yet it was true. If he heard anyone saying anything nasty to Pinkie he'd go for 'em. Even if they was as big as... as big as Boy-boy, even. He'd get bashed up, but he wouldn't care.

It was disappointing to see that their old table was being used by a gang of road-workers, but Pinkie walked straight past and sat at a corner table. It was just like the old times. Again Jimmy carried the two cups of tea, again Pinkie smiled and pointed to the chair at her side. Her eyes were glowing and she'd never looked prettier.

Jimmy sat down, looking suddenly unhappy.

"It's funny, Pinkie. I used to walk past your house, but I never saw you once. Till last Tuesday. You got in a sports car."

He stopped speaking and stared at the table, with the rings of dried tea and the cigarette ash. He was asking her to explain, yet he was afraid of the explanation.

... That was a hard one... oh, well, no more lifts-to-work from Mr Andrews. She realised that somehow Mr Andrews had seen Jimmy that day, that that was the beginning of his plan. Just because Johnny Burton had

been told that he was fit to go in the Forces after all. ...
She realised too that Jimmy hadn't recognised Mr
Andrews, and that was a good thing. Her instructions
were not to tell Jimmy exactly who she worked for, and
never to recognise Johnny Burton if they met anywhere
accidentally. But she hadn't expected this. ...

"Last Tuesday?" She wrinkled her straight nose,
fighting for time. "Oh yes — I remember. It was a date I
had — one of the customers from where I work."

"Oh. I s'pose he's rich, is he?"

"He's... well-to-do. But I don't like him," she added with
sudden venom, and that was true. She was beginning to
hate Mr Andrews.

"Where do you work? What at?"

"Well... about a week after the wedding party I got a
job as a salesgirl in a dress shop." Her voice faded and he
saw that she had gone off into memories; almost
immediately she was back with him, smiling. "It was
terrible. I used to get all the prices wrong, and I couldn't
wrap the parcels properly —"

Jimmy smiled with her; he could just imagine her,
wrestling with sheets of brown paper and balls of string.

"— So I gave it up, before they gave *me* up... then I got
a job in an all-night restaurant, where I am now."

"You work all night?"

"Mmmm — except Sundays, my day off. Now and then
I get an extra day off in the week, too."

"What's it like, working at night?" Jimmy had often
wondered about it.

"I like it, really. It's only a small place, but there's a
little dance-floor and a band — they call it an orchestra,
but it's only a four-piece. And —" She shot him a careful,
guarded look before adding: "Well, some of the customers
are well off, and now and then I go out with one of them...
nothing serious," she added defensively, "— just for
something to do." The miserable look was back on his face
but, hoping to avoid any further questions, and partly to
carry out her orders, she forced herself to go on: "I *like*

268

going out in cars, to clubs and places... don't you, Jim? You can't just sit at home and never go anywhere."

"You could... if there was something special you wanted, something you was savin' up for."

He looked up, straight into her eyes, but she had understood his meaning even before he finished speaking. "That's why I do this night work," she said quickly. "I earn two or three times as much as I could get in any ordinary job."

"Do you? As much as that?" He was interested already, but she didn't want him to be. He went on: "If I got a job in a restaurant, would I earn as much?"

It was her cue; she should have said 'Yes — in some jobs, if you work for the right boss', but she couldn't. She felt sick.

"It — it takes a lot of training," she said. "If you want to be a waiter — a *good* waiter — you have to go to a special school... it takes months."

"Oh." The interest faded from his face, and she was glad. For Peggy's sake she'd have to go through with it, but not now, not so soon.

She was afraid of saying too much, of giving herself away, and she was just as afraid of saying too little. She'd have to watch every word... there was a big net round them, herself, Jimmy, Peggy... she hoped Jimmy wouldn't get into any trouble, or even get involved, yet she herself had to lead him into it.

Trying to avoid any more questions, she changed the subject: "Why aren't you working today, Jimmy?"

"Me?" He laughed, with a short, bitter edge to his voice. "I've been out of work for nearly two weeks now."

He didn't know what he'd said that was so terrible, how it happened. Her eyes were wide open, her face was grey.

... So that was it. Through Janey, and then through Johnny Burton, Mr Andrews had found out that Jimmy was unemployed. This, he thought, was his chance. ... Nononono... staring at Jimmy, thinking of his drive to *be* someone, she knew she liked him. But how, she wondered

269

frantically, *could* she like him, when she was already in love? Even that was something she couldn't tell him about... her life had become a knife-edge of do's and don'ts; one wrong word, one false step, and they'd all end up in disaster.

She was tired, sick of the whole thing. Where were all the hopes and plans Peggy had made for her? What had happened to the flat they were to have shared in Kensington? What had become of the rich Indian merchants she was to have met, the people from the Embassy and the wealthy students?... Gone, all gone in a war that did nobody any good. Nobody, except people like Mr Andrews... when he first suggested this plan she'd rushed off to Peggy and asked if Peggy herself couldn't afford to pay for the operations... somehow Peggy had always given the impression that she was comfortably off. But Peggy had less than eighty pounds, and she was so excited about even the possibility of plastic surgery that Pinkie had been caught up in her excitement... what could she do...?

"Pinkie? I'll have to go now — it's dinner time. ... You're not working tomorrow, are you — it's Sunday."

"That's right. I never work on Sundays." She knew what was coming, and there was no way to prevent it. Pictures, or...

"Well, seein' as it's Sunday... they have dances at Saint Mary's — the club... well, if you're not doin' anything else, would you come with me?"

He was so earnest, so hopeful, like a little dog wagging its tail and hoping for a crumb, that suddenly her eyes misted. Yet looking at him, smiling at him, she resolved once and for all to do what had to be done. It was for Peggy.

"I'd like to. I'd like to very much."

Jimmy walked her back to her door, but didn't go inside, and she was glad. As soon as it closed behind her she burst into tears.

The Club, when they went in, was almost empty. It looked, Jimmy thought wryly, as if it had a hangover. Some of the chairs were broken, and there were the nice boys and girls who had attended regularly since it was opened. They were dancing and jitterbugging lazily, as though it was too much effort. Perhaps, he smiled, they were afraid of incurring the wrath of the Lord. After all, it *was* Sunday.

The radiogram was turned down and barely audible, and from the dais at the far end of the drill-hall came the smell of weak tea, of stale cakes and buns, of orange-juice. Behind the counter Mrs Gapley moved with quick, bird-like movements, wishing that Mr Brown, the vicarage handyman, would hurry up and relieve her. She had thought the Club was a wonderful idea, until a few months ago. Then, instead of the usual crowd of *nice* young people, strangers had come. They were rough and loud-voiced and violent, and Mrs Gapley was terrified of them. Although she knew that they brought small bottles of rum and gin and whisky, she had never dared to tell Mr Gapley. But Mr Gapley knew, and was powerless. He had thought for a time of closing the Club altogether, but that would have meant admitting defeat. The Club had become a snowball and then an avalanche, and now it was beyond his control.

Jimmy, who had only been there two or three times, shortly after it opened, wasn't sure what to expect; hoping that Jimmy's dancing had improved, and smilingly prepared to be bored to death, Pinkie sat at one of the small tables along the wall. They danced once or twice, and both of them tried hard to look as though they had enjoyed it.

Gradually, almost imperceptibly, the few became many; the radiogram was turned up and there was the rising level of shrill and emphatic young voices. Mrs Gapley disappeared and was replaced by Mr Brown.

Pinkie set herself out to be light-hearted, and Jimmy was so absorbed in her that it was some time before he

271

noticed the thickening crowd, and then he was surprised to see among them several faces he knew from his schooldays. He hadn't expected to see the young toughs of the neighbourhood, or the school bullies. They seemed to vary in age from fourteen to eighteen and were mostly in little cliques, and each clique seemed to have two or three girls — painted, high-heeled, raucous-voiced, attached to it.

The chatter rose to a high, continuous babble; the radiogram was at full blast and the dancing was quicker, suggestive. Nobody drank tea or played ping-pong, but everyone appeared to love orange-juice. Jimmy realised why when he saw the small bottles being passed from one to the other under the tables, and he stiffened when Knocker Williams came in with an under-dressed girl Jimmy vaguely remembered from school as Eye-leen Someone or other. With them was a slender but vicious-looking crony, who reminded Jimmy of Boy-boy; they had the same way of moving, as though their power and all their muscles were tensed up and ready to fly at any moment. But he relaxed again as Knocker's eyes slid over him and Pinkie and past, without any flicker of interest or sign of recognition.

Pinkie too had noticed Knocker and his group come in, and the surreptitious passing of bottles, and she was nervous. She reached across the table for Jimmy's hand.

"I... I don't like it much, do you?" She sensed, she *knew,* that Knocker's eyes were fixed on her, and her nervousness increased. Jimmy, staring calmly at Eye-leen, didn't hear her. She shook his hand urgently.

"Jimmy, let's go home. I've got some beer. ..."

Jimmy brought his eyes back to Pinkie, and there was a hard little smile touching his mouth. "Why should we? You're not frightened of *him,* are you?" He nodded his head at Knocker, but his words were both a question and an accusation. He stood up suddenly, pushing his chair back so that it screeched loudly against the french-chalked floorboards. "Come on, Pinkie. Let's dance."

272

"No, Jimmy. It's asking for trouble —" Her eyes were wide and a little pulse beat at the base of her throat. He leaned over and pulled her to her feet. "Nothin' to be scared of. I c'n take care of *'im*." He grinned, confident that he could look after himself, and Pinkie, too, if Knocker started anything.

They danced. The dance ended and nothing had happened, and she thought she was worrying over nothing. The next record began before they reached their table and again they danced. They had only taken a few steps when Jimmy felt a light tap on his shoulder.

"This is an excuse-me," said a thin, lifeless voice. "— *if* you don't mind."

Jimmy glanced quickly round the hall. Several couples were dancing, but nobody else was being excused.

"You go an' dance wi' one o' the tarts," he said evenly, pleasantly. "You try an' cut in 'ere, an' I'll bust you wide open. Tell Knocker I said so."

"Jimmy." Pinkie was pulling his arm, trying to drag him away, and he said sharply to her: "Stop tuggin'." But he put his arms round her and they were dancing again. Knocker's crony blinked and Jimmy said triumphantly, "See? They won't try anythin' if you stand up to 'em." Pinkie smiled weakly.

"Tell you what. We'll stay a bit longer, so's they don't think I've run away, then we'll go. O.K. ?"

Pinkie smiled again, but there was an icy feeling inside her. Then, looking at the door, her smile faded as she saw Johnny Burton. She stared.

She had to work with him for Mr Andrews, but she disliked him as much as ever. She did not know it was Johnny who sold the half-bottles of spirits to the Club-members. Most of the boys had gone straight from school into war factories, and so had plenty of cash, and Johnny had worked up a good connection at Saint Mary's. Despite all this, when Pinkie and Johnny met in public they had been instructed not to recognise each other.

Jimmy noticed Pinkie's stare and slowly his head

turned. Johnny was just inside the door; his brother-in-law, and they hated each other. And Johnny had that ugly, oily smile.

Jimmy felt the old tightening in his belly. He could take on Knocker Wilson, or his crony, but he would think twice about tackling Johnny Burton. Johnny's eyes were sparkling and his face opened in a wide grin as Knocker Williams and his crony and Eye-leen joined him by the door. They spoke loudly, with considerable animation, with Jimmy watching carefully from the corner of his eyes.

For some time nothing happened, then with a light scream Eye-leen left them and hipped and flaunted her way down along the wall to where Jimmy and Pinkie were sitting. She surveyed Pinkie with green, gold-flecked eyes, but when she spoke it was to Jimmy.

"Well, if it ain't ole comic-cuts Wilson 'isself! Doin' all right for yerself, ain'cha?" Her voice was insinuating and derisive and still she eyed Pinkie up and down. "— Never did see why white boys wanta get stuck into black —"

Jimmy's fingers bit into her wrist so savagely that she stepped back, her blood-red mouth wide open. Pinkie reared backwards in her chair and when she spoke her voice was soft yet vindictive: "You dirty little slut. You —"

Jimmy's fingers dug even deeper into Eye-leen's arm. "They tell you to come down 'ere an' start somethin' ?" he demanded, his voice thick and muffled with fury.

"Them? 'Course not. I c'n start trouble meself." Eye-leen paused, filled with righteous indignation, staring again at Pinkie. "D'you know Johnny Burton? 'E said 'e wantsa talk to yer."

Jimmy let go of Eye-leen and said quickly: "Stay where you are, Pinkie. You don't want nothin' to do with 'im." There was a slight twitch at the side of his jaw, the muscles of his thighs and biceps were jerking and quivering like cut worms. Abruptly Eye-leen turned and sidled back to her group near the door.

Pinkie shifted slightly, so that she could watch both

274

Jimmy and the door. There was going to be trouble... how could she prevent it? What did Johnny want her for, and why was he defying Mr Andrews' instructions? If she went, could she stop the fight she could feel developing? She could sense, she could *taste* and smell the violence that was in Jimmy... his mouth was a narrow, compressed line. She moved hesitantly towards the door.

"Stay there," Jimmy snapped. "If you go up to them, there's no tellin' what they'll do. Wait till they come down 'ere — they'll 'ave to take me first. If they do, you run. Get 'ome as fast as you can."

Desperately her eyes sought another door, another way out, but there was only the one entrance. Jimmy was determined to shield her, and again the knowledge of her agreement with Mr Andrews made her feel sick. She knew that Johnny Burton wouldn't touch her, nor let the others touch her, because of Mr Andrews. ... There was something wrong, something that didn't fit... breathing quickly, frightened yet excited, she halted. The radiogram blared on and others were dancing. Nobody seemed to have noticed anything unusual.

Seconds passed in tight-lipped silence that stretched and stretched between them, until she wanted to scream. Jimmy turned sideways-on to the door and moved slowly to the next table, and in a smooth sweep slid an orange-juice bottle into his trouser pocket. One against two was bad enough, but one against three was a bit too much. He turned to Pinkie with a bitter smile: "Might as well get it over with. You run as soon as it starts," he added warningly, as together they moved along the wall.

There was a smile fixed on Pinkie's face, but her knees were trembling as they came to the door. Johnny Burton still smiled.

"'Lo, Jimmy," he said lightly, and added softly: "It's dark outside, y'know."

"You're kiddin' me," Jimmy said. "It's not dark yet. Besides, I'm not goin' anywhere. I'm just seein' my friend to the door."

"She goin' 'ome?" Knocker inquired, "— all on 'er own?"

He grimaced. "— I wouldn't do that to a nice-lookin' gel. Think I'll see 'er 'ome meself."

Jimmy knew he couldn't win. If they'd let Pinkie go it wouldn't've been so bad, but Knocker and his pal moved through the door ahead of her. Jimmy went after her, slowly, one hand on the bottle in his pocket, and last came Johnny Burton. In a slow, tension-tight cortège they went past the concrete slabs reinforcing the wall. Knocker and his pal stopped suddenly, so that Pinkie almost walked into them. It was not quite dark, but the door of the Clubroom opened and spilled weak light over the rough ground. The black-out was bad, but no one worried now that the raids had ended. The entrance to the Clubroom couldn't be seen from the street.

"Johnny. Let Pinkie go 'ome. You know she's never done you any 'arm."

"No? What about Boy-boy's weddin'? Besides," Johnny added, his voice light and mocking, "— I might know 'er better than you think."

So that was it, Pinkie thought. He's going to tell Jimmy about me working for Mr Andrews. Breathlessly she waited.

The insinuation was not lost on Jimmy, but he thought Johnny was just being clever, just trying to make him lose his temper.

Johnny was happy. Very happy. For over two years he had waited to pay Jimmy back for that swipe with the brick in the City ruins, although he had done nothing because of Mr Andrews. But a week earlier he had received a letter stamped O.H.M.S., telling him to report to an Army Training depot in two days' time. He hadn't really thought that Mr Andrews would *do* anything, and now he was past caring. In any case, before Mr Andrews did anything — even if he *did* try — Johnny would be a member of H.M. Forces. Meeting Knocker tonight was a bit of luck... he'd never forgotten the way Pinkie had slapped his face, even if they were forced to work

276

together. ... He'd have to show Janey his call-up papers in the morning and say they'd just arrived. She'd be upset about Jimmy getting bashed up, but she'd never know who did it; it was part of the code not to split, unless you had a brother or a pal who was interested in a return match. He thought fleetingly of Pinkie, then dismissed her. She wouldn't dare run for the Law, and as for her ratting to Mr Andrews... well, balls to him. In two days Johnny'd be a soldier, and who could tell *what* might happen before he came back from the war?

Knocker and his crony moved warily back towards Jimmy, but again Johnny spoke: "Pinkie, you'd better go on 'ome. Jimmy's got some business to see to. 'E's always bin a big-'eaded bastard, an' we're goin'ta take 'im down a peg or two... go on, before I change my mind."

Jimmy pushed her gently but firmly, then she was running; she wanted to scream, she could hardly breathe. But the trouble was partly through her... perhaps there were some passers-by in the street who would help. ...

The street was deserted. She went back the way she had just come, until she could see the four figures standing in the shadow of the wall.

Jimmy slid the bottle from his pocket, so that it was partly up his coat-sleeve, and he tried to watch his three enemies together.

"'Ang on, Knocker," said Johnny, standing directly in front of Jimmy, who was waiting with his back to the wall as the three closed in. They stopped at Johnny's order.

Enjoying his moment of revenge, Johnny went on: "Remember, Jimmy, this 'appened a long time ago? The day you won the scholarship... didn't do you much good, did it, big-'ead?" As his words ended Johnny's fist flickered forward and back without doing any damage. Jimmy waited quietly; he'd need all his breath before long. The palms of his hands were sweating so that the bottle was slippery. Johnny's fist flicked again, then he stepped back. Jimmy moved away slightly, nearer to Knocker's pal. Jimmy didn't see the fist that came from behind him and crashed down on his shoulder, but he knew that it was Knocker, and that Knocker's hand was wrapped round a stone, or something hard. Johnny stepped in and crashed a left-hander into Jimmy's ribs, and Jimmy pulled out the bottle.

"Look out," came the quick shout from Knocker's pal, "— 'e's glassed up." Johnny and Knocker leaped in together and Jimmy was forced to face them, trying to jab with the bottle and at the same time to protect himself from the fists and feet that seemed to come from everywhere.

Jimmy got one sharp jab into Knocker's face, then from the corner of his eye he caught the dull gleam of metal as Johnny's fist curved down on to his forearm; there was a shattering crunch and the bottle slid from his nerveless fingers. "That got you, you bastard," Johnny said with great satisfaction.

The three attackers paused, all breathing heavily, and Jimmy used the break to shift further along the wall. If he went down, he didn't want his face crunched on the broken glass. Johnny smiled, a grim, taut smile: "You shouldn't use glass," he mocked. "— It's not fair."

Jimmy feinted towards him and in the same moment swerved right round, taking Knocker by surprise. He got both fists in just under the ribs, and still in the same motion dived at Knocker's crony. There was the *whoof* of air screaming explosively from lungs, there was a flurry of kicks and punches and they were all writhing on the ground. Knocker whipped away to one side then slid upwards, and Jimmy was spread-eagled. Johnny gradually shifted upwards, then leaned all his weight with his elbows on Jimmy's face, grinding his nose. Then he stood up and kicked, and through closing eyes Jimmy caught once more the gleam of metal, on tips under Johnny's boots. Pinkie. ...

There was another explosion in his ribs, and Knocker's fist rammed into Jimmy's mouth and split his lips, then someone jumped on his ankles. Now hardly able to see, Jimmy sensed rather than saw the metal-shod boot rise and fall. This time the pain made no difference, but he knew the foot was landing low down, right in his groin. He tried to curl up, away from the foot, then he could see nothing clearly, just drifting black fog. ...

He heard Johnny's voice, seeming to echo on itself: "O.K., Knocker. We don't wanna kill the little bleeder. Not so easy as 'e looked, was 'e?"

Through the deep pit of pain Jimmy tried to grin. Bloody flattery!

"If I'd 'ad me 'dusters, I'd've broke 'is bloody jaw," Knocker grated. Jimmy tried to speak, to tell them he'd get them, one by one, and it seemed to him that he did actually speak. But the others heard only a groan.

"Let's move," Johnny said, "— across the road." His voice was sharp and incisive. The darkness filled with revolving pinpoints of light, and Jimmy knew he was going to be sick.

Pinkie moved away as Johnny and the others came to the street. She saw with satisfaction that Johnny's nose was bleeding, that one of Knocker's eyes was puffed and closed. The crony seemed to be untouched. She moved to go back to Jimmy, but when she saw that the three had simply moved across the street and stood there waiting, she stopped. Could they be waiting to get her too? She thought they couldn't be because if they'd wanted to beat her up they could easily have done so already, but she was uncertain. Why couldn't she run, why couldn't she *do* something?

Johnny sauntered back across the road and she stiffened.

"I wouldn't tell anyone, if I was you," he said casually, then walked back and rejoined the other two, still waiting.

She saw Jimmy crawling on hands and knees towards the street but she leaned against the wall, unable to think or move. Jimmy reached the kerb and his arms collapsed so that he fell on his face, and he retched and then vomited.

279

"It's all right," Johnny said loudly, "— 'e'll live," but still they stood waiting.

The gutter smelled of dried and musty cabbage water and there was blood in his nose and mouth. Pinkie stared at his bloodied face and swollen eyes in horror, then she began to laugh and the laugh went higher and higher and echoed in his brain; still like a musical-box, but now out of tune. She saw two people approaching through the street's deepening shadows.

"Pinkie," Jimmy moaned, his hands waving pitifully, "— 'elp me up." She stared wildly round her and saw the three across the street, all staring with their eyes focused on her. Her laughter stopped as though switched off.

Blood... she hated blood, she hated Jimmy Wilson, she hated herself. And she couldn't bring herself to touch him. The two people were closer now, and suddenly she recognised the couple — Mr and Mrs Clarke? — who had been at Boy-boy's wedding party. She panicked. If they saw her here with Jimmy in this state they'd go straight to the Court and tell the Wilsons and it would be her fault. "Get up yourself, you fool," she hissed, trying to give the impression that Jimmy was putting it on. "— You trying to make me look small?"

Jimmy forced his eyes open and he saw the tears streaming down her face and he saw Johnny Burton still across the road. At the back of his mind was a great wonderment that Pinkie should be ashamed to help him because Johnny Burton and the others were watching... she was part-Indian, she worried about funny things... he heard the sharp and rapid striking of high heels, and she was gone. There were two voices that he thought he ought to know, yet they sounded wavy and distorted and he couldn't place them: "Christ... someone's bin done up... it's the Wilson boy. ..."

And there was the woman's voice, hard and strident: "Don't you interfere, Fred. It's none o' your business — betcha life 'e arst for it. These 'ooligans an' ruffians. ..."

The voices faded and there was a sickening wave of

280

pain and sharp stabbings that rose through his chest with each breath. He dragged himself back, against the wall.

The next time he opened his eyes the street was empty, so far as he could judge, and darkness was purple and shadowed.

With jerky, agonised movements he dragged himself homewards along the wall, stopping now and then to bring up the sourness that was in him, and an hour later Tom and Addie Cooper, on their way to the Wilsons for the usual Sunday-night drink, found him at the top of the Court.

... He was lying naked on the big bed downstairs. Only his mother was there, going backwards and forwards to the gas-stove and bringing back rolls of clean and steaming rag which she put all over his body, and she was making a thin and high whining-noise all the time.

The gas-light seemed to grow and grow until it filled all the world, then there was nothing.

# 7

For three days Jimmy lay downstairs, while his mother applied fresh and steaming-hot bread poultices to the bruises which erupted all over him. In the meantime she and the old man slept on Jimmy's bed upstairs. The old man didn't like it and objected loudly, his faded-blue eyes standing out and his ginger moustache quivering in indignation, but with a few quiet but sharply-pointed remarks Mrs Wilson put him in his place.

To all their questions he said nothing whatever, and he spoke only to Johnny Burton, who came with Janey on the morning of the second day, to say good-bye to his in-laws before going off to become a member of H.M. Forces.

Janey's concern when she saw Jimmy and heard from the old lady about the beating-up was understandable, and he didn't really mind being exposed as the old lady, marvelling, and not without pride, pointed at the cuts and bruises. After all, Jimmy and Janey had dressed and undressed in the room upstairs ever since they were kids. It was knowing that Johnny Burton was looking too, his eyes glinting and gloating, that Jimmy couldn't bear.

Christ, Jimmy thought, you should've been a bloody actor. Johnny looked incredulous, astounded, and his voice was filled with sympathy as he stared down at his brother-in-law. Very carefully he moved so that his back was towards Janey and the old lady, then he smiled his vindictive smile.

"Who done it, Jim? Tell me — I'll get some o' the boys to go after 'em." He was filled with joy, something close to ecstasy. He knew Jimmy wouldn't talk — certainly not while any of his family were there. Jimmy jerked his head slightly and, his face reflecting the emotions he didn't feel, Johnny leaned down with his ear close to Jimmy's mouth.

"I'll get you, you bastard. I'll get you. ..." Jimmy said faintly, his puffed eyes slitted in hatred.

"— What's 'e sayin'," Mrs Wilson demanded quickly.

"I — I dunno, Mum. I can't make it out." Johnny moved away from the bed, but Jimmy's eyes remained fixed on him until at last he shook hands with Mrs Wilson, promised to write from his training camp, and went off with Janey. Jimmy saw now why Johnny had joined in the beating-up; he thought he was safe.

Again Jimmy went back into his wall of silence, doing nothing but stare at the wall or the ceiling, and slowly the old lady's bread poultices drew the pain and the swellings from his body. The bruises round his eyes and on his cheeks turned to yellowish-blue and then began to fade, and Mrs Wilson thought he looked even worse than when Addie and Tom carried him home. If on'y Boy-boy was 'ere — 'e'd take care of 'em, 'ooever it was. ...

On the third day Jimmy sat up and swivelled himself round to sit on the edge of the bed. Breathing very gently because of the sharp pains that still came he slid into his underpants, then staggered weakly to the table. He shook his head, trying to clear it of the buzzing that hadn't left him since he found himself in the old lady's bed. He walked slowly twice round the room, then went back to the bed.

Mrs Wilson watched in silent approval. Her boys were strong as oxes — it'd take more'n a bashin' up to put 'em out of action for long... but there was something she had to do. She left her chair and walked across to him, standing in front of and over him, her feet spread apart.

"Feel better now, son?"

Jimmy nodded, knowing what was coming, and it came immediately and with a complete change of tone:

"Now, 'oo was it? I've arst yer dozens o' times an' you wouldn't say... '*Oo was it?*"

Wearily Jimmy shook his head. The old lady's face whitened, her mouth dropped at the corners, her eyes glittered. She stuck her hands on her hips. "Tell me 'oo done it," she insisted. "Jeeesus, they nearly crippled yer for life. ..."

She didn't even realise *why* she wanted to know, for there was nothing she could have done. Yet, although she would have despised Jimmy if he'd split of his own accord or asked for help to get his own back, now she herself *had* to make him talk. She was aware of the dull fury underlying his uncanny, frightening silence and she knew it was bad, that it meant more trouble. So she *had* to break him down *now,* while he was still weak.

"You gettin' mixed up in them gangs?" It was more an accusation than a question, but again Jimmy shook his head.

"It wasn't anyone you know," he said. "I'll look after it meself."

"You'll getchorself killed, you mad bastard. 'Aven't they done enough to yer already? 'Oo was it — what'd they do it for?" Her voice was rising, the words bursting in little explosions. The misery in his eyes weakened her, sickened her, but she had to go on. Quickly she ran to the chest-of-drawers and pulled the broken chair-leg from behind the wireless. "Tell me," she insisted again, then she screamed: *"Tell me!"*

Jimmy simply stared at the upraised arm and the chair-leg, which shook slightly with his mother's anger.

... This was her last child, her youngest son, the boy who'd won a scholarship, who everyone said was clever, who wanted to talk posh and work in an office with clean collars every day... obsternit, 'ard as a poker... yet she loved him, for all his strangeness, and as she laid into him her heart broke. The chair-leg rose and fell and she made little moaning noises.

... She was so small and already there was so much pain, rivers and waterfalls and volcanoes of pain, that somehow Jimmy's mind became detached from it; he felt an insane urge to laugh even as his tears ran unchecked... poor Mum. She wanted to help, to keep him straight, and this was all she knew. How could he tell her that it was partly because he and Johnny Burton had always been enemies, partly because Pinkie was unwhite, because... there were so many different things that had led up to it all, how could be explain? He loved his mother, he knew she loved him, yet there was nothing either of them could say. She didn't understand... no one understood. Except Peggy... and, he thought, Pinkie. ...

With a little cry the old lady threw the chair-leg across the room, and collapsed on the edge of the bed. Then she cried her eyes out. Jimmy reached out and gently pulled her to him and his arm went round her shoulders. "It wasn't your fault, Mum... you couldn't 'elp it. ..." His voice was thick and broken with pain and sorrow. She made some little choking sounds, unintelligible sounds, and cried harder, and he soothed her as she cried.

"One day I'll be all right, Mum. You see, it'll be worth it. ... I'll buy you a fur coat. ..." Was he mad? Half dead and in bed and out of work, and talking about fur coats. ...

"Jimmy..." Her voice was soft and agonised and low: "Why don'cha listen to me..." That was the trouble. He *was* listening, but her words seemed to be meant for somebody else: "Why don'cha get a job in a fact'ry an' get more money... keep out o' trouble... ?"

"I didn't wanta get in trouble this time," he answered. They were crying together, both beginning to feel better.

"Well, why —?"

His hands waved sadly: "— It's just the way things are." It was the way things always had been. No matter what you wanted, what you tried to do, someone or something bigger and stronger always stopped you. *That* was the way things were. The pain rose and soared through him like a great rushing wind.

She left him suddenly and put the small saucepan on the gas-stove.

"Another poultice, Mum?" He wasn't really interested,

285

but he wanted her to forget. She nodded dumbly.

"Come 'ere, Mum." He raised his arms a little and she went to him.

"I'll — I'll get you some skate an' chips, eh?" She knew he liked skate. He nodded.

"Jim, why doncha try'n settle down, like all the other boys?"

... Like all the other boys. ... You worked in a sawmill or the brewery or the factory and you earned enough to keep alive, but no more than that. He remembered Peggy telling him years ago that that's how life was for most people, unless you worked hard and learned and made something better for yourself... like the other boys. ... That was just what he *didn't* want. In spite of what had happened, he and his mother were as far apart as ever.

She made him slip his underpants off and put the poultice on, then went and rinsed her face under the tap in the yard. She put on her coat, picked up her shopping-bag, and came over to the bed. Unexpectedly she leaned down and kissed him, as she stroked his hair, and this alone almost broke him, made him want to tell her what she had been so determined to know. But she didn't realise, and went out without another word to get the shopping in Brick Lane.

Lost in her thoughts she turned from the Court into the street and stopped, face to face with the girl Pinkie, the girl Jimmy had brought to Boy-boy's wedding party. She was lovely, in a hard and jewel-like way, exotic in the colours of her hair and her mouth and the smart clothes she wore. Did Jimmy still have anything to do with her? Did she know what had happened to him?

Pinkie stared, surprised at this unexpected meeting; she stared at the red-rimmed eyes, at the drawn yellow skin, and didn't know what to say.

"Did you want to see Jimmy?" Mrs Wilson's voice was cold, restrained; "Did you know someone set about 'im?"

"I — I heard, Mrs Wilson. I wondered how he was getting on." Mrs Wilson smiled faintly. "Why doncha go

286

an' 'ave a look?" she said. "— 'E's in bed. Go'n then — the door's on the latch."

"I... thank you, Mrs Wilson. I'd like to."

Jimmy thought his mother had come back for something she'd forgotten, then he caught the perfume, the same perfume. He was dreaming...

Pinkie took off her coat and, turning away, undid the top button of her blouse. She moved to the bed, and when Jimmy suddenly opened his eyes her own were all he could see, huge and dark and luminous.

"Pinkie..." he sighed, and she slid her arm under his head. She stretched herself out beside him, on top of the bedclothes, but her other arm slid down across his chest with a light, electric touch.

"Pinkie... why'd you run away?"

She pressed her cheek to his before replying: "I couldn't think. I was nearly in hysterics, and when those people came along I knew they'd tell your mother —"

"What people? Who?"

"That loud-voiced Mrs Clarke and her little husband — they were here that night, when Boy-boy got married."

So that's who those voices belonged to... they hadn't done anything to help, hadn't said a word. ...

"— But don't worry about it now. Try to sleep, and hurry up and get better."

A weak grin spread over his face. "How can I sleep with you there like that?" The words were slightly suggestive, a thing he'd never attempted before, and he realised that her silence, her soft smile, were tacit acknowledgements. Where her fingers traced over his ribs the flesh quivered as though from electric shocks, and again she smiled.

"Try to sleep," she repeated, drawing her hand away. "When you're better, I've got a surprise for you." Remembering the reason for her visit, she added softly: "When you're able to get out, come round to the flat. Will you?"

"You try'n stop me." He longed to call her Jalani, but was too uncertain of himself. His happiness was too real, too great, to risk. He could wait.

"I'll 'ave — *have* — to go round the Labour Exchange first. I was s'posed to sign on yesterday... ne'mind. ..."

"Come round early in the afternoon, before I go to work. And don't worry about the Labour business. I think I can help you... that's my surprise."

She stood up, then leaned down and kissed him, not lightly, as his mother had done, but full on his split and swollen lips. She looked down at him as she put her coat on again; his eyes were closed and he was smiling. She didn't know how it could be, but in spite of everything she liked him. But even more, she pitied him. There was nothing she could do now; this morning, just as she was ready to leave the club, Mr Andrews had told her that Peggy's operations could start almost immediately — provided that somehow Jimmy was led, or forced, into working with her. It need only be something easy, like helping her with the checking, as Johnny Burton had done occasionally, and as soon as Mr Andrews knew that this had been done the operations could start. But not until then. It was a gentle but definite ultimatum.

She wished she could dislike this strange boy — boy? He was a man now... that would have made everything easier... yet apart from that, her life had opened out so much... she was in love, and in a few months Peggy would be as well as the surgeons could make her. ... She wondered yet again why Mr Andrews was so determined that Jimmy, and Jimmy alone, must be drawn into the world of stolen goods and black market materials, of clubs and booze and prostitutes... with a hurried touch of her hand on his cheek, she left.

That evening Jimmy was sitting by the fire, wrapped in a blanket, when the old man came in. He stood by the table, whistling soundlessly, as he undid his coat.

"Well," he said at last, "— they done you up all right, didn't they?" He waited for some reply, but Jimmy stared at the glowing coals.

"Don't you carry anythin', Jimmy?"

Jimmy frowned. "What d'you mean? Knuckledusters?"

"Well, anythin' like that. Three 'alf crowns is as good as anythin', an' the Law can't touch yer, even if they do catch yer. 'Alf crowns is good because o' the edges — rip anyone's cheeks an' ears open wi' no trouble... don't s'pose you've got three 'alf crowns... but three pennies'll do nearly as good... 'Oo was it done it? Whaffor?"

The old man waited expectantly as Jimmy studied him with veiled and guarded eyes. Did he know anything?

Jimmy shrugged. "I'll look after it meself."

The old man started his silent whistling again, his watery blue eyes searching for his tea. The old lady'd gone to Janey's for her weekly visit; the potatoes were simmering on the gas-stove, and on the big plate were two thin slices of corned beef. Mr Wilson helped himself to his meal. He'd given Jimmy the benefit of his advice, and now his responsibility was ended. Youngsters never listened to their elders these days, anyway. ...

Jimmy remembered his father's advice, but thought he could improve on it; on the Sunday he prowled along Bethnal Green and down Mile End Waste, where the stalls and weekend vendors sold almost everything imaginable, and when he returned home a set of smooth and shiny knuckledusters were in his pocket. He'd be ready next time. ...

Another week had passed before Pinkie heard Jimmy's old signal-tap on the door. She glanced quickly round the room, then opened it: "Jimmy! I'm so glad... come in."

He came wondering into the flat, his eyes darting everywhere. It had been nice, the way they'd done it out before, but it was never like this... it was bright and colourful and warm, and sparkling with mirrors. There was a small cocktail cabinet, and an electric radiogram... a great, soft-toned Indian carpet covered almost the whole of the floor. There were two stuffed armchairs, and by the far wall was a curved, Oriental-looking divan. Jimmy whistled in admiration.

"D'you like it, Jimmy?" Her voice was deep with concern, as though his opinion was of the utmost importance.

"*Like* it?... I've never seen anything like this... must've cost a mint. ..."

She smiled at him with glowing eyes. She led him to one of the chairs, noticing that a faint yellowness round his eyes was all that was left of Johnny Burton's ganging-up.

"It's so nice to see you up again, Jimmy... but let's forget all that. Like a drink?"

She darted, a flash of brilliance, to the cabinet and brought back two whiskies. "Cheers," she said, laughing her tinkling laugh.

"Cheers." He winced as the spirit bit into his still-raw gums and, noticing it, she came and perched on the arm of his chair.

"What's the news about Peggy? Is she any better?"

"She's a lot happier now. They should do the first operation in three weeks time."

"Poor Peggy. Remember me to her, won't you?"

"I always do." Together they smiled. "Come and see the kitchen and the other room," she invited him.

She took his hand and led him, laughing and feeling lightheaded, along the passage and into the kitchen, and from there into the bedroom, which she liked most of all. There was a double divan covered by a brilliant bedspread, a soft thick carpet, and heavy, rich-looking tapestry panels depicting elephants and camels decorated two of the walls. The other two were absolutely bare, but washed in pale blue. The ceiling was of deeper blue. Jimmy gasped.

"Oh, Pinkie... it reminds me of Peggy's old room, but it's even better. ..."

"That's why I had it done like this. She'll love it."

Jimmy's face clouded. "It must've cost you a for..."

She looked at him quizzically, then burst into laughter. "It *did* cost a fortune — for me, at least," she said, not at all disconcerted. "— But I told you, I earn good money, and besides..."

Jimmy gazed at her with his head on one side, frowning. She took his hand and led him back into what she now called the lounge. She pushed him gently back into his chair and again perched on the arm. His tongue flickered round his lips.

"Pinkie, what were you going to say about... besides?"

"Besides... ? Oh, now and then I do extra jobs for my boss — I go round checking the stocks in the store-rooms, and things like that, and then I get a bonus."

He went suddenly tense, and she knew she would have to be careful, very careful. He was no fool.

"What stocks? What store-rooms?"

She laughed lightly, airily. "I told you — they have a restaurant, and there's the bar and the dance-floor. With things being so hard to get, they buy their stocks months in advance, and store them. I just have to check them — there's always somebody looking for things like that... it's mainly spirits and cigarettes." Even as she finished speaking, she knew she had said too much.

"Spirits and cigarettes? I thought you couldn't get things like that, except on the black market?"

She shot him a quick, angry glance, but his face showed only open curiosity. She looked serious and her voice when she spoke sounded doubtful, troubled. "To tell you the truth, Jimmy, I've thought about that too. I wouldn't be surprised if that's where all the stuff comes from, but I'm not sure. In any case, it's nothing to do with me. I just check the amounts, and sometimes I arrange for stuff to be collected or delivered.

"... That's why I get the bonus. ..." Her hands fluttered and indicated the room: "I couldn't have done all this, otherwise."

"Hmmm — you know it could be dangerous if you're picked up, Pinkie? If the Law catches you. ..."

"Dangerous? For me?" She laughed coolly, confidently. "How can it? I'm only doing what my employer tells me to do. I don't know where the stuff comes from, or how they buy it. ..."

He stared at her with level, intent eyes, and she slid from the arm of the chair and crouched down with her hands on his knees. "Look, Jimmy, I get good money, and it's worth it." She looked right into and through him, her voice filled with earnestness and conviction. "Look, Jim. If you want something very much, you've got to work for it, and you've got to take a chance. What's the use of working all your life and getting nowhere? You've got to be able to save, to buy clothes, to be able to go out to a club now and then, somewhere decent... to *live*. If you like," she added, as though the idea had only then occurred to her, "— I could ask my boss if you could help me. I think — I'm *sure* — he'd pay you, if you did." She paused, then went on, her voice rising with excitement, "Think of it, Jimmy — being able to *save* money... what can you save on thirty shillings a week, or whatever you'd get in an office."

He smiled gently. "I'd get twenty-five bob, that's all. I know, because I got myself a job this morning. I start work on Monday again."

For a moment she was nonplussed, then she added as though his job was of only minor importance: "Well then! Look at the extra money you'll have... new clothes... don't you see that if you want to get on, as you say you do, you've *got* to have money?"

"Money's not much use if you're doin' six months inside."

The matter-of-fact way he said it showed that he knew near enough what she was doing, but that was inevitable... with earnest face and voice, her hand tightening on his knee, she gambled: "Think of it, Jimmy! We could go out to lunch, we could go out dancing on my night off, we could ride in taxis... we could..."

Each time the word *we* was slightly emphasised, and registered deep in his mind. *We* could... that decided him.

"All right. We'll see how it goes."

Elated, she kissed him lightly and again he almost called her *Jalani*. As he left she kissed him again.

***

For three months they worked together, and soon he had a new suit. He started a savings account at the post office, and he noted the places they went to, the amounts of spirits, the thousands of cigarettes... he knew what was going on.

Trying to protect him, Pinkie told Mr Andrews that — as he knew from other reports — Jimmy was helping her. She also told him that Jimmy was still a bit suspicious, and she didn't think he would do anything more than checking the stocks. Mr Andrews laughed, and made his plans.

Jimmy was not happy about what they were doing, and sometimes he tried to persuade Pinkie to leave it all and take an ordinary job, but her reply was always the same. Didn't he like the clothes, the savings, her company, their few evenings out at shows? He did, that was the trouble. He loved his suit, his bank account, the feeling of power, of superiority, that the extra money gave him. He was even going to night school, learning correct English. ... Sometimes, despising herself, she allowed him to kiss and caress her, never allowing him to take any liberties. He was at once happy yet miserable.

On odd occasions he told her of his hopes and plans... to become a manager of something, somewhere... to have a little car... if you went to a college or to a high school it was easier — you automatically became the Personal Assistant to someone, or you became the Assistant-Trainee for something, but you never started off being the office-boy. She encouraged him in these beliefs.

Sensing his determination, his will to become someone, Pinkie never failed to point out the advantage of money, of perhaps being able to take his employer or manager out to lunch should there be a good opening in his firm, some opening that would get him started on the road to success. Always she listened to him, always she was sympathetic, and meanwhile Peggy was operated on twice.

Sometimes Jimmy talked guardedly about being in love. What was it all about, what did it do for people, what did it do *to* them? And sometimes in answering Pinkie's face softened. She told him how wonderful it must be to love somebody, no matter who or what they were, no matter what they did, despite right or wrong. Jimmy watched her expression as she spoke and he believed, in spite of her talk about the man — the rich man — she was going to marry one day, that it was *him,* Jimmy Wilson, that she really liked. Not *love,* really, not yet, but if he went on saving, if he worked at his office job and got promoted... his belief made his life wider, greater. He would do big things, he would be someone, all for Pinkie. ...

It was on a Tuesday that Mr Andrews gave Pinkie her final orders. A ship had arrived at Liverpool Docks from India, and there was a special package to be collected. Two of the Indians — one of them was Firoz, who had once kept an Indian café in Luxton Street — would bring the package to London, where the Indians were to join another ship at Millwall. Pinkie was to meet them in a pub in Shadwell, and she was to take Jimmy. Whatever happened, no matter how she achieved it, Jimmy himself was to take delivery of the goods. Once that was done, Mr Andrews would be able to control him, and Pinkie's job would be done. Further, Mr Andrews would see that, when the surgeons had done everything possible for Peggy, she was given a good job. Mr Andrews knew that the East End was ripe for further development, or would be very soon, and he was running out of patience. Pinkie put on a new dress, laid some beer and glasses on a tray and, putting a soft classical record on the radiogram, sat down and waited for Jimmy. She hummed lightly to herself, and when Jimmy saw the new dress he whistled in admiration.

"Hallo, Jimmy. You're late."

"Me? Late? I'm not, y'know." He looked at his new wrist watch. "It's only five-to-six."

She looked puzzled, then her face broke into a smile. "Oh... I must have been wanting you to come round early..." Their eyes met and Jimmy felt something strange, a tingling. ...

She brought the tray over and as they sipped he asked about the record. What was it, who was it by? She told him what she knew of the composer, of other works he had written. She sat again on the arm of his chair and fondled him gently.

"Jim," she said at length. "There's a special job I have to do. Will you help me?"

"I s'pose so. Which bank you going to rob?" He laughed, holding his glass up high. Then, with sudden seriousness: "Pinkie, why can't we stop all this — live like ordinary people... ?"

She frowned, appearing to consider his suggestion, then replied slowly: "How can I? I must be able to keep this place going. And besides," she added with inspired deftness, "— there's still Peggy's operations to be paid for."

He was surprised, astonished. "Peggy's... you mean, *you* pay for 'em?"

"I do now... Peggy's money ran out... she's broke. I've *got* to go on as I am, even though I don't like it."

As her words sank in his admiration for her grew wider and deeper. That Pinkie should do all this, take the chances she was taking, all for Peggy... it was a wonderful thing.

"I... I didn't know," he said lamely.

"There's nobody else will help her, Jimmy. That's what daughters are for. ... But the thing is, will you help me?"

"Well... what is it? Is it different, or worse than what we've been doing?" He thought about this question and before Pinkie could reply he repeated it, changing the wording: "Is it different from what we've been doing?" Different *from*, not different *to*. The way posh people would say it.

"In a way. ..." There was no way out for her; their lives

295

had led up to this point ever since the day, when she was eleven, she had come to the house near the brewery in a taxi and seen all the East End kids gazing awe-struck at her.

"... the stuff we've been doing, I think, all came from the Black Market, but this... it's new stuff."

"New? You mean it's been pinched from a factory, or something like that?"

"No. It's been brought in from overseas. ... I'm supposed to meet the seamen who brought it and collect it, but I'm nervous." She moved restlessly, to show how disturbed she was, adding: "I'm supposed to meet them in a pub, and I've never been in a pub. Not in an ordinary pub. This one's in Shadwell."

"— But... what is it?"

"I'm not sure... perhaps it's diamonds, or something like that. I know it's in a small packet. ..."

He slammed his glass down on the tray and jerked to his feet, away from her. "I don't like it, Pinkie. You said yourself, with the other stuff you was — you *were* — only doing what your boss asked you to do. But this must be worth a lot, if one or two blokes can smuggle it off the boats. ..." His eyes widened as he realised what it might be. "You don't know what it is — you're *sure*?"

"Of course I'm sure. It's just a packet —"

"And you'll still go, even if I don't come?"

She moved slowly towards him. "I must," she said sadly. "I've got no choice, the way things are." He stared away from her, at the radiogram. It was a nice record. ...

"I don't see why you're so worried, Jimmy. The risky part's over, the stuff — whatever it is — is already here, off the boat... I've just got to meet the Indians in —"

"Indians?" His tone and his manner told her that he had guessed. "That settles it. I've done all sorts o' things to 'elp, Pinkie — things I wouldn't of done, except for you..." His *h*'s had gone, but he couldn't help them any more. ... "I've done all I could, because I like you so much. ..." He strode jerkily up and down across the carpet, and suddenly he rounded on her: "D'you know what people who take drugs are like?" he demanded. "They're dead, except they still walk an' talk —"

"— Jimmy. ..." Her voice was honey, soft and appealing. "You don't *know* what it is... you've made your mind up for no reason... you've just — I mean, *I've* just to meet these seamen. ..." She stood in front of him, so that he couldn't even push past her, and her perfume was in his head, in his brain, her blue-black hair caressed his face. She looked up at him with wide, melting eyes.

"Jimmy," she murmured. "You're always a bit frightened of me... why don't you ever kiss me — properly, the way I want you to?"

Her hands slid up and behind his head and she drew him to the divan. He forgot that when he'd wanted to kiss her properly it was she who always evaded him. Her hands slid inside his coat, he was going to explode. He thought of Rosie. ...

She kissed him passionately, her tongue trembling on his lips. She moved and untied the bow at the throat of her dress, pulled it down and he felt the soft yet firm breasts pressing. ..." Jimmy, don't run away from me any more. ..."

There was a wild, soaring elation. If she liked him so much as this, if she wanted him, then surely now he could call her... "Jalani," he whispered, "— Jalani. ..."

With a dumb, nerveless sensation he felt the immediate stiffening of her, sensed the repulsion as her head reared back.

"Not to you," she spat at him. "To you I'm Pinkie. That's all I'll ever be to you. ..." Her voice rose until she was screaming, choking on words she wanted to shout but which stuck in her throat.

Slowly he drew away, rose to his feet. Without a word, as she lay panting and hating him he put on his coat, switched off the light, and went out. She heard his steps mounting heavily, unevenly, to the street. She lay on her back, staring at the ceiling.

When he reached home he thought at first that nobody was at home. The gas was only a gleam, and he didn't notice the outline of the old lady as she lay in bed. He heard the weak, bubbling cough.

"Whatsamatter, son?"

Staring, he saw that she was wearing a nightgown and that on her head was a clean calico cap: a thing he had never seen before.

"Mum. ..." He threw himself down beside her, disarranging the pillow, and then he saw the dark-spotted handkerchief.

"Don't worry, Jimmy. It's time now... run round for Addie, and look in the Two Bakers for yer father." Her claw-like hand stroked his hair. "Don't cry, Jimmy. ..." Her voice was a whisper, faint and pain-racked. "Hurry up, boy. ..." He couldn't speak for the tears that blinded and choked him. "... Jimmy, promise me... if you go in the war, don't ever kill no one... promise... ?"

Her body arched suddenly, then relaxed.

With the last of her strength her nails bit into his arm: "... promise, Jimmy... don't never kill no one. ..."

Exhausted, she could no longer speak. Her eyes carried a faint reflection from the gaslight, her hand wandered slowly up to her frilled little cap. "Jimmy, go round for Addie. ..."

She turned her head away, aware that he still hadn't said a word, hadn't promised... again she stiffened. "Jimmy, promise me. ..."

"I promise, Mum..." He was shaken by a storm of grief deeper than he had ever known, as again she whispered, "Jim, try'n look after things, an' the old man. ..."

Abruptly he stood up, staring with wide and frightened eyes, then he rushed out.

Mr Wilson, who because of the war now earned more than he'd ever earned in his life, and so was able to spend more than ever in the Two Bakers, needed only one look at Jimmy's stricken face. He ran, forgetting the bottle he'd already ordered to take home for Lizzie... and when

Jimmy arrived in Addie's kitchen she too needed nothing in the way of explanation. But when they arrived at the Court the old lady was dead.

Addie sent Jimmy and the old man back to the Two Bakers while she put water on the gas-stove and set about laying-out Lizzie Wilson, her old pal of so many years.

The next morning, instead of going to work, Jimmy travelled to Edgware. Lying successfully about his age, he volunteered for the Royal Navy.

# Book 3

# 1

There was the damp and acrid bitterness, the writhing streamers of steam and smoke, the lazy flapping of half-smoked pigeons, the air of rush and bustle; there was the usual man who had put his money in the cigarette machine, only to find it empty; there were the usual last frantic rushes to the buffet or to the Gents for a last quick one before the train went, or before it arrived... a great railway terminus in the heart of London. Old, grimed by years of service and still with the soaring glass dome black-painted according to war-time regulations, although the war had ended almost two years earlier.

There was an impatient scream in the distance. A moment later the express rounded the far bend, snaked along the platform and came gently, tiredly to rest. There was the smug, self-satisfied hiss of yet more steam.

Even before the train finally halted doors and windows were thrown open; cases and kit-bags were hurled to the platform and bodies, all shapes and sizes of bodies, hurtled after them. Jimmy Wilson, sitting calmly in the third-class compartment, felt apart, insulated from the excitement. Most of the other blokes had to rush across London to other termini, to catch other trains to other cities, and already the mad bastards were screaming for porters or taxis or both. But Jimmy was almost home.

"If you swallow any more of that, Ken," he said with the shadow of a smile, "instead of getting out at Kettering you'll wake up in Glasgow. If not worse."

The near-empty half-bottle of whisky gurgled happily as ex-Telegraphist Kenneth Taylor took another mouthful. Carefully wiping his mouth with the back of his hand he pushed the cork into the neck of the bottle, and immediately pulled it out again.

"What —" he asked quizzically, "— could be worse than ending up in Glasgow? In any case, who cares? We're not likely to get de-mobbed again in this lifetime. I hope."

His face cracked in a happy grin as he offered Jimmy the bottle. "Have some? Going, going, gone. ..." Before he could put the neck of the bottle to his mouth Jimmy snatched and emptied it.

"Bloody good-oh, Ken. Cheers."

"Cheers," Ken replied regretfully.

Bloody old Ken. Good old Ken. Bloody good old Ken... Jimmy burst into what had been the unofficial signature-tune of H.M. Frigate *Cotswold,* one which had seemed designed for him and Ken:

'Pal of my brothel days,
I know two hundred ways. ...'

They broke into a great burst of laughter, which faltered gradually into silence. The crowd had gone; the compartment was shabby-looking, empty and dead. Ken hoisted himself to his full six-feet-one-inch height, saying with false heartiness: "Well, ex-Telegraphist Wilson, James, R.N., this is the end of the road. No more middle-watches, no more dhobey rash, no more First Lieutenant's Report. ..."

That was it. There would be no more rushing down the port-side alley to the bathroom to get washed and shaved before the quartermaster piped Libertymen; no more cooks-to-the-galley, no more rum, no sippers-of-tots on birthdays, no more of Leading Tel Acutt waving the remains of his tot and shouting in mock seriousness 'Rum for bum, anyone? Rum for bum... ?' And his synthetic disgust as he turned away shaking his head: 'Never sailed with such a crowd of bloody he-men!' There would be no more sitting in the D/F shack on the upper deck, the earphones so hot your ears filled with sweat and you couldn't hear anything. ...

"I dunno, Ken. It wasn't so bad, was it? We had some good times —"

"It wasn't so bad," Ken agreed, "— if you don't mind bombs and torpedoes —"

"But all that was years ago. Still, we were lucky to get away with it..."

They looked at each other intently, thinking of their service as North Atlantic convoy escort, of the nine shipmates killed in the sudden blast as the torpedo hit the stokers' mess, the shriek of torn and twisted metal... silently they pulled their kit-bags from the racks, left the train and walked slowly along the platform.

"What time's your train go, Ken?"

"I'm not worried — we're going in for one for the road. Come on, matelot."

The buffet was crowded, filled mainly with men who that day had also been demobilised from the Services, and looking at them — several of them already weaving on their feet — Jimmy thought they had some strange, unaccountable similarity. Then he placed it; their de-mob suits, the reward of a grateful government in return for four or five years of their lives. Jimmy smiled wryly. Each suit must have cost all of thirty bob.

As though reading Jimmy's thoughts, Ken raised his pint and stared at the sleeve of his jacket. "Look at this 'ere rubbish," he said scathingly. "All we want now is the ashes — we've got the bloomin' sack-cloth."

Sometimes Ken too left off his h's and g's, but when he did it was always lightly, with a laugh, in such a way that you knew it was deliberate, that he didn't usually talk like that... Ken Taylor, rugby-playing public schoolboy, son of a Kettering shoe-manufacturer. ... Jimmy had only to close his eyes to see the big detached house, the garage with Ken's little M.G. sports car and his father's big saloon, as they were in the photograph Ken always carried in the lining of his cap. ... Ken Taylor, who scornfully regarded most of the ship's officers as jumped-up bank-clerks; who skilfully and obstinately defeated all recommendations for a commission, who was known to all and sundry as Shag-'em-all Taylor, who could argue with the officers about Freud or Bach or the Ethics of Aristotle, who almost always won. ... Ken hadn't a thing to worry about. After a while at home he was going to the continent for a holiday and eventually, when he felt ready, he would go into his family's business.

"Drink up, Ken. We'll have one for the other road."

Ken looked at him curiously. "How long will it take you to get home, Jim?"

Jimmy shrugged. "About half an hour — all the way by bus."

Knowing that Ken was in the mood for a night out, Jimmy would have liked to invite him home, but it couldn't be done. The old man, who had lived on alone in the Court until he was blown out of bed by a buzz-bomb, had been forced to move into a furnished room. Jimmy wasn't even certain that he was expected, or that there would be a bed ready for him.

"You know, Jimmy, I think we were lucky, don't you? We've been through part of the war, and two years of peace, and we've come through without a scratch. Except the ones I collected from that nurse in Capetown.".... Ken thought in silence, then added: "One of my brothers was blown out of a bomber, but he was all right in a couple of days... any of your family get hurt?"

Again Jimmy shrugged, this time with attempted carelessness. "Not so far as I know... if it wasn't for my sister Janey writing now and then, I wouldn't've known a bloody thing. My oldest brother Boy-boy's been demobbed over a year — stayed home long enough to put his wife up the spout again, then disappeared. And I know my brother-in-law — Johnny Burton, the one I told you about — he's been back about six months. That's all there is to know, I think. Except that the old man went on the dole when the war-work ended, and he's been on it ever since. My mother died in forty-two, but not from the raids. ..." Jimmy's voice tailed away and sensing his uneasiness Ken changed the subject.

"I was joking before, about the bombs and the torpedoes. Most of all I'll remember the good times — the shore-runs in Aden and that wog village where the sluts were so dried up you couldn't tell if they were six or sixty... that time in Bombay when the Indians challenged us to the water-polo match at Breach Candy... remember that night when we were in Colombo and we took the Wrens swimming in the governor's pool —"

"— And got chased all over the beach for trespassing. ..."

The whisky and beer had lost what little effect they had had; in the packed and noisy buffet they were marooned on an island of reminiscence, and although they were going home their memories were tinged with sadness.

"Remember the first time we ever saw the Gateway to India?"

Ken was still running on, but abruptly Jimmy was lost in his own personal memories. The long and bitter first months of training at H.M.S. *Collingwood,* near Portsmouth, when, no matter what he did or where he went there was only the memory of Pinkie... yet going away was a good thing. Naval training routine makes no allowance for private worries or despair, and gradually Jimmy became involved in the affairs of his class, in the study of Morse code and cyphers... the passing-out parade when training was completed, with the third-highest marks; joining the *Cotswold* at Londonderry and the long, freezing trundling across the Atlantic... the refit at Sunderland, after they'd been hit by the torpedo, and the eventual routing to Bombay, via Capetown and Mombasa... funny thing, he never did recall the sound of the torpedo exploding, only the scream of the ship's side as it opened like a sardine tin... and he thought he'd got over Pinkie.

Ken was already one of the crew, and in no time they teamed up and became known as the Terrible Tels, ever ready for a fight or a drink or a new brothel. Jeesus, Ken could move, for all his size... and then, three days out from

'Derry, the click of the mess-deck speaker and Jimmy The One telling them they were going East, to India.

... Looking back, Jimmy thought he must have gone out of his mind; he neither slept nor ate, and the image of Pinkie was as clear and vivid as ever. He drank harder, he fought more often, he went bagging-off as often as he could, trying to lose Pinkie in a welter of women and arrack and warm beer and violence... and always there was Ken to help him out, Ken, with a worried frown on his amiable, craggy-looking face. Good old Ken who knew you were in dead trouble and gradually got the whole story out of you... who told you Pinkie was no good. ... Tommy Cooper told you that, once, but you didn't believe him either. ... Ken, who told you that to dream of revenge on Johnny Burton was a waste of time and energy, who pointed out that when at last you got home again you'd have a job to settle down, that there would be thousands of others like yourself who had joined up with little or no experience of office or factory life, who would need work as you did, who also would have dreams of getting on, of making something of their lives. The only way was to forget everything else and concentrate on working and learning, on improving yourself. There was no short cut to success.

Without being condescending, Ken had talked and taught him something of the old philosophers, of painting and music and books... you admired and respected Ken, but you couldn't help thinking that for Ken it was easy. Plenty of money, public school, a family business... what else could anyone want?... No more lazing in the hot sun on deck, Jimmy Wilson, no more leaves to be spent in the rest camp at Diyatalawa in Ceylon, no more invitations to tea — offered mostly through Ken — from the tea-planters... It's over, Jimmy Wilson. You've got a life to make, a living to earn. ...

"... too late now. It's closing time." Serious-faced, Ken drained his glass and together they shouldered their kitbags and left. Outside the station Jimmy halted.

"I'll say good-bye here, Ken. I get my bus just across the road."

They shook hands, as many thousands of ex-servicemen had done when the times of death and danger and the times of pleasure were over; like those other thousands, they promised to write, to keep in touch, and like those other thousands they knew that they would not do so; the letters, if any, would spread further apart, then stop altogether. Ken would be swallowed up by his family, by the Country Club and the Golf Club, while Jimmy vanished in the masses of Stepney and the docks and the warehouses and the Markets.

He wouldn't waste any time. He must get a job, look after the old man — who through the service years had been paid an allotment from Jimmy's pay. The first thing was to get a job, one with some sort of prospects, and work and work... As he boarded the bus and sat in the back seat upstairs once again he was grateful to Ken, who in various canteens had taught him something of music, had shown him how to make better use of his left hand on the piano; he could even do tenths, as they did on the wireless, and of that he was proud... he would live on the wages from his job and he could work at week-ends playing the piano in a pub, and he would save and save.

With the slow and thoughtful deliberation of a liner leaving the jetty the bus drew away, heading for Whitechapel, and the first strange thing was that the conductor was a negro. Jimmy had never seen that before, but he shrugged. People were born, and they had to live somewhere... it might just as well be here as anywhere else.

As the bus passed through the West End Jimmy had the vague feeling that something was wrong, that there was something missing, and as Bond Street and then Oxford Street slid past the windows he realised what it was. He had expected the shops and streets to be blazing with lights, but instead the shop-windows showed only one or two low-powered bulbs and the street lamps seemed to be subdued. England came victoriously out of the war, but rationing was as strict as ever and there was an acute power shortage. Jimmy sighed.

The bus drifted through the City and soon turned along Aldgate, Jimmy staring through the window to spot Rosie Gates's tea-shop. The windows were all steamed up and he could see nothing. Finally, along Whitechapel, he knew a rising excitement. His sense of smell, made acute by the years of fresh sea air, picked out the warm heady smell of the brewery. At last he was home.

Janey had sent him the old man's new address — he had written occasional letters to his father, but there had been no reply — and eventually, at what he judged to be the nearest bus-stop, Jimmy lifted his kitbag and rang the bell. He left the bus slowly, heavily, wondering what he would find. He had written to Janey, telling her what day he'd be home and even giving the time of the train, in the faint hope that she or the old man would be at the station, but as it turned out it was just as well. As he and Ken had done their de-mob routine and the journey to London together, Jimmy was glad that neither Janey nor the old man had been waiting. Ken wouldn't have liked either of them. I'm not ashamed of them, Jimmy told himself angrily but defensively. It's just that... and there he left it.

The street ran parallel to Whitechapel Road. Dark and narrow, there was a long row of identical three-storeyed houses on one side, on the other the long charred wall of a furniture factory which twice during the air-raids had been set on fire. It struck Jimmy that the street must have looked the same in the black-out, when the raids were on.

As he walked through the shadows and beyond the pool of light shed by the single street lamp, Jimmy knew that at last he had to do what he had tried to avoid doing ever since he learned the date of his demobilisation; he had to take stock of himself, to determine exactly what he was going to do, to become; to drive himself to work and learn, to master a position so that in the end he would be able to leave the East End and move out to the suburbs, where there was grass and fresh air. And he would take the old man with him. He was thankful that he no longer dreamed of a little car, or even of a wife... the way he had chosen would be difficult, would demand all his time and all his ability, but it was enough. And it was honest.

When he arrived at the house he looked at it searchingly. There was no sign of life except through the window on the left, from which came the steady rose-glow of a bright-burning fire. The window was so caked with dirt that nothing but the glow could be seen.

He knocked loudly on the door and the knock was hollow, empty. Again he knocked, louder, and this time there were muffled footsteps shuffling downstairs and a woman's voice complaining aloud. A light flooded the passage and as the door opened Jimmy was dazzled. The woman was fat and slovenly, with a voice that sounded like rusty nails being scratched on glass: "'Oo d'ja want?" She peered at him with weak, myopic eyes, then added plaintively, "— Don't see why them people on the ground floor don't open the door, 'stead o' leavin' it for me always." A slight breeze stirred her ragged-grey corkscrew curls and brought from the passage the smell of boiled cabbage and overfilled and rotting dustbins, and above this was the sourness of damp washing. Jimmy felt sick and weak; it was as though his years in the Navy were unreal, as though he had never been away.

"Could I see Mr Wilson, please?"

"Wilson? Wilson...?" She scratched her head with long, black-rimmed finger-nails. "— You mean ole gran'dad, 'oo talks to 'isself all the time?"

Jimmy swallowed. The woman turned and went back up the passage. "First door on yer left," she said with supreme indifference, but pointing as she passed it. She padded her way upstairs, leaving Jimmy to close the door. He dragged his kit-bag along the floor and knocked on the first door and then, suddenly impatient, he turned the handle and pushed.

The small box-like room was stifling hot, yet stale and damp. Immediately opposite the door was a square window with on the left a huge, old-fashioned gas-stove and on the right, in the corner, a chocolate-brown sink above which a cold-water tap dripped and gurgled. Along the left wall was a single iron bedstead, and Jimmy shook as he noticed that the sheet and pillow-case could not have been changed for weeks. The right wall was taken up by the fireplace, and on either side of this were tall wooden cupboards. A naked, unlit electric bulb swayed gently in the draught from the open door, above a small plain table and here, on a rackety old chair, sat the old man, his feet stretched towards the blazing fire. Leaving his kitbag still in the passage Jimmy closed the door, noticing that the window-panes were so dirty that only the reflection of the room could be seen in them. The old man's head turned and his watery blue eyes stared in vacant surprise at the door.

"That you, Boy?" he queried hopefully and then, as though unbearably disappointed, "... Jimmy?... oh."

Jimmy was already aware of his striking resemblance to Boy-boy, but he hated to be reminded of it so soon. He forced himself to smile.

"'Lo, Dad," he said, moving to the table and putting his arm on his father's shoulder. "I'm back."

The old man stared at the fire. The evening was far from cold and Jimmy was sweating. "— Thought you was Boy-boy," the old man said sadly.

"You thought I was...?" Jimmy laughed without humour. "Is Boy-boy supposed to be coming round tonight? Didn't Janey tell you I'd be back... ?"

"Mmmmm... but I thought you was Boy-boy."

There was a moment of blank silence, then Jimmy asked casually: "You seen Boy-boy lately, Dad?"

"No. No one 'as. 'E's vanished, but I thought you was 'im." The old man dragged his eyes away from the fire and focused them on Jimmy, adding: "'E come 'ome a year back an' everythink seemed to be all right, 'cept 'e stayed

312

out once or twice like 'e did before. Then 'e put Maisie in the pudd'n club agen, an' then 'e vanished... must be two or three munce ago, now. No one's seen 'im since." He giggled with feeble, sickening malice. "Pore ole Maisie's in dead trouble."

"But... what about the police? Can't they do anything?"

The old man shrugged. "Maisie says it's no use draggin' 'im back if 'e don't wanta come. 'E'd on'y knock 'er about an' bugger orff agen."

Jimmy had that cold, prickly feeling he'd had that night in the ruins when Johnny Burton followed him and Tommy, like the nights in the Atlantic when he heard the U-boats signalling to each other and there was nothing to do but wait for the attack to start... just sit there and listen and wait... he hadn't wanted to get involved in anyone else's affairs, yet he knew he would have to help. He had his ex-service gratuity — about seventy pounds — in the Post Office, he could give Maisie a few quid... he swerved away from his thoughts.

"Dad, why don't you try'n clean this place up a bit? Look at your bedclothes — the old lady'd never let you sleep on a sheet like that!"

"Lizzie? Lizzie...?" Rigid with shock Jimmy saw his father's eyes cloud over, saw the two fat and heavy tears roll down the seamed face and lose themselves in the whispy moustache. He knew it was wrong, but he began to feel angry and ashamed. Jeesus, what was wrong with the old man? He was getting on a bit, but he had a couple of years to go before he got the Old Age Pension. Why didn't he try to get a job — even a part-time job, instead of sitting in all this dirt and feeling sorry for himself? Again Jimmy swerved away from his thoughts.

"Dad, is there anything I can sleep on?"

"'Ere? Yer not sleepin' 'ere, are yer?"

It was a moment before Jimmy could speak. Then: "'Course I am. Where else can I go?"

Mr Wilson shrugged aimlessly. "Dunno... why din'cha stay in the Navy?"

Jimmy wanted to hit him, to force him into some movement, into life, but instead he walked to the window and
then turned and savagely ripped the sheet from the bed.
Having done this and calmed down he went and stood in
front of his father.

"Look, Dad. I've come back... I'm goin'ta get a job an'
try'n look after you, make things a bit easier. Tomorrow
we'll get that sheet washed and we'll clean the windows
an' scrub the floor an' try'n make the place a bit decent...
and I'll get meself a camp-bed. ..."

As Jimmy spoke the old man listened, frowning. He
was happy the way he was... he had his dole money, and
Janey always slipped him a quiet pound a week. He'd had
ten bob a week from Jimmy's allowance as well... why
don't Jimmy leave me alone an' stay in the Navy...? He
was fretting with the self-centredness of the old and
lonely, thinking only of himself, and it was difficult for
Jimmy to draw out of him any news about Janey and
Maisie. ...

Maisie came round now an' then with the two kids. ...
Little Billy was a sod already, just like 'is ole man, an'
Eunice was like Maisie. ... Janey generally comes round
on Tuesdays. She used to do the old man's washing each
week, till Johnny come out o' the Army an' stopped it...
right bastard 'e was... 'e'd on'y bin round once, when 'e
come 'ome... Janey said 'e 'ad a smashin' job, doin' well fer
'isself... works in a club somewhere. ...

Jimmy digested this with mixed feelings, but in silence.
He'd have to go easy on the old man at first, but he had
to be livened up, made to live again... smarten the place
up a bit... get a second-hand bed... should be easy to get
one along Bethnal Green, or in one of the little shops off
Brick Lane. ...

The old man moved slowly, restless under Jimmy's
questions; at length, saying he was tired, he undressed
and slid into the sheetless bed. Jimmy made a bed for
himself on the floor in front of the fire, using his naval
greatcoat and an old blanket from the cupboard beside

314

the fireplace, and in taking it out he saw the string-tied old cardboard box. He was suddenly glad the old man had kept it — inside was his dictionary and his personal possessions.

The old man watched with a curious envy as Jimmy undressed before the fire; he noticed the strength and symmetry of Jimmy's chest and shoulders, the flat belly, the tapering legs and the rounded, muscular arms. Jimmy was taller than Boy-boy and not so solid, but the muscles rippled as he moved and he looked strong and fit. I bet he can look after himself now, all right, the old man reflected, and the most surprising thing of all was when Jimmy stood up in his underclothes; seen in the glow of the firelight, and in contrast against his evenly-tanned skin, they were startlingly white, just as if Lizzie'd washed 'em 'erself. Flexing his thighs and arms, Jimmy too was proud of himself, of his strength... he was young and as fit as a buckrat, he had a big job to do, and these tendons and sinews would help him... he was glad that in spite of the bombs and torpedoes and duty-watches, the Navy taught and insisted on personal cleanliness, on regular and efficient dhobeying... looking critically at his singlet and pants Jimmy thought they were as white, or almost as white, as his mother could have done them...

For two days Jimmy worked on the room, pressing the old man into helping: the floor was scrubbed, the washing was boiled on the gas-stove and rinsed in the yard, the window washed and polished. Jimmy gave the old man some money and sent him out to buy new curtains, and they bought a camp bed. The old man began to feel as though once again he had a purpose, happier than he'd been for a long time.

Janey came round for her weekly visit and congratulated them on the room's changed appearance, and Jimmy smiled. He hadn't liked doing it but a couple of days, a bit of effort, and it was done. Effort, that's what it took... if you made your mind up and put all you had

315

into the effort, sooner or later you'd win. You couldn't help it.

Janey gave the old man her usual pound-note and unashamedly he took it. Tight-lipped, Jimmy watched but said nothing. The crafty old bastard. ...

"How's the baby, Janey? he asked, "— and Johnny?"

"The baby?" Janey laughed proudly, "Gawdelpus, she's five now — the boys're whistlin' already. ... Johnny's doin' well an' all. Why doncha come round one night an' see 'em — Johnny might be able to 'elp you get a job."

"Johnny might?" Despite himself Jimmy's lip curled. "What's he doing then — staff-manager or something?" He'd rather stay on the dole than ask Johnny Burton for help. Janey bridled.

"'E's got a good job," she said. "— Managing a club for one of 'is old Army pals — name of Andrews. On'y trouble is, 'e's always on night work an' don't get much time off. But 'e gets smashin' money, an' 'e does a bit of fiddlin' on the side —"

"I bet." The old tension was back, his dry words were out before he could stop them. Immediately Janey took him up:

"You startin' already? What's 'e ever done to you? What've *you* got to be so clever about? Bein' a manager's a bloody sight better'n' bein' an overgrown office boy!"

Jimmy swallowed the quick reply that rushed to his throat. "I didn't mean anything, Janey. ... I know Johnny don't mind a bit of fiddling, like anyone else. ..." He tried to sound reasonable, to avoid quarrelling so soon, and quickly Janey calmed down.

She made Jimmy promise to go round to her flat to see little Elizabeth and Johnny, and even as he agreed to go, Jimmy knew he had no intention of doing so. The further he kept away from Johnny Burton the better for both of them. ... Ken had made him see the futility of revenge, of a nursed and nurtured hatred, and he had no wish to start any more trouble. He and Johnny would never be able to get on together. ...

Surprised at himself, he wondered if Janey had heard anything of Peggy or Pinkie... *not* Pinkie, he told himself angrily, he didn't want anything to do with *her,* but Peggy? Had she ever come back to London, did the operations go off all right? He wanted to ask whether Janey had any news at all, but decided against it.

On the third morning he reported once again to the Labour Exchange and was faced with the immeasurable superiority of the men behind the counter, with the inevitable tea-time delays. And he was surprised at the number of young men, wearing de-mob suits like his own, who waited patiently but anxiously in the long queues. Jimmy didn't know it, but following the Almighty Dollar had come another American creation, called a Recession; as day followed day the queues grew longer, the suits a little more creased and baggy, but there were no jobs. Most surprising of all was the arrival at the Labour Exchange of a long imported saloon car, driven by a negro and with other negroes in the back. It drew up with a squeal of brakes, they all walked in and signed for their dole, then drove off. There was a soft murmur of resentment, which died away as quickly as it had started.

At the end of the first week Jimmy went to the Post Office and drew out ten pounds, which he went round and gave to Maisie. She was so silent, so sad that he couldn't stand watching her moving miserably about. Both the children were out playing in the streets, and as he left he gave Maisie a few shillings for them. She cried in her gratitude and he felt himself growing irritated. If only she could stop being ever-pregnant, he thought, perhaps Boy-boy would have stayed with her. She had heard nothing from or about him, and she seemed resigned to bringing up the children alone. The room was poorly furnished but spotlessly clean, and Jimmy saw on the window-ledge the electric iron Addie Cooper had bought as a wedding present. It had never been used, but Maisie often polished it, still loved it. Perhaps one day she'd be able to move to a house with electric. ... Jimmy shivered suddenly, although the small gas-fire was lit, and as soon as he could he escaped.

He went each day to the Labour Exchange and also began watching the Positions Vacant sections in the daily newspapers, and as a result at the end of the second week he started work as an invoice clerk. There was to be a three-month trial period, during which the pay was not too good, but at least it was a start; fiercely he drove himself to learn all about the different types of wallpapers and paints and varnishes, the uses of valves and joints. Working for a company of builders-merchants was varied and interesting, and swiftly his life fell into a routine; Jimmy worked and paid the rent and the bills and expenses, while the old man got up first in the morning and made the tea, cooked their evening meals, and kept the room tidy. Jimmy's evenings were spent poring over the stock charts, over the fat catalogues of patterns of wallpapers, of plumbing equipment, of various types of tubing, of cisterns and tanks with their allied valves and joints. Within a month he had found himself a job as a regular pub-pianist — ten shillings a night, and he was allowed to go round once each evening with a collection box which brought him a few more shillings. He settled down to save money, to increase what was still in his post-office account.

On a Saturday afternoon, soon after Jimmy had returned from his regular jaunt to the public baths, he was sitting indoors and waiting for the old man to come back from Mile End Waste, where he often sauntered along looking for small bargains — cut-price groceries, tinned foods, and sometimes little envelopes of black-market clothing- or petrol-ration coupons, which were fairly easy to dispose of. Jimmy was almost asleep when there was a loud knock on the front door.

As he went up the passage he heard young voices shrilling and he knew that for some reason Maisie had called and brought the children. She looked worse than he had ever seen her — in only a few weeks her face had

318

thinned, her hair was badly in need of more peroxide. She had put on make-up without bothering to wash and her eyes were red-rimmed and swollen. She grabbed the yelling children and pushed them in and into the room.

"Jimmeh," she began as soon as he followed her in, "would you an' gran'dad look after the wee'ns for a coupl'o days? Ah wanta go'an see mah relations up hoam... ah think ah'm goan' out of mah mind. ..."

Her scarlet mouth trembled and Jimmy thought she was going to cry again. She moved slowly, as in a dream.

"Here, Maisie?" Where could they sleep, what would they do in the daytime? "I — I don't know, Maisie. ..."

"It'd oan'y be for a couple o' days, Jimmeh. Ah just wanta get away for a rest... Ah can't eat, ah can't sleep. ..." She was so earnest, so close to tears that Jimmy didn't know what to say.

"I s'pose it'd be all right. Little Billy'll have to share the old man's bed, and Eunice can have the camp-bed for a coupla nights if I sleep on the floor. ..."

"Ah'm sorreh, Jimmeh..." She collapsed into a chair and cried and cried, and little Eunice added her piping cries to Maisie's deeper sobbing. Maisie waited for half an hour, to see the old man, but Jimmy told her that it would be all right and in the end she went home, leaving Jimmy giving the children piggy-back rides round the floor.

Maisie was surprised to find herself back in the tidy, shining room she had shared for so long with Boy-boy, and as she thought of him again the tears rolled down her cheeks. She hadn't seen her family, nor even written to them for years, but she had suddenly had the intense wish to go north again. She had taken the two children round to gran'dad in an unthinking, spur-of-the-moment decision, and now that they were gone she no longer wanted to see her family. She didn't want to move, but she didn't want to stay here in this empty room, to lie awake for hours staring at the pale ceiling, at the walls, waiting hopelessly for the sound of Boy-boy's feet on the stairs. ...

At the foot of the bed was a folded blanket — Boy-boy had loved to lie on the floor in front of the gas-fire, often pulling Maisie down with him. Sometimes he made love to her there, gently or violently according to his mood... she remembered his soft voice, the sparkle of devilment in his clear eyes, his strong, compelling hands... she crossed to the window and brought Addie Cooper's electric iron back and put it on the floor by the gas-fire, then she brought the blanket from the bed. Sobbing uncontrollably she stroked the iron, her most precious wedding present, and unfolded the blanket. She shuddered in the cool evening air, then reached up for the matches; she stopped her slow movement and instead she spread the blanket over her head and over the gas-fire. She pulled the iron under the blanket with her and then, blindly reaching forward, she turned the gas on.

Early the next morning there was a loud knocking, and a policeman told the horrified Jimmy that Maisie was dead. There was still no trace of Boy-boy so Jimmy drew almost half of his savings from the Post Office; Janey helped him and together they saw that Maisie had a decent funeral. A day later Little Billy and Eunice were called for by a woman from the council and they were taken to an orphanage.

The weeks passed and congealed into months, and still Jimmy studied the catalogues and stock-charts. But he began to doubt his own purpose. It seemed that each and every member of the office-staff was glued immovably into his position; no one died, no one seemed to leave for other or better jobs elsewhere, but still Jimmy sorted and collated and dispatched the endless flow of invoices.

When he overheard two of the typists discussing the resignation of Mr Johnson, one of the firm's travelling salesmen, he shook with excitement. That was a job he could do: he felt it, he knew he could do it. He was familiar with the ranges of goods, he knew the prices and delivery dates by heart... more important still was that the salesmen didn't earn wages, but were paid their salaries by monthly cheque, to which was added commission on their sales, which in itself put them far above ordinary office-staff. And, Jimmy knew, after a brief training period the firm provided them with a little car and a limited expense account. The thought alone, the realisation that such a position would be the answer to all his hopes and dreams made him feel sick. He knew that if Mr Johnson — a red-faced, over-hearty man in his early thirties, who told the unfunniest stories Jimmy had ever heard — could be a successful salesman, then so could he. Not only *could,* but *would.* He went immediately to see Mr Hackett, the office manager.

He was slightly uneasy standing in front of the desk watching Mr Hackett's long spidery arms crawling over the desk, hearing the perpetual dry cough, feeling the colourless eyes fixed on his face with the unblinking stare of a dead crab.

Mr Hackett had himself started as invoice clerk with the firm more than forty years ago, and defensively he despised the sales-staff while being unable to admit that he would never have made a salesman. He was hostile, in a reserved way, to Jimmy's application for a transfer; he pointed out that the sales-staff were appointed only after an interview with the Sales Manager in the firm's Head Office in the West End, that representatives of the firm were expected to be well-dressed; that naturally they were required to have something better than an elementary-school education. On top of which he coughed even more than usual.

Jimmy countered these objections with quiet insistence. He had enough money to buy a new suit, he was of good appearance and spoke reasonably well. He hadn't had much of an education but he had read a lot. In any case, he already knew all the firm's products and prices. Surely that was a great advantage, Mr Hackett? Besides, he was a good worker, he had never lost a day's work through illness. ...

Finally, with reluctance, Mr Hackett reached for his phone and arranged an interview for Jimmy at Head

Office for three o'clock the next afternoon. Filled with excitement and optimism, Jimmy thanked him.

The rest of that day passed by with Jimmy dreaming of being the firm's Top Salesman, having a bank account and living in a little house in the suburbs, of driving to work each morning in his little car... he'd have to take his Test to get a driving licence, but there was nothing in that. ...

When the office closed that evening he ran straight to the barber's to have his hair cut and trimmed, and he spent the rest of that evening at home, pressing and re-pressing his suit. The interview was of supreme importance; nothing could be left to chance.

He arrived at Head Office well before time, to find two other applicants already waiting. One was an elderly man with a rubbery blue-veined nose, who Jimmy felt would be no rival at all. The other was a quiet-looking young man of about Jimmy's own age; neatly and respectably dressed, yet entirely inconspicuous. Examining them both, Jimmy felt his chances soaring. He moved and sat in one of the old and dusty armchairs. He reached in his pocket for a cigarette but a hurried look round showed that there were no ash-trays. Then he was glad he had looked first, for on the wall opposite the door was a printed notice: *No smoking*.

There was a tapping of high heels from the corridor and a pretty but cold-looking girl put her head round the door and called, and old blue-nose vanished after her. The young man smiled and cleared his throat nervously and looked as though he was about to speak. Instead his fingers began to twitch and he ran them round the inside of his too-stiff collar. The girl reappeared and he too vanished. Jimmy wanted a cigarette more than ever, and suddenly he noticed the silence; it seemed to grow and press in on him.

There was a rising sound of laughter and the same girl came back, this time leading a tall, well-built man who appeared to be in his late twenties. Jimmy took one look at the bright, dice-checked sports coat and the pale green

322

gaberdines, then came the rich and fruity and immeasurably superior voice: "Well, if you'll tell him. I really can't sit here all afternoon."

"Certainly, Mr Lewis," the girl said with a great fluttering of her eye-lashes. "I'll tell him right away." Jimmy hadn't looked at the man's face, but the mention of the name made him stare. Even then he found it difficult to believe what he saw.

The man looked at Jimmy and for a moment their eyes locked, then the man looked away with a frown. Almost immediately he spoke:

"Isn't your name Wilson — Jimmy Wilson?"

"I... yes, that's right. You're —"

"Lewis. Tony Lewis. I remember you from Saint Mary's — I was in the same class as your brother Billy. Not that I ever think of Saint Mary's."

His voice and manner showed that he had gone far beyond Saint Mary's and Stepney, and suddenly Jimmy remembered him clearly. He was the boy who had won the scholarship three years before Jimmy himself had won it. But Tony's parents had sent him to the High School. They were both at work and they saved their money instead of going to the Two Bakers. And then — dimly he recalled the details, which had filtered back to Stepney, of Tony's success story, the public school and University education, the commission in the Army. Now, looking at his lounging elegance against the wall, Jimmy realised the stories had all been true. With his bright clothes and his suede shoes and soft-collared shirt, Tony gave the impression of immense assurance, of absolute confidence in his own ability.

"You... have you come about the job — the sales job?" Jimmy asked diffidently. The coldness in his belly was growing into resentment, yet still he could be wrong.

"Why else?" Tony negligently drew a silver cigarette case and lighter from his pocket and lit up, without offering a smoke to Jimmy.

"There's no smoking allowed," Jimmy said quickly, too

quickly, pointing to the printed notice. Tony raised a quizzical eyebrow and blew a long dribble of smoke at it. "That's for clerks and office-boys," he said. "Or for those people who have to be told what to do and how to do it. It isn't really important." He left the wall and sat in a chair immediately opposite Jimmy, smiling gently to himself.

Jimmy relapsed into dark, brooding silence. I've still got a good chance, he thought. I've worked several months for the firm, and I still know a lot more than anyone coming in from outside. Won't that be in my favour?

Already the time fixed for his appointment had passed. He himself would see Mr Alexander, the Sales Manager, before Tony did; he would have to create the best impression possible, to emphasise all he knew of the firm's system and organisation, to offset the advantages that Tony, despite his ignorance of these things, automatically possessed by reason of his education and Army rank.

There was the sound of high heels tapping along the corridor, and as the door opened Jimmy took a deep breath, steeling himself for the most important interview of his life.

"Mr Lewis?" the girl asked brightly, "— Mr Alexander will see you now." Tony was grinning, as Jimmy spoke up in protest: "Excuse me, miss. I was here first — I had an appointment —"

The girl stared at him coldly, with arched eyebrows. "Mr Alexander will send for you when he's ready," she announced, turning to the door. Still grinning, Tony turned. "You should never rely on routine," he said. "Always go straight to the top. I rang Mr Alexander this morning."

The door closed on the sound of their echoing footsteps and Jimmy was alone. Again the room seemed to close in, to restrict him; there was nothing he could do, nothing to think about. Simply sit and wait until after Tony had played all his cards, shown all his assets.

In spite of the notice, Jimmy took out and lit a

cigarette. When it was half-finished he heard a door slam and there was the sound of two male voices. One of them was Tony's, raised in loud emphatic laughter.

... Didn't last long, Jimmy thought hopefully. Perhaps Tony's played his cards *too* well, perhaps he's *too good* for this job. ...

Quickly he stubbed out the cigarette and rose to his feet, straightening his tie. Any minute now...

Several minutes passed before he heard once again the tapping of high heels, and excitedly he went to the door to meet the girl.

"I'm sorry, Mr Wilson," she said. She was not sorry, nor glad; she was completely disinterested. "Mr Alexander asked me to tell you the position's been taken."

Jimmy stared at her in disbelief, stupefied. "But... but I 'ad — *had* — an appointment with —"

"Mr Alexander never sees anyone without an appointment," she said irritably, "— but the job's gone."

"Please... could I see him? Even if that job's gone, there might be something else... assistant or something. ..."

Her expression remained cold. "You can't see him now," she said. "He's just gone out with Mr Lewis." With a disdainful shrug she turned and tripped back along the passage. Jimmy stood without breathing, without thinking, and then at last, slowly and sadly, he turned and with misty eyes walked out, away from Head Office, towards home.

... It was no use, it was never any use, to keep trying. He felt a brief surge of hope as he walked: perhaps something else would turn up, perhaps something even better, if he worked and struggled. But the fleeting hope died almost as it was born.

Gradually, irresistibly, as time passed Jimmy felt himself growing restless, feeling shut-in. His week-ends were taken up in playing the pub piano, but it was during the week, after he'd had his evening meal and there was nothing much to do, that he began smoking too many

325

cigarettes, moving jerkily to the door and then back to the table. The old man, who usually sat mumbling by the fire, brought it to a head.

"Fagawsake siddown," he said suddenly. "You're like a cat on 'ot bricks."

"Mind your own bloody business," Jimmy snapped, and for the first time he realised the power of the forces inside him that he was fighting against. He had intended, *determined,* not to quarrel. ...

Instead of being offended, the old man smiled. "It ain't nat'chral for a young bloke to be shut up indoors all the time," he went on relentlessly, "— why don'cha go an' getcherself a bit o' stuff? Do yer good."

Jimmy glared at him and then, without another word, he stalked out of the room and into the street. A walk would cool him off.

He wandered aimlessly through the ill-lit streets, angry at himself and at his father. He rounded a corner and then stopped dead, feeling the sweat break out in his armpits, feeling suddenly sick. The row of houses in which Pinkie had once lived was now a series of jagged and broken walls, through which he could see the rest of the shattered block. He leaned against the wall, pressing his burning face to the cool bricks as the blood drummed and pulsed in his ears. He had tried to forget Pinkie, to take Ken's advice. Was it any use?

Could Pinkie have escaped — could she be alive? In sudden inward fury he told himself that she was probably dead, that it would be better for him if she was, and the thought was enough to make him groan, almost to stop his breathing.

Walking slowly he crossed the street from Pinkie's old house, searching for a lighted window, and when he found one he knocked loudly, rapidly on the door beside it. It opened immediately.

"I... excuse me, missus, but... I used to have some friends lived over there. Number twenty-eight... d'you know if they're all right, or... ?" The lump in his throat

326

threatened to choke him. "Number twenty-eight?... oh, Mrs Rubens? No, they're all right. They was all out when it 'appened... one o' them rockits. One minnit everythin' was all right, next minnit there wasn't nothin' left. They moved to 'Ackney."

"Oh... do you know anything about the girl who lived in the cellar — an Indian girl... ?"

The woman smiled knowingly. "She's all right — she come back next day with a coupla blokes an' they poked in the ruins. Don't know where *she* went to. It killed fifteen people," she added, "— but they was lucky this side o' the block."

"Thanks. Thank you very much."

"'S'all right, son. On'y wish I c'd tell yer. ..."

"Thank you."

As the door closed he turned away, his thoughts confused and running in all directions at once. He walked back and along Whitechapel, wondering again at the gloom of the wide thoroughfare, noticing almost unconsciously the deeper shadow in a pool of shadows, the burnished hair that reflected a distant gleam of light. Lost in his thoughts he walked on... he saw the awkward movement and then he heard the voice, soft and inviting:

"Good evening. ..."

He shrugged in irritation, then stood stock-still as the realisation flooded through him, burning and stifling. She moved stiffly, with a pronounced limp, to his side, adding, "— I just thought you..." And then she recognised him.

A car glided along the road, pressing the silence on them, showing their shocked faces, forcing them out of the silence.

Through numb, frozen lips he said simply, "Hallo, Peggy."

"Jim! Jimmy Wilson!" He knew that she wasn't afraid or ashamed, yet it was hard to believe. He noticed that although her hair was piled high over her face, the back of her head and her face itself were covered by a thick headscarf. Seeing his stare she turned her head away.

327

"Peggy,"... he said gently, "— have you been doing this long?" He was quiet and sympathetic and she knew that at least he was still friendly.

"No. ... I don't do it often," she said, her voice soft and muffled-sounding. "Just sometimes I get so lonely, so miserable. I can't bear it. And I can't bear myself either."

"But... shall we go up the road and have a cup of tea?"

She stared at him carefully, searchingly.

"I don't live far away," she said, her tone a mixture of hope and yet of doubt, "— we could go back there if...?"

He groped for her hand reassuringly. "If...?" he mimicked, smiling. "I'm not scared, if that's what you mean. I'm a big boy now."

She eyed him critically. "You certainly are," she agreed, and they smiled. Then, with Jimmy walking very slowly and Peggy with her sideward limp, they walked back to the house where Peggy rented two rooms, near the London Hospital. He noticed that even inside the living room she didn't discard her headscarf. The room itself was neat and tidy, though in a shoddy, down-at-heel way.

"Sit down, Jim... how long have you been home?"

He knew that at last, because of Ken and the years of trying to learn how to speak well, there was very little difference between Peggy's way of speech and his own, yet now there was no pleasure in that knowledge. He knew too that Peggy was no longer the full-bodied, beautiful and gracious woman who had impressed him so deeply. That had only been because she was different from all he knew, from all he had seen; and he knew in a moment of sharp-focused clarity that in spite of all her hopes and promises Peggy would never leave the East End, never be able to share that flat in Kensington she had promised Pinkie. She was shattered and broken, she would spend the rest of her life wandering round the narrow gloomy streets searching for companionship. In the same frightening moment he saw himself wandering these same streets just as hopelessly, old and alone. It had been a great thing, to have dreams, but being intelligent wasn't enough. You had to be able to find new sources of information, to absorb and so to develop. If he'd been able to go to the high school when he won the scholarship... with his dictionary and his h's and g's he was just a shell, an imitation. He was the same underneath as he had always been, and he would never change. You couldn't just throw the East End off, forget it — it wouldn't let you. It could be done, but you needed help. ...

"— About three months, now." He glanced up, then asked slowly: "Why were you down in the street, Peggy?"

"Why?" She laughed shortly, bitterly, then suddenly dragged off her headscarf and turned the left side of her face to the light. "Because of this. ..." She gulped, then the words came in a rush. "I'm just forty, Jimmy... I live on my own because no one would look at me in daylight, because no one wants to share. ..." The words strangled in her throat; staring, he saw the livid red-blue scar that crept from her jaw in a sweeping curve towards her eye. "Look at it!" she told him, tracing it with her fingertips. The scar ended abruptly beneath her eye... it didn't actually end there. It became no more than a hairline.

"I... the operations didn't work, then?" She stared at him, surprised. "Of course they worked — the three I had. But... the money stopped. ..."

He frowned. "Don't Pinkie ever come up an' see you?" He tried to sound casual, disinterested, but he knew his voice had betrayed him.

Peggy laughed scornfully. "I haven't seen Pinkie for years — not since soon after you joined the Navy." She looked into his eyes and was suddenly saddened. "Did you know about the operations, and who paid for them?" she asked. "Did you know what the price was?"

Her soft questions threw him off balance. "I... I knew Pinkie was helping to pay —"

"*Pinkie* was?" Her face set and Jimmy heard the ticking

of her clock growing louder and louder.

"So that's what she told you? Well, she didn't help at all. To tell you the truth, Jimmy, it was because of you that the money stopped."

Amazed, speechless, he could only stare.

"You liked Pinkie, didn't you, Jimmy?" she asked gently. "She told me you helped her when she first came home from the convent."

Jimmy waved her words aside: "I didn't do much."

"But you liked her... did you know she was working with your brother-in-law, for the blind man who used to live near the brewery?"

At first he wondered whether Peggy was in her right mind, but the look on her face convinced him. "Pinkie was? But..."

"— He wanted you to be his contact man in the East End."

"— I knew that. He even tried to get me to work for him when I left school —"

"And Pinkie was supposed to get you to work in with her. In the end you were supposed to take over. That's why Blind Billy paid for the operations. ... I didn't know that you were mixed up in it until you'd already gone away. We had a big row in the hospital and I told Pinkie never to come near me again. ..." Her sadness was so deep, so real, that Jimmy almost choked. There was no hatred in him, only sorrow that Pinkie had been in such a trap, and he remembered saying to her jokingly: "Which bank are you going to rob?" It didn't help much now, but he knew that if only Pinkie had been honest he would have done whatever she asked... so much for going straight, he thought sadly. But whatever Pinkie'd done, whatever anyone said about her, he knew she'd liked him. He was sure that she would like him again, if only he could find her. ...

As the full implications of Peggy's words sank in his face softened. "I'm sorry about everything, Peggy. ..."

"I still don't know all the details, what happened in

the end. I only want you to believe, Jimmy, that I didn't know what they were doing at the time. They told me after you joined the Navy... in a way, you ruined what hopes I had —"

"For Chrissake, Peggy, I didn't do nothin' o' the sort. I didn't know either —" His words failed and suddenly Peggy smiled. A ghastly, ghostly smile.

"I didn't do *anything of* the sort," she corrected him as she had done years before. "— If I'd known what was going to happen, I'd never have started it, Jimmy. ... I used to make nearly a hundred pounds a week," she said wonderingly, "— but I never saved much of it. I was so sure of myself... now I'm an office cleaner in the City. I start every morning at half-past four. I hardly ever go out, no one ever comes to see me. The doctors give me tablets. ... I've thought of taking the lot at once, but I can't do it... it's all my fault that you got into this, Jimmy. I'm sorry —"

"— But you couldn't help it, either —"

"It's funny, Jimmy. ..." She was a long way away, thinking back over years gone but still fresh in her mind: "There I was, making plans for Pinkie, giving you advice... and it was wrong. All of it. *We* were wrong too... we didn't believe in anything real. We didn't believe in anything long enough or hard enough... but it's all done now." She was crying gently and he wanted to touch her, to comfort her. Yet he couldn't move.

"Don't... don't you know where Pinkie is, or what she's doing?"

"No. I haven't seen her — or Blind Billy — since the day we had the row." That was not quite true, but seeing the hope in Jimmy's eyes she lied deliberately.

"Oh... I was wondering... she might've met that rich bloke she was always talking about. ..." He spoke carefully, his eyes riveted to the floor.

She put her hands on his shoulders and spoke with terrible, searing earnestness: "Jimmy, have you heard anything — anything at all?"

Off guard again he answered too soon: "No, not a word. When I saw the block was in ruins —"

"So you went and looked for her?"

"No, I didn't —" he began, but stopped.

"Jimmy, whatever you hear, keep away from her. Will you do that for me?"

"I'm not likely to 'ear anythin'." Ken, the Navy and the dictionary were all sloughed off, like a snake shedding an unwanted skin. He was beginning to be himself again, but even that had to be learned.

"But if you... promise me... ?"

Abruptly, fiercely, he pushed her hands away and rose to his feet. "I'm sorry, Peggy... I can't. I thought I'd got over it, but I've not. When I was in India I couldn't think of anyone else, I couldn't think of anything except Pinkie... I went ashore wi' me mates, we used to go... but I always thought it was Pinkie... I can't promise you, Peggy. If she was to come in the door this minnit I'd..." His voice broke, and Peggy knew that he was ashamed the tears were so near. But she understood.

"Jimmy, don't. ... I've heard that she's thinking of getting married." It was Peggy's last hope, her only weapon to keep him away; her words were in his ears, in his brain, but he couldn't believe them. Pinkie *couldn't,* she *wouldn't,* not if she saw *him* again. ...

"Is she?" He gave a sickly smile, his tongue running over his lips. Then he said brokenly, "Peggy, I'm sorry... I still love 'er, in spite of ev'rythin'. That's all there is to it. I'd've stopped if I could, Christ knows. ..."

He knew suddenly that if anyone knew where Pinkie was living, or working, it would be Johnny Burton, who was managing Mr Andrews' club.

"I'll 'ave to go now, Peggy. Can I come up 'ere nex' week?"

His words and speech were of no importance, and Peggy didn't even try to correct him. "If you like," she said dully. "I'm sorry we didn't get round to having that cup of tea."

Jimmy laughed, suddenly happy. "Ne'mind. I'll 'ave it

nex' week instead. All right?"

Without waiting for a reply he vanished through the door.

# 2

Jimmy tried, with a futile desperation, to take Peggy's advice. But the more he tried, the more he remembered the way Pinkie's face had softened when they had talked of love, and he was certain that it was he himself Pinkie had loved. Or would have done, if only he hadn't been such a fool as to run away and join the Navy. She *wouldn't* — she *couldn't* admit it because she had still hoped to marry someone rich, the ideal she had all her life... it was stupid, to have run away just because he couldn't call her Jalani. He had forgotten the way she spat the words at him, as he had forgotten Ken and his advice; he *had* to see Pinkie. He only half believed this story of Peggy's, because she told it to him only a couple of minutes after she'd said she hadn't seen or heard of Pinkie for years.

The old man watched him, sometimes cynically, sometimes sadly, with a knowing look in his eyes; he heard the restless turning and twisting through the nights, he heard the half-awake mumbled words, and at last he spoke. "Why doncha go out dancin' or somewhere..." And then, as though he'd only just thought of it, "S'time you was thinkin' o' gettin' married. When I was your age, I already 'ad two kids."

I know you did, Jimmy thought, glaring at his father angrily, but where are they now? Why did old people think they knew everything? Why did they think they were wise when they were simply old? There was television, there were jet planes and rockets and atomics, and of these things the old man knew nothing beyond that they worked. Wise?... Jimmy wanted to vomit. He slammed the door behind him and flung himself along the street.

Some minutes later he paused uncertainly, recognising the tall figure just in front of him, then he quickened his stride.

"How's goin', Tommy?" he asked, clapping the figure on the back.

Slowly Tommy turned his head and Jimmy went cold, a deep shivering coldness that went right through him. The hair was as dark and as neat as ever and there was a nauseous sweetness of pomade. The eyelashes would put a Hollywood actress to shame, and it was the eyes and the face that were so frightening. The look in Tommy's eyes was at once a plea and a rejection, the face was an unearthly mixture of childish innocence and ancient decay, like a cherub fallen too soon. But that look. Jimmy had seen it all over the world, wherever he'd been.

"Don't... don't look at me like that, Jim."

Jimmy's throat was full of seaweed and sand and mud; they turned and walked on with slow, hesitant steps. Jimmy tried to think of something to say, but his mind went round in dizzying circles.

"I'd of bin all right, Jim, if they'd let me alone," Tommy said. There was a dreadful desolation in his voice as he added: "I was goin' steady with a gel — remember Susie Tomkins? —"

Jimmy didn't remember her, but he shook his head affirmatively.

"Well, I was goin' with 'er for a year, after you joined up... then I was called up. They stuck me up in the middle o' Scotland, miles from everywhere, there was 'undreds of us all together, nowhere to go... it just 'appened." Tommy halted and stared, adding accusingly "— I wasn't the on'y one, either." Then he swung back into their walk with a curiously graceful, sidling movement.

There it was. The war 'ad even got Tommy, as it'd got Peggy an' Pinkie an' Boy-boy... no one was the same. The

335

war dragged everyone into its maw and when it was all over it spat them back where they came from, but no one was the same; nothing had changed yet everything'd changed. Jimmy swallowed. "I — there was... one on the ship, Tom. It didn't make any difference."

Tommy shot him a sidelong glance and quickly looked away again. "Don't you think it makes any diff'rence to me?" he asked bitterly.

"Couldn't you... what 'appened to Susie?"

"Got stuck up the spout by an Italian prisoner." The words were soft and gentle, heart-breaking. At the next corner, hoping to escape any further revelations, Jimmy halted. Tommy smiled almost to himself.

"I'm goin' up Bethnal Green, Tom. I'll see yer later on." Tommy looked at him hopefully. "Why not come up 'ome — we could 'ave a game o' cards or somethin'... ?"

"I — I can't tonight. I'm goin' out on a date." Jimmy hated himself for being so weak, for feeling embarrassed and ashamed, but the feeling was beyond control.

"Oh... what about termorrer?" Tommy was so pathetically insistent that Jimmy couldn't hurt him any more.

"Mmmm, all right. Termorrer."

They parted and Jimmy hurried back home. The old man had gone out somewhere and the house was deadly quiet. Except for the unending drip of the tap. Jimmy sat at the table and stared blankly at his reflection in the window and the dripping grew louder and louder, filling his ears, the whole room. He'd go and see Johnny Burton, ask him if he knew where Pinkie was... if Johnny wouldn't tell him, there was always the card with Blind Billy's address. Jimmy went to the cupboard and took out the old string-tied cardboard box. Slowly, carefully and dreamily, he untied the knots. His heart-beats seemed to synchronise with the dripping of the tap as he took out his old dictionary, as he stared at the set of knuckledusters he'd bought after Johnny Burton and Knocker and his pal had beaten him up.

He lifted the dictionary and shook it gently, and from

inside the pages fell two small pieces of card. One was the photograph of Pinkie when she was twelve years old, and it lay at an angle, just as he'd first seen it the day Peggy dropped her handbag years ago; the other was the card Blind Billy had given him on the night of Boy-boy's wedding, with the address of the billiards saloon. Jimmy thought for a moment, then with slow deliberation he slid the knuckledusters one into each coat pocket. He knew enough about clubs, as they were called, to know that there were usually one or two toughs, or bouncers, and although he didn't intend causing any trouble, with Johnny Burton you could never tell. And you couldn't be too careful.

Quickly memorising the address of the saloon, he slipped Blind Billy's card and Pinkie's photograph into his inside pocket. He put some coal on the fire and then went out, going quickly round to Janey's flat. It was his first visit since he had been demobbed.

Janey was pleased and surprised to see him, and in no time he was admiring little Elizabeth and the new cocktail cabinet and seeing, for the first time in his life close-to, a television set in action. Janey proudly showed him the various glasses and bottles of spirits, then suddenly she remembered the curtains Johnny had bought a week earlier.

Jimmy forced himself to appear casual and interested in all these things as he sipped the whisky Janey had poured him, but an hour of polite but wasted time was all he could stand. He stood up.

"I'll 'ave to go now, Janey... by the way, remember you said Johnny might be able to 'elp me get a job?" He made himself sound curious, but not too curious: "Well, I thought I could go an' see 'im about it. I don't seem to be gettin' any-where, an' I'm fed up wi' bein' a clerk," he explained. "Where does 'e work?"

Gladly, thinking that at last her brother and her husband might become as friendly as relatives — even relatives by marriage — should be, Janey told him. He was not surprised to hear that the address of Johnny's club was the same as that of the billiard saloon on Blind Billy's card. He'd go and see what was what.

Unable to find a trolley bus he flagged a cruising taxi and leaped inside. Trying to keep calm, yet cursing at every red traffic-light, lighting and heel-grinding one cigarette after another, he made himself draw in slow and deep breaths of the cool air. The taxi made its way through the streams of evening traffic and finally pulled up in a dingy street not far from Shaftesbury Avenue. Jimmy leaped to the pavement, paying the driver and giving him a good tip, and as the cab drew away again he looked up and down the street.

He knew very little about Soho, and he thought it wasn't very different from Stepney. There were the tall and narrow houses, with an occasional shop-window gleaming in subdued light. It was just that there were more red and blue and yellow neon signs flickering, inviting.

Looking through the open street door, there was only a bare and uncarpeted passage, with a flight of stairs at the far end. On the right a series of printed cards nailed or pinned or glued to the wall told him that the billiards saloon was on the first floor, while the club Janey had named, where Johnny worked, was in the basement. He smiled, his throat suddenly dry and aching. It looked as though Blind Billy owned, or leased, the whole building.

He halted uncertainly in the passage, then decided on the spur of the moment to look in at the billiards saloon first. If you had to move fast, you could move faster downstairs than you could *up* 'em. ...

He heard the cold voice of the marker calling out the scores, he heard the clicking of the balls and there were other voices. Turning from the stairs he was framed without warning in the open door of the saloon. The voices all stopped at the same instant and a greasy-looking man with a fat belly jutting over his trousers eyed him carefully before moving with incredibly swift and light steps to the door, still staring. The voices picked up again.

Cursing himself for being such a fool as to stick his neck out, Jimmy made himself smile. "Evenin'. Any 'ope o' seein' Mr Andrews?"

The little pig-eyes studied him carefully, focusing for a moment on his pockets, then the man smiled.

"Someone's always lookin' for Mr Andrews." His voice had a curiously thin and piping quality, and Jimmy wondered why Blind Billy employed him. He didn't know that the fat man had once been an international-class wrestler.

"Hey, Chunky," came a voice from one of the tables, "— 'urry up. We ain't got all night."

Chunky glared round at the tables, then swung back to Jimmy. "What d'you want Mr Andrews for?" he asked.

"Well, I was wond'rin' if 'e might 'ave somethin' for me. I used to work for 'im before I joined up," Jimmy lied. He dug into his inner pocket and, feeling carefully, he brought out Blind Billy's card and offered it to the fat man. Chunky glanced at it and then at Jimmy, who added: "'E told me to look 'im up after I was demobbed."

"Oh." Reassured, Chunky smiled. "I dunno where 'e might be nah — 'e on'y comes 'ere Sat'dy nights. 'E's got a coupla noo dives dahn east — that's the place nah. S'all finished up 'ere, what wi' the Law gettin' busy an' everythin'." He shrugged sadly and added deprecatingly: "Not much cop dahn there. No class, yer might say, just seamen an' wogs. Seem to be doin' all right, though... I c'd ring up'n find out, if yer like."

"Tha'ss all right — I'm in no 'urry. Ain't spent me demob money yet. I'll call back on Sat'dy. Ta just the same."

"Okay. We'll see yer."

Jimmy turned to leave, then stopped. "I s'pose," he queried as though it was not really important, "— I s'pose you don't know what 'appened to the Indian girl? Used to work for Mr Andrews, name of 'Arcourt. Pinkie 'Arcourt?"

Chunky frowned in laborious concentration. "Oh, I remember. She used ta work dahnstairs, never useta come up 'ere... she's not bin up this end o' town for more'n a year, far as I know. I think she's runnin' one o' the noo dives dahn east... whyncha go an' ask dahnstairs in the cellar? You a friend of 'ers?"

Jimmy couldn't avoid a thin, tight-lipped smile. "Used ta be... wouldn't mind seein' 'er again."

Chunky smiled and explained apologetically, "I'd 'elp yer if I could. Ole Andrews 'as got 'is fingers in ever'rythin' what's goin' — we're not s'posed ter know what goes on anywheres else, but there's always someone as talks. Ask dahnstairs."

"I might do that," Jimmy said slowly, as though giving the suggestion some serious thought. "— I bin savin' it up fer a long time."

"You'll be lucky," Chunky warned, grinning.

"I always did like chancin' me arm. If I don't, I'll be back Sat'dy."

"Okay, boy. By the way, 'oo shall I say called?"

"Alfie... Alfie Thompson," Jimmy said easily, "— from Aldgate."

"Okay. I'll tell 'im you was askin'."

Jimmy went downstairs and waited for a moment, looking at the down-pointing red-and-green arrow. There was the sound of an over-brassy band and a veil of stale cigarette smoke hung over the stairs. Drawing a deep breath, feeling the weight of the 'dusters in his pockets for reassurance, he went to the bottom. He didn't want trouble, but...

It wasn't such a bad idea, after all, goin' upstairs first. At least he knew he wouldn't run into Blind Billy, and that was all to the good.

His footsteps sounded clearly and when he reached the bottom a young, hard-faced girl in a very brief costume, with a cigar tray hung from her neck and balanced like a shelf on her chest, was waiting for him.

"Good evening," she drawled, her eyes going over him

340

from head to toe, her appreciation written all over her face. "— Looking for some fun?"

Jimmy studied her as carefully as she had studied him.

"I might be," he said, with a double meaning she didn't understand, "— one way or another."

She raised an eyebrow. "There's only one way to have fun down here." Her voice was hard and brittle. Jimmy guessed that she too came from Stepney or somewhere like that, but was determined to hide her ordinary accent at all costs... just like he used to do.

"Straight through the door," she said, pointing,

"Thanks. I'll see you later."

The door was open but blocked off by a thick crimson curtain; the noise of the band was louder and there was the faint hum of voices. Jimmy pushed the curtain aside and went in, and found himself in an ante-room in which the most impressive thing was the bar which curved out from the right-hand wall. It was backed by a series of glittering mirrors with here and there bottles of straw-coated Italian and Spanish wines. The floor was carpeted all over, and on the far side were a few small tables with chairs. In the far corner another heavily curtained doorway led into the inner room, and a small extension-speaker relayed the sound of the band and the voices from inside.

At the far end of the counter were two women he recognised from Aldgate. He had seen them often, parading up and down with their sharp and probing eyes, their enamelled faces split by empty, meaningless smiles. And he had seen them once or twice in Rosie Gates's tea-shop, had occasionally said 'How's tricks?' So they too worked for Blind Billy... the nearest one, he recalled, was named Geordie. She was the one who had told Rosie about the prossies' club, who had been mixed up in that airman-murder case. ... Johnny Burton was behind the counter, and as Jimmy entered their three heads swerved as one.

Geordie smiled appraisingly. "Hi, lover-boy," she said, "— come an' join the ball. We always 'ave balls." She

341

giggled explosively. "It's a bit early. ..." Her voice was harsh and cracked and Jimmy wondered how she had managed to smother her north-country accent so successfully, where Maisie never had been able to. ...

"— Shut up, Geordie," Johnny snapped. "'E's my bruvver-in-law."

"'E's nice," Geordie said thickly, "— pass 'im on when you've finished with 'im." Johnny scowled but she was supremely indifferent. *She* and Sheila brought in the business, not pig-face Burton. ...

Jimmy stared at them frostily, and moved to the counter, where it flared out from the wall. Johnny smiled at the two women and moved down towards him and his face was flushed and sweating. He was looking very prosperous in a black jacket and black bow-tie.

"Hi, Jim," he said amiably, yet with his voice loaded with dislike. "Whassup — you on a night out, or 'ave you just got lost?" He paused, expecting some reply, but as Jimmy stayed silent Johnny added: "I thought you might've come up 'ere before."

Seeing him again, even after all these years, Jimmy still hated him. He remembered lying bruised and naked under Johnny's derisive mocking stare as he offered to go and get some of the boys to take care of whoever it was had beaten Jimmy up... it's funny, Jimmy thought, after all that's 'appened, I've got to crawl to *'im* an' ask him a favour. He decided to waste no time.

"Johnny, Janey told me where you was workin'. I've come up just for one thing — d'you know where I c'n find Pinkie?"

Johnny's eyes, looking like hot little stones, blinked in astonishment, then he smiled and the smile was full of malice. "Won't you 'ave a drink, brother-in-law?" he queried heavily.

"— 'Course I will. But I just wanta know where Pinkie is." Seeing that Johnny was unaffected, Jimmy pleaded: "Look, Johnny, I'm not playin'. I've *got* to see 'er." It was difficult to speak, almost impossible to go on with

Johnny's cold blue eyes set deep in their flush-pink flesh staring and staring, but he had to. To plead, to beg if necessary. But he had to see Pinkie.

Johnny pulled a whisky bottle from under the counter, poured a double and pushed it across to Jimmy. "I *could* tell yer where she is, if I wanted to... don't see why I should. I'm not a information-centre."

"Johnny, I'm askin' yer. Will yer tell me?" Jimmy felt a sudden, icy calm in what he said and did. Johnny could make the most of this moment, but Jimmy's time would come later.

"Well," Johnny reflected, enjoying playing cat-and-mouse, "*you* wanta see Pinkie, but s'pose she don't wanta see you? Bloody fool I'd look, would'n' I?" Johnny had already decided not to tell Jimmy where Pinkie was but now, with his extra knowledge, he saw all the makings of a lovely big mix-up, one Jimmy couldn't win. Johnny added, just for the pleasure of it, "'Specially after she made you look such a bleed'n monkey."

White-faced, with a tight-lipped smile, Jimmy answered: "I won't tell 'er you told me, Johnny... please, where is she?"

With the wonderful sensation of being carried on rushing, soaring winds, Johnny taunted his enemy further. He saw Jimmy's hands slide into his pockets but thought nothing of it. Along the counter Geordie was listening with her ears flapping.

"I wouldn't see 'er if I was you, Jimmy. She's gettin' married soon."

It was a shattering, unbearable pain, fierce and white, but Jimmy tried, and tried hard, not to show it. "Is she?... who to?"

Johnny's grin spread all over his face. It could have been his moment of triumph, of revelation, but he had to twist the knife. He hadn't enjoyed himself so much for years. ...

"Oh," he said, "— that's not my business... someone you know, anyway. Went to Saint Mary's."

Jimmy gasped. "Someone I know?" It didn't make sense. Who was there... not Tommy Cooper? Tommy and

Pinkie had always disliked each other, besides... Tommy wasn't the sort of bloke. Who else did Pinkie know... the thoughts ran round in his head but there was no sense in any of them. It occurred to him that it might be one of the boys who was a year or two older than himself, and frantically he tried to recall someone who he thought Pinkie might like, might even fall in love with, who would make her a husband, a lover... he shook his head dazedly. He knew Johnny was playing with him, leading him on, and the gentle pressure of the 'duster in his pocket was comforting. He had never hated Johnny quite so much as he did at this moment.

"She's known 'im for years," Johnny went on, with vicious, calculated cruelty. "Didn't you know? All the time she was makin' up to you, before you joined the Navy, she was goin' with... wi' this bloke." He shrugged lightly. "Everyone else knew, even if *you* didn't."

Jimmy could hardly breathe, to speak was an effort that took all his strength. "... Where is she, Johnny? Just tell me, that's all." But Johnny wouldn't give in so easily.

"Know where she went with 'im Chrissmas?" he demanded. "They went to Brighton — an' Pinkie paid. She always does... an' d'you know what 'e gave 'er for a present? Real Yankee bras an' knickers... I c'n just see 'er walkin' roun' the room in 'em, wi' that coffee skin of 'ers... 'an 'e gave 'er a pair o' gold earrings, big as waggon-wheels, they are. Looks smashin', she does. ..."

Jimmy spoke between tightly-clenched teeth. "All right, Johnny, you win. Who's the bloke?"

Johnny smiled, then the smile became a loud laugh. But he shook his head. After a moment Jimmy said: "All right — *where* is she? Fer Chrissake, Johnny, tell me. Please."

That last *'please'* was worst of all. Did Johnny want him to get on his knees, to lick his boots? If that was the price, Jimmy'd pay it —

"Eh, Johnny, givus a drink. We're dyin'..." Geordie was getting fed up with the game, and bored. Jimmy had forgotten about her and Sheila, but they must have heard every word. He was past caring. As Johnny turned away to get drinks for the two girls Jimmy suddenly reached across the counter and grabbed him, almost pulling him over the top. Their eyes were only inches apart, and still Johnny smiled.

"You makin' all this up, about Pinkie gettin' married, about me knowin' the bloke? If you are, Johnny, I'll kill yer. Tell me — *tell me!*"

"— Why should I make it up? Don't mean nothin' to me. Why should I tell yer, if all yer goin'ta do is go an' bash 'er up a bit?"

Close to defeat Jimmy swallowed, letting Johnny slide back. "Y'know I've bin in love with 'er fer a long time, Johnny," he said brokenly. "I wouldn't 'urt 'er, you know that. I just... I just don't believe it."

Johnny smiled. "I don't care if you believe it, or not. It's true, tha's all. She's bin wi' this bloke for years an' years, an' she made you look a right bleed'n charley."

Immediately, unexpectedly, Jimmy grabbed Johnny's coat lapels. His face was dead white, his eyes blazing, he was almost choking. "If it's true I'll kill 'er... I don't believe it, but if it's true. ..."

Spent and exhausted, again Jimmy let go of the lapels and Johnny still smiled his malevolent smile. "It's all true, Jimmy. S'welp me Gawd."

"Johnny, facrissake givus that bottle... why doncha tell 'im to go to Eva's place if tha's what 'e wants?" Geordie, feeling sorry for Jimmy, put an end to Johnny's enjoyment.

Jimmy stood by the counter, miserable and full of doubt, as at last Johnny took the whisky up to the two girls. Then he came back, as a party of young, half-drunk revellers came in. They went straight through the ante-room and through the heavy curtain into the club-room itself. There were a few shrieks of greeting, then once again only the shrill noise of the band and the distorted hum of voices.

345

Johnny simply stood, watching and still grinning. "Well," he said. "Why doncha go — y'know where she is. Eva's place, near Cable Street. Yer askin' fer trouble," he added, "— but you always did."

Swiftly, like a striking snake, Jimmy's hand whipped up in a rising, glittering curve, and there was the deep satisfaction of feeling the bones of Johnny's nose crack under his steel-plated knuckles. Johnny reared back, his nose streaming with blood, and Geordie gave a little half-scream.

"Thanks, bastard, I will," Jimmy said. He turned and pushed through the curtains, upsetting the startled cigarette-girl's tray. He took another taxi down to Cable Street, but when he asked the driver if he knew Eva's Place the man shook his head. "There's so many o' these joints goin' now, you don't know where you are these days. All wogs and Malts, an' all... time the Law did somethin', I reckon."

Jimmy left the cab and walked slowly along, listening carefully for the sounds of raised laughter or of loud music. He found no less than seven clubs or dives that might have been Eva's, but which guarded inquiries from passers-by proved were not. He walked right along to the junction of Cable Street and Commercial Road, then turned and retraced his steps. Must be in a side street somewhere. ...

Although only a few blocks from where he was born, Cable Street was an unknown area to him. A lot of Irish had moved in, and there was the unending stream of seamen who came and went — usually sadder but rarely wiser. He walked back and at last, not far from the offices of the Shipping Pool, where the merchant seamen reported when their leaves and their money were gone, he found it. *Eva's* was all it said above the door, and there was noise and the blare of a radiogram. It was in a side street, with one side blocked almost entirely by the black rearing walls of warehouses and factories. He made as though to go in; then, halting for an undecided moment,

346

he crossed the road in a slight diagonal. There was a house without sign of light or life, with a small tree in a tiny front plot.

The doorway was in shadow and a weak street lamp shone and showed the entrance to the club, and he leaned against the door and lit a cigarette. A sudden spatter of rain beat on the leaves of the tree, and he shivered as he settled down to wait. These clubs were supposed to close officially at eleven, but people like Blind Billy paid protection money. Shortly after eleven had struck on a nearby church clock the noise decreased, but the door remained open.

As he waited his mind ran over all the different Pinkies he had seen; Pinkie getting out of the taxi, that first time he ever saw her, with her portable gramophone; the day she caught her dress on the nail, when she was cleaning her first little basement flat; Pinkie sadly telling him about Peggy's injuries, Pinkie smiling and dancing on the night of Boy-boy's wedding party... he would never forget that night, with Boy-boy's furious white face and the sudden slam that sent him reeling across the room, and he would never forget the night Johnny Burton helped to beat him up... time ran on and still there was the muted sound of voices and music from the club. Later, much later, there was a burst of raucous laughter and cheerful good nights; a crowd of people left the club and quickly split into small groups, some going to cars parked further along the street, others vanishing singly or in pairs down alleyways and near-invisible passages. The music stopped, the rain fell harder and became a monotonous London downpour... there was a final burst of shouts as yet more people left. Then there was nothing; nothing but darkness and rain and the melancholy wail of a tug on the river. ...

He saw her, he caught the angles of her face in the distant lamplight as she turned and carefully locked the door. He watched as she walked to the end of the street and turned the corner, then he left the doorway. Running swiftly and silently he followed. She was half-way along the block, walking with that smooth and easy movement he remembered so well, that was part of her. He paused and let her get further ahead and again he ran as she turned into the next street. As he himself turned the corner he thought with a choking fear that he'd lost her. Then his eyes caught a reflection of movement in the shadows of a tall and narrow house. She was at the top of a short flight of plaster steps leading up from the street, fumbling in her handbag for her keys.

He slid after her and as her hand inserted the key into the lock his own closed over it and twisted, hard, opening the door. In one long continuous movement he forced her inside, following swiftly. She gave a startled cry then spread herself along the wall. Her eyes were wide and frightened and she was even more beautiful than he remembered.

He pulled her to him in a savage, bruising kiss. Then he moved away.

"Hallo, Pinkie," he said lightly, almost flippantly. "— Bet you never expected to see me."

"Jimmy. ..." There was fear in her, all through her, yet she was completely under control. "Jimmy," she repeated urgently, "— you mustn't come here."

"*No*? I'm 'ere, anyway." He turned abruptly and faced along the passage. "— Let's go an' talk a bit."

"Jimmy, you mustn't. There's someone waiting for me —"

"— Your boyfriend?" he said mockingly. It was a time for gambling, for taking chances, and he took yet another. "I've already seen 'im."

Before she could reply he pulled her along the passage. She led him up to the first floor and halted.

"This is my flat."

There was something expressionless in her voice and in her actions, as though she was a wooden doll.

The door opened into a bright kitchen, and she pointed to another door. "In there."

It was just as he had known it would be — bright and colourful; he had never seen it yet he felt that he had been here before; he expected the brilliant contrasting colours, the table radiogram, the soft chairs and the expensive-looking cocktail cabinet. With her stiff, curious movement she switched on the radiogram and a moment later the tragedy of the slow section of Balakirev's first symphony wept into the room.

No... he thought helplessly. She's done it all before, she's still the same as she was, nothing's made any difference to 'er. But he was beyond her, out of reach. Yet seeing her now, in this bright room, with her honey-skin and her blue-black hair and her brilliant dress he thought of the butterflies he had seen in the forest near Mombasa and in the jungles of Burma; brilliance and colour surrounded by other overpowering colour, so that you couldn't really take it all in. He pulled her to him and kissed her again. "What're you nervous for, Pinkie? I know all about it."

"All about... what?"

"All about the... the boyfriend." Jimmy sighed with cool, calculated effect. "I know all about it," he repeated, lying easily. "— About the Crissmas at Brighton, an' them earrings 'e gave you. They look nice," he added critically.

She stared at him uncertainly, suspiciously. "How — ?" she began, but he interrupted quickly. "— I know." He smiled. He had to smile, to try and pass it off as though it was unimportant, and the skin on his back rose in little ripples. He had to smile, just as he *had* to find out who it was who had the right to buy her gold earrings. Did she let *him* call her Jalani? he wondered suddenly.

"I met 'im not long ago, in a pub," he said casually. "We 'ad a few beers... you should've told me when it all started, Pinkie," he said almost archly. "After all, I've known 'im fer such a long time... d'you love 'im, Pinkie?" His smile was a dreadful travesty, glued on and fixed by nothing but will-power and the irresistible drive to find out *who* it was...

Pinkie was still uncertain. She had been told so often that she must never say anything to Jimmy about it all, even before he went into the Navy. Yet if he knew so much...

"Do I love him? Of course I do. He's lazy and he spends too much money he never earns, but I love him. I've loved him since the first time I ever saw him. ... You're a funny one, Jimmy," she said, swerving in her thoughts. "— I used to think *you* loved me, once."

"I did. I still do." Agony and love and hatred, all held in a few words she hardly noticed. ...

"— And you don't mind, now you know?"

Jimmy's hands fluttered aimlessly. "'Course I mind. But if you love 'im, not me. ..."

She shook her head sadly. "I couldn't, Jimmy. You were always so good, so young... and you always did what I wanted. But I never wanted you to love me —"

"What about Peggy?" It was a shot in the dark and it jolted her.

"I used to think the world of her. But she was such a failure... all those plans about a nice flat and rich men... she just ran away in the end. Did you know that?"

He was calm, supremely confident again. Deliberately he moved and sat in one of the stuffed chairs. "No," he said, "— that's not what Peggy told me when I was talkin' to 'er a coupla days ago. She said it was you an' Blind Billy who run away."

Her eyes held that soft, melting look, and her voice was deep and persuasive. "Jimmy, I had to do it... at first because it was the only way I could help Peggy, and then... because I had to have more money. I couldn't stop."

"You didn't care what 'appened to me."

"No," she said simply, her hands fluttering like pale moths. "At least, I did, but it wasn't so important. You were just a boy I knew, and liked a bit. Mr Andrews wanted to get you involved in what he was doing because he thought you'd be a sharp worker, and he was willing to pay for me to play up to you... I *had* to try, but I was glad when you ran away and went into the Navy. Glad. ..."

"So you could carry on with your boyfriend? It's all right, Pinkie — he's told me all about it, 'ow long it was goin' on. ..." How low could you get, how many lies must you tell to find out something you'd be better off not to know? But he couldn't stop.

She came over and sat on the arm of his chair as she had done years ago, and once again her hand ruffled his hair, and she was almost crooning: "I liked you, Jimmy, and I never wanted to hurt you. But I never loved you."

"What about when I was in bed an' you come down the Court to see me — did you love me then?"

"I've already told you," she said irritably, her hand still doing things to the back of his neck and his ears. "I did it because I wanted to get you to work in with me. I *had* to try to get you to come to that pub with me... for Peggy."

"For Peggy?" His lips curled. "You never loved Peggy — you never loved anyone but you."

She thought for a moment, then she shrugged. "Perhaps you're right... until I fell in love myself. Then it didn't matter what I did... I think I'd have killed someone if it came to it."

"But, Pinkie..." he made a last effort, trying to find once again the pleasure just being with her had once brought. "Are you *sure* 'e loves you? Do you *know* it?"

"Of course I know it. He left Maisie for me... he said she must've been mad to kill herself. ..."

Jimmy didn't hear the rest of what she said. Her words had dripped with shocking paralysis into a mind gone dark, vacant. Except for one thought that whirled and raged.

"Boy-boy," he said dully, "— it was *Boy-boy!*"

"Jimmy," she said. "I couldn't help it. Neither of us could — it just happened, right from the night you took me to the party in the Court. Even then I didn't know, until he came out of the Army prison and began his ordinary training. I met him just by accident when he was on a week-end leave —"

351

"— So that's why 'e started stayin' out all night?"

"It didn't matter, Jimmy. I loved him, and he loved me. That's all that counted."

The dead feeling, the numbness, had gone. He was suddenly alive again, vibrantly and powerfully alive again.

"But, Pinkie," he said, "— it won't work. 'E's a lot older than you — it never does work like that."

He reached out and pulled her head and kissed her again. At first she resisted and pushed against him, but the kiss went on and she relaxed, sighing. His hands were swift and urgent and again they kissed. "Jalani," he whispered, and this time she said nothing.

There was the sudden slamming of the front door and a moment later heavy and slightly-faltering footsteps on the stairs. She jerked upright, her eyes wide and staring.

"Jimmy! It's Boy-boy! Quick — run in the bedroom."

He was dazed, unable to understand. "Me? Why? I never —"

"Jimmy — if he sees you here... there's lipstick on your face... he'll kill you."

Slowly the footsteps came closer. Panting, horrified, she tried to drag him from the chair. "Jimmy — for God's sake hide. He'll —"

"'E c'n try," Jimmy said slowly, calmly, "— but 'e won't get very far." His right hand slid into his pocket and felt the 'duster. All his life he'd been running away from something, from someone, but he couldn't run any more... if it came to a fight, he wasn't even scared. He'd enjoy it. ...

"Jimmy. ..." she pleaded. He saw her expression change suddenly, he saw her cream-coffee throat-muscles tighten and her mouth as it opened and showed her coral-bluish tongue and he heard the hissing breath she drew before screaming. Without thinking he hit her, his fist flying upward in a swift and graceful arc. And the arc was edged with the gleam of steel.

Her head twisted sidewards and away and there was a dull, muted little click. She looked so surprised, like a

352

child caught stealing the jam, as she slid down the chair to the floor, and there was a thread of blood running down her chin. Then the door opened. Not quickly but very slowly; the handle turned, the door pushed gently inwards... standing there was not Boy-boy but Johnny Burton.

Jimmy saw Johnny's face with the purple bruises and the flattened nose, he saw Johnny's slow and expansive smile as he looked from Jimmy to Pinkie and back again.

"Well, sonny boy. You've done it now, good an' proper." His voice was soft yet incisive and his smile grew and grew.

The door slammed and Jimmy heard footsteps rushing downstairs, the wrenching of the front door, and Johnny's voice frantically screaming *"Pleece... pleece. ..."*

Jimmy sat staring at his steel-ridged knuckles, the ghost of a smile on his face. And he knew he was crying, and the tears rolled down and down *inside* him, not outside. But still there was the ghost of a smile. ...

# Finale

There is no cold like the cold of a prison cell.

In only a few days it eats into you, first your body, then your mind, then your spirit, and as it does so something in you dies. I think that's a good thing — it makes it easier for you when the time comes.

All I want to do is stand on my cot and look out through the bars at the big square brewery, at the two tall and slender chimneys with their veils of smoke. Usually the smoke is the same colour, but today one of them is pumping out a great, thick black plume that stays in the still air, coiled and curling over London, and it makes me think of Pinkie. And there is still the same wonderful and comforting smell of hops and malt and barley and sugar, and this I love above everything.

All I want to do is stand on my cot and look out at the soft English-blue sky and the soft white clouds drifting past the two chimneys, but they won't let me. I'd be quite happy on my own, but the two Screws, who will be with me all the time now, won't let me. They keep asking if I want to play cards, or write a letter, or would I like a cup of coffee, and every time I say *no* they look as hurt as if I'd kicked their teeth in. If one of them was Old Wetlips I would have done.

I had a letter from my brother Billy — the one who vanished just before Boy-boy got married — saying he always knew I'd do something unusual. Sarcastic bastard. It took him three lines to say that, the other two pages were all about this bird he's knocking off and how they're thinking about getting married, although the neighbours think they already are. I wonder why?

I stand looking and looking, and I don't seem to think of anything much — not Pinkie, or Peggy, or Janey... out there Johnny Burton is managing the club and Mr Andrews is still coining the cash. I didn't have much of a defence, because I didn't talk. What good would it have done? The two prostitutes told the Court they'd seen me hit Johnny with the 'duster, they heard me say I loved Pinkie and that I'd said I'd kill her...

I've had interviews with Miss Social Worker and Mr Prison Psychiatrist; she showed her teeth and looked as if she was going to be sick, and he just looked worried to death. Then they got together and said there's something wrong with my generation.

They may be right. But if they are, it isn't our fault.

Sometimes I think Peggy was right. We didn't believe anything real enough, hard enough, long enough.

# Available from New London Editions

*Scamp* by Roland Camberton
(introduction by Iain Sinclair)

*The Furnished Room* by Roland Camberton
King Dido by Alexander Baron
(introduction by Ken Worpole)

*Rosie Hogarth* by Alexander Baron
(introduction by Andrew Whitehead)

*October Day* by Frank Griffin
(introduction by Andy Croft)

*The Furnished Room* by Laura Del-Rivo*

*Baron's Court, All Change* by Terry Taylor*
(introduction by Stewart Home)

*Adrift in Soho* by Colin Wilson*

*This Bed Thy Centre* by Pamela Hansford Johnson
(introduction by Zoë Fairbairns

*also available as ebooks

**Available from bookshops or, post free,
from www.fiveleaves.co.uk**